D0572713

Black Was the Ink

Michelle Coles

Tu Books

An Imprint of LEE & LOW BOOKS Inc.

New York

Copyright © 2021 by Michelle Coles
Jacket art and interior art copyright © 2021 by Justin Johnson

TU BOOKS, an imprint of LEE & LOW BOOKS Inc.,
95 Madison Avenue, New York, NY 10016
leeandlow.com

Manufactured in the United States of America
Printed on paper from responsible sources

Edited by Elise McMullen-Ciotti
Jacket art and book design by Sheila Smallwood
Typesetting by ElfElm Publishing
Book production by The Kids at Our House
The text is set in Dante MT
Interior illustrations by Justin Johnson

10 9 8 7 6 5 4 3 2 1
First Edition

Cataloging-in-Publication Data is on file with the
Library of Congress

To my darlings J.T., M.E., C.D., L.M.,
You come from Kings and Queens.
Know your greatness.

# PROLOGUE

Malcolm fell for an eternity before landing with a thud on his back—his arms stretched out in a snow angel and his stomach in his throat. He gingerly peeled his fingers off the cold, hard ground and checked his body for broken bones. Surprisingly, he was fine. He stood up and felt his way around the dark, cavernous space, searching for a door, a light, anything to let him know where he was. He couldn't see a thing but the stench was overwhelming. Malcolm covered his nose and stumbled forward, banging into a wall.

He felt along the wall's hard, ribbed surface looking for a way out. His fingers found a metal latch. Relieved, he lifted it. A door swung open, and he was momentarily blinded by a burst of sunlight. Malcolm felt disoriented. He gave his eyes a second to adjust and then stepped forward onto a step, then another, and then down onto the dusty ground. Malcolm turned about to see he had just stepped out of a rusted-out train car. He had never seen a train like it.

Suddenly, a potbelly pig charged past him kicking mud and muck onto his clothes, spinning him back around. A short old man with dark, sun-weathered skin wearing a straw hat and brown cotton overalls soon followed chasing after the pig at full speed, cursing the whole way. Across the road people scurried in and out of a barn tucked into a dense cluster of trees. Malcolm could see a white dome above the trees that reminded him of something, but his memory failed him. Malcolm felt a push from behind.

A tall, middle-aged, light-skinned Black man stood at the top of the train-car steps Malcolm had just descended. The man had broad shoulders and a full beard that grew all the way back to his ears, yet he had no mustache. He wore a three-piece blue cotton suit held up by suspenders with a white pleated shirt underneath and a red silk handkerchief folded into the front jacket pocket. He tapped Malcolm's hip with a knobby cane.

"Come on, Cedric, you've stood there gawking long enough. Now let me through!" the man said, nudging Malcolm again. "Don't forget my bag," he called, pushing his way past him.

Who's Cedric? Malcolm looked around. He felt confused, dizzy, and nauseous. He slapped his face to see if he was awake and immediately felt the sting. He glanced down to find he was wearing a tattered brown suit and homemade-leather boots. Looking back up, he caught his reflection in the open train door's glass window. The person peering back was not Malcolm—similar in appearance, but not him. He looked about Malcolm's age, sixteen, and had Malcolm's same tall, lean frame, ruddy brown skin, and embarrassingly long eyelashes. He even had the same chin dimple, but his hair was off. Way off. It was cut short and featured a strange side part, instead of Malcolm's tightly coiled jet-black hair, usually worn in braids or in a loose crown on top of his head. Most disturbing was his super-weird, caterpillar-thick mustache that twisted up at the ends, like an actor in an old movie.

Where am I? Malcolm wondered. He grabbed the side of the train and braced himself, no longer able to suppress the gush of vomit that flew from his body. Then in a blink, he was in bed with his head resting on his sketch pad, pen still in hand.

Cock-a-doodle-doo!

It was still dark outside when the rooster's crow jarred Malcolm from his sleep. A few seconds later, an engine roared. He pulled a pillow over his head to block out the noise, but it didn't help. He reached for his phone and checked the time: 5:57 a.m. He put the phone down and pulled the pillow back over his head. No way was he getting up this early, especially after that crazy dream with a train, a pig, and some man with a weird mustache. He was more tired now than when he went to bed last night, but his curiosity got the best of him.

Malcolm sat up in the twin bed against the wall and peered out through the window blinds. A pink haze was emerging on the horizon. He'd arrived at his family's farm late the night before, making this the first time he'd seen the property in years. It was bigger than he remembered. Green pastures adorned with giant pecan trees stretched out for acres. Behind the farmhouse was a wide-open backyard that led to a short red metal barn. A couple of small fenced-off areas for different farm animals—goats, cows, and a horse—marked the path between the house and the barn.

This farm had been in Malcolm's family forever. His grandma Evelyn and her sister, Carol, had grown up there, raised by their mother, who everyone called Mama Lucille. Malcolm was too young when Mama Lucille died to remember her, but he'd seen a picture of her cradling him in her arms when he was a baby. Now Grandma Evelyn was also gone. That was six years ago. He knew Aunt Carol missed her. He missed her too.

Malcolm spotted Uncle Leroy, Aunt Carol's husband, sitting on a tractor near the barn chewing on a piece of straw. Even from this distance, Malcolm noticed how Uncle Leroy's imposing stature stood out with his tall, lean frame, square jaw, and neatly trimmed beard. Malcolm chuckled. It may have been six years since he had last visited the farm, but Uncle Leroy still looked the same—like he lived in a country music video, complete with a ten-gallon hat, cowboy boots, and overalls. Uncle Leroy glanced up at the window, but Malcolm quickly ducked down to avoid being seen. No way was he helping this early. He sincerely doubted that he could survive an entire summer working a farm. He buried his head back under the pillow, determined to get more sleep.

Malcolm woke a few hours later feeling better, grateful for a dreamless slumber, and checked his phone again: 10:00 a.m. *Finally, a respectable time to get up*, he thought, and stretched his arms out toward the walls, recoiling when his hand grazed a poster. If he didn't know better, he could have easily been back home in his own room in D.C. The same iconic pictures hung on his bedroom walls: Martin Luther King Jr. and Malcolm X shaking hands in a friendly embrace, Muhammad Ali issuing a knockout punch, and runners Tommie Smith and John Carlos raising their fists in the air while accepting their 1968 Olympic medals. But Malcolm wasn't in D.C. He was in his dad's old room at the family farm in Natchez, Mississippi—a room his aunt Carol had obsessively kept in pristine condition like a museum for the past sixteen years, even leaving an extra twin bed on the other side of the room that his dad must have had for when friends slept over.

Malcolm kept his eyes off the posters. They reminded him of why he was there. He still couldn't believe his mom had exiled him to the boonies for the summer. Aunt Carol didn't even have Wi-Fi. He checked his phone again. Zero bars. How was he supposed to survive a summer without the 'Gram? So what if he had gotten into a fight at school . . . or a few. People were always testing him. And maybe he could've tried harder in his classes, but why should he if his fate was sealed? Nobody he knew ended up doing anything dope anyway.

The final straw had come when some guys shot up the basketball court where he and his best friend, Damian, had been playing hoops to

celebrate the final day of their sophomore year of high school. The dudes
had fled, and for no reason, he and Damian were arrested as suspects.

When his mom had arrived to pick him up at the police station, she
was shaking. She had squeezed him tight and said she didn't know if
she was more afraid that she had come so close to losing him or relieved
that he was still alive. Malcolm, on the other hand, was just pissed. Only
a few minutes after ducking the bullets of some fools trying to settle a
beef that didn't concern him, he'd found himself on the wrong side of
a cop's pistol pleading for his life.

Later that night, he'd flown into a fit of rage. "All these people are
dead and gone," Malcolm shouted, ripping the posters off the walls while
his mom looked on. "Is this the future that these Black people dreamed
of and died for? It's 2015, and we're still getting shot in the streets like
dogs! Getting hauled off and thrown in jail, no questions asked." He'd
swung then, punching a hole in his wall. "Living in beat-down apart-
ments in broke neighborhoods!"

"Malcolm, stop!" his mom had screamed, horrified by the ripped
posters lying about the floor in shreds. His dad had put up the posters
in his room just before he was born to inspire him to believe in himself
and his potential while growing up. But Malcolm saw it as pure fiction. A
lot of good those beliefs had done his dad. A few months after Malcolm
was born, he had been shot and killed by the police in a case of mistaken
identity.

"Why'd they even bother dreaming?" Malcolm had asked, looking at
his mom like she should've known better. "Nothing changes and nothing gets better. You thought having a Black president would make things
better, but even President Obama can't change that."

His mom had darted out of the room. When she returned, she frantically tried to put the pieces of the posters back together with Scotch
tape, but it was useless. She was so angry she couldn't even look at him.
Malcolm looked on defiantly. He didn't feel bad because he'd meant
every word he'd said. And just like that, Malcolm was on a bus traveling
from Union Station in Washington, D.C., to Jackson, Mississippi, where
his great-aunt Carol had picked him up and driven him to Natchez—and
then even farther, to her farmhouse in the middle of nowhere. That was

last night. Now here he was, halfway across the country surrounded by those same posters on the wall, as if they had hitched a ride.

Malcolm grabbed his sketch pad and pen off the bed and placed them gently on the dresser. At least he had his sketch pad with him. To some people, drawing may have just seemed like a fun way to pass the time, but it was more than that to him. Whenever he felt like the world was spinning out of control and he couldn't take it anymore, he would pick up his charcoal pencil or his favorite black pen and draw things the way he wanted them to be. Sometimes he drew comic book characters taking on his enemies at school, sometimes he drew the smiling faces of friends who had passed away, and sometimes he drew pictures of himself making the winning shot in a basketball game.

But sketch pad or not, Mississippi was the last place Malcolm wanted to be. First, it was all hot and muggy outdoors and even when you made it inside, you couldn't keep the sweat from dripping from your fingers. Thankfully there were the occasional spurts of cool breeze from the window AC units and the large box fans about the place. And second, he didn't have any friends around. What was he supposed to do on a farm all summer? Hang out with the goats? Not to mention his allergies would probably get the best of him. He needed to be in D.C. with his boys playing basketball and video games, but those fools on the court had messed that up.

Malcolm opened the dresser drawers, which were stuffed with his dad's old T-shirts and basketball shorts that Aunt Carol said he could use. How she kept them in such good condition, he had no idea. He threw on a black pair of gym shorts—which were a little big, so he pulled the drawstring tight—and walked over to the closet. Not much was in there besides his backpack, one of his dad's old navy-blue suits and a pair of beat-up sneakers. He finally threw on a white tee, his favorite pair of Jordans, and checked himself in the mirror. An old Polaroid picture stuffed between the dresser mirror and its frame caught his eye. He pulled it from its spot and looked at it. There was his dad playing basketball with a group of friends, his confident allure radiating off the fading square. Slowly, sadness crept in like a river filling with rainwater. Malcolm quickly put the picture down before the levee could break.

As soon as Malcolm stepped out of his room into the second-floor hallway, the smell of homemade buttermilk biscuits and sausage gravy hit him. *And grits?* He couldn't remember tasting grits since his grandma died. He hurried into the bathroom across from his room to brush his teeth and splash some water on face.

"Good morning, Aunt Carol!" Malcolm called as he hopped down the stairway that led directly into the kitchen. For a second, seeing Aunt Carol standing at the stove, he thought it was his grandma Evelyn. Although Aunt Carol was a few years older, they looked almost identical and were frequently mistaken for twins. They both had been pretty, petite ladies with short, wavy, auburn hair and cappuccino-colored skin. But their personalities had set them apart with Grandma Evelyn having a light, carefree demeanor while Aunt Carol, as the stereotypical older sister, seemed weighed down by the stresses of life.

Grandma Evelyn had been all that anyone could ever ask for in a grandma and more. Her presence had filled every room with love and laughter and she had filled everyone's bellies too. Malcolm smiled thinking about what he would give to taste her peach cobbler again, even better with homemade vanilla ice cream.

"Good morning, Malcolm. Did you sleep well?" Aunt Carol asked, turning toward him and smiling, a red rubber spatula in her hand.

"Yeah, mostly, till the rooster woke me up at the crack of dawn."

Aunt Carol laughed. "Just like a broken clock, that rooster's right at least twice a day." Aunt Carol motioned for Malcolm to have a seat at the small round kitchen table covered with a red-and-white-checkered tablecloth. "When Herman crows, it's time to get to bidness. I hope you feel rested because there's plenty of work to do." She walked over to the table and set an empty plate down in front of him. "Hurry up and eat, now. Uncle Leroy's waiting for you," she said, nodding at a platter of biscuits stacked high on the table.

Malcolm groaned as he sat down in one of the four chairs and grabbed a biscuit off the platter.

"Excuse me?" Aunt Carol challenged, whipping her head around. She snatched the biscuit right out of his hand.

Malcolm's mouth fell open in shock before he remembered his mom's admonition about how strict Aunt Carol was about manners.

"I mean, yes ma'am," Malcolm squeaked out sheepishly. Aunt Carol squinted her eyes and nodded, returning the biscuit to Malcolm's plate.

● ● ●

Two platefuls later, Malcolm headed out the kitchen's back door onto the screened-in porch. He paused, looking for Uncle Leroy until he spotted him out in the yard hard at work hefting a small bale of hay. "Good morning, Unc," he called out, leaving the porch and carefully stepping over mud puddles on his way over to him.

Uncle Leroy looked Malcolm up and down, his gaze landing on Malcolm's feet. "I hope those're not your favorite sneakers. They ain't gonna be nearly as pretty when we done."

Given how quickly Malcolm had packed, his Js were the only pair of sneakers he'd brought, and he loved them more than anything else he owned. Uncle Leroy laughed seeing Malcolm's crestfallen face and sent him back inside to borrow a pair of work boots.

As he made his way back in, Malcolm had to admit it was a cute little farmhouse. It looked like its white wooden exterior had been freshly painted, and the rectangular planter boxes that hung on every window were blooming with flowers.

Aunt Carol was surprised to see Malcolm return so quickly.

"Uncle Leroy sent me for some work boots?" Malcolm asked. Aunt

Carol chuckled and pointed him toward her and Uncle Leroy's bedroom, which was through the kitchen and down a hallway to the right of the living room. By mistake, he accidentally opened the door to his grandma's old room, which was across from Aunt Carol's, and smiled, vaguely remembering her reading him a bedtime story on her lap in the rocking chair that sat in the corner. He shut the door softly and moved to the next door. He found the work boots in Aunt Carol and Uncle Leroy's closet.

By the time Malcolm got back outside, Uncle Leroy was leaning against the tractor rolling what appeared to be a joint.

"What is that?" Malcolm exclaimed, surprised to discover Uncle Leroy smoked weed.

"Boy, you ain't never seen a cigarette before?" Uncle Leroy asked incredulously.

"Yeah, but, you mean that's just tobacco?" Malcolm clarified.

"What else would it be? Why? You want one?" Uncle Leroy asked, offering him a freshly rolled cigarette.

"Um, no sir."

"Suit yo'self." Uncle Leroy quickly pivoted to the part of the day that Malcolm had been dreading the most. "Lookee here, I'm gonna need you to move the rest of the hay from the barn to the stable for the horses, grab the feed for the goats from the barn and spread it around their pen, and depending on when you're done, we'll see if you have time to mow the grass." Uncle Leroy handed Malcolm a pair of gloves. "Put these on. If you need me, I'll be over there tending the garden." Uncle Leroy pointed to another indistinguishable plot of land in the distance.

"Man, are you kidding me?" Malcolm asked, looking at him in shock. "I'm from the city. I don't do farms and animals and stuff."

"You do now," Uncle Leroy said, tossing Malcolm a hayfork. "Didn't yo momma tell ya, you gonna earn yo keep around here? You best believe that, city boy."

Malcolm grunted as he took the hayfork and tried to recount Uncle Leroy's list. Number one: Move the hay from the barn to the stable. He walked over to the barn and peered inside. Loose strands of hay covered every inch of the floor. He headed toward the small square bales of hay that were stacked on top of each other in the back and nearly tripped over a chicken that was running around, maniacally flapping its wings.

"What am I doing here?!" Malcolm shouted into the dusty air, fuming, knowing exactly why he was there and hating every second of it. "The sooner I'm done with this, the sooner I can be back inside chillin'." Malcolm told himself, stabbing the bale of hay with the fork. He tried to lift it, but it didn't move an inch. Thinking it might be easier to just carry it, he wrapped his arms around the bale, but immediately started sneezing and itching all over as the blades of hay poked his arms and chest. He tried to return the bale to the pile, but it rolled back toward him, knocking him to the ground.

Lying on his back, Malcolm stared up at the ceiling of the barn stunned at how terribly his morning was going. He got a weird feeling that someone was watching him. *Maybe Uncle Leroy?* He sat up on his elbows and glanced around, but didn't see anybody. He felt the peck of a tiny beak on his arm.

"Arghhh!" Malcolm screamed, scooting out of the way as Uncle Leroy walked in.

"Boy, what is you doing? The horses out there hungry, waiting for their breakfast, and you in here taking a nap? Playing with the chickens?" Uncle Leroy asked, hovering over him.

"Naw man. That thing was trying to eat me! And I'm allergic to hay. I was sneezing and itching . . . I can't do this!" Malcolm shouted, jumping to his feet.

"Fool, everybody is allergic to hay! It's *hay*! And you sooner gonna eat that chicken than it's gonna eat you! Come over here and give me a hand," Uncle Leroy said. He grabbed the hay by its twine and tossed it over his shoulder. "Now go grab a bale and follow me out so we can finish up. I 'bout had enough of you and your tomfoolery today."

"Look, Unc, I tried, but I'm just not cut out for this. Let me know if there's something you need help with inside," Malcolm said as he started backing toward the door.

Uncle Leroy stared at him dumbfounded. "So that's it. You been out here barely five minutes and you quittin'? That's mighty ungrateful of you," he huffed.

"Look, I'm sorry, but I didn't ask to be here, and I never said I wanted to be a farmer," Malcolm scoffed.

"We brought you down here to save you from that city your momma got you living in. You know how lucky you are to have this land in your family? You know how hard it is for Black people to have something of their own, and you don't even want to learn how to take care of it?" he asked, narrowing his eyes in disgust.

"Why would anyone want a farm? You know they have places called grocery stores now? Sorry, Unc. I tried, but this just ain't for me," Malcolm said as he pulled his gloves off and threw them down near the door.

"Fine. Leave. I don't need you here disturbing my peace no way. 'Scuse me, you're in my way," Uncle Leroy snapped as he stormed past Malcolm fast enough to leave a cool breeze in his wake.

Relieved to be done with farming, but still fuming, Malcolm blazed back to the house. As he stormed through the yard, a flicker of movement behind a round upstairs window caught his eye. *What was that?* he wondered, hoping Aunt Carol didn't have some cat in the house. That would mess with his allergies too.

Malcolm marched up the back porch steps, but stopped in the kitchen doorway when he caught sight of Aunt Carol. She was flitting around like a bird with its head on backward. One second, she was digging in her purse, and the next, she was picking up her old-school, corded phone, holding it to her ear a few seconds, then hanging it back up and returning to her purse. She was literally spinning. Malcolm had never seen her so frazzled.

Aunt Carol froze in midmotion, startled that Malcolm had entered the kitchen without her noticing.

3

Aunt Carol plopped down in a chair at the kitchen table and resumed searching through her purse, muttering absentmindedly. "Where are my glasses? They should be . . . "

"Aunt Carol, is everything all right?" Malcolm asked.

Aunt Carol kept digging. "Oh baby, yes. No. Well, it will be. I just got a call from the prison about your uncle Corey. He's being released today." She glanced up momentarily. "They shaved a few years off his sentence because of good behavior combined with the prison getting overcrowd—. The reason doesn't matter. I'm just grateful that he is, praise Jesus! Oh, if only Evelyn were here to see this day." Aunt Carol paused her frantic energy for a moment to kiss her fingertips and hold them up to the ceiling.

"Uncle who?" Malcolm asked, confused.

"Dear God," Aunt Carol said, staring at him in shock. "I forgot you've never met your dad's little brother. He got locked up right before your dad and mom moved to D.C. to make a better life for themselves . . ." Her voice trailed off.

"Uh, okay. Why is this the first time I'm hearing about him?" Malcolm asked, trying to wrap his mind around the fact that his dad had a brother he didn't know about—and that neither his mom nor grandma nor *anyone* else had ever even mentioned him.

Aunt Carol stopped searching in her purse to give Malcolm her full attention. "I'm sorry, baby." Her eyes were full of compassion. "When Corey was a junior in high school, he started hanging with the wrong crowd. He happened to be at some fool's house one day, and the cops busted him for selling marijuana. The state threw the book at every person in that house, and Corey wound up with a twenty-year sentence. They took that baby's whole life away," Aunt Carol said, shaking her head as the eyeglasses she had been looking for slid down from the top of her head onto her forehead. "Here they are. Lord have mercy." She held up the glasses in the light to check for fingerprints and then wiped the lenses with the soft side of her checkered apron. "Your grandma and I used to visit him regularly but your mom asked us not to mention him to you. After your dad died, she thought it was better if you didn't know his only brother was locked up for your whole childhood."

She grabbed her purse and checked inside it once more, letting out a sigh as she retrieved her keys. "She didn't want you to live in fear of growing up as a Black man, but instead wanted to keep you focused on all the good things life has to offer. Evelyn and I thought you could handle it, but it wasn't our call." Standing back up, she announced, "I'm on my way to pick him up now. Want to come with me?"

"Yeah!" Malcolm answered decisively. It was a lot to take in. He was mad and shocked and excited all at the same time. His mom knew how much he missed having a father. He would have given anything to know his dad's brother while growing up, even if it was through prison walls.

"Okay. Let me just run to the bathroom real quick," Aunt Carol said, excusing herself, putting her purse down on the table. When she got back, she grabbed her purse and her car keys, but before she made it to the door, she set her things down and went to use the bathroom once more.

"Are you okay?" Malcolm asked. They were finally out the back kitchen door and making their way down onto a short sidewalk that led to an outdated but sparkling-clean, champagne-colored Buick sedan parked a few yards away in the driveway.

"What are you talking about, baby?"

"I mean, you went to the bathroom like three times in five minutes. You okay?"

Aunt Carol laughed as they climbed inside. She placed her purse on the armrest and buckled her seat belt. "Oh, did I? I didn't even notice. Old habits die hard, I guess."

"What do you mean?"

"Well, back when things were segregated, whenever my family would take a long trip in the car, we never knew where we could stop along the way. Never knew if we would be allowed to use the restrooms at the gas stations or be allowed in a restaurant. So your grandma and I always made a habit of peeing three times before we left the house, just in case we'd have to hold it for a while." Aunt Carol looked left and then right before slowly turning from her gravel driveway onto the country road.

Malcolm welcomed the cool gush of air from the car's AC and tried to imagine a world where he couldn't stop at a gas station to pee. Sometimes the cashier made him buy a candy bar first, but the main color gas attendants seemed to care about was green.

Once on the highway, Aunt Carol motioned to the expanse around them. "This out here used to be our land too," she said.

"Really? We owned a highway? Why would we sell it?" he asked incredulously.

"We didn't own the highway. We owned the land the highway is on. The land has been in our family for generations. We used to have about thirty acres, but the state took a chunk of it to make space for the highway when I was a teenager."

"Oh," Malcolm responded, disappointed. "Did we get good money for it at least?"

"Not really. We didn't want to sell. But the state did some study. They first decided to run the highway through nearby land owned by wealthy White people, but wouldn't you know it? They suddenly had a change of heart. Then they concluded that our land was best location for the highway. So they took it and paid us what they felt like paying. Wasn't nothing we could do to stop it.. We've got five acres left, but they took the best parts."

"Aunt Carol, that doesn't sound right," Malcolm said, scrunching his face in confusion.

"No, baby. It doesn't," she said, smiling weakly.

It was a long, dreary drive to the prison. Foreboding clouds slowly danced across the dark gray sky. Aunt Carol popped in a cassette tape.

"Aunt Carol, how old is this car?" Malcolm asked, his eyebrows raised in surprise as he tried to remember if he had ever seen a cassette in person before.

"Boy, hush. Ain't nothing wrong with my car. Waste not, want not." She shrugged lightheartedly.

Soon Malcolm fell asleep listening to a medley of classic tunes from Nina Simone, Sam Cooke, and Ray Charles. When he awoke, Aunt Carol had already parked in front of the drab concrete prison and was gathering her purse.

"You coming?" she asked impatiently.

Malcolm hurried to follow her out of the car. They walked past a sniper tower and through a tall steel fence covered with rolled barbed wire at the top. Malcolm shuddered at the thought of spending sixteen years trapped inside these menacing walls. The couple of hours he'd spent at the D.C. police station being questioned after the basketball court shooting had been scary enough. In the distance, Malcolm could see dozens of Black men clinging to the inside of a towering metal fence, seemingly longing for someone to rescue them.

Once inside the waiting area, Aunt Carol walked straight up to the front desk and announced matter-of-factly, "I'm here to pick up my nephew."

"And your nephew is . . .?" the lady guard behind the counter asked nonchalantly while smacking on some pink bubble gum.

"Corey, Corey Johnson Williams."

"Mmmph. Please have a seat. Somebody will be with you soon," she said, and pointed at two blue plastic chairs against the wall.

They sat down and waited.

And waited and waited. Aunt Carol crossed and uncrossed her legs for the umpteenth time, staring intently at the round clock hanging on the wall behind the guard's desk. Every now and then she cleared her throat to remind the guard that they were still there. Malcolm concentrated on figuring out the perfect thing to say when meeting his dad's only brother for the first time, but as the minute hand on the clock went round and round, he began to wonder if it would even happen today. Just when he was about to give up hope, a tall, muscular man with mahogany skin, short braids, and a magnetic smile walked through the door carrying a small cardboard box.

As soon as Aunt Carol saw him, she burst into tears. The man dropped his box on the ground and wrapped his large arms around her and wept just as hard.

Finally, he looked up and saw Malcolm standing there. "You must be Malcolm," he said, looking deep into Malcolm's eyes.

"How'd you know?" Aunt Carol asked. "Do you recognize him from the pictures?"

"Naw." Tears formed again in the corner of his eyes. "I'd recognize my big brother anywhere."

Malcolm had mastered the art of being stoic in the face of everyone else's pain, but in that moment, all he wanted to do was collapse into his uncle's arms and sob like a baby, grateful for a connection to his dad that he never even knew existed. But instead he stood there stiffly and confused with his arms by his side, trying to decide what to make of this stranger.

His uncle hugged him nonetheless, but not for long. "All right, we'll have plenty of time for this. Let's get the hell out of here," Uncle Corey said, heading for the doors without looking back.

It was drizzling when they got outside, but Malcolm could see the sun shining through a dark cloud, leaving a bright yellow outline in the sky. Uncle Corey climbed in the car and rolled his window down, leaning his head out and shaking his braids in the rain. Aunt Carol pursed her lips and looked like she was going to admonish him for getting the inside of her car wet, but as the look of ecstasy spread across Uncle Corey's face, she relaxed and said nothing.

From the back seat, Malcolm examined his uncle, comparing him to pictures he had seen of his dad. They definitely resembled one another, but his mom had always described his dad as extremely focused and driven, to the point of being almost uptight. Uncle Corey, on the other hand, exuded serenity beyond what one would expect from someone just released from prison. His calmness didn't appear to be situational; it just seemed like a part of who he was.

When they were pulling up to the house, Uncle Corey asked, "Malcolm, you ball?"

"Hell yeah!" Malcolm enthused. Catching a glimpse of Aunt Carol's eyes narrowing in disapproval in the rearview mirror, he corrected himself. "I mean, heck yeah."

"Not before you eat a home-cooked meal, you won't." Aunt Carol chided as they climbed out of the car. "I got a pot of red beans waitin' for us on the stove."

"You're right. Let me put a little food in my belly, and then we'll head around back." Uncle Corey winked at his nephew.

Malcolm continued to observe Uncle Corey closely, looking for any signs of trauma but not really finding any. More than anything, Uncle Corey just seemed happy and relieved to be back. Malcolm watched him walk slowly toward the farmhouse, pausing on the back porch steps to take in the sight of his home, then smiling reflectively before heading into the kitchen.

Malcolm lingered by the table for a minute but then remembered he needed to change out of Uncle Leroy's work boots. He ran upstairs and put on a pair of his dad's old-school sneakers—not wanting to scuff up his Js. Thankfully, the sneakers fit perfectly and were in good condition after sitting untouched in the closet for at least sixteen years.

The picture of his dad on the dresser caught Malcolm's eye. He picked it up and took a closer look. The teen with his arm swung over his dad's shoulder was a younger version of Uncle Corey. A smile crept over Malcolm's face. With Uncle Corey out, this was the closest to his dad that he had ever been. He respectfully placed the picture back on the dresser and ran downstairs to the kitchen. Uncle Corey was already devouring a heaping plate of red beans and rice.

"Want a bite, Malcolm?" Aunt Carol offered, stirring the steaming pot of red beans.

Malcolm shook his head, but sat down at the table anyway. He was way too excited about getting to know his newfound uncle than to be distracted with eating.

Aunt Carol shrugged and walked over into the laundry room that was just off the kitchen. "Corey, you gonna sleep in Evelyn's old room. I'm gonna let Malcolm keep you and Michael's room to himself this summer."

So that's who the other twin bed was for, Malcolm noted.

Aunt Carol reappeared with a fresh set of sheets in hand and headed down the hallway to the first-floor bedrooms. Suddenly, sunlight filled the kitchen. The rain and clouds were finally passing. Malcolm rose from the table and went over to the sink to glance out the window. *Where could a basketball hoop be hiding?* he wondered.

"You ready?" Uncle Corey asked, scarfing down the last few bites from his plate.

"Sure you don't need more time to digest?" Malcolm queried.

"Naw. I need to stretch my legs. Been cooped up way too long. Don't worry, I'll take it easy on you." He smiled, getting up from the table and placing his plate in the sink. Then he ducked into the laundry room. "If I'm right, Aunt Carol still keeps balls and games and such in here." A few seconds later, he emerged. "Some things never change," he grinned twirling a basketball in his hand.

Malcolm followed Uncle Corey out to the barn, perplexed. He would have surely remembered seeing a hoop in the barn, and maybe would've stayed in there a little longer that morning if he had. But instead of going inside the barn, Uncle Corey walked around it, stopping on a square patch of packed dirt. Nailed to the back of the barn was a bottomless milk crate.

"Your dad and I put this up when we were kids. We both thought we were going to be the next Michael Jordan," he said, grinning while taking a shot that bounced off the rim.

"Were you guys close?" Malcolm asked.

"Thick as thieves. I wanted to be just like him . . . when I wasn't trying to take him out on the court," he laughed, catching the rebound and tossing the ball to Malcolm. "First to twenty-one?"

Malcolm nodded but then held the ball to his chest for a second. "What was he like?" he asked, feeling the familiar pang of sadness he got whenever he thought of his dad.

"Awww man. Your pops was the man. He was cool with everybody: nerds, thugs, grandmas. Everybody loved him cuz he never tried to fake the funk with nobody. Love him or leave him, he didn't care. He was just gonna be himself."

Malcolm took that in. It was nice hearing more about his dad. Malcolm looked around. "You liked growing up here in the country?" he asked, trying to imagine growing up on a farm. He glanced at Uncle Corey, dribbled, and then shot the ball. Nothing but net.

"Okay. He's got some game," Uncle Corey teased, grabbing the ball and dribbling. "It was cool. We did some farming, and we played a lot of sports—mostly football and basketball. Your dad was more into his studies than me. When he wasn't playing sports, he had his head buried in a book." Uncle Corey made a basket from a makeshift three-point line barely visible in the dirt.

"Oh yeah?" Malcolm asked, snatching the rebound and remembering a stack of books he'd found in his dad's room with titles like *The Mis-Education of the Negro* and *The Autobiography of Malcolm X*, which stood out because it was his namesake.

"He was real nice with numbers too. That's how he got into a smarty-pants math program over at Alcorn State and became an engineer."

"That's where he met my mom, right?" Malcolm said, making another shot.

"Not bad, Mal! I see you inherited some of your dad's skills." Uncle Corey grabbed the ball, moved up under the basket, leaped, and dunked it. "Yeah, he met Alesha at Alcorn. Around the time me and your dad started drifting apart. I was hanging with a different crowd who liked a different kind of numbers," Uncle Corey said, laughing. He scooped up the ball and held it tight, looking earnestly in Malcolm's direction, as if making a confession. "Your dad took it hard when I got busted. That's why I think him and Alesha moved to D.C. Once they found out she was pregnant, they didn't want you growing up here—where there's not much to get into besides trouble."

There's plenty enough trouble to get into in D.C., Malcolm thought, *trust*.

"Alesha could teach anywhere, and your dad found a good job with the federal government. So I owe you an apology. If I hadn't been such a knucklehead and gotten myself locked up, maybe your pops wouldn't have gone off to D.C. and . . . maybe he'd still be alive today," he said, tossing Malcolm the ball.

Stunned by his uncle's reasoning, a whiff of air escaped Malcolm's lips as if he had been punched in the gut, and the ball brushed past Malcolm's outstretched fingers to land with a thud in the dirt. He reached down to pick up the ball, gathering his thoughts in the process. Had his whole life been affected by Uncle Corey going to prison? Something he didn't even know had happened before today? *Naw*, he decided, *my dad's death wasn't Uncle Corey's fault*.

"Man, you can't think like that," Malcolm said. "You're not the one that pulled the trigger." Malcolm brooded, his mood getting darker. They were on some serious ground.

"I don't know, Nephew. If he wasn't running away from my mistakes, he wouldn't have been walking home from that dark bus station in D.C. when the cops stopped him. And they wouldn't have confused him for another brother and shot him and left him to die in the street like a dog."

Malcolm didn't respond. Sadness and anger mixed inside him.

"Did your mom even tell you about me?" Uncle Corey asked, his eyes pleading for absolution.

Malcolm averted his eyes, and took a shot instead. It was a brick. "Naw, I didn't know my dad had a brother until this morning."

Uncle Corey nodded, grabbing the ball and dribbling it in place. "I get it. It's hard enough raising a Black boy in this country without him having to know his dad was murdered by the cops for no reason and his dad's only brother was locked up for decades over some bull. I get it."

Malcolm shook his head in disagreement. He felt the void from his dad's death constantly and maybe knowing his uncle would've filled it a little. He could've told him what his dad was like growing up and helped him understand how they were alike and different.

"You gonna shoot that thing," Malcolm teased, eager to move on to a happier subject. He swooped in, stealing the ball from Uncle Corey before making another shot.

Uncle Corey quickly took the ball back. Malcolm stepped near the basket, watching him line up the shot.

"You out now, man. How's it feel?" he asked.

"Feels good, can't lie. But everything reminds me of how much I've missed. Like, this is the first time I'm meeting you and you damn near grown." The ball went through the basket easily. Malcolm picked it up and dribbled it back. "But I didn't want you to see me in there like that either. Alesha did the right thing keeping you away."

"I don't think so, Unc. I would've understood," Malcolm said, pausing before taking his shot.

"Maybe, but prisons are no place for kids, even though they sho nuff got enough kids in 'em. They suck the soul out of you and leave you a shell of yourself. Even if you had met me while I was in there, you wouldn't have known me." Uncle Corey returned the favor by snatching the ball away from Malcolm and shooting, making another basket effortlessly. "Yes!" he said, pumping his fist in the air.

"And man, have things changed since I went in!" he continued enthusiastically. "Like, we got a Black president? What?!? That was something that we only rapped about in the '90s. I never, never thought it would happen! And everybody got a cell phone, not just the drug dealers. And you got the world at your fingertips with the Internet and everybody's all connected to one another. It's wild! It's like living in the future, which I guess is what this is."

"Good luck getting a signal here." Malcolm groaned, rolling his eyes. "Only thing my phone is good for is telling time, but yeah, I guess a lot has changed in sixteen years, which is my whole life, so I didn't notice."

"I got a lot of catching up to do, but I'll get there. Maybe my nephew can teach me a thing or two," he said, smiling. "All right. What are we at, nine to eight? First to twenty-one buys the other ice cream."

"You're on," Malcolm said, sinking another shot.

After a couple of hours of playing ball, Malcolm was suddenly parched. He ran back to the house to get him and Uncle Corey something to drink. Uncle Corey trailed behind, saying he wanted to hang out on the back porch to savor every breath of fresh air during his first full day of freedom.

When Malcolm entered the kitchen, he was surprised to find one of the prettiest girls he had ever seen, in a purple cotton shift dress, standing beside the kitchen table. Her radiant brown skin, wide toffee-colored eyes, high cheekbones, and fluffy jet-black hair casually pulled back with a folded tie-dyed bandanna stopped him in his tracks. *Please don't let this be another surprise relative*, Malcolm silently pleaded while trying not to stare.

"Uh, hi," Malcolm said to no one in particular as he made a beeline to the refrigerator.

Aunt Carol looked at Malcolm, amused by his apparent discomfort.

"Malcolm, this is Jasmine. She lives on the farm next door. Jasmine, this is my great-nephew, Malcolm."

Malcolm gave her a nod and mouthed *Sup*, before proceeding to grab a couple of plastic cups from the cabinet and the pitcher of lemonade from the fridge. He filled his cup to the brim. "This is some good lemonade," he said, taking a long sip. He refilled his cup, poured Uncle Corey's cup, and began to return the pitcher to the fridge.

"Malcolm, do you want to offer Jasmine some?" Aunt Carol prompted while clearing space on the counter.

"Oh, my bad. You want some?" he asked.

"No, I'm okay. Thank you. I was just stopping by to drop off some dessert for y'all's family reunion. My granny sent her best pineapple upside-down cake, and sweet potato and pecan pie."

"I love cake," Malcolm said clumsily. "Um, what family reunion?" he asked, turning to Aunt Carol.

"We're having our annual family cookout tomorrow. It's going to be extra special this year with you and Corey here. I didn't know either of you would be in town when I picked the date—I always pick a Saturday in June when most folks are free." She beamed. "And this year it's gonna be right on time," Aunt Carol said, suddenly looking away. She pursed her lips while lining up the desserts neatly on the countertop.

"Okay. So you won't be there?" Malcolm asked Jasmine, wanting to officially confirm that he was not salivating over a cousin.

"Naw. I got other plans. Do you live here now?" Jasmine inquired as she sat down at the kitchen table and made herself more comfortable.

"No. I live in D.C. I'm just down here for the summer." Malcolm leaned against the fridge sipping his lemonade.

"Ooh, D.C. What's that like?" she asked, her eyes lighting up. "I've never left Mississippi," she added in a cute Southern drawl.

"It's cool. There's mad shi—I mean stuff, to do," Malcolm said quickly correcting himself, catching Aunt Carol's eyes narrowing in disapproval.

"Wow. I'd love to see it one day. I have an aunt that moved up there a long time ago and cousins I've never met. Maybe I should see if they'd let me visit."

Malcolm entertained the idea, but figured a pretty farm girl like her would get eaten alive in D.C. with its fast pace and cutthroat atmosphere. She'd probably get lost on its sprawling Metro system.

"Yeah, you should come. You'd love it," he lied.

"Cool. I gotta go. My granny asked me to hurry back to help her prep some cakes. Enjoy the treats, Miss Carol. Nice to meet you, Malcolm. Hope to see you around," Jasmine said, standing up suddenly to excuse herself.

"Yeah, me too," he said, not sure if that made any sense.

As soon as Jasmine left, Aunt Carol looked over at Malcolm and clucked her tongue before smiling and walking out into the living room. Malcolm was smiling too as he headed out to the porch to give Uncle Corey his lemonade.

Later that evening after dinner, Malcolm was still thinking about Jasmine. He sat down on the floor next to his bed with his pen and sketch pad in hand. He flipped past the images of the basketball court shootout and his police interrogation that he had sketched during the bus ride to Mississippi.

The door to Malcolm's bedroom opened and he turned to see who it was. No one. *Weird old house*, Malcolm thought. He got up and shut the door, then made his way back to his spot on the floor by the bed, picking up his pen and sketch pad. He tried to capture Jasmine's beauty. He focused first on her eyes before moving down to her sculpted cheekbones. The sketch was all right. It would be better if he saw her again. He'd see her again. Right?

"Malcolm, I need a little help setting up," Aunt Carol said with her hands deep in the refrigerator. "Could you go over to the buffet cabinet that's in the living room and get me three trays and two large bowls? Make sure you bring back my silver platter that's got the flowers engraved around it."

Aunt Carol had spent the whole morning in the kitchen cooking for the family reunion. Uncle Corey was outside giving Uncle Leroy a hand with the grill, and Aunt Carol put Malcolm to work sweeping and mopping the floors.

Malcolm knelt down to open the double doors of a squat old oak cabinet, and a pile of trays, plates, bells, and silverware boxes began falling out. He pushed everything back inside and brought her the platters and bowls that she had requested.

The front doorbell rang. "Who's that?" Aunt Carol called out when she heard people piling into the living room.

"So glad y'all could make it." Aunt Carol beamed upon seeing who was entering the kitchen. "Malcolm, meet your second cousin Cynthia, and her oldest boys, Keith and Kliff." She added, "Cynthia, you can put that there on the table."

Malcolm reached over to help, taking an oversize bowl of potato salad out of Cynthia's hands and setting it on the kitchen table. Then he turned to greet his family.

"Waddup, Mal," Kliff said while giving Malcolm dap. The brothers looked to be around Malcolm's age and bore a slight family resemblance, each standing a little over six feet with curly jet-black hair. Kliff even shared Malcolm's chin dimple.

"Cynthia is the only person I allow to bring potato salad to the cookout," Aunt Carol said, winking at her. "Malcolm will you take that on out?"

"Sure, Aunt Carol." Malcolm carried the bowl of potato salad outside into the steamy Mississippi afternoon. A dozen other people were already mingling around a picnic table in the backyard, fanning themselves with paper plates. A group of folks had surrounded Uncle Corey and were hugging him and welcoming him back home.

"I'm just grateful to escape that place alive," Malcolm overheard Uncle Corey say as he set the bowl down onto the picnic table. "I saw way too many good brothers leave in a body bag long before their time. Half the time the guards were worse than the inmates, always trying to start fights and selling illegal stuff inside. It was real hard to figure out who the real criminals were. One of these days, I'll be able to sleep with my eyes shut again," he said, chuckling bitterly.

A freckly-faced aunt with bright red hair gently stroked Uncle Corey's hand. "We're just glad you're home, baby," she purred soothingly. He smiled back, soaking up all the love like a sponge.

Aunt Carol brought out a cooler filled with lemonade and placed it on the far end of the picnic table next to the plastic cups. Foil pans overflowing with barbecued ribs, grilled chicken, and well-done burgers crowded the table, with baked beans and rolls rounding out the menu.

Malcolm looked around, admiring the intimacy the family shared—the kind that only comes from knowing someone your whole life. The truth was it got lonely in D.C. sometimes without any other family members around. Holidays spent with just him and his mom were quiet. His mom's parents had been long gone before he was born and with his dad dead, she didn't seem interested in maintaining past relationships. Instead, she put all her focus into her job and raising Malcolm. She worked hard as a teacher and doubly hard as a mom, and that seemed to be enough for her. Malcolm wondered if his close brush with death had forced her to reconsider. Maybe she'd come to realize that she couldn't provide him everything he needed and that quality time with family could help.

As the oldest person at the reunion and the clear matriarch of the family, Aunt Carol was the first stop for any new arrival to greet with a kiss. Noticing Malcolm awkwardly standing off to the side of the picnic table, Aunt Carol cleared her throat and casually announced, "Family, this is Malcolm, Michael and Alesha's boy. Malcolm, this is your family." Folks glanced up from their conversations to smile and wave. "There's a T-shirt for you in the cardboard box over there," she said, pointing to an adjacent picnic table that, besides the shirt box, also had on it a woven basket filled with brightly colored flowers.

Malcolm walked over and pulled out a bright blue *Johnson Family Reunion* T-shirt emblazoned with an outline of the state of Mississippi from the cardboard box. He looked at the shirt quizzically, questioning how much this family reunion really had to do with him. He didn't know hardly anyone here. He never thought of himself as being "a Johnson from Mississippi" since D.C. was all he'd ever known, and his last name was Williams. Still he couldn't deny how familiar everyone seemed, even if life here couldn't be more different than back home.

After putting on his T-shirt, he made himself a plate and walked over to a cluster of teenage cousins joking with one another under a towering pecan tree a few feet away.

"Hey fam. I'm Malcolm. What's up?"

"Mal, this is Brian and Tyrone," Kliff said, nodding at the cousins Malcolm hadn't met yet while balancing an overflowing plate of ribs in one hand.

"So you're our cousin? How come we never seen you before?" Brian, the smallest one asked.

"I live in D.C. I'm just down here for the summer."

"Oh yeah? I've heard good things about D.C. What made you want to come down here? I can't imagine you're having more fun at Aunt Carol's than you'd be having there right now. Huh bruh?" Tyrone chuckled.

"I just needed a little time to .chill out, get my head straight. You know how it is."

"Yeah man. I feel ya." Kliff nodded knowingly.

"So what's D.C. like, for real?" Keith asked.

"Man, it's cool, I guess. I never really been anywhere else." Malcolm shrugged his shoulders. "Tourists love it. They're always coming to D.C. to see stuff. Over by the Capitol, it's all shiny and nice, but it's little rougher in my hood, but that's why it's called a hood, right? One of my homies got killed over some bull last year, and you know cops always trying to lock a brother up for somethin'."

"Damn. That sucks. Don't get it twisted. It's bad down here too. Shoot, Parchman penitentiary is right up the river, and I know mad folks in there. I guess there ain't too many places where it's good to be Black," Kliff commiserated.

"Maybe Hawaii," Brian joked.

"Man, shut up, Brian," Kliff said, playfully punching him in the shoulder. "Ain't no Black folk in Hawaii."

"What about President Obama? They must have *some* Black folks out there," Brian said, laughing. "Naw, I'm just playing."

"So what y'all do for fun here? I know there's gotta be more than mowing lawns and milking cows," Malcolm teased.

"Ha! Okay. You wanna call us country?" Keith laughed back. "Man, we prolly do the same things you do. Chill, holla at shawties, play basketball. Just kick it."

"No doubt. No doubt. Me too. What's up with that girl Jasmine who lives next door? Y'all know her?" Malcolm asked casually.

"Oh she cool. She don't really give nobody round here the time of day though. You know how them siddity girls are," Keith said, rolling his eyes.

Malcolm nodded hoping that meant he might have a shot.

Malcolm and his cousins spent the rest of the afternoon hanging out, eating, talking smack, and listening to music. By the end of the day, he felt like he had known them his whole life. Malcolm suddenly felt a pang of loss for the family he had never known growing up so far away, and for the first time, wished his mom had brought him back to visit Mississippi a little more often.

A nice breeze blew through the air as the evening approached.

The sun began its descent into the horizon, and the sky obediently followed, shifting like a kaleidoscope from fiery orange to mellow purple to celestial blue. As the reunion began to wind down, Malcolm grabbed a trash bag and walked around collecting the empty plates.

Aunt Carol waved her hands to summon everyone to the picnic table for an announcement. "Well, I just want to thank y'all for taking the time to come to this year's reunion. I can't tell y'all enough how much joy it brings me to see everyone all together like this. We've got so many different branches of our family tree here, but at the end of the day, we're all Johnsons. I know Mama Lucille would have liked to know that we kept the annual cookout going after she passed, even though this one might be our last . . ." Her voice trailed off.

"What are you talking about, Carol?" the red-haired aunt asked.

"Well, I've been praying it wouldn't come to this, but . . ." She paused and appeared to suppress tears as she tried to gather her composure.

Malcolm leaned in, wondering what she was about to say.

"But," she resumed, clearing her throat, "the state has made the decision to expand the highway, and I got a letter saying they're gonna be taking the rest of our family's land by the end of year to do it."

Gasps rang out in the crowd.

"No, Carol. Not again!" an old man in a wheelchair hollered out.

"They gonna pay?" someone asked.

"Yeah, they gonna pay. But what difference does it make? We can't afford to buy land like this again. Plus, I don't want money. I want my home." Aunt Carol's lips tightened and tears glistened in the corner of her eyes.

Uncle Leroy walked up and put his arm around Aunt Carol's shoulders. His small show of support appeared to restore her and give her strength. She pulled her shoulders back and lifted her chin. It sucked that Aunt Carol and Uncle Leroy would have to leave their home in their eighties, but they'd be all right, Malcolm figured. At least they had each other and maybe it was time for something new.

"Okay, enough of that," Aunt Carol said, visibly shaking the negative energy from her head before continuing. A full smile returned to her lips. "I'm so happy that Malcolm was able to join us this year and get to know everybody and that Corey is back home." She looked at each of them wistfully. "I know our family's future is bright. As always, before everybody leaves, I would like us to pay respect to our past." She pulled a handful of flowers from the basket on the table and began walking toward the back of the property in the direction of the barn.

Everyone followed her as if they knew where she was going, each person picking up a couple of flowers from the basket on their way. Malcolm brought up the rear, wondering where they were headed, as the cacophony of mating crickets echoed in his ear.

Malcolm followed his family down a well-worn path that ran along-side the barn past a section of the property covered in overgrown brush. Aunt Carol pushed open a little chain-link gate and stepped inside a plot that was hidden from view from the farmhouse. Everyone followed her quietly. Illuminated in the moonlight, Malcolm could see twenty, maybe thirty headstones on a neatly maintained patch of grass. They were in a graveyard.

Aunt Carol walked right up to a particular headstone, neatly arranged the flowers on top of it, and turned to address the group. "For years our family has owned this land. Countless relatives were born here, raised here, and died here. The sacrifices they made to make our family strong guide me and give me strength. As always, I'd like to take a moment to let them know that while they may be gone, they are not forgotten."

Aunt Carol leaned over the grave and whispered, "I love you, Mama," before turning to walk out of the little graveyard and back up the path to the house. One by one, folks stopped to say a prayer or lay a flower on top of different headstones before heading back to the farmhouse. By the end, Mama Lucille certainly had the most flowers, but tokens of appreciation were scattered around the graveyard. Uncle Corey lingered in front of Grandma Evelyn's grave, wiping away tears, no doubt trou-bled that he had missed her passing while he was locked up. Malcolm waited until he was done and then laid a rose on Grandma Evelyn's grave as well, kissing her headstone with the palm of his hand.

As he stood up to leave, he noticed a looming headstone at the rear of the graveyard and walked toward it. The inscription carved into the stone read:

CEDRIC JOHNSON	ISABEL JOHNSON
CIRCA 1851–	DECEMBER 17, 1855–
OCTOBER 19, 1902	MARCH 6, 1906

BORN IN SLAVERY, DIED IN FREEDOM

Malcolm stepped closer and leaned down to get a better look. A cool gust of wind blew across his face. The hairs on the back of his neck stood straight up. His heart raced. He looked around suspiciously, but no one was there—not even Uncle Corey. Apparently, the rest of his family had made their way back to the house. He could hear people off in the distance saying their goodbyes and getting into their cars. Just when Malcolm thought he should rush to catch up, he heard a baritone voice clear as day:

"Don't let them take my farm."

8

Malcolm leaped a foot into the air and then fell on his butt. He scrambled away from the headstone trying to get his feet underneath him. Finally, he was able to shoot up and run back to the house. Once he was within the ambit of the kitchen lights, he slowed down. A rush of relief came over him when he felt the crunch of backyard grass under his feet again. He took a breath, dusted his hands off, and tried to make sense of what he'd heard. "I must be losing my mind," he murmured.

Still unsettled by what had just happened, Malcolm walked up the porch steps in a confused daze and stepped into the kitchen. All was normal inside. Aunt Carol was busy tidying up the kitchen and putting food away. He could hear the buzz of the TV in the living room over Uncle Leroy's loud snore. Uncle Corey must have already gone to his room because Malcolm didn't see him around. Lost in his thoughts, Malcolm drifted over to the stairs leading up to the second floor.

"Excuse me! Good night, Malcolm," Aunt Carol said, interrupting his thoughts.

"Oh, I'm sorry." Malcolm said, turning back to Aunt Carol who was standing with her hands on her hips in front of an open refrigerator door. He shook his head to clear it. "Thanks for today. It was really nice."

"I'm just glad you were here," she said, drying her hands on her apron. "Everybody should know their family."

"Yeah." He nodded, wondering if he should tell her that an unexpected relative might have tried to crash the family reunion. "I'm pooped," he said, deciding against it. "Gonna get some sleep. Good night, Aunt Carol."

"Good night, baby," she said, covering a serving bowl with foil.

When Malcolm got to the top of the steps, another cool breeze moved behind him, just like in the graveyard. He glanced around in the upstairs hallway. "Man, I'm tripping," Malcolm said, shaking his head again. He quickly went into his room and shut the door behind him. He tried to stop thinking about what had happened in the cemetery, but it was impossible. Spotting his sketch pad on the floor, he picked it up to sketch for a while and calm down. He admired how nice Jasmine's sketch came out, even if he wasn't quite finished with it. If he could figure out a way to see her again, maybe this trip wouldn't be so bad after all.

Turning to a fresh page, Malcolm began sketching some of the more memorable faces from the family reunion—Uncle Donny seated in a wheelchair, Aunt Peaches with her bright red hair, the cousins gathering around Uncle Corey in adoration. Soon the incident in the graveyard was behind him. He was in the zone. He began drawing Aunt Carol but paused when he couldn't figure out what expression to give her. Should he try to capture the joy she emanated while greeting loved ones or the haunted look in her eyes when she told the family the state was going to take their land?

THUMP! A loud sound erupted from somewhere in the house above his head. Malcolm sat there for a moment wondering what could've made that noise. Maybe it was the cat he thought he'd seen in the round window from outside yesterday. After a few moments of silence, Malcolm went back to drawing, but no sooner had he picked up his pen than he heard another loud THUMP. He glanced around for a

round window, but his bedroom window was rectangular. *Maybe the window is in the hallway*, he thought as he got up to investigate with his pad and pen tucked under his arm. He still didn't see a round window, but he noticed a hall closet and opened the door to see if the window was inside there. To his surprise, he found himself standing at the foot of a staircase. *I didn't know this old house had an attic*, Malcolm thought as another cool breeze blew, sending chills down his spine.

Malcolm proceeded up the stairs to a landing shrouded in darkness, the floorboards creaking with every step. He instinctively felt along the wall for a light switch, but nothing. Finally, his eyes adjusted and he could see a string in front of him hanging from the ceiling. He pulled on the string and the soft glow from a dim light bulb revealed a decent-size attic with solid wood floors spanning the length of the room. An old oak desk and matching wooden chair occupied one corner, and an oversize bright yellow beanbag chair and box fan were in another. His childish fears subsided, and he began to see the room as a cool place to hang out and draw. He'd even have a whole fan all to himself.

He finally spotted the small round window on the far wall and noticed a slight crack in its pane. *That must be where the breeze was coming from*, he thought, even though he knew it was warmer outside than in the attic. Malcolm brushed this fact from his mind, satisfied that one mystery was solved. Next, he looked around to figure out what had caused the banging sounds, but nothing stood out. No cat was lurking in the shadows. It was an old house, maybe he just had to get used to its sounds. He walked around the room, dusted a handful of cobwebs off the wall, and turned on the fan, which was as refreshing as an ice-cold washcloth after a long day playing hoops. Then he plopped down onto the beanbag chair, sending up a dust plume around him. He coughed a few times, chuckling. "Man, I've been tripping." He settled in and began concentrating on drawing Aunt Carol's expression in his sketch.

A shadow appeared, looming over his sketch pad.

"Nice drawing."

"Aaaauughhhhhhhh!!!!" Malcolm screamed, scrambling to get away, but the beanbag chair was too deep and swallowed him whole. He pulled his knees up to his chest and covered his head with his hands. "Please don't hurt me," he repeated over and over again.

"Boy, calm down. I'm not the one you need to be afraid of," the baritone voice said, then snorted.

Malcolm peeked through his fingers. The man's face hovered above him and slowly his full body, dressed in a chocolate suit with suspenders, came into view. He looked a lot like Malcolm, but with a weird mustache that twisted up at the ends, which was eerily familiar.

"You need to understand something," he said, raising his hand into the air. "You and your uncle think y'all got it bad?"

"What? Stay away!" Malcolm shrank back farther, so scared he could hardly breathe.

"You'll be fine, son," he said, touching Malcolm's forehead with the tip of his index finger. "Trust me."

Then . . . all went black.

• • •

Malcolm felt the floor open up and swallow him. He was falling, falling, falling before finally landing with a thump. Thankfully, it didn't hurt. It was more like when someone slams hard on the brakes in a car. He was in a dark room with loud booms and bangs echoing all around him. His head felt dizzy. It took him a moment to realize the booms and bangs were gunshots, but as soon as he did, his instincts from surviving the shootout on the D.C. basketball court kicked in. He ducked and felt around for cover. The only problem was he couldn't see a foot in front of him and had no idea where he was. Gradually, his eyes adjusted to the dark, and he could see that he was crouching on a hardwood floor under a pitched roof with exposed rafters, like an attic.

His mind raced, trying to put the pieces together. He must be dreaming. That kind of dreaming where you know you're dreaming. He must have passed out in the beanbag chair and dreamed he was falling, but was still in the attic at Aunt Carol's house. If he was dreaming, he'd never dreamed of anything as real as this.

After about ten minutes, the booming stopped and was replaced by the moans and wails of people in agony. Then the wails stopped. Outside, Malcolm could hear the excited yelps of people celebrating and the clack of horse hooves smacking the street fading into the distance. Then all was silent. Malcolm waited a few minutes more before slowly getting on his feet. In the darkness, he could faintly make out a door on the other side of the room and walked toward it. He pressed his ear to the door first to make sure he was alone. Nothing. He opened it slowly, an inch at a time, and sunlight streamed in revealing a short landing before him and a set of descending stairs. Malcolm walked to the stairs and began making his way down, but came to a quick halt. He couldn't believe what he saw lying before him at the bottom of the stairs. Strewn all over the floor were Black men in suits riddled with bullets and beaten beyond recognition.

Malcolm's nostrils stung from the stench of gunpowder and burning flesh. He braced himself against a wall, overwhelmed by the sight, and vomited. He gasped, tears forming in his eyes. "Where am I?" He stood up and wiped a lingering trail of vomit from his mouth and tried to get ahold of himself.

"This is just a dream. It's a dream."

He carefully stepped over the corpses of the men whose faces and bodies were contorted in final pangs of agony. As he tried to escape the room, his shoes left a trail of bloody footprints behind. Only, the floppy brown loafers he was wearing weren't his shoes—he'd never buy anything like them. He made his way down a hall where he finally found the front door of the building, but there were bodies piled up in front of it blocking his exit.

He stood there for a moment staring, willing himself to remain calm, and trying to figure out what to do. He walked over to a nearby window and peered outside. The coast looked clear. Taking a deep breath, he decided his only option was to clear a path to the door. He began nudging the dead bodies aside as gently as he could as his stomach lurched. When he was finally able to pry the door open, he stepped through a set of columns onto the sidewalk. He stooped over with his hands on his knees, gulping in fresh air like a fish out of water. As he descended the steps to the packed-dirt street, he nearly tripped over the bodies of two more men who lay crumpled together, discarded like trash. Both had stab wounds all over their bodies and their heads were smashed beyond recognition.

Malcolm took off running aimlessly through the abandoned city streets, trying to get as far away from the building as he could, but it was starting to get dark, and there were no streetlights. He had no idea where he was, or where he was going. Exhausted, he collapsed under a tree in a park a few blocks away. Pulling his knees up to his chest, he began rocking back and forth, as tears poured from his eyes. He couldn't shake the horrific images he'd seen inside that building.

"Wake up. Wake up," Malcolm whispered over and over. "I want to go home. Please take me home," he pleaded.

In a flash, he was back, curled up on the bright yellow beanbag chair in Aunt Carol's attic. The strange man with the twisted mustache lingered over him, watching closely to see if Malcolm was okay.

"What did you do to me?!" Malcolm screamed angrily. "Where did you send me?"

Looking at Malcolm with compassion and a hint of regret, the man pointed to the corner of the attic. "It seems I have your attention. My answers are in the desk," he said, and then vanished before Malcolm's eyes.

10

Gasping to catch his breath, Malcolm sat in the beanbag chair, staring at the place where the man once stood before disappearing. He didn't understand. He was hearing and seeing people who weren't real and traveling to places that didn't exist. He touched his face with his hands expecting his cheeks to be wet from the tears he'd cried under the tree, but his face was dry. The images of the bodies were still too clear in his mind to ignore. He needed answers.

The phantom had said something about his answers being in the desk. Malcolm stood up, but felt a surge of blood rush to his head. He sat down again to breathe and get ahold of himself. When his heartbeat and breathing had slowed, he shakily walked over to inspect the desk. After running his fingers over the ornate carvings in the wood, he opened the center drawer to see what was inside. It was empty. He then tried to open each of the three side drawers, but they were all locked. As Malcolm was about to close the center drawer, he heard something clang and reached inside to see what it was, but didn't feel anything. He got down on his knees, took his cell phone out of his pocket, and pointed the flashlight toward the desk. At least his phone was still good for something without a cell signal.

He spotted a shiny object stuck between the back of the drawer and the frame of the desk. Malcolm pulled the drawer out slightly, reached up from underneath, and withdrew a key. He immediately tried it on the locked drawers and found it unlocked all three. The first two were empty, but as he was feeling inside the third drawer, his fingertips brushed against something leathery.

Malcolm hesitated for a moment, questioning what he was getting himself into. Maybe it would be better to go back to his room and forget this ever happened. Chalk it up to another strange dream. But part of him knew he had already seen too much to turn back. Filled with trepidation, he reached in farther and pulled out . . . a book.

Malcolm wiped off a layer of dust and read the word *Diary* embossed in gold on the worn, black leather cover. He flipped open the book and stared at the first page, which was filled with twisted cursive writing that he could barely read. His jaw dropped when he finally deciphered the date in the top left corner: *July 30, 1866*. Intrigued, Malcolm sat down in the desk chair to give the book his full attention. He glanced around the room to see if the phantom had returned, but after confirming he was alone, he began reading.

July 30, 1866

It was a massacre. Wounded men lay about, howling in pain; many more with their cries silenced forever. All because free men wanted to exercise their right to vote, to organize, and have our voices heard. But the white folks in Louisiana wouldn't stand for it. And so they slaughtered us like pigs. Pa was one of hundreds of negroes murdered at the Mechanics' Institute today.

It's not right. It's not fair. I still need him. I spent the evening going through Pa's meager belongings. His pocket watch, his Bible, his flask, his journal. Each one brought back a flood of memories of the times we shared. On the last page of Pa's journal, he wrote his favorite scripture: "If ye have faith as a grain of mustard seed, ye shall say unto this mountain, Remove hence to yonder place; and it shall remove; and nothing shall be impossible unto you."

I woke up this morning with all the faith in the world, but today my faith was shattered. This morning, I stood shoulder to shoulder with my brothers, demanding Louisiana pass a new state constitution that would recognize that negroes are equal with whites in the eyes of the law. But instead of enjoying freedom with Pa by my side, as we were promised at the end of the war, I sit here writing his eulogy. I can't

Malcolm paused reading, completely befuddled. The writer appeared to stop mid-sentence. And what war was he talking about? "Wait, the Civil War?" Malcolm gasped as he revisited the date at the top of the page. "1866. What?!," he exclaimed, and continued reading.

August 2, 1866

We buried Pa today. I had the hardest time writing his eulogy. How do I sum up who he was in just a few words? Above all, he was a survivor. Born a slave on a plantation outside of New Orleans, his master called him Sam. He renamed himself Isaiah—meaning God is Salvation—Johnson when he went to register at the Freedmen's Bureau. His mother was a tall, slim woman who toiled in the sugarcane fields from sunup to sundown for the better part of her life. Pa was also tall and slim, but fairer than his mother. Even though he never knew for certain who his pa was, he had some idea given how much he looked like the master's white sons.

As a young'un, he served the master's children and went everywhere they went. When he was sittin' in the back of the tutor's house, he'd pretend to fall asleep, but hung on to every word. He learned how to read that way, something he hid from white folks so they wouldn't tan his hide, or worse, and practiced on an old Bible that nobody noticed went missing.

And boy did Pa love the Bible. He couldn't stop talking about the faithful servants like Abraham, Job, Jonah, and Moses who never doubted the Lord, no matter what troubles they faced. They gave him hope that our living nightmare would also end and that one day, the Lord would deliver us from the evils of slavery, as he had the Jews. From the time he was barely as high as a water pump, Pa preached the gospel to all the slaves on the plantation who still held out hope that they'd one day know freedom. He taught me how to read with his old Bible, and made sure I learnt that while white folks may be able to control our bodies, they could never control our minds.

I'll never forget the day we got the news that the North had won the war, and we were free! Never before had I seen Pa cry, but that morning he dropped to his knees and wept like a baby. He hugged me so tight he almost squeezed the breath out of my lungs. When I asked him why he was crying, he said, "If only your ma had lived to see this day." Even on the happiest day of his life, he carried my ma's memory with him. He always said she was the prettiest and kindest woman he knew. I never met her because she died while giving birth to me, but he always said that I have her dimpled smile.

As soon as Pa learnt that slavery was over, he set out to lay claim to his freedom and all that came with it. He summoned his flock to meet at his shack to discuss what was needed most, with me by his side taking notes: land on which to build our homes and plant our gardens; schools so that our children could thrive; and more than anything, the right to vote so that we could elect people who understand us and our needs. Surely our centuries of labor and sacrifice have at least earned us this modest remittance!

What does this have to do with all the strange things that have been happening to me? Malcolm wondered, setting the diary back down on the desk. He wasn't any closer to understanding why he was having crazy visions that felt so real. And all this slavery talk was weird to read about. It all happened so long ago. Why was he being forced to read about it now? Who knew if this diary was even real. It could all be some prank. *I guess it wouldn't hurt to read a little further to find out*, he figured.

We were so excited to hear that the freemen of color in New Orleans had formed an Equal Rights League and had sent a petition to President Lincoln demanding the right to vote. The Louisiana government had a different idea about what to do with all the newly freed negroes in the state and began passing law after law trying to find different ways to put us back in chains, losing the war be damned. A couple of days ago, Pa and I joined thousands of negroes all across Louisiana to descend on New Orleans like a swarm of bees and attend a Constitutional Convention at the Mechanics' Institute where our rights would be decided. It started out such a glorious day, but it came to such a tragic end.

We met on Canal Street, and I couldn't believe my eyes. Never before had I seen so many negroes marching through the streets of New Orleans, all dressed in their Sunday best—not even on Easter. In full celebratory spirit, folks were tooting their horns, banging their drums, dancing, laughing, cheering, and proudly hoisting the American flag as high as they could. But by the time we arrived at the Mechanics' Institute hundreds of armed white men decked in Confederate battle gear were waiting to arrest us, looking like they were preparing for the last battle of the war. But we hadn't come prepared for war, only a peaceful march.

We rushed inside the Mechanics' Institute for safety and barely beat the mob who immediately began ramming the front doors, screaming for blood. I looked around for anything I could find to protect myself: chairs, flags, drums, horns. A group of strong men blocked the door using tables and their bodies, but it was a poor defense from gunfire. Men were falling on my left and right. Women and children were frantically looking for places to hide.

I lost sight of my pa in the commotion, and went upstairs to find him. Never one to give up without a fight, I found him firing rocks with a makeshift sling out the window at the mob below. Then I heard a loud scream behind me, and turned to see a man jump out a window trying to escape. I ran over to the window and was relieved he landed safely. Just as I was preparing to make the jump myself, a mob surrounded him and stomped him into the ground. One miscreant even pissed in the poor man's eye. Disgusted, I turned away, hoping that this man's fate wouldn't soon be my own.

In that moment, I realized that these men were not here to arrest us for standing up for our rights. They were here to send us to our maker! I heard the large oak doors give way downstairs. Panicked, I asked my pa what we should do. Pa pointed to a door on the opposite side of the room and said it led to an attic. He told me to go up there and hide until everything was quiet. I'll never forget his last words: "I love you, son. You will survive this. You must survive this so that you can tell the world we were here and what we stood for." Before I could respond, Pa ran back downstairs to help fend off the attack.

I felt awful about abandoning the fight, but I knew that Pa had sacrificed his life so that I and others could live. He had done all he could to protect me for the first sixteen years of my life. The least I could do was listen and hide.

"Sixteen!" Malcolm shouted as it dawned on him that the person writing the diary was the same age as him. The way he wrote, he sounded like he could be twice Malcolm's age.

I came down from the attic the following morning ill prepared for the horrors below. Men I'd known my whole life lay dead before me. Gone was the vigor and vitality that they had possessed that morning, when we eagerly marched to the Mechanics' Institute ready to assert our rights. Pa was near the front door, caked in blood, nose broken, and clothes ripped to shreds. Kneeling before him, I said a prayer for God's mercy before lifting him over my shoulder to begin the long trek home. His lifeless body was only half as heavy as my heart.

Malcolm stopped again. What he was reading was starting to sound very familiar. A few minutes ago, Malcolm had felt like he was in a large, dark room that looked like an attic as gunfire blasted around him. And when he went downstairs, dead bodies were everywhere. "Impossible!" Malcolm said, turning the diary over in his hands to inspect it before resuming.

Tears streamed down my face as I carried Pa over my shoulders through the eerily quiet streets of New Orleans. It was a typical sweltering July morning, but the day was anything but ordinary. The streets were empty, save the undertakers, gravediggers, and clergy. Crows circled overhead, their squawks the only sound puncturing the silence. The shotgun shack that Pa and I shared was a little over a mile from the Mechanics' Institute, and before long, my shirt was drenched with sweat. Neighbors gossiping about what had just happened gathered on their front stoops. One said it took the federal troops several hours to get to the Mechanics' Institute, even though they were stationed only a few miles away. That was several hours too late.

After I laid Pa down on his bed and covered him with a sheet, I started going through his belongings, which is when I found this journal. I picked it up again tonight after his funeral. This time, as I read his favorite scripture about nothing being impossible if you have faith, I couldn't help but smile. If Pa was anything, he was hopeful. Suddenly, his last words came back to me: "You must survive this so that you can tell the world we were here and what we stood for." Now I know what I have to do.

Pa, I promise to do everything in my power to help our people and bear witness to our truth. If we ever get blotted from the pages of history, let this diary serve as proof that, come what may, negro men stood tall with an unyielding thirst for true freedom and justice in the land of our fathers.

—Cedric

"Cedric," Malcolm said, repeating the name aloud as he stared at the diary in awe. *Cedric from the headstone? And that wild dream with the train?* he wondered. Even though it seemed impossible, he knew the diary was describing exactly where he had just been: at the Mechanics' Institute in New Orleans in 1866.

"I must be losing my mind," Malcolm said. His hands were clammy and his whole body was tense with anxiety. His eyes found his sketch pad and pen on the floor. Relief washed over him. He grabbed them and returned to the desk chair and began sketching the gruesome scene that he had witnessed, wiping tears away as he drew. He had to get what he'd seen out of his head. It was too heavy to carry. As he was transposing the final images from his head onto paper, he heard someone yell his name from below. He was so focused on his drawing, it took him a second to recognize Aunt Carol's voice calling him, and from the sound of it, she must have been calling his name for a while. "Malcolm!"

"I'm up here, Aunt Carol," Malcolm shouted back.

As she came upstairs, he hid the diary under his sketch pad, wanting to keep the discovery to himself for now. There was no way he was going to tell anyone what was happening. He was already doubting his own mental health. What would other people think?

"Sorry, Aunt Carol," he responded. "I didn't mean to make you come upstairs. Were you looking for me?"

"Malcolm, what are you doing up here?" Aunt Carol asked sharply from the top of the stairs.

"I found this great desk, and I was just hanging out, doing some sketches," he explained.

"Did you ask if you could work up here?" Aunt Carol berated, placing her hands on her hips.

"No, I—I—" Malcolm stammered. "I'm sorry. I didn't know I was doing anything wrong," he said, looking down at his sketch pad. He hoped she couldn't see how shaken up he already was.

Aunt Carol paused and took a deep breath. "No, I'm sorry. You didn't know. How could you? It's just that my mother was always very protective of this room. She never let me or Evelyn play in here as children. She said it was a special place."

Taking another deep breath, she continued, "But Mama Lucille has been dead for over a decade, and I never understood that rule, even way back then. Of course, you can hang out in here, you should stay. I'm sorry I fussed at you. Old habits," she said as she shook her head, appearing embarrassed by her initial reaction.

"Are you sure? I could go back to my bedroom if—"

"No, no," Aunt Carol said cutting Malcolm off. "You stay. Might as well put this attic to good use. I was just coming to bring you some fresh towels. I set them on your bed."

"Okay. Thank you. I was about to go to bed anyway," Malcolm said

as he got up and followed her down the attic stairs. Before shutting his bedroom door, he looked back toward the attic door, wondering if the man he'd seen really was Cedric—and wondering if he'd see him again.

11

Malcolm was exhausted. As he aimed the water hose at the cooler to rinse off the soap he'd been using to clean it, all he could think of was what he'd seen and read the previous night. His drawings sitting on the nightstand that morning proved that whatever was going on wasn't just something he'd dreamed.

Malcolm tried to process the surging sea of questions swirling in his mind: Who was Cedric? What did he want? Why was this diary in the attic? Did anyone know it was there? He knew this house had been in his family for a long time. The desk certainly looked old and the diary was caked in dust, but he had a hard time believing that he had discovered something that had been hidden for well over a century.

Malcolm still didn't think he should tell anyone about his visions, but there had to be a way he could figure out what was happening to him. Maybe Aunt Carol could shed some light on the family history. He finished up with the coolers, propping them open and upside down to dry, and went inside. He found Aunt Carol in the kitchen, a room she never seemed to leave, washing dishes.

"Hey Aunt Carol. How's it going?"

"Boy, don't you see I'm busy. What you want? There's some fresh-squeezed orange juice in the fridge. Pour yourself a glass and then get," she said.

Malcolm chuckled, wondering how in the same breath she managed to be hospitable while also telling him to get the hell out.

"I'm sorry, Aunt Carol. I didn't mean to bother you. I was just wondering, if you have a sec, I wanted to learn more about our family and like, where we came from."

Aunt Carol responded smartly without turning from the sink, "Well, we started out in Africa, then a boat came along, picked us up for an all-expense-paid, one-way trip to hell, dropped us off in Mississippi, and that's where we've been ever since. That about answer your question?"

"Thanks, Aunt Carol. I knew that part. I was wondering more about what our family has been doing since we got to Mississippi. Like, how long have we had this house?"

Aunt Carol sighed at Malcolm's persistence. She wiped her hands on her bright floral apron and turned halfway toward Malcolm. "We've had this house a really long time. I'm not quite sure how long, but I know I was born here, and my momma, Lucille, was born here. Maybe her momma before that. I didn't know my grandparents. They died before I was born. Why you got all these questions? What are you trying to say? The house needs fixin'? I know it could use some work. Why don't you make yourself useful and put a fresh coat of paint in the upstairs bedroom? Asking me all these doggone questions. You must have too much time on your hands. I got more than coolers that need cleaning. You know what they say, an idle mind is the devil's playground. Now stop pestering me and *get* before I tell Uncle Leroy you're free." She grabbed another handful of dishes from the counter and submerged them in the sudsy water.

Malcolm knew that wasn't an empty threat and decided to take his juice upstairs. When he got to the landing, he paused, looking first at his bedroom door and then down at the door to the attic. *Maybe if I check out the attic in the daytime things will make more sense*, he mused.

He stood at the top of the attic stairs for a moment peering into the room to see if anything looked awry before entering—but it was just as he'd left it. Dusty yellow beanbag chair on the floor. Desk in the corner. Diary on the desk. No creepy ghost named Cedric. Malcolm slowly walked over to the desk and picked up the diary. If Aunt Carol had any answers for him, she wasn't giving them up easily. He might just have to read a little further to figure out what was going on. He hesitated. What if he began reading and weird things started happening again? Only one way to find out. He opened the book.

February 3, 1870

Let me start by first apologizing. I know it has been a while since I've written, but I promise I have good reasons. But now that I am on a multi-day train ride to Washington, D.C., I finally have time to write about everything I've neglected to record over these last several years.

First and foremost, I must recount how I met the love of my life, Isabel. We met at the old St. Louis Cemetery in New Orleans on All Saints' Day a year after Pa's passing, so even in death, Pa continued to look out for me. The cemetery was bustling when I arrived, and I was glad to see I wasn't the only one keeping our traditions alive. Just as we did for Ma every All Saints' Day on the Johnson plantation, I brought flowers and cleaned up around the communal mausoleum where Pa is buried. A few hundred yards away, a band was playing a slow funeral dirge. Some folks swayed to the music while others passed around plates of ribs and bottles of whiskey. As I was paying my respects, I caught a whiff of begonia and looked up to see the most beautiful lady praying beside me.

She was pretty as a bluebird with two long charcoal plaits and almond-shaped eyes. She wore a violet dress with a white lace collar and lace around her midriff as if to show off her small but curvy frame. I was immediately drawn to her and knew I had to introduce myself, but couldn't figure out how to get her attention without being insensitive to her grief. I spotted my chance when I saw a tear fall from her eye and summoned all of my courage to ask if she needed a handkerchief. Thankfully, she accepted, and we've been inseparable ever since.

Not long after, I began my work at the *New Orleans Tribune*. Pa always held a special place in his heart for newspapers. Whenever old Massa Johnson would leave one behind, Pa would do everything he could to get his hands on it. He'd pretend like he was going to use it to stoke a fire, sweep up debris, or cover a table for crawfish, but as soon as the white folks looked away, that newspaper would vanish. Now instead of hiding newspapers, his son worked for one. Imagine that.

My first assignment was no disappointment as I was asked to cover a special congressional election where a negro candidate named John Willis Menard was running. I didn't even know that was possible! On election day, I dusted off Pa's old suit and arrived at the schoolhouse just before dawn. I wanted to get there early so I didn't miss anything, but by the time I arrived, dozens of negroes were already lined up around the block giddy about their first vote.

Most of them looked like they had just come out of the field, except for a handful of well-dressed light-skinned negroes who spoke to each other in French. Rich or poor, it didn't matter. It was everyone's first chance to vote.

One elderly man in overalls and a straw hat was so excited he waved his voter card in the air for all to see and hollered about how he couldn't wait to send a negro to Congress. Out of nowhere, a young white boy rode by on horseback and snatched the card out of the old man's hand. "Who's laughing now? If my pa cain't vote, you cain't neither," the boy taunted as he dangled the card above the old man. If his pa couldn't vote, it was for good reason. He must've been one of many who lost their right to vote because they committed treason by joining the Confederacy to wage war against their fellow countrymen.

The old man jumped as high as he could on his wobbly knees trying to get his card back, but it was useless. Everyone in line watched what was happening, but we were all too afraid to make a move.

Just then, a tall white man in a Union uniform walked

up and snatched the card out of the white boy's hand and gave it back to the old man. Unwilling to challenge a soldier, the white boy rode off humiliated, and the officer tilted his hat and returned to his post in the shadow of the schoolhouse. Menard ended up winning that election. Or rather, he got the most votes, but Congress refused to seat him, claiming that it wasn't ready to admit negro members yet.

Malcolm was gripping the diary so firmly that his thumbs had imprinted little craters in the top corners of the pages. "That's messed up. I thought in a democracy the person who wins the most votes wins the election!" Malcolm looked around hoping his outburst hadn't summoned Cedric. Thankfully, he was still alone. He went back to reading.

A few years later, the *New Orleans Tribune* folded, leaving me jobless, but fortunately, thanks to Isabel, another amazing opportunity arose. Isabel came to New Orleans from Natchez, Mississippi, after the war to teach at a primary school for negro children, and as an added benefit, learned to make some of the best jambalaya this side of the Mississippi! Her cousin had recently opened the first negro school in Natchez, and Isabel really wanted to go home to teach there. Around the same time, her uncle, Hiram Revels, was elected alderman of Natchez and needed an assistant. I recognized his name right away because he used to serve as a pastor at an African Methodist Episcopal church in New Orleans that Pa and I attended on occasion. After reporting on politics for so long, I was excited for the chance to experience it firsthand. Little did I know how close to the action I would get. Only a year after Pastor Revels became alderman, he won a seat in the Mississippi State Senate and asked me to come with him!

He tasked me with putting together a legislative agenda that would promote economic development and educational opportunity for his district. I enthusiastically set to the task, inspired by his focus and seriousness of purpose, and drafted a couple of speeches to help make our case. I thought I had a gift with words, but Pastor Revels took my drafts and perfected them. When he spoke, you could feel the clouds in heaven part so that God himself could lean closer to hear him better. He delivered the opening prayer at the start of the Mississippi State Senate session, and God must have been listening closely that day, because he decided he had other uses for him.

Barely a month into Pastor Revels's State Senator term, we were dining at a small café across the street from the Mississippi State Capitol when a young white boy walked up to our table and asked whether Pastor Revels was that nigger Senator. I almost spit out my coffee when I heard him say that. Just as I started to get up to shoo the boy from our table, Senator Revels held up his hand firmly to stop me and then extended his hand to the child. The boy stared at the senator, confused, before shoving an envelope in his face.

After signing the receipt, Pastor Revels smiled and slapped the boy on the back a little harder than necessary before he winced and scurried away. I was infuriated at the child's disrespect, but Pastor Revels held up his massive hand and, with a twinkle in his eye, reminded me that he was a State Senator. That child just delivered HIM a note. He was about to read said note, in public, across the street from the State Capitol, where we were both EMPLOYED, earning our keep for a service rendered to the public. He said we was doing just fine.

His words sank in as I glanced across the street at the Capitol, where a Union soldier was completing a patrol round. I opened the letter and began to read it, but halfway through, my mouth fell open in shock. The Mississippi State Senate had selected Pastor Revels to be its representative in the United States Senate!

And with that, Pastor Revels was headed to Washington to join one of the most powerful governing bodies in the world, and I, a former slave, along with him. As hard as it was to say goodbye to my beloved Isabel, I knew this opportunity was too rare to pass up. As a legislative aide in Washington, I could help write laws that would make the world safer for Isabel, all our loved ones, and hopefully our future children too.

But even as we travel now to Washington for such a noble purpose, there is no forgetting that we are negroes. Pastor Revels and I presented our coach-class train tickets to the conductor, and he took one look at us and laughed, saying, "The nigger car is at the end." I started to protest. How dare he disrespect a soon-to-be United States Senator like that, but Pastor Revels tapped my hand to silence me.

With complete composure, he turned away and led me toward the last car. As we walked to the back of the train, he cautioned, "What good can we do our people if we never make it to Washington? Never let them get the best of you." Then he closed his eyes and dramatically took a deep breath in before slowly releasing it. I copied him and instantly felt calmer.

Malcolm stopped reading for a second and tried the breathing technique as well. He felt himself relax a little too.

As I write this, I am sitting on a pile of hay that has spilled out of a filthy pigpen. Across from me is a crated boar and above me a chicken coop. Apparently, the car for negroes is also the car for livestock. The stench of all these animals in such close quarters is nauseating, but somehow Pastor Revels has managed to sleep through these indignities. I can think of no better way to pass the time, and so I must put down my pen and do my best to keep my eyes shut for the remainder of this trip.

"Man, this diary is ridiculous!" Malcolm whispered as he closed it. He obviously knew Black people had been slaves in America, but he never thought about what happened to them once they were free. He was shocked to discover that way back then, Black people were voting, and running newspapers, and serving as senators. *Seems like a strange thing to leave out of the schoolbooks*, Malcolm thought, perplexed. He pondered: *Just whose history have I been learning in school this whole time?*

"Malcolm!" Aunt Carol yelled from the kitchen. "Someone is on the phone for you."

Malcolm had no idea who it could be other than his mother. He slid the diary into the top desk drawer and went downstairs to answer the phone.

"Hello?"

"Hi Malcolm." It was a female voice and definitely not his mother's.

"What's up?" Malcolm asked, waiting for the caller to identify herself.

"This is Jasmine, from the other day. I have to go to a county fair, and I wanted to see if you'd like to ride with me. I'm bringing some of my grandma's cakes to sell and could use an extra set of hands."

It took Malcolm a moment to even process what she was asking. A haze had settled over his brain ever since he started having strange visions. He shook his head, trying to focus.

"Hello?" she asked, her voice filled with doubt.

"Oh my bad. Yeah. Sure. When is it?" Malcolm asked. With everything he'd been through the last couple of days, he didn't really feel like hanging out, especially at some lame Mississippi county fair, but the last thing he wanted was for Jasmine to think he wasn't interested in her, because he was. Very interested. And getting out of the house sounded better than waiting around for ghosts to show up and freak him out again.

"In about an hour. How about I pick you up at 3:00 p.m.?"

"Cool," Malcolm said, "see you then."

Malcolm ran upstairs to take a much-needed shower, brush his teeth, and get dressed. By the time he made it back down in his pristine Js, Jasmine was waiting in the living room with Aunt Carol, looking as pretty as ever in cutoff jean shorts and a sleeveless denim button-down shirt tied in a knot at her waist, teasing him with peeks of her smooth abs.

"Thanks for coming with me," she said, smiling when she saw him. "These fairs can be so boring when you're by yourself."

"Any excuse to get out of the house," Malcolm replied before realizing he'd probably offended both Jasmine and Aunt Carol at the same time with that statement. "Um, I mean, I guess we should go?" He thought about asking for a little extra cash, but figured he'd have to trade in some chores for it and decided to keep it moving.

Jasmine stood up next to him. "Sure!"

"Bye, Aunt Carol," Malcolm said, waving on his way to the front door.

"Okay, baby. Y'all be safe. Don't come home too late. Supper will be ready around 6:00 p.m. Jasmine, you're welcome to join. We gonna have pot roast."

"Thank you, Miss Carol, but my mom is expecting me home for dinner tonight," Jasmine responded sweetly as she and Malcolm headed out the front door.

An old, bright blue Chevy pickup truck was parked in the driveway. Malcolm climbed inside next to Jasmine. The smell of delicious cakes was wafting through the open window behind his seat.

"Is this your truck?" Malcolm asked, surprised, having a hard time picturing such a pretty girl driving a muscle truck.

"It's my dad's, but I use it when I need to. So how's your summer in Mississippi going so far?" she asked.

"It's cool. I haven't done much besides help Aunt Carol clean. This is probably the first time I've been off the farm since I got here a few days ago."

"Well, sounds like it is time for you to see the 'Sip!" Jasmine rallied enthusiastically.

Malcolm laughed. "So you like living here?"

"Oh yeah. It's quiet and slow, but it's peaceful. I've had the same friends since preschool and our families have been friends for generations. And I love getting out in nature, riding horses, going fishing and hunting with my pa."

Just as she mentioned this, they entered onto a long bridge that stretched across a never-ending swamp, and all kinds of dangerous images came to Malcolm's mind. "You ride horses and fish and hunt?" Malcolm exclaimed, completely caught off guard by that revelation.

"'Course I fish and hunt! How else we gonna eat? Don't you? And after hunting, I usually get busy churning butter."

Malcolm looked at her, trying to hide his surprise, and noticed she was smiling coyly. They both fell out laughing.

"I'm just messing with you," she said. "I do like to fish every now and then, but I mostly leave the hunting to my brothers. But I love riding horses. I used to compete when I was younger."

"So what else do you like to do?" Malcolm asked, intrigued by her sense of humor.

"I just hang out with my friends mostly. We go to the mall, the movies, out to eat, normal stuff. I volunteer at the Boys & Girls Club sometimes tutoring kids. What do you like to do?"

"Hang out with my boys, play basketball, video games, go to concerts, normal stuff," Malcolm responded playfully.

After exiting the highway, they pulled onto a long two-lane road lined with weeping willows. They continued through marshy bogs and open pastures until they arrived at their destination. Jasmine pulled into a gravel parking lot in front of a tall chain-link fence that enclosed the fairgrounds. Bright lights and fast-moving rides beckoned just beyond the gate.

"Give me a hand with the cakes?" Jasmine asked as they climbed out of the truck.

"Sure. Which one is mine?" Malcolm asked, eyeing all the delicious treats.

"Funny! These are strictly for sale. It's my grandma's business."

"Hey Miss Madeline," Jasmine said, carrying cakes over to a portly, middle-aged White lady with a pleasant smile and short auburn hair that looked like it had just come out of rollers. She was sitting at the first table they reached upon entering the fair.

"Hey shugah," she replied, while giving Jasmine a kiss on the cheek. "Your granny sent some of her delightful treats?"

"Yes ma'am. She sent a couple of pecan pies, a few carrot cakes, a German chocolate cake, and a rum cake." Malcolm's eyes lit up as Jasmine recited her grandma's best treats.

"My, aren't we lucky?" she said, placing Jasmine's cakes in front of the other desserts already on the table. "Her rum cake is my favorite! I might have to set that one aside for myself!" she exclaimed with glee. "Who's your friend?"

"Do you know my neighbor, Miss Carol? This is her nephew, Malcolm, visiting from D.C.," Jasmine said. Malcolm nodded a hello.

"I'm not sure if I do. Well ya'll kids have fun. It's a nice afternoon. Not too muggy. Even felt a nice little breeze earlier."

"Thanks. Enjoy your cake!" Jasmine waved as they walked off.

"So what's next?" Malcolm asked.

"Now we can enjoy the fair!" Jasmine exclaimed, skipping forward with excitement like spending the day at a local fair was one of the premiere things to do in town and never got old. But for Malcolm, once again, he knew he was in a very different world.

Looking around, he couldn't remember ever being surrounded by so many White people, definitely not in D.C. He tried to suppress his unease. "Ummm, you sure it's cool for me to be here?" Malcolm asked skeptically.

"Yeah! Why?"

"I mean, are we the *only* Black people here?"

"My grandma sells her cakes at all the local fairs, and I've been dropping them off with her for years. Some of the fairs are Whiter than others, but they all love her cakes! Don't worry. The South gets a bad rap, but we're fine. Trust me!" she said, laughing at his nervousness.

As they walked around the fairgrounds, Malcolm took in the unfamiliar sights, like the competitions for largest hog and biggest tomato and the mechanical bull ride. Malcolm was thankful for the distraction. The past few days had been so weird. Now, he finally felt like he was getting back on track. He was with a girl, a pretty one. And although it wasn't his preferred place to hang out, he'd take it over a dusty attic, any day. Cedric popped up in his mind, reminding him that things weren't as normal as he'd like to think, but he pushed the thought aside. Jasmine led him to a Ferris wheel in the distance. "Want to ride?" she asked.

"Sure, why not," Malcolm said hesitantly, while looking up at the rickety structure. It wasn't nearly as impressive as the one at National Harbor, but as was abundantly clear, this was not Washington.

As they stepped onto the platform together, Malcolm caught a whiff of Jasmine's pleasant floral perfume. He gently took her hand to guide her into the carriage and, after noticing a faint smile grace her lips, held on to her hand a few seconds longer than necessary.

When they got to the top of the ride, Jasmine shivered.

"Are you cold?" Malcolm asked.

"A little," she said. "It is kinda chilly up here."

"Want to wear my windbreaker?" Malcolm offered as he took it off.

"Sure!" She happily accepted. "What do you think?" she asked, spreading her arms wide to showcase the fairgrounds and sun setting in the distance.

"It's beautiful," Malcolm replied, staring into her eyes.

All too soon, their carriage reached the bottom and the ride was over. Malcolm took Jasmine's hand to help her down off the ride in a daze. Completely distracted, he bumped into someone at the bottom of the steps.

Before he could say *Excuse me*, someone yelled, "Watch where you goin', nigger," and pushed him hard to the ground.

Malcolm looked up and saw he was surrounded by a group of country White boys, some wearing T-shirts emblazoned with the Confederate flag. Jasmine reached down to help him up, but Malcolm jumped quickly to his feet, not needing any assistance.

Seething, he dusted the dirt off his pants. Adrenaline raced through his body. His jaw tightened, and his fists instinctively clenched at his sides.

"Hmmm, that's a pretty flower I'd love to pluck," another White guy said, staring at Jasmine and slowly licking his lips.

"Come on, Mal, let's go," Jasmine said, grabbing Malcolm's hand and trying to pull him away.

Malcolm could smell the beer wafting off them and knew they were itching for a fight. He wanted nothing more than to swing at them and see how many of them he could take out at once. At least two, maybe three, but there were five or six in their crew, so the odds were not in his favor.

All of a sudden, he remembered the calming technique that Mr. Revels had taught Cedric. He took several deep breaths to regain his composure. Finally feeling clearheaded, Malcolm glared at the one who had pushed him and coldly said, "I see you," and proceeded to follow Jasmine.

But the guy blocked his path. "I said watch where you goin'." He sneered menacingly.

"I heard you the first time. Now move out of my way," Malcolm barked, feeling his temperature rise again.

"You got a real smart mouth, nigga. Somebody oughta teach you a lesson," the guy said, shoving Malcolm again in the chest. Instinctively, Malcolm swung and hit the guy dead in his eye.

The guy leaped back, covering his eye with his hand and hollering, "That nigger just sucka punched me!"

One of them pushed Jasmine aside and another kicked Malcolm's legs out from under him and jumped on his chest. Another took his turn at Malcolm, punching him twice in the face while another held him down. As Malcolm lay on his back bleeding, his eyes locked with one of the guys in their crew who stood off to the side with a pained expression on his face. He reached toward the others as if he wanted to tell them to stop, but pulled back before anyone besides Malcolm noticed.

After suffering numerous blows, Malcolm heard a whistle and two cops sauntered over with a panicked Jasmine in tow. "All right, boys, break it up. Looks like y'all have had enough fun. Get off the boy."

The White boys dusted themselves off and obliged, leaving Malcolm a bloody mess on the ground.

The officer walked over to Malcolm and helped him up.

Just as Malcolm was about to thank him, the officer took out his handcuffs and snapped them on Malcolm's wrists.

"What are you doing?" Jasmine screamed. "Don't you see he was just attacked?"

"From what I can tell, it looks like these guys were just restraining him after he hit that guy first," the cop said, pointing at the one with the bloody eye, who looked on with a half grimace, half smirk.

"But they were—"

"Save it, young lady. Tell it to the judge."

Malcolm couldn't believe his bad luck. For the second time this summer, he was headed to the police station for something that was not his fault. He tried to suppress the tears brimming in the corners of his eyes and wondered how things could go so wrong, so fast, as the cop patted him down, took his cell phone and wallet, and tossed him into the back of a police car in handcuffs that were far too tight. Running behind the police car, Jasmine yelled that she would get him out, but how that was possible, he didn't know. Malcolm's second time in a police car was about the same as the first—dark, scary, and alone.

He didn't even bother trying to argue with the cop. He knew it wouldn't get him anywhere, so he just rested his head on the back seat, closed his eyes, and tried to use the collar of his shirt to apply pressure to his bleeding lower lip. He couldn't help but think of Uncle Corey and how one ride to a police station had changed his life forever. A knot in Malcolm's stomach tightened, and he tried to brace himself for the unexpected.

Once inside the station, the officer stopped at the security desk to fill out some paperwork and then led Malcolm over to large metal door. Through the yellow haze of a blinking fluorescent light, the cop led him down a long dimly lit hallway past a row of empty cells and deposited him in one at the end. The rancid stench of urine mixed with bleach stung his nostrils, and he tried to suppress the urge to vomit.

"Don't I at least have a right to a phone call in Mississippi?" Malcolm asked pointedly.

"Watch it, boy. Just wait your turn. Hands through the bars," the officer said, smiling as he uncuffed him through the cell bars. "You'll get your call."

Malcolm walked over to a small metal sink in the corner and looked into a steel mirror screwed into the wall above it. Half his face was covered in dirt and blood from the fight. Malcolm turned on the water and splashed some water on his face. He tried to remove the grass and twigs that were stuck in his mountain of black hair. Before he knew it, a tear trickled down his face carving a trail through the dirt. He sat down on the bench and cradled his head in his hands and began to cry. He willed himself to stop. He refused to give the cop the satisfaction of knowing that he had broken him.

Eventually, he'd get his phone call, everything would be cleared up, and he'd be released. Or maybe they'd throw a bunch of charges at him, just like his uncle, and he'd never make it out of Mississippi. Malcolm's breath quickened at the thought and the cell walls started closing in on him. "No," he whispered, refusing to let panic set in. There were witnesses. People saw what happened. He would be fine. Just then, he heard a booming voice coming from the front of the police station.

"You let him out this instant or I will bring the NAACP and every camera crew in Mississippi in here and have you tied up in litigation till kingdom come!"

Who could that be? They had to be talking about him. There wasn't anyone else back here. But Malcolm didn't recognize the voice. It wasn't Uncle Leroy, and he doubted Uncle Corey had the nerve to talk to police like that after all he'd been through.

After a few minutes of back-and-forth conversation that Malcolm couldn't quite make out, a door flung open, and the cop who'd locked him up not thirty minutes before made his way back with keys in hand. Grabbing Malcolm firmly by the shoulder, he escorted him to the front of the police station. As soon as Malcolm's eyes adjusted to the harsh light, he saw Jasmine standing next to a tall Black man in a pin-striped gray suit and horn-rimmed glasses. Noting a resemblance, Malcolm realized he must be Jasmine's dad and hung his head in shame that this was how he was meeting him for the first time.

"Sorry about that confusion, Mr. Rogers. It seems like there was a lot going on at the fair, and my officers must have misunderstood the situation. I'm glad we were able to sort it out."

"Try to stay out of trouble, son," a different cop with a sheriff's badge said as he walked them out the station.

"Thank you, sir," Malcolm said to Jasmine's dad as soon as they were outside. "How did you get me out?" he asked, surprised.

"I've been around Natchez long enough to know the right people. Are you okay?" he asked, focusing his gaze on Malcolm's swollen lip.

"I'll be okay. I'm Malcolm," he said, extending his hand.

"I'm Mr. Rogers, Jasmine's dad."

"I told you I'd get you out," Jasmine said, grinning as Mr. Rogers led them to his silver Cadillac DeVille. They all climbed in.

"Malcolm, I told Miss Carol what happened, and she's worried, but I told her that my dad was taking care of it." Malcolm nodded and smiled appreciatively, hoping that this ordeal hadn't worried Aunt Carol too much. Between losing the house and trying to help Uncle Corey get settled, she already had enough troubles.

15

When Malcolm got back, Aunt Carol was sitting at the kitchen table talking nervously on the phone. "Oh Alesha, he's back. I'll let you talk to him," she said, handing him the phone.

"Hi Mom," Malcolm said sullenly as he stretched the cord to his seat at the kitchen table.

He had barely finished his greeting when his mom interrupted nervously. "Ohmygod baby. Are you all right? What did they do to you? I can't believe I thought you would be safe down there. What was I thinking?"

"Mom, please calm down. I'm fine. I've gotten hurt worse in gym class. Don't worry about me," Malcolm said, adding some extra pep to his voice to put her at ease. Aunt Carol passed him a pack of frozen peas, which he gratefully placed on his busted lip.

"How could I not worry? Aunt Carol said they took you to jail after some boys beat you up?" Malcolm could hear the tears in her voice as she choked on those last three words. "What in the world? Did anybody mess with you in there? I swear to God I will walk to Mississippi if I have to if somebody touched my baby!"

He was sure if he didn't convince her that everything was all right, she would be on the next flight out of D.C. "No Mom. Nobody messed with me. I'm fine. I sat in a cell by myself for a few minutes before Jasmine's dad got me out."

"Thank goodness. Whose dad did you say?" his mom asked without missing a beat.

"Aunt Carol's neighbor. No big deal." Malcolm shrugged, trying to deflect her question.

"I'll have to thank him because those places are not safe, especially for children. Maybe you should come home. I don't know what I was thinking sending you to Mississippi. This is exactly why your daddy and I . . ." Her voice trailed off.

"Mom, I'm okay," Malcolm said, surprising himself that he wanted to stay in Mississippi after all that had happened—farmwork, the fair, being put in jail, visions of ghosts. Still, he felt like there was something there for him. Plus, he had just met his uncle Corey. "I'll be home at the end of the summer, like we talked about. I'll be fine."

"I don't suppose Miss Jasmine next door has anything to do with your sudden fondness for Mississippi, huh?" his mom prodded.

"Uh—uh," Malcolm stammered, caught off guard. "Actually, I've really been enjoying getting to know my family better. Like, why didn't you tell me about Uncle Corey?"

His mom was silent for a moment and now the one caught off guard. "You know about Corey?" It was clear that she was not prepared for this conversation.

"He got released early from prison the other day," Malcolm informed her.

Her voice lifted for the first time during this conversation. "Thank God. He got a twenty-year sentence around the time I found out I was pregnant with you. I thought maybe once he was out . . ."

"I wish I would've gotten the chance to know him growing up," Malcolm said, mindlessly twirling the phone cord around his fingers and staring down at his shoes.

Silence hung heavily between them. Finally, she blurted out, "I'm sorry. I did what I thought was best. And after your dad . . . How's Corey doing?"

"He's okay. Glad to be out," Malcolm answered, realizing he didn't know much about his uncle's adjustment outside of that. Uncle Corey was having to navigate through a whole new world quite different from the one he'd left behind. Uncle Corey had only been a couple of years older than Malcolm was now when he was locked up. Malcolm had already lived through two close brushes with the law. Who knew how much longer he could escape that fate? His mind was drifting off, deep in thought, when his mother's voice on the other end of the line snapped him back.

"Good. I'm glad you're getting the chance to know him. He never deserved to be locked up like that. He was a good kid." She paused and cleared her throat. "Now, back to Miss Jasmine . . ."

"What's that you say, Aunt Carol? You need me for something? Be right there," Malcolm shouted away from the phone.

"Boy, don't you try to play me!"

Malcolm laughed. That felt good. "For real, Mom, I love you, but I gotta go. I'll call you later, all right?"

"Bye!" she said indignantly, followed by "Love you too," as her voice went soft again.

Malcolm went upstairs to take another shower and wash the filth from the fair and the police station off his body. When he was clean and dressed, he grabbed his sketch pad and pen off the nightstand and fell onto the bed. He heard a knock at his door.

"Yeah," he answered hesitantly, slightly afraid that the mustached ghost was back and had decided to knock this time.

Uncle Corey poked his head in the door. "How you doing, Nephew?" he asked, looking genuinely concerned as he walked over and sat down on the other twin bed, facing Malcolm.

"Man, I'm all right," Malcolm replied, shrugging his shoulders, sitting up straighter in bed. "They didn't do nothing to me that hasn't been done before. I'm not scared of those fools."

Uncle Corey sighed. "I know that tough talk, Mal. Shoot, I thought I invented tough talk when I was your age, but you don't have to play that game with me. I know how lonely it is when you're locked in a cell not knowing when or if you're gonna see daylight again. Even though you weren't in there long, it's okay if you were scared."

Now Malcolm let out a sigh as he tried to fight back tears. "You know . . . it was just so messed up. Here I am chillin', mindin' my business, got this pretty chick on my arm, we vibin', you know. And just like that," Malcolm snapped, "I'm getting my butt kicked by these country White boys and thrown in jail by some racist cop. He didn't see me, a kid getting jumped. He just assumed it was my fault or didn't care enough to find out. Think what would've happened if he saw a White boy getting stomped on by a bunch of Black kids."

"Oh we know what would've happened. You'd have been lucky to make it to the jail," Uncle Corey scoffed derisively. He took note of the posters his brother had hung up in the bedroom decades before and grimaced. "Their fight, our fight, is far from over."

"Yeah man. Every time a cop comes around, I'm afraid I'm gonna end up like my dad, just a memory. I can't do that to my mom. And what if Jasmine's daddy didn't show up at the police station? I'd probably still be there right now. All I did was defend myself, but who knows what they would've said I did. How can you live when the whole system is working against you?" Malcolm felt like he was rambling. He gripped the edge of the bed, struggling to explain himself in a more concise manner. "When I was in that cell, I just felt so alone and so . . ." He paused to think of the right word. "So powerless."

"Yeah man," Uncle Corey said, nodding in agreement. "That's how they want you to feel. Powerless. So you just give in and stop standing up for yourself, 'cause you know it's useless. It's messed up. But we Johnsons. We don't give up, right?" he asked, lightly punching Malcolm on the shoulder.

A smile crept onto Malcolm's face. "Naw. Thanks, Unc."

"No problem. Now get some sleep. You gonna feel better in the morning," Uncle Corey said on his way to the door.

"All right. Bet," Malcolm said, leaning back on the bed. He was so tired he felt like he could fall asleep sitting up. But just then, a cool breeze blew past his feet.

"We had power once," the voice purred. "And so much hope for good things to come."

And then everything went black.

16

Malcolm found himself lying in a narrow bed in the corner of a small, dark apartment with low ceilings. Someone rapped insistently at the door.

"No, no, no," Malcolm cried out as he sat up in the bed and cradled his head in the palms of his hands. "No, not again! This can't be happening. I don't even know where I am."

"Come on, now, Cedric. I don't have all day," the visitor demanded from outside. "Get your butt up and come answer this door."

Malcolm thought about hiding and waiting until somehow he was brought back to the farm, but then he remembered the massacre at the Mechanics' Institute. If Cedric was trying to show him something, he wasn't going to see it hiding in the room. Not that he really wanted to see whatever it was, but if it got him home faster . . . Pulling the blanket back, he reluctantly rose from the bed and walked over to the door.

The apartment was bare inside—nothing but a bed, dresser, wood-burning stove, sink, and wicker chair. On his way to the door, he caught his reflection in a small mirror hanging above the sink. It was Cedric—weird mustache and all. That meant *he* was Cedric, but he had no idea how to act like Cedric.

As soon as Malcolm cracked open the door, the man waiting outside used his knobby cane to push through, making his way boldly into the room. "Cedric, your pappy always rose early to study the Bible before beginning his day. I figured you'd be up already," he bellowed.

"I'm—I'm sorry," Malcolm stammered as he examined the man,

trying to figure out who he was. Full beard but no mustache. It dawned on him. He was the man who pushed past him while getting off the train in his dream—if it actually was a dream—from his first night in Mississippi. But who was he?

"Everything okay with you, Cedric? I thought you'd be more excited and ready to go. It isn't every day that a Negro has a chance to become a US Senator," he said, beaming.

That's when it clicked. The journal. He was standing before Hiram Revels, Cedric's boss.

Malcolm thought quickly. He was pretty sure he didn't want to be committed to an insane asylum in the 1800s, so pretending to be Cedric was his best bet, at least until he found his way home. He thought back to Cedric's diary. What could he say that would make sense?

"Yeah, yeah, I'm fine. It's just, the train ride really, umm, wore me out. I'm just, uhhh, still trying to clear my head. Must be all the animal fumes I was smelling," Malcolm ad-libbed. "So you're about to be America's first Black senator? That's cray . . . crazy."

Pastor Revels raised his eyebrows and sat down on the edge of the wicker chair. "Let's not get ahead of ourselves, Cedric. We don't know that they will accept my credentials. Don't forget, John Willis Menard won his election for that New Orleans House seat, but Congress refused to seat him. Didn't you cover that story for the *New Orleans Tribune?*" he asked.

"Oh yeah, yeah."

"Yeah?"

"I mean, yes. Yes sir, Pastor Revels."

"Son, I'm not quite sure what's going on with you this morning, but make sure your head is clear by the time we get to the Senate. I need you to be sharp in there," Pastor Revels chided, tossing a garment bag onto the bed. "We need to get going. The vote on my appointment is happening soon, and we can't be late for that. Now hurry up and get dressed."

Malcolm glanced at the bag, unsure what to do with it.

"What? You didn't think I'd let you wear those tattered rags you've been wearing every day into the Senate chamber."

Malcolm opened the bag and pulled out a black suit and a pair of suspenders. He dressed quickly, getting the suit on easily, but he couldn't figure out what to do with the suspenders.

Noticing Malcolm struggling, Pastor Revels walked over, laughing. "Look, son," he said as he fastened the suspenders in place. "I guess you haven't had too many opportunities to dress in fine clothes before, but this is Washington, so we've got to look the part." He plucked his own suspenders with his thumbs as he made his way to the door. Malcolm glanced at himself in the mirror. The suit was slightly too big and Cedric's mustache and hair were strange, but it would have to do. He quickly followed Pastor Revels out the door and tried to ignore the butterflies fluttering in his stomach.

They emerged out of a basement apartment and climbed steps leading to a cobblestone street lined with connected row houses. As soon as they were aboveground, Malcolm instantly knew where he was. In the light of daybreak a few blocks away, rose the same white dome that he had seen in his dream—the dome capping the US Capitol. He was home—kind of. Gone were the limousines and fancy town cars with government license plates that he was used to seeing in this part of town, and in their place were men in top hats rolling by in horse-drawn carriages. Malcolm followed closely behind Pastor Revels, dodging more than a few mud puddles that had accumulated on the soggy ground. He tried his best to navigate around piles of horse poop, as well as people selling fruit and peanuts from carts.

"Paper! Get your paper!" a young Black boy hollered on the side of the street as they passed.

Malcolm took a copy from the boy and skimmed the front headline hoping to find clues about this world he was suddenly thrust into: "Fifteenth Amendment Becomes the Law of the Land!" Malcolm racked his brain trying to remember what the amendment was from history class. He suddenly regretted spending so much time doodling and dozing off.

Pastor Revels snatched the paper from Malcolm's hand, smiling and giving the paperboy five cents. "This must be a good sign. Iowa just ratified the Fifteenth Amendment, taking us over the threshold to amend the Constitution. Now, instead of our right to vote being decided state by state and subject to the whims of the mob, it is baked into the highest law of the land. Now and forever, as long as there is a United States, Negroes will have the right to vote! Isn't that something?" Pastor Revels beamed.

"Yeah!" Malcolm agreed. "I mean, yes!" But something didn't make sense. He didn't remember a lot from history class, but he did remember learning about the civil rights movement. Wasn't that when Black people fought for the right to vote, in the 1960s?

"First, Congress passed the Thirteenth Amendment, outlawing slavery, then the Fourteenth Amendment, giving all who are born on American soil the rights of citizenship, and now this one, guaranteeing our right to vote," Pastor Revels continued, excited. "Now we are one step closer to ensuring that the American decree that all men are created equal rings true. God willing, today I will be sworn in as the first Negro senator, but I will surely not be the last to cross this threshold and for that, we should be truly grateful."

Malcolm nodded, appreciative of the quick history refresher, and followed Pastor Revels up the steps of the United States Capitol. When they got to the top, Pastor Revels turned around to take in the scenery.

"Isn't it beautiful?" Mr. Revels marveled.

Malcolm turned as well and was shocked speechless at what he saw. From this vantage point, Washington, D.C., looked nothing like the city he knew. Instead, it looked like a city on its way to greatness suddenly struck by one of the ten biblical plagues. For as far as he could see, the streets were half brick, half mud and swarming with livestock. He couldn't tell if he was looking at the National Mall or a petting zoo in a swamp. He was even more confused when his eyes landed on a half-erected marble structure that stood in the distance surrounded by dirt and a handful of beat-up shacks.

"What's that?" he asked pointing.

"I read that they are building a monument to George Washington. I think that's the site for it," Pastor Revels replied.

That can't be the Washington Monument, Malcolm thought, staring at it in disbelief. He couldn't picture the D.C. skyline without the looming obelisk and its two beady red eyes that kept watch over the city.

"What happened to it?" Malcolm asked, horrified.

"I heard they started building it, but couldn't finish because they needed all the money in the Treasury to go toward the war effort. Maybe they'll get back to it soon."

"Let's hope so." Malcolm grimaced.

At the bottom of the Capitol steps, a crowd of Black people had assembled and were cheering loudly for the arrival of Pastor Revels. Some were dressed in their Sunday finest, with men in suits and top hats and ladies in wide-skirt dresses, but even those wearing rags were just as excited. Several were crying tears of joy. Pastor Revels waved and walked down a few steps toward them. Not missing an opportunity to give praise to the one on high, he said, "This is the day the Lord has made. Let us rejoice and be glad!," before making his way to the top of the steps.

Near the entrance to the Capitol, a lanky elderly Black man with a round navy felt hat and a broad smile stood beside a shoeshine stand. "Senator Revels," he gleefully proclaimed, "would you do me the honor and let me shine your shoes, suh?"

Smiling, Pastor Revels replied, "The honor is all mine, sir," to which the man clapped his hands and grabbed his brush.

Tipping his bowler hat humbly, the shoeshine man said, "Senator, my name is Buddy, at your service. We do aim to please, now relax, this will be a breeze!" Buddy knelt and made quick work of Pastor Revels's shoes. "How you doing today, suh?"

"I'm fine, Buddy, God is good!"

"All the time, Senator! All the time."

Malcolm stood nearby watching people moving up and down the steps. Buddy shined Pastor Revels's shoes with as much vigor as one would expect for a king or perhaps President Washington himself. Then, just as Buddy was buffing on the last bit of shine, Malcolm watched him lean into Pastor Revels's left ear, and, completely devoid of his earlier servile accent, he whispered, "I hear you got forty-eight votes secured. That's way more than you need, so try to relax." Taken aback, Pastor Revels's eyebrows arched in surprise. Malcolm too stood wide-eyed. Buddy looked over at Malcolm and winked while closing up his shoeshine kit.

After the odd exchange, Pastor Revels paid Buddy for the shine, and then he and Malcolm proceeded into the Capitol Building and down a long hallway. On the surface, the Capitol looked pretty much how he remembered it from a school field trip he'd taken a few years ago. The ornate marble floors, grandiose granite columns, winding staircases, and extravagant artwork hanging on the walls were all the same. But the people looked very different—different hairstyles, different clothes, different ways of speaking—which made the visit feel vastly different from before. Soon they were entering the Senate Chamber.

Old White men were huddled around desks that spread out in a semicircle pattern across the room. Their boisterous conversations came to an abrupt halt the moment Malcolm and Pastor Revels walked in. Pastor Revels motioned for Malcolm to take a seat at a table near the front of the room that had been reserved for them. Malcolm marveled at the crowded balcony that encircled the room, filled with spectators and reporters of every hue.

An older senator seated on an elevated chair at the head of the room surrounded by American flags gaveled the session to order, and one by one senators lined up at the lectern to address the room.

"The carpetbaggers who have taken over the Mississippi government do not have the authority to send a Negro to Congress," one man shouted. "In the nearly one hundred years since our nation's founding, there has never been a Negro in the House or the Senate, for good reason!"

"The Constitution requires that one must be a United States citizen for nine years before serving in the Senate. Pastor Revels, here, has only been a United States citizen for two years, since the adoption of the Fourteenth Amendment gave Negroes the right to citizenship. He is therefore ineligible to hold a seat in Congress," shouted another.

Why did that sound so familiar? Malcolm wondered. He suddenly remembered protesters on the National Mall demanding to see President Obama's birth certificate. *Didn't they claim he didn't meet the citizenship requirements either?*

"*Dred Scott*, which is still the law of the land, made clear that the Negro has no rights which the White man is bound to respect. Therefore, Negroes are unfit to serve as equals in this great body," echoed another.

As the dehumanizing speeches wore on throughout the morning, Malcolm sank farther and farther down in his seat, wishing he could disappear. Just when Malcolm thought everyone in the room opposed Pastor Revels becoming a senator, an older White gentleman with gray sideburns and a beak-like nose limped his way onto the Senate floor.

"The vote on this question will be a historic event, marking the triumph of a great cause. From this time there can be no backward step. After a prolonged and hard-fought battle, beginning with the Republic, convulsing Congress, and breaking out in blood, the primal truths declared by our fathers are practically recognized. All men are created equal says the great Declaration. Today, we make the Declaration a reality. The Declaration was only half established by Independence. The greater duty remained behind. In assuring the equal rights of all, we complete the work."

Malcolm was in awe. "Who is that?" Malcolm asked Pastor Revels, unable to recall ever hearing a White man advocate so forcefully for the fair treatment of Black people.

"You don't know?" That is the great Charles Sumner," Pastor Revels whispered, "the senior senator from Massachusetts. You are looking at an American treasure and a true friend of the Negro. He once took a beating on the Senate floor from a South Carolina congressman who felt his honor had been insulted when Senator Sumner compared the South's love of slavery to the way one loves a whore."

"Yeah, those were probably fighting words." Malcolm chuckled quietly.

Senator Sumner continued, "What we do today is not alone for ourselves, not alone for that African race now lifted up; it is for all everywhere who suffer from tyranny and wrong; for all everywhere who bend beneath the yoke; for all everywhere who feel the blight of unjust power; it is for all mankind; it is for God himself, whose sublime fatherhood we most truly confess when we recognize the Brotherhood of Man."

Suddenly, silence settled over the room. One by one, senators stepped forward to record their vote, some glaring contemptuously at Pastor Revels as they walked past, others offering reassuring smiles. Finally, the Senate Majority Leader called the vote: forty-eight yays, and eight nays.

17

"Yes!" Malcolm shouted, jumping up excitedly. But not everyone looked pleased. Some were slumped over in their chairs and had turned pale as ghosts.

"The Senator Elect shall present himself at the chair of the Vice President to take the oath of office."

Pastor Revels rose slowly to full stature and, grasping his cane with a firm grip, began moving steadily toward the front of the room. Every eye in the Capitol was affixed to Pastor Revels, watching his every step and no doubt wondering, can it be? Is it possible?

As Pastor Revels raised his hand to accept the oath of office, Malcolm's chest filled with pride. He didn't know Pastor Revels well, but the significance of the moment was not lost on him. A few minutes later, Malcolm was following Senator Revels off the Senate floor and spotted the man who had said Pastor Revels hadn't been a citizen long enough to be a senator. He was sitting at his desk with his head cradled in his hands. Unable to help himself, Malcolm leaned down and whispered in his ear, "Boo!" The frightened senator leaped three inches into the air and nearly fell out of his seat. Stifling his laughter, Malcolm hurried the rest of the way out of the room and into the hallway.

Malcolm couldn't believe how happy he felt. After watching Pastor Revels be sworn in as the first Black senator, he suddenly felt invincible. Still, he hoped he wouldn't see that senator he just spooked again. Looking around as they made their way through the Capitol building, he shook his head. Was he really in a jail cell only a few hours ago?

Wasn't he just telling Uncle Corey how often he felt powerless? The strangeness and impossibility of being in the past, being Cedric, began to seep back into his thoughts. He had nearly forgotten he was living as Cedric, until he felt the mustache tickle his upper lip. He ran his fingers over his strange, side-parted hair.

When they got outside, Malcolm and the man who was now Senator Revels passed Buddy again, who glanced at them knowingly, smiled, and tipped his hat.

"Strange fellow," Senator Revels whispered.

Waiting at the bottom of the Capitol steps was a tall Black lady Malcolm had seen earlier with the group cheering their arrival.

"Congratulations, Senator Revels. We are just so proud of what you achieved today. Please accept this invitation for a reception in your honor that is already underway at my home," she said, handing him a shiny red envelope.

"Why, thank you. You are too kind. What is your name?" Senator Revels inquired, humbled by the invitation.

"I am Serena, better known as Mrs. George Downing. My husband manages the dining room for the US House of Representatives so there will be plenty of people there that you should know."

"Again, thank you for this honor. There is no place I'd rather be. This is my trusted aide, Cedric, who I assume can join?"

"Why, certainly! If you'd like to head straight there, I have a carriage waiting at the corner."

"I'd be delighted. After you, madame!" Senator Revels said, clasping Malcolm by the shoulders and ushering him along. When they reached the horse and buggy, Senator Revels jumped right in, but Malcolm hesitated, doubting the safety of such a primitive mode of transportation.

"Cedric, are you coming?" Senator Revels asked, sounding exasperated as he made an apologetic expression to Mrs. Downing.

Realizing he had little choice, Malcolm stepped forward and into the carriage. While Senator Revels and Mrs. Downing chatted comfortably, Malcolm held on to the side of the door as tightly as he could and tried to stay calm as the carriage bounced all over the cobblestone street.

"How are you finding Washington so far, Senator Revels?" Mrs. Downing asked.

"It is quite a town—a little muddier than I expected, but still something to marvel at. But to be honest, Mrs. Downing, I haven't had a chance to see much of it. We arrived late last night and went straight to the Capitol this morning."

Malcolm kept quiet. He glanced out the window while they spoke, searching for landmarks he'd recognize. He was still trying to wrap his mind around what was happening to him. He was beginning to believe that it was something between a dream and actual time travel, but really, he had no idea. After racking his brain for several minutes, he diverted his attention back to the conversation taking place in front of him.

"Oh, I hope you get a chance to go into town soon. We have some of the best restaurants around," Mrs. Downing bragged enthusiastically.

"Really, even ones that serve Negroes?" Senators Revels inquired.

"Well, there are certainly nice Negro-owned establishments, but you can dine any place you like." Mrs. Downing smiled.

Malcolm perked up, again completely confused by how this knowledge conflicted with what he had learned in school. He was 100 percent certain restaurants were segregated before the civil rights movement. He distinctly remembered the pictures of people holding sit-ins at lunch counters. "Blacks and Whites eat in restaurants together?" Malcolm asked.

"Yes, ever since the Washington City Council passed a law prohibiting racial discrimination in places of public entertainment," she said, her eyes twinkling in delight.

The carriage stopped in front of a stately redbrick house with wraparound balconies and manicured flower beds. Malcolm was in awe. It was more beautiful than any home he'd been inside and he couldn't believe Black people lived there—in the 1800s no less.

As soon as the three entered the home, an army of servants swarmed to greet them. One butler took their coats; another hastily poured them drinks, followed quickly by a third who offered oysters and other delicacies from a tray. A string quartet played in the living room. They came to an abrupt stop the moment Senator Revels entered the room, and their music was quickly replaced by the sound of thunderous applause.

Everyone raised their glass and toasted "To Senator Hiram Revels," followed by echoes of "Hear! Hear!" Malcolm raised his glass of ginger ale in salute. Besides whiskey and gin, he didn't see hardly any drinks he recognized—no Coke or Pepsi or POWERADE. Ginger ale seemed like the safest option, but upon taking a sip, he nearly choked on its spiciness. The ginger was so fresh it burned through his throat. He thought about ordering a shot of whiskey to mix with it since he was older after all, being Cedric, but he decided against it. He'd need to keep his wits about him, especially if he had to pretend to be someone else from a different century.

A hush fell over the crowd as Senator Sumner, the man who'd spoken so well of Senator Revels earlier in the Chamber, clinked his glass with a spoon and took command of the room. "Not too long ago, the State of Mississippi sent to Washington a fellow named Jefferson Davis to serve in the United States Senate."

The crowd groaned their displeasure at the mention of Jefferson Davis's name.

Relishing the crowd's reaction, Senator Sumner paused for a beat before continuing, "That Senator did not take to heart the oath he swore to support and defend the Constitution. Instead, he decided to resign from the nation's most esteemed legislative body and commit treason by waging war on his brothers. And he did all of this so that he and his brethren could continue to subjugate and enslave millions of human beings who happened to be of a darker hue. Well, the State of Mississippi is working to make amends and has sent to Washington no finer a specimen than Senator Hiram Revels. I can personally attest that the state has lost nothing in the way of intelligence or character in their representative."

Turning to Senator Revels, Senator Sumner raised his glass higher. "To Hiram, the Fifteenth Amendment in flesh and blood." The cheers that followed were deafening. Something about those words stirred in Malcolm. Constitutional amendments hadn't ever felt personal before.

Well-dressed Black people and a handful of equally polished White ones floated from room to room enjoying the evening of revelry. Malcolm stood taking it all in. An attractive middle-aged lady with freckles and perfectly coiled sandy-brown hair walked over to him. "So you came all the way from Mississippi to Washington to work for Senator Revels? What do you think of all this?"

"So far, my time in Washington has been amazing," Malcolm said, clearing his throat as he tried to play Cedric's role of dutiful staffer. "I have to pinch myself every second to make sure it's real. I still can't believe I got to see the first Black person sworn into the Senate today. I have a feeling he won't be the last. One day, we might even have a Black president!" Malcolm couldn't resist the urge to drop a hint about the future.

The lady broke out into laughter. "Well, it certainly seems like Senator Revels picked the right aide. You're not short on optimism! Have you met my husband, Doug Syphax?" she asked, motioning her husband over.

Malcolm extended his hand. "Hi, I'm Ma—, excuse me." He paused to clear his throat. "I'm Cedric, most people call me Cedric," he said, quickly correcting himself.

"Welcome to Washington, Cedric," Mr. Syphax said with a note of authority.

"Thank you. Are you from D.C.?"

Mr. Syphax looked at him incredulously before turning to his wife. They both fell out laughing.

"You could say that," his wife interjected, answering for him. "His great-grandfather, George Washington Parke Custis—they called him Wash—was the grandson of Martha Washington, you know, the first First Lady? President Washington raised Wash as his own, but Wash ended up dippin' his banana in the chocolate sauce," she said, laughing.

"Excuse me?" Malcolm asked, confused.

"Oh lawd. You gonna make me say it. Wash had a baby with one of Martha's slaves, but he claimed his baby girl, Mariah, gave her land and everything. Well, Mariah is Doug's grandmother," she said with exasperation, as if everyone already knew all of this.

Malcolm's eyes flew wide in shock and he tried to keep from spitting out his ginger ale.

"Yes, Great-Granddaddy used to regale us with tales of growing up in the presidential mansions in both New York and Philadelphia, before Washington became the capital city. He told us all about how kind President Washington was to him and his sister and how much the president loved spending time in Mount Vernon tending to his plantation and distillery. I hate to say it," Mr. Syphax continued with a smirk, "but I don't think President Washington would be too pleased with the recent developments of a Negro joining the Senate, but he probably also wouldn't care for the fact that the only part of his family that remained loyal to the country he founded were the Negroes." Mr. Syphax erupted in laughter, which Mrs. Syphax heartily joined in.

Seeing Malcolm's confusion, Mrs. Syphax explained, "George Washington Parke Custis's other daughter, his White one, married Confederate General Robert E. Lee." She giggled.

"Goodness," Malcolm exclaimed. "Is there anyone in your family who didn't start a country?"

Mr. Syphax smiled politely and suddenly excused himself.

"I hope I didn't upset him," Malcolm apologized to Mrs. Syphax.

"Nonsense," she said. Taking it upon herself to be his social ambassador, Mrs. Syphax asked, "Have you met Christian Fleetwood?" Malcolm shook his head. "Oh, Christian . . . ," she called, summoning the man walking by.

"You are looking ravishing as usual, Abbie," Mr. Fleetwood said, stopping and leaning in to kiss her on the cheek.

"Thank you, darling. Christian, I'd like you to meet Cedric, Senator Revels's aide."

"Nice to meet you, sir," Malcolm said, shaking his hand, consciously straightening his posture to look more professional. He could already tell it would be hard to get anything past this guest.

"So you work in Congress?" Mr. Fleetwood asked. His eyes scanned Malcolm up and down but then he looked away, seemingly deciding nothing was off.

"Yes sir. I just got here. It is all very new to me."

"I see. It's been a while since I was at the Capitol," he said, waving his hand aloofly. His voice was carefree, but his demeanor was stern, like someone who was tried and true.

"Oh, you've been there before?" Malcolm asked, surprised. Knowing that Senator Revels was the first Black member of Congress, he wondered how this could be.

"Oh yes," he responded coyly.

"Were you there to watch a hearing?" Malcolm asked, increasingly intrigued.

Again, Mrs. Syphax flashed a knowing smile as if she enjoyed watching him squirm.

Finally, Mr. Fleetwood relented, "The last time I was at the Capitol was to accept a Congressional Medal of Honor for my gallantry during the War of the Rebellion."

Malcolm's cheeks burned with embarrassment. "Wow, it's an honor to meet you. Thank you for your service."

"No need. Many Negroes died fighting for the Union. I'm one of very few who were recognized, but I wear this medal for all of us. You give them your best in Washington. No excuses," he said with a wink.

"None, sir," Malcolm said, shaking his hand again.

As the evening came to a close, Malcolm realized that he had successfully impersonated Cedric for a whole day and nobody seemed to know any better. He sat down on a stool near the bar and relaxed a little, beginning to feel slightly more comfortable in his new skin, but wondering how long all this would last. His last couple of trips had been over in a matter of minutes, but this time he had already been stuck in Cedric's body for a full day. He couldn't help but think about what was going on back at the farm. What if he had disappeared and everyone was trying to find him? Malcolm was lost in this thought when Senator Revels tapped him on the shoulder.

"Doing okay there, Cedric?"

"Yes sir," Malcolm said quickly, snapping back to attention. "I hope you enjoyed your evening. I had a great time."

"I did. Very much so. In fact, the Downings have been kind enough to offer me use of their guest quarters for the remainder of my time in Washington, so no more dingy basements for me! My apologies," he added, seemingly acknowledging that Cedric was not so fortunate. He patted Malcolm on the back. "Anyway, Mrs. Downing has arranged for a carriage to take you back to your apartment on Capitol Hill whenever you're ready. See you bright and early tomorrow morning at the Capitol."

"Thank you. Good night, sir," Malcolm said, leaving Senator Revels at the bar and making his way outside into the cloudless night. Stars, undiminished by streetlights, lit up the sky like supercharged fireflies. He had never seen the D.C. sky look so beautiful.

18

Rays of sunlight flooded the room, warming Malcolm's face. A rooster let loose his call, rousing Malcolm from his sleep. He stretched his arms and smiled, relieved to be back in his bed at the farm. He rubbed the sleep from his eyes—only to discover that he was still in Cedric's basement apartment. Same wood-burning stove, same dresser, same wicker chair.

Malcolm jumped up in horror. "No, no, no! I can't still be here!" he screamed, pinching himself. "Wake up, wake up, wake up, Malcolm. You gotta wake up."

Nothing happened.

"How am I going to get out of here?" He hopped out of bed, walked over to an empty bucket under a water pump, and stared at it not knowing what to do. He tried turning the handle left and then right, but it wouldn't budge. Then he lifted it up and down and a trickle of water came out. Faster and faster he pumped until a small pool of water gathered in the bucket, but by then he had worked up a sweat. "All that to wash my face!" he shouted in frustration. "Get me out of here, Cedric!"

Deflated, he sat down on the foot of the bed, covered his face with his hands, and began to cry. He was trapped in a world 150 years before he was born where he didn't know anyone and where people who looked like him had been slaves only a few years before. He didn't know how to act like these people or talk like them. What if he did something that got Cedric killed? Would that mean he would never even be born?

Would he be killing his dad and Uncle Corey, Aunt Carol and Grandma Evelyn too? It was just too much.

Malcolm stood up and paced around the room, catching a glimpse of the base of the Capitol from the small front window. *I know at least one person in this world*, he thought, and he knew where to find him.

"If I can't get back . . ." He sighed, thinking about what to do next. *Cedric would go to work. He'd be happy about it. He'd be on time.* With that, Malcolm got moving. He went to Cedric's suitcase and pulled out the least tattered shirt he could find. He put it on along with the suit Senator Revels had given him the day before. Then, marshaling his bravest face, he walked out the front door, up the steps, and across the street to the US Capitol.

Standing in the middle of a wide hallway unsure which direction to go, he saw a familiar face. The kind senator whose impassioned speech had persuaded the Senate to accept Senator Revels stopped in his tracks to greet him.

"Cedric, so nice to see you again! It's going to take a while for Senator Revels to get through all his paperwork. You are welcome to pass the time with me. I'm working with a very special person that I would love for you to meet. We just finished breakfast, but we have a few cornbread muffins left," Senator Sumner invited him warmly.

Malcolm's eyes lit up. He was starving, and he figured he needed as many friends as possible in this strange world. "Sure," Malcolm replied enthusiastically.

"Wonderful!" Senator Sumner said, leading Malcolm down a corridor and into a meeting room with a marble fireplace that was lined wall-to-wall with books. A light-skinned Black man with short wavy hair, a nicely trimmed beard, a pinched nose, and beady eyes sat at a large oak table in center of the room covered with sheets of paper.

"Mr. Langston and I were just discussing some ideas for a civil rights bill and your feedback would be most helpful," Senator Sumner said, motioning Malcolm to sit down with them. "Have you had the privilege of meeting John Mercer Langston before?" he asked, handing him a muffin.

"No sir. Good morning. My name is . . ." He paused for a second, not wanting to repeat last night's mistake. "Cedric, Cedric Johnson. I'm Senator Revels's aide. It's a pleasure to make your acquaintance, Mr. Langston," Malcolm said in the most formal language he could muster.

"Of course, I know who you are," John said, extending his hand. "Please call me John. The whole town is abuzz about Senator Revels's arrival—well, the side of town I live on is. I apologize that I wasn't able to attend last night's reception. I'm just getting back into town from visiting my ailing mother in Ohio."

"You're from Ohio?"

"Yes, well, I'm from Virginia, but I went to college in Ohio."

"Oh, I didn't know Black people went to college back then, I—I mean now," Malcolm stammered. "I mean, I didn't know they let slaves go to college."

"Well, fortunately, I was never a slave."

Malcolm winced in embarrassment. He took a large bite out of the muffin so he wouldn't feel pressured to speak right away. It was a little dry, but still pretty good.

John explained: "My father was a White plantation owner, and he freed my mother before I was born, so I was born free, but then both my parents died when I was young. Before their death, my father made arrangements for my brothers and me to move to the free state of Ohio, and he set aside money for our education. My older brothers were the first Negroes to integrate Oberlin College, and I followed in their footsteps."

"Cedric, John is being overly modest," Senator Sumner interrupted. "He is not only an Oberlin graduate, and what a fine institution that is, but also an attorney with a master's degree in theology and the first Negro elected to public office in the United States. You are looking at a bona fide living legend right here, and I am fortunate to have the benefit of his vast intelligence and experience while we draft a bill that will change the lives of Negroes in this country forever."

"Wow," Malcolm replied, dumbfounded. "It's really nice to meet you! I don't even know what to say."

"Well, how about saying, 'What's this bill about?'" Senator Sumner teased.

"Okay." Malcolm laughed and grabbed another muffin. "What's this bill about?" he asked.

"Very well, since you asked," Senator Sumner said, seizing the opening and scooting a chair up to the table for Malcolm. "We are drafting a bill that is going to make Negroes full and equal citizens before the eyes of the law and all mankind. It will prohibit discrimination in jury selection, schools, transportation, cemeteries, and all places open to the public. We might not be able to change what's in people's hearts, but we can sure as hell raise the stakes if they act on their malignancy—get them to think twice, so to speak."

"What I'm most passionate about is education," John chimed in excitedly. "Institutions of higher learning are the key to creating generations of Negroes who not only understand their rights, but know how to access them. Just this past year, we opened a law school at Howard University, a law school dedicated to educating and uplifting Negroes, former slaves and freemen alike. But we are not going to discriminate in our admission. Men, women, Negroes, Whites. We'll accept anyone who is interested in advancing the cause of justice. As a matter of fact, our inaugural class of six students has two women.

"Just imagine a world where there are legions of Negro lawyers who can defend other Negroes when they are railroaded by the so-called justice system, vindicate the rights of those who have been wronged, and advocate for laws to protect our communities. How could we lose?" John said, beaming with pride.

Briefly forgetting he was in the past, Malcolm chimed in with his two cents. "I've been to Howard. They got a dope homecoming." He began to reminisce about a concert he and his homies went to on the yard once before remembering he was thinking of the university in its modern form.

"Excuse me?" John asked, his eyebrows arching into a confused expression.

"I mean, that sounds incredible. I've been wanting to visit Howard. I'm sure it would feel like a home coming," Malcolm corrected himself, trying to cover up his goof.

"Anytime you like. The door is always open," John replied kindly.

John began flipping through the ink-filled pages of the bill. Parts of the text were crossed out here and there and notes written in the margins. Malcolm had no idea so much work and dedication had gone into ensuring his freedoms were protected.

"But do you think this country is really ready for Blacks and Whites to go to school together?" Malcolm asked suspiciously, thinking about how hard White people fought integration a century later. Shoot, his high school still looked segregated in 2015.

"The salvation of this country depends on it," Senator Sumner interjected as he stood up and started pacing the room as if he were before a jury. "When I was in private practice in Boston, I took the case of a little Negro girl way back in 1849. She wanted nothing more than to attend a good school, but any school worth its salt was, of course, all White. Her little school was grossly inferior, with dilapidated classrooms, hardly any books, nothing in there to stimulate one's mind beyond sheer will. When I took the case, I was prepared to argue how much inequality harms Negroes, but I was shocked to learn that it hurts Whites as well."

"How? They don't seem to be hurting too bad where I'm from," Malcolm asked confused.

"Well, it might not be apparent, but Whites are nursed in the sentiment of caste, receiving it with the earliest food of knowledge, and are unable to eradicate it from their natures. It is like a disease that eats through our core and perverts our appreciation of humankind." Sumner looked down dejectedly before continuing. "Don't get me wrong, segregation hurts colored children plenty. It fosters in them the idea that they are not as good as other children and embeds in them a near unshakable feeling of inferiority. The sooner this country accepts that no matter how our ancestors arrived on these shores, we are in the same boat now, the sooner this dark shadow of oppression can be lifted from our nation."

"You really believe what you preach. You're all right by me," Malcolm said admiringly.

"Well, thank you," Senator Sumner said, waving his hand to dismiss the praise. "I love my country and want to see her reach her full potential, but we never will as long as we're divided. By the way, where did you say you were from? You have the most curious dialect."

"Oh, umm, I—" Malcolm said, trying to think quickly, "am from New Orleans." He decided it would be better to tell the truth, at least Cedric's truth.

"I see. I haven't made it down there in my travels yet, but they do have an interesting dialect, what with the French influence and all," Senator Sumner replied, nodding thoughtfully.

"*Oui*," Malcolm agreed, hoping his French wouldn't be tested any further since that was the only word he knew.

Senator Sumner laughed and pointed to a draft of the bill on his desk. "What do you think?" he asked proudly. It was in a strange cursive that Malcolm could barely read and used a whole bunch of words that he didn't know. He couldn't understand a lick of it.

"It looks great!" he replied nonetheless, after staring at the page for a few moments.

Senator Sumner and John spent an hour tossing around ideas on how to improve the bill, with Malcolm mostly nodding along, but every now and then, he chimed in on how important certain parts of the bill were. He couldn't imagine being told he couldn't go into a movie theater or a McDonald's. If this bill would make sure that was possible, he was happy to help them draft it!

As they were wrapping up, John mentioned, "I'm heading back to Howard if you'd like to join me."

"Yes, you might as well," Senator Sumner agreed, glancing at the grandfather clock standing in the corner. "Senator Revels won't need you for at least another couple of hours."

"Sure. Thank you," Malcolm said, interested to see more of what D.C. looked like in the 1800s.

Malcolm followed John a couple of blocks to 7th Street, where they hopped onto a streetcar heading north with John graciously covering Malcolm's five-cent fare. The streetcar looked a lot like the electric trollies he'd seen in pictures of San Francisco, except for one big difference. The conductor wasn't inside driving it along, but on a bench outside using two horses to steer the streetcar along a track!

Malcolm and John sat down in a row in front of an elderly White couple and both pretended to ignore how tightly the husband wrapped his arm around his wife's shoulders while glaring fiercely in their direction.

"Should we move?" Malcolm whispered, not wanting to take a chance on getting arrested like Rosa Parks. He wasn't sure how he'd fare in a nineteenth-century jail. *Twenty-first-century ones are bad enough,* Malcolm thought, remembering his arrest a few nights before.

"No. Some folks still haven't gotten used to it, but the law is the law. We have just as much right to sit here as they do," John said, turning to tip his hat at the couple and mouth, *Good day.*

The man snorted loudly in response and turned his head in the opposite direction.

To Malcolm's surprise, no one bothered them or made them move. Then he remembered the recently passed D.C. anti-segregation law that Mrs. Downing mentioned the night before.

It was strange riding through a city he knew so well while recognizing nothing. They passed what could have been Gallery Place based on how far they'd ridden, but instead of the Chinatown archway, Verizon Center, and legions of restaurants and stores, all he saw was a couple of drab concrete buildings.

A few blocks later, they passed a large grassy field filled with Black people. Young women stood around wood fires, stirring pots and turning meat; children ran in playful circles, shrieking with laughter; and elderly women sat making quilts together. Something was off though. Malcolm looked closer. Among all the tents, he didn't spot any men.

"Where are the men?" Malcolm asked.

"Most of them were probably either sold away during slavery or died fighting in the war. The few who survived are probably off looking for work. There are tent cities like this all over town."

Malcolm realized these were people's homes. His stomach turned.

"Ever since President Lincoln signed the Compensated Emancipation Act, prohibiting slavery in Washington—nearly nine months before he issued the Emancipation Proclamation, mind you—Negroes have been flocking here for refuge. They came with nothing and live in squalor—desperate, isolated, and largely forgotten in the capital of one of the greatest nations on earth."

"So the slaves were compensated? Why don't they just use the money they got when they were freed to buy a house?" Malcolm asked.

John winced. "It wasn't the slaves who were compensated. It was their owners."

"Ohhh." Malcolm groaned, feeling like he had been sucker punched in the gut. He couldn't help but think about how D.C. still had tent cities scattered all over that didn't look much different from these. "Why doesn't anyone do something?"

"We are working on it, but it takes far more money and resources than Negroes possess. My hope is that by opening the doors of education, more people will be able to save themselves. Speaking of which, welcome to Howard," John said as the streetcar pulled to a stop.

Malcolm had only been on Howard's campus once for that homecoming concert, but the lush green campus at the top of a hill brimming with students eager to fill their thirsty minds with knowledge still felt familiar. Time slipped quickly by as John led Malcolm through the campus, pointing out the library and undergraduate buildings and where medical and law school classes were taught. Malcolm had always thought of Howard as a place where people went to party. Now he realized how revolutionary it was to have a school built right after the Civil War dedicated to educating former slaves—people forbidden from learning how to read just a few years before.

An hour after they arrived, John walked Malcolm back to the university's entrance. "Mark my words, education is freedom, and Howard is the road to liberty," John said, smiling.

"Man, this was really great. Thanks for showing me around," Malcolm said, surprising himself that he was so interested in a college. "I better get going. Senator Revels is probably wondering what happened to me."

"Of course. I have a class about to start. Can you manage getting back to the Capitol by yourself? Any streetcar you hop on headed south will take you back downtown," John said. "And here," he added, handing Malcolm another five cents. "The fare's on me."

"Thank you!" Malcolm said, happily accepting the coin since he didn't know where Cedric kept his money.

"You should think about teaching a class here one day," John encouraged him.

Malcolm laughed before collecting himself. "What could I possibly teach?"

"I'm sure before your time is up in this city, you will have soaked in plenty of knowledge that needs to be passed on to the next generation."

Malcolm chuckled as he walked back to the streetcar trying to imagine himself as a teacher. He barely paid attention in class. Imagine trying to teach a bunch of knuckleheads like himself all day long. *No thanks!*

Malcolm stared out the streetcar window mesmerized by the old D.C., but he didn't feel like a tourist. Instead he was beginning to panic. When would he be whisked back to Aunt Carol's? Was he stuck in the 1870s for good? The streetcar was nearing the Capitol and came to a halt. He took a deep breath to calm himself down and then descended out into the street.

Once inside the Capitol building, Malcolm approached a security guard to ask if he knew where he could find Senator Revels.

"The Negro senator?" the guard asked matter-of-factly.

"Yes," Malcolm confirmed tersely.

"He would likely be on the Senate floor at this time," he said, pointing to a nearby staircase.

Malcolm proceeded up the glistening marble stairs and past framed portraits of countless old White men until he arrived at the entrance to the Senate floor. Malcolm looked inside the room, but didn't see Senator Revels. Finally, he spotted him in an adjacent room comfortably reading a newspaper in a chestnut-colored leather armchair and smoking a cigar.

Senator Revels's face lit up when he saw Malcolm approaching. "You found me! I was just beginning to worry about you. What do you think?" he asked, obviously pleased with his surroundings.

"It's incredible, sir," Malcolm answered honestly, looking around the gilded room with dark mahogany walls. Malcolm sat down on a matching leather couch next to a coffee table covered in newspapers. "I still can't believe I'm standing in front of the first Bla—I mean Negro senator," he said, correcting himself as "Negro" appeared to be how everyone in this time referred to Black people. "Congratulations. You did it!"

Beaming, Senator Revels replied, "No, son. *We* did it! Truthfully, I'm still in shock myself. It wasn't until they told me I could make full use of this Senate Reception Room that it finally sank in that this is real. And boy, do we have our work cut out for us. I might be here to represent Mississippi, but you know as well as I how much our people's hopes and dreams are hinging on the lone member of Congress who looks like them and can give voice to their troubles. I pray that I am up to the task."

"You'll do great. You were chosen for a reason," Malcolm reassured him confidently.

"Thank you. As were you."

Just then, a security officer put his head in the room. "Senator, there is someone at the reception-room entrance who would like to meet with you."

"Who could that be?" Senator Revels asked, looking expectantly at Malcolm.

Cedric is Revels's aide. Assist! Malcolm told himself. "Wait here, sir. I'll check," Malcolm said. He walked briskly toward the entrance. Just outside the door, he found an elderly Black woman he didn't know wearing a long brown dress with a high ruffled white collar pacing the room. Her jet-black hair was swept up in a bonnet, and her skin was as dark and as smooth as ebony.

"Excuse me, ma'am. Can I help you?" Malcolm asked.

"I'm here to see Senator Revels," she demanded, her eyes flashing with a feistiness that warned she was prepared to fight until she got what she wanted.

"Okay. And your name?"

"You don't recognize me? Most people do these days. Please let Senator Revels know Miss Truth is here."

"Yes ma'am," Malcolm said, finding the lady a bit odd, but he returned to Senator Revels to pass along the message nonetheless.

Immediately upon hearing her name, Senator Revels jumped to his feet, hurried to put out his cigar in an ashtray, and straightened his suit. "By all means, what are you waiting for! Bring her on in!" ·

"Sure, right. Yes sir," Malcolm said, returning to the door confused by his reaction. Malcolm timidly tried to catch the woman's gaze with apologetic eyes, but she stared straight forward, determined to get her message to the senator. "Right this way," he summoned her.

"Miss Truth, thank you for stopping by to see me. It is such an honor to make your acquaintance. To what do I owe the pleasure?" inquired Senator Revels.

"Senator Revels." Miss Truth grinned. "Pardon me, sir, but I do get such a tickle out of seeing a Negro and calling him Senator. If you don't mind, I think I will just keep calling you Senator until my throat gets sore."

"By all means, but it is I who am honored by your presence. God only knows that I wouldn't be sitting here today, and millions more wouldn't be free, if it wasn't for the sacrifices of Miss Sojourner Truth. So you can call me whatever you like for as long as you like."

So that's who she is, the famous abolitionist! Malcolm realized, finally recalling something useful from school.

"Thank you, Senator," Miss Truth said, smiling sheepishly as she took a seat on the leather couch beside Malcolm. "What brings me to Washington is quite simply land. Today I met with President Ulysses S. Grant and told him that Negroes need land if we're to have any chance at building a life of worth. You know as well as I how we tilled the soil of this country for centuries and reaped nary a reward from its rich harvest. White folks seem to think that freedom alone is payment for our service, but what they gave us was never theirs to give. We're human, created equal as any man or woman before the Lord. We was born free, and they took that from us."

"You're right about that," Senator Revels agreed.

"That's why today I asked President Grant to imagine if he had a garden, and every day a thief came in and took all his most precious produce, and that thief went off and sold what he stole for a profit and then bought himself a big fancy house on the hill. Now you're broke 'cause you've been workin', tillin', and weedin' the garden, but you don't have nothin' to show for it. So one day, that thief comes up and says, 'You know what, I've been stealin' from you for years, but today I'm gonna stop. Have a good day.' Are you gonna feel grateful that the thief finally decided to stop stealin' or are you gonna want some of your produce back so you can buy your own fancy house on a hill? Of course, it wasn't just produce that was taken from us, but our lives and the lives of our ma and pa and children and so on, so shouldn't we be owed all the more? Mr. President, I said, you know as well as I that Negroes are the only reason this country is rich, yet what do we have to show for it?"

"You're right, as always, Miss Truth," Senator Revels said, nodding in agreement. "General Sherman had the right idea when he set aside four hundred thousand acres of land along the coastline of South Carolina, Georgia, and Florida for Negro families to have for themselves to govern and farm."

"Forty acres per family was a fine attempt to compensate us for all we've suffered, but President Andrew Johnson forced those poor Negroes off that land after barely a year and then gave it back to their former masters!" Miss Truth said, squinting her beady eyes and testily pursing her lips.

"'Forty acres and a mule'?" Malcolm asked incredulously, wondering if this was where the familiar expression came from.

"That's right." Miss Truth nodded briskly before continuing. "This country oughta finally do right by us and give us our own land as payment for our labor. I passed by those poor Negro camps where folks are living in tents and have seen the desperation in my people's eyes. They've fled the most horrifying places imaginable only to end up here to wallow in a shallow grave. This can't be the best this country can do," Miss Truth said, shaking her head in disgust.

"So what are you suggesting? Are you thinking of something along the lines of the Homestead Acts?" Senator Revels inquired.

"That's exactly what I'm thinking, Senator."

"Excuse me, but what's a Homestead Act?" Malcolm interjected.

"Boy, you betta read your history if you're gonna be working at the United States Capitol! Right at the beginning of the war, Congress gave away millions of acres of land out West for nothin', but they wouldn't give none to Negroes, 'cause only citizens could apply, and they said we weren't that. Then, right after the war, Congress passed another

Homestead Act. Negroes could apply for that one, if they knew 'bout it, but the cost was too high and the land too poor, so it didn't do us no good. So what I told President Grant was, we need a new Homestead Act, this one especially for Negroes so that we can till our own soil and, for once, be the ones to profit from our own labor."

Malcolm remembered Uncle Leroy telling him in the barn that day about how hard it was for Black people to even own land—land like his family's farm. Malcolm was beginning to understand why the farm was so special to him and Aunt Carol.

"That would be amazing, Miss Truth. Did he like the idea?" Senator Revels asked from the edge of his seat.

"Maybe. You never quite know what them politicians are thinking. You know, I was real good friends with that nice abolitionist fella John Rock, God rest his soul, and something he said always stayed with me. Now let me see if I can get this right," she said, clearing her throat. "'When the avenues of wealth are opened to us, we will then become educated and wealthy, and then the roughest-looking colored man that you ever saw will be pleasanter than the harmonies of Orpheus, and black will be a very pretty color. It will make our jargon, wit—our words, oracles; flattery will then take the place of slander, and you will find no prejudice in the Yankee whatever,'" she concluded, sitting up straighter in her chair, clearly pleased that she had recounted his words so eloquently.

"John Rock was a very intelligent man," the senator noted.

"Yes, he was," echoed Miss Truth.

"Yes ma'am," Malcolm answered as well. He didn't know who John Rock was, but he wasn't going to ask either. He didn't want to seem like he didn't know *anything*.

"Miss Truth, I want you to know that I fully agree with everything you said today. I will certainly use this perch to advocate with all my might for the land rights of Negroes. I can think of little that would do more to turn our race from one of paupers into princes."

"Thank you kindly, Senator Revels. If we all do our parts, we'll get to where we're goin' sooner or later," she said as she pulled herself up from the seat, waving away Malcolm's offer of assistance.

"Thank you so much for this surprise visit," Senator Revels said, escorting her out. "You have reaffirmed that I'm exactly where I'm meant to be."

As Malcolm waited for Senator Revels to return, he couldn't stop thinking about what Miss Truth had said about Black people needing land to be truly free. Was that why Cedric had asked him to save the family farm? Malcolm's mind skipped around like flat stones tossed into the sea. But what could he possibly do? He wasn't an adult like Cedric with senators around to get things done. He was sixteen. *There has to be something, though*, he thought. *Something I can do. Why else would Cedric bring me here?*

"You hear that, Cedric?" Malcolm whispered under his breath. "If you take me back home, I'll try to figure out a way to save the farm." He closed his eyes and waited, hoping he'd be instantly transported away, but nothing happened.

Senator Revels sat back down in the leather chair, pulled a piece of paper out of his pocket, and handed it to Malcolm. "Here's an advance," he said. "I know you need a little money to help you get settled."

"Thank you, sir!" Malcolm exclaimed. Even though the money was Cedric's, Malcolm was still excited. It was the first paycheck he'd ever received. "What do I do with it?"

"Just open yourself an account at the Freedman's Savings Bank. They'll take care of you."

"The what?"

"I'm guessing you never had enough money to bother putting in a bank before?" Senator Revels said, teasing gently. "Well, Congress and President Lincoln created the Freedman's Savings Bank after the War of Rebellion so that Negro soldiers would have a safe place to deposit their pension payments from their service. Now thousands of Negroes, not just soldiers, deposit their money there and can feel safe knowing that it is protected by the United States."

"It's in D.C.?"

"Head out the Capitol down Pennsylvania Avenue. Keep going about fifteen blocks, and you'll see it just before you get to the White House. Don't forget your credentials," Senator Revels said, handing him a card that showed Cedric worked for the US Senate. "You go on and make your deposit and do what you need to do. See you first thing tomorrow morning?"

"Yes sir, Senator Revels. And thank you!"

• • •

Malcolm knew exactly where he was going. He had taken countless bus rides around D.C. with his mom as a child. Half an hour later and damp with sweat, Malcolm approached a tall redbrick building with turrets on the roof. He stepped inside a grand oak doorway onto white marble floors surrounded by dark wood panels lining the walls and counters. All the employees were Black, dressed in the finest wool and linen suits.

Malcolm walked up to a teller and handed her his check. "I'd like to open an account," he said hesitantly.

"I'm happy to assist. I just need to see some identification," she said, smiling back amicably.

Malcolm fumbled in his pockets for a second before pulling out Cedric's business card.

"My, my," the clerk noted approvingly. "I don't recall ever meeting a customer who worked there. Congratulations!"

"Thank you. I was wondering, how long has this bank been open?" Malcolm asked.

"Since 1865. We currently have thirty-seven offices in seventeen states and nearly fifty million dollars in deposits. Nearly seventy thousand depositors, most of whom were once slaves, bank with us now."

"That's incredible," Malcolm said, wondering if he could ask his mom to open an account for him at the bank when he got back home—if he got back home.

"Don't lose this," she said, handing him a card with his account number along with a few coins for pocket change. "You are holding your future in your hands."

On his way out, Malcolm spotted a row of food vendors parked on the other side of the street and made a beeline to them since he finally had some pocket change. He ordered a sausage link and a pretzel and devoured them in seconds. Then, still tired from his walk to the bank, he decided to splurge on a trip home and hailed a carriage.

"To the Capitol," he said to the coachman, figuring he could direct him to Cedric's basement apartment from there. The driver tipped his top hat and opened the door to the carriage for Malcolm. Malcolm climbed inside and heard the crack of the driver's whip. As the carriage bounced along, Malcolm reclined back, smiling and stretching his arms across the full width of the seat. He couldn't believe how well he'd adapted to this strange environment. In the couple of days he'd been trapped in the 1870s, he hadn't gotten himself, or Cedric, killed. He had a job, had met with important people, and had opened a bank account. Not too bad. If he had to, he could probably survive a little longer as Cedric—not that he really wanted to. He still didn't know what was happening at home. He couldn't bear to think about making his mom or Aunt Carol worry about his absence.

Just then, the carriage picked up speed. The coachman shouted, "Whoa boy, whoa!" But instead of slowing, the horse went faster and faster, as if it was trying to outrun the carriage behind it. Malcolm peeked through the curtain and watched in horror as the coachman leaped from his seat and into the road. Now the horse tore ahead even faster, careening around other carriages and people and food carts, completely out of control. As the horse made a sharp right turn, the connection between the horse and the carriage broke. Malcolm covered his eyes and screamed as the carriage slid through the street toward a sidewalk filled with people. He braced himself for impact and then . . . blackout.

20

"Aaauugh!" Malcolm yelled, but there was no crash. He opened his eyes. Instead of lying in a mangled carriage, he was flat on his back in his bed in the dark at Aunt Carol's. He let out a huge sigh of relief, taking in his dad's posters on the walls and the stacks of books. *Wait. What day is it?*

Malcolm jumped out of bed alarmed. "Aunt Carol," he screamed as he flung open his door. He flew down the stairs into the kitchen and down the hall leading to the other bedrooms. "I'm back! I'm back! It's okay. You don't have to worry!"

Aunt Carol stepped out of her bedroom into the hallway. She was in her nightgown, slippers, and silk cap. "Malcolm, what in the world are you hollering about at this time of night? What's wrong with you?"

"How long have I been gone? Were you worried about me?"

Uncle Corey stepped out of his bedroom too, rubbing the sleep out of his eyes.

"You all right, lil man?" he asked, concerned.

"Yeah. I just thought y'all might've been looking for me. I was gone so long," Malcolm responded, looking confused.

"Boy, I just saw you in the kitchen two hours ago, and I'll see you again in a few more, God willing. Good night, dear. Get some rest," Aunt Carol said, slamming her bedroom door shut. Uncle Corey stretched his arms and yawned before stumbling back into his room.

Malcolm lingered in the hallway a second, still confused, before returning upstairs to his room. He lay down on his bed, staring up at the ceiling, trying to make sense out of his experience. He was here until he wasn't, and then he was there until he wasn't. Did it even really happen? The last thing he remembered here at the farm was Uncle Corey leaving his room and then hearing Cedric's voice before he blacked out. Even more confusing, he had been stuck in the past for at least two days. How was it possible no one here had even noticed that he was gone?

Maybe he hadn't gone anywhere at all. All the stories he'd read in Cedric's diary could have seeped into his head and given him crazy dreams, although something in his gut told him that he could never in a million years have imagined what he'd seen. He had no idea Black people were doing such incredible things right after slavery ended—like serving in the US Senate, fighting for newly freed slaves to have land, and running banks. In fact, all that was contrary to everything Malcolm had learned about his people's history. How could he have imagined a world that he had no idea existed?

"It had to be real," Malcolm said, assuring himself. And if it was, Malcolm had promised Cedric he'd try to find a way to save the farm once he returned, but he didn't even know where to start. Malcolm slowly drifted off to sleep, slightly afraid that returning home was the dream, and when he woke up, he'd be stuck in the past again.

＊ ＊ ＊

Malcolm stood in front of the medicine cabinet in the bathroom with his head pounding. His lip was still bruised from the events at the fair, and his ribs hurt. He'd forgotten about his injuries while he was Cedric. He found a bottle of Tylenol and popped a couple of pills, swallowing them with some water from the sink. He wished he could just sleep the morning away, but he wanted answers—some kind of confirmation that everything he'd witnessed wasn't just in his head. Given how tight-lipped Aunt Carol was the last time he tried to ask questions about their family history, he decided to give Uncle Leroy a try. He was old too, after all. He should know something.

"My, Malcolm, you're up bright and early," Aunt Carol greeted him while flipping bacon and stirring grits at the stove. "I'm surprised to see you up on your own before eight."

"Good morning," he said, stopping to kiss her on her forehead. "I just thought maybe I could get out of the house a bit, help Uncle Leroy with some chores."

Aunt Carol looked up at him with surprise in her eyes. "You want to do chores? Don't tell me that. I could make you a long list. But I didn't think you wanted to do anything except draw—that's nearly all I seen you doing since you got here. Your momma didn't tell me you were all artistic," Aunt Carol observed wryly.

"Yeah, well, you know . . . ," Malcolm said, his voice trailing off. He was thankful his headache was beginning to subside. He debated whether or not to tell her what was really going on, but he still didn't feel ready. He wasn't sure if he ever would.

After having a big glass of orange juice, Malcolm went out back to find Uncle Leroy. The sound of metal clanging was coming from the tractor by the barn. He could barely see Uncle Leroy's legs sticking out from underneath. Malcolm headed over.

"Hey Unc," Malcolm said once he was closer.

"Who's that?" Uncle Leroy hollered from under the tractor. Straw covered his pants, poking out of the woven crevices like he was half porcupine.

"It's me, Malcolm."

Uncle Leroy slowly scooted himself out and looked up at Malcolm expectantly from the ground.

"Ummm, I just wanted to apologize for, you know, how I acted last week. And I was checkin' to see if you needed any help out here."

Uncle Leroy eyed him suspiciously and then slowly sat up, wiping his greasy hands on his pants. "What's your angle, boy?"

Malcolm's face flushed briefly from embarrassment over the reputation he had earned on the farm. He straightened up and deepened his voice slightly, hoping this might make his uncle take him seriously. "Nothin', sir. I just, umm, wanted to earn my keep, like you said, and was wondering if there was anything I could do to help."

"If that's what you say," Uncle Leroy said, raising his eyebrows skeptically.

Unaware that he had been holding his breath in anticipation,

Malcolm let out a sigh of relief, thankful that he was being given another chance to help his family and prove to himself that he could meet the challenge.

"There's a few things I could use your help with. I'm almost done changing this tractor oil. Cows need milking. I got some new fencing I need to put up around the perimeter of the chicken coop, and Sally needs a brush out. Take your pick."

Malcolm almost immediately regretted offering his help once he heard the list, but he was curious about the unfamiliar name. "Sally?"

"You ain't met my horse, Sally, yet? She's my best girl, but don't tell your auntie I said that." He chuckled and winked at Malcolm. "She's a beauty. And as loyal and gentle as they get."

Malcolm paused for a minute. He hadn't had the best experience with horses lately, but he didn't have the faintest idea how to milk a cow or put up a fence. A brush out seemed like the only thing he could handle.

"Lead the way to Sally."

As Uncle Leroy led Malcolm over to a fenced-in field to the right of the barn, Malcolm attempted some conversation. "So have you always lived in Mississippi?"

Uncle Leroy glanced over at Malcolm quizzically and snapped, "Son, Black folks don't *move* to Mississippi."

Malcolm mulled over his uncle's response for a moment and soon realized he had asked the wrong question so he tried again. "If it's so bad, why don't you leave?"

Uncle Leroy's eyes closed as he seemingly recounted a mental list of all the obstacles he had overcome in order to arrive exactly where he was that day. He kept them closed for so long that Malcolm wondered whether he had fallen asleep standing up, but then his eyes popped back open. "It ain't all that different down here from where you and your momma live. Anywhere you're a Black man in America, you better watch yo back."

Even at his young age, Malcolm knew that better than most, but he wanted to know more about his uncle's perspective. "What do you mean?" he pressed.

"I mean I just do the best I can to mind my business and stay out of trouble, even when trouble is doin' its best to find me." He kept his eyes focused on the path ahead in order to discourage Malcolm from asking for more details. Sally started to whinny when she saw them approaching.

"Do you ever want more than that?" Malcolm continued to probe.

Uncle Leroy sighed, accepting that Malcolm was not going to let this conversation go. He placed his hand gently on Malcolm's shoulder and spoke genuinely, as if imparting a piece of wisdom. "I done seen plenty of people who want more get cut down to half they size. It's best to just be thankful for what you got and hold on to that, if you can." He turned and unlatched the gate to Sally's pen.

A beautiful black mare stood at the opposite side of the small enclosed pasture near the fence, eyeing them as they entered.

Malcolm picked up on the sensitivity of the conversation, but still wanted to know more. He decided to approach the conversation from a different angle. "How long have you been farming?"

Uncle Leroy's guard seemed to come down slightly as he answered casually, "All my life. Ever since I can remember. Started when I was around three."

"Three-year-olds can't farm!" Malcolm exclaimed incredulously. Sally snorted.

The corners of Uncle Leroy's lips briefly curled up in a half smile at Malcolm's naivete. Then his smile dropped and he clarified sternly, "My parents were sharecroppers, so the whole family would be out in the field from sunup to sundown trying to make our tally."

"Unc, that sounds like slavery," Malcolm remarked. Suddenly, he noticed the signs of decades of wear and tear on his uncle's body that he had subconsciously skipped over before. His eyes darted to the intense swelling of his uncle's calloused hands, the sheer width of his shoulders when he stood up straight, and the scattering of scars on his arms and neck that had refused to fade over time.

Uncle Leroy chuckled. "Boy, slavery didn't end. It just changed names." He paused reflectively, grabbing the brush hanging on the fence and pulling out a carrot from his pocket to summon Sally toward them.

At the sight of the carrot, she slowly trotted over. Uncle Leroy used a rope to tie her to the fence post and handed Malcolm the brush.

"What do I do?" Malcolm asked, trying to hide how intimidated he was by Sally's humongous size.

"Just brush her. Start with her mane and work your way back. Whatever you do, don't find yourself behind her. That won't end well for you." Uncle Leroy snickered as he stepped aside to give Malcolm more space.

"Anyway, the thing about sharecropping was we had to hand over most of what we grew to the White man so he could either eat it or sell it. If we fell short, he'd write us a promissory note and we'd owe more the next month, but we was already farming the land as hard as we could. Eventually, we fell further and further behind till we got kicked off the land altogether. Lucky for me, I had an aunt in Natchez who was an old maid and decided to take me and my brothers in. We started going to school regularly for the first time." Uncle Leroy smiled. "It was all worth it because that's how I ended up meeting your aunt Carol."

Malcolm slowly reached up to Sally and lightly patted her neck. "That's nice," Malcolm replied, trying to move the old man's story along to the family's farm. "Is that when y'all moved here?"

"You sho got a lot of questions this morning. You up to something?" Uncle Leroy asked incredulously, raising an eyebrow.

"Nope, just curious," Malcolm denied. He stared into the horse's dark saucer-shaped eyes and wondered what kind of horrors these types of animals had witnessed in the South throughout the years.

"Uh-huh, why don't you get more curious about that brush out?"

"My bad," Malcolm said, and slowly began running the brush through Sally's mane, hoping not to upset her.

"That's right. There you go. Just move the brush from top to bottom. Then think front to back," Uncle Leroy said, eyeing his work.

Malcolm held the brush firm and tried to concentrate on the mane of hair in his hands. The horse's ears gradually relaxed, indicating that Sally had reached a point of comfort with Malcolm. Though Malcolm was still a bit tense, he could tell the horse was unlikely to hurt him—at least as long as his uncle was near.

Not wanting Uncle Leroy to leave him there without answering his question, he continued. "You were saying?"

"Boy, patience. Let's see, where was I . . . ? Right. Carol and I got married in '59. Your great-grandma, Mama Lucille, was still living here then. We got ourselves a little place not far from here, but we couldn't afford no land. This here land's been in Carol's family, your family, a long time, but there weren't no menfolk around to farm it good, so I started helping out, planted that garden you see over yonder, bought some live-stock, till we finally decided to move in and help your grandma raise her boys after your grandpa died and help take care of Mama Lucille."

Uncle Leroy smiled broadly. "It's been my pride and joy to turn this into a nice farm we could live off of. We don't hardly need nothing out-side this property. We got peas and carrots, okra, tomatoes, squash, eggs, fish, pork, chicken, and milk. We ain't never gonna go hungry, I'll tell you that. And anything we don't eat, I sell down at the farmers market."

Malcolm had finished brushing Sally's mane and began focusing on her shoulders.

"Okay, Malcolm, you got it from here? I got other things to do," Uncle Leroy confirmed as he was already halfway out the gate.

"Sure, I think I can handle it," Malcolm said hesitantly. If someone had told him a month ago that he'd be on a farm in Mississippi tending livestock at 8:30 a.m., and not completely hating it, he would have said they were out of their mind.

Malcolm was slowly putting together the pieces. It sounded like Uncle Leroy had been through a lot and seen a lot, but at the same time was content with where life had taken him. He was a man who could keep what he grew for himself like Sojourner Truth wanted for former slaves all those years ago. Even if Cedric hadn't benefited from the Homestead Acts, he still managed to buy something of his own that continued to bless his family after all these years. *But now the state's even trying to take that away*, Malcolm thought, remembering his mission. He hurriedly wrapped up with Sally and went back to the house to see if he could squeeze any more information out of Aunt Carol.

21

"You were out there helping Leroy a good while. Want some breakfast?" Aunt Carol offered as soon as he walked into the kitchen. She was standing in front of the oven, peeking inside. "The biscuits and bacon are ready. I can reheat the grits and scramble some eggs real quick."

"That sounds great! Thanks!" Malcolm took a deep inhale of the savory smells.

"No problem, baby. Fix yourself some orange juice and have a seat." She pointed over to a clear glass pitcher filled to the brim with juice from fresh-squeezed oranges on the counter. The leftover rinds were still lying there, so Malcolm pitched in, picking them up and throwing them away.

As soon as his food was on the table, Malcolm decided to cut straight to the chase. "Aunt Carol, what's going on with the farm? At the family reunion, you said it might be one of our last ones because the state's trying to take the land to expand the highway." While waiting patiently for her to answer, he stirred his eggs into his grits and crumbled his bacon on top like he used to do when Grandma Evelyn made this breakfast.

Aunt Carol plopped down in a seat next to him and exhaled a puff of air. "Yes. I'm sorry you found out that way. I didn't want to worry you, but it looks like we are going to lose the farm by the end of the year. I told you this happened before, fifty years ago, when they first built the highway. We fought tooth and nail to keep it then, had lawyers and everything, but it didn't matter. We just ended up losing money on top of land. Well, now they want to expand the highway and surprise, surprise, they need our land to do it. Hey Corey, baby. Want some breakfast?" Aunt Carol asked, standing up as Uncle Corey entered the kitchen. She handed him a plate and motioned toward the stove where steam was rolling off the buttery grits.

"Thank you, Auntie. You know this was one of my favorite breakfasts growing up!" he said, grinning. He sat down at the table with his plate loaded with food. "Morning, Nephew." He greeted Malcolm with a nod. "You feeling better?"

"Yeah," Malcolm answered sheepishly, remembering how wild he must have looked waking everyone up in the middle of the night. "I just had a weird dream." He grabbed another biscuit from the plate in the center of the table and lathered it with butter and homemade strawberry preserves. "Aunt Carol, why can't they expand the highway on the other side?"

"Well, I suppose 'cause White folks live on that side. They not gonna inconvenience them," she said matter-of-factly as she joined them at the table. "Could you pass the preserves, Malcolm?"

"Have you tried fighting it?" Malcolm passed them, and then took a huge bite of his biscuit. "Ohmygoodness, this is so good!" He almost forgot he had asked a question.

"Thank you, baby. Of course I have, but when the state claims eminent domain, there isn't much you can do. You don't need to worry yourself about this. Ain't nothing gonna happen till you get back to D.C. nohow. I'm just glad you got to spend our last summer in the house with us. Evelyn would've wanted it that way." Aunt Carol looked over lovingly at Uncle Corey as she watched him eagerly devour a biscuit.

"Aunt Carol, I'm so sorry. Is there anything I can do to help?"

"There isn't, baby." She shook her head hopelessly and then stood up. "Would anyone else like some more juice?" She got up and grabbed the pitcher off the counter and returned to her seat.

"No, thank you. Where are you guys gonna go?" Malcolm persisted.

"There's an assisted living facility in town I've been looking at." She sighed. "We might go there," Aunt Carol said dryly, chasing an egg yolk on her plate with a biscuit.

After seeing how hardworking a man his Uncle Leroy was, Malcolm knew this was the worst idea. "But Uncle Leroy will be bored out of his mind at a place like that," he objected.

"We all gotta do what we gotta do. Didn't nobody promise life would be easy, especially not for us. Sooner you accept that, the better off you'll be."

Sucking his teeth, Malcolm got up to put his plate in the sink and then returned to the table. How in the world would he, a sixteen-year-old Black kid, save the family farm? And if he couldn't figure it out fast enough, would Cedric return and send him back to the past again?

"So Corey, how you adjusting? You doing okay?" Aunt Carol asked, turning her attention to him.

"It's going all right. I'm just trying to get my job search together. Turns out knowing how to make license plates isn't a hot market skill. And I don't have none of the papers I need to even apply for a job." He reached for a napkin and dabbed the grit that was stuck to the stubble of a beard that was growing in.

"What you need, baby?" Aunt Carol asked, concerned.

"Everything! I need a driver's license, a social security card, my GED certificate, an email address, and my own phone number. Everything," he said again, sighing in frustration. "I've been locked away for sixteen years and now I have to prove that I still exist."

"One step at a time. One step at a time," she said, patting his hand reassuringly. "A lot of this stuff you can do on the computer now, so we can go down to the library, and I can help you with that."

"But doesn't it cost money to get all these things? I don't have a job because I don't have the paperwork, but if I can't afford the papers, how I'm gonna get a job?" he asked, exasperated and throwing his hands in the air.

"You know, Aunt Carol, you could always get Wi-Fi and then you-all wouldn't have to go to the library to get everything done," Malcolm offered with a smirk.

Aunt Carol snorted and replied haughtily, "I've been doing just fine for eighty years without them people from the internet spying in my house. I suspect I'll do just fine for however many more years I got left. Thank you very much."

Malcolm rolled his eyes, but smiled. It was worth a try.

"Now Corey, it's going to be all right. We'll get everything sorted out," Aunt Carol continued.

"All right." He nodded and took a deep breath. "Thank you."

"You don't have to thank me. We're family. My job is to make sure you're okay. It's what Evelyn would've wanted," she said.

"Thank you, anyway," he replied, taking her hand and squeezing it.

Just then, the phone rang.

22

"Malcolm, it's for you," Aunt Carol said, smiling at him with a glint in her eye.

Malcolm took the phone. "Hello?"

"Hey. How you doing? I was really worried about you last night." It was Jasmine.

A huge grin spread across Malcolm's face when he heard Jasmine's voice, causing Uncle Corey and Aunt Carol to start giggling. Malcolm stretched the phone cord out of the kitchen and into the living room.

"I'm all right. Swelling's gone down and everything," he answered, keeping his voice low for privacy.

"Thank goodness. What are you up to this afternoon?" she asked.

"Nothing much!" His voice squeaked. Embarrassed, Malcolm coughed loudly into his fist and then pushed his voice down to a sultry level. "The usual."

"Would you want to come with me down to the Boys & Girls Club?" Jasmine asked hopefully. "I volunteer there sometimes, play with kids, teach them things."

"Really? Why?" There were so many things he'd rather do than hang with some random little kids.

"It's fun. The kids are sweet. It's a good pick-me-up."

"I guess," Malcolm conceded reluctantly, knowing full well he would have gone almost anywhere to spend more time with her.

"I'll take that as a yes. Scoop you around 3:00 p.m.? It feels good to give back. You'll see."

● ● ●

That afternoon, Malcolm followed Jasmine into the local community center. After checking in at the desk, they went into a recreation room. She was greeted like a celebrity.

"Miss Jasmine! Come see the braids I just put in Latanya's hair. They cute!" a petite girl with colorful barrettes said, leading Jasmine away.

Malcolm looked around the room and tried to figure out what to do with himself. A couple of kids were hunched over a foosball table, some were playing a game of Uno in the corner, while others were just sitting around chatting and laughing. A couple of older kids hung out at a back table loosely keeping an eye on things. Malcolm heard the screech of sneakers against a waxed floor coming from another part of the center and perked up. He followed the sound out of the room and around to a basketball court in the adjoining room. Some middle school kids playing ball looked up when he entered the room.

"Yo, old man," one of them called out, "you ball?"

"I got your old man!" Malcolm hollered as he stormed onto the court. "Check me."

Before he realized it, he was having a good time. Jasmine was right. Giving back did feel good. *Maybe becoming a teacher wouldn't be the worst thing in the world*, he thought, remembering John Mercer Langston's suggestion when he was at Howard.

After embarrassing the kids with his skills on the court for a few minutes, Malcolm decided to take a break to see what Jasmine was up to. He found her seated at a table with the girl who had pulled her away, braiding her hair.

"You look nice," Malcolm said as he walked up in a good mood.

"Thank you!" Jasmine and the little girl said in unison before bursting into giggles.

"I want to braid someone's hair!" Another little girl pouted. "Jeremy," she said, turning to a thin freckly-faced White boy who looked to be around eight years old, standing near the table behind her, "let me braid your hair."

As she reached over to touch Jeremy's chin-length strawberry-blond hair, he started screaming uncontrollably and then began banging his fists over and over on the plastic table, the papers from the table flying down to the floor.

"Oh no!" Jasmine said, jumping up. "He's having an episode. We need a counselor!" she called out, hoping someone would hear her from the front desk.

"Whoa, Jeremy, whoa!" Malcolm said as he stooped down to Jeremy's level. "It's okay." Malcolm noticed Jeremy was wearing a Snoopy shirt. He quickly grabbed a piece of paper and a pencil from the table, knelt next to him on the floor, and began sketching Snoopy.

When Jeremy noticed what Malcolm was doing, he stopped screaming. He stared at the drawing transfixed.

"You like to draw?" Malcolm asked. "I can show you how," he said, and slipped Jeremy some paper. "First, you start with a circle, see, and then you add a little loop here." Jeremy picked up a crayon and began to follow along. "You got it!" Malcolm said encouragingly as Jeremy mimicked the shapes. Before long, Jeremy had drawn his own Snoopy and was beaming as he hugged his drawing.

"I didn't know you were good with kids," Jasmine whispered admiringly.

"Me neither," he said, smiling.

Malcolm and Jeremy sat drawing cartoon characters for another twenty minutes until the door opened and a teenage boy stepped into the room. Jeremy jumped up and ran into the teen's arms. The teen was a taller, lankier version of Jeremy, strawberry-blond hair, freckles, and all. Jeremy pulled the teen over to Malcolm, holding his drawing outstretched with pride.

As the teen approached, Malcolm had the feeling he knew who he was, and he noticed a flicker of recognition in the teen's eyes as well. But how would he know a random White boy in Mississippi— *The fair! He was the one standing on the side when those jerks at the fair attacked me!*

Suddenly, Malcolm was up and storming toward him enraged. The teen quickly stepped back, putting a hand up in defense while Jeremy instinctively hid behind him. "Look, I'm sorry," he blurted out.

"Oh you're not so tough without your boys, huh? You wanna finish what y'all started last night? Let's go," Malcolm challenged him, walking toward the door.

"Naw man. I'm sorry. We were drunk. It's no excuse. One of my boys had just lost his job and wanted to blow off some steam, so we got drunk and . . ." His voice trailed off. "Look, it's no excuse, but I'm sorry." It was clear he knew what his friends had done was inexcusable and possibly unforgivable. Jeremy poked his head out from behind his brother, and looked up at both of them warily.

"I got arrested because of y'all fools," Malcolm hissed back. Jasmine walked over and gently took Malcolm's hand. Others stared intently in their direction.

"I know, man. That was messed up. I didn't see that coming." He stared down at his shoes ashamed, unable to look Malcolm in the eye.

"Hmph," Malcolm huffed angrily. He wasn't buying this half-assed apology. "Jasmine, I'm ready to go."

"Look, man, I got a call from the counselors that my little brother was having an episode, and I needed to get here as fast as I could. But then they called back to say some new volunteer was able to calm him down. Was that you?"

Malcolm took a breath, still angry, but nodded.

"Thanks, man. I really appreciate it."

"Yeah, whatever," Malcolm said. He pulled his hand away from Jasmine and headed straight for the community center's doors.

Jasmine was on his heels, following him through the doors and stopping him just outside. "Malcolm, wait. I know you're mad, and you have every right to be, but I can't leave yet. They expect me to be here another hour."

"Well, I can't be in the same room with that dude. I'll lose it," Malcolm snapped.

"Okay, could you wait out here for a little bit? Please, for me? I could probably leave thirty minutes early today."

"Fine. I'll be here." He plopped down on a nearby bench and pulled out his cell phone.

"Thanks, I appreciate it," Jasmine said and returned inside.

Malcolm was surprised he actually had a signal for the first time since arriving in Mississippi and watched as text messages started blowing up his phone, grateful for the distraction.

Ten minutes later the door opened and the teenage boy stepped out with Jeremy following closely behind. Jeremy ran up to Malcolm. "I'm Jeremy. This is my brother, Jason. What's your name?" he asked.

"I'm Malcolm," he said, unable to rebuff Jeremy.

Jason stood a few feet away. "Look, man, I'm real sorry about what happened. But you know, I wasn't one of the dudes who hit you. I tried to stop 'em!"

Malcolm shot back up from the bench. "Yeah, well, you didn't try hard enough. You didn't say nothing when they called me a nigger. You didn't pull them off me when they were jumping me. And you didn't speak up to keep the cops from arresting me. You could've told the cops the fight was all your friends' fault and kept me out of jail. But instead you did nothing." Malcolm's eyes narrowed in anger and his fists curled into tight balls as he waited for the slightest provocation from Jason to justify the beat down he was itching to inflict.

"You right, man. I should've, could've done more," he said, hanging his head in what appeared to be genuine sorrow. "Thanks for helping with Jeremy though. He's autistic and sometimes things set him off, and it can be hard to get him to calm down again," Jason explained.

Malcolm let out a deep sigh. His beef was with Jason, not with Jeremy. Turning to Jeremy, he shared: "When I get upset, sometimes drawing helps me calm down. 'Cause then I can focus on the small details that I can control, instead of whatever else is bothering me."

Jeremy smiled up at him, hugged his Snoopy drawing close to his chest, and then returned to Jason's side.

"Well, I owe you one, man. If there is anything I can do for you, just let me know. I know I'm 'bout to swing by the dollar store and pick up some notepads and color pencils for Jeremy."

Malcolm nodded, wishing they'd leave already. He sat back down on the bench and resumed scrolling through his phone.

"So do you go to school around here? I've never seen you before," Jason asked, taking a step closer.

"You keep track of all the Black kids in town?" Malcolm harshly retorted without looking up.

"Naw, I didn't mean it like that. It's just, you know, not that big of a town. You tend to know folks," Jason said, stuffing his hands in his pockets and shuffling his feet.

"Yeah, well, I'm just visiting, thankfully."

"I guess we didn't give you the warmest welcome. We can be a little leery of outsiders down here," he said, shrugging.

"Seems like outsiders need to be more leery of you," Malcolm quipped, finally returning his gaze.

Jason laughed. "That's fair. Where you from?"

"D.C."

Jason's eyes opened wide. So did Jeremy's. "Wow, that's far. Big city. Well, we don't have all the fancy stuff that y'all got, but it ain't that bad down here. There's a cool spot to play paintball, and a bowling alley just opened. Oh, and there's an old-school video arcade not too far from here."

"It's lots of fun," Jeremy chimed in before bending down to collect pecans that had fallen off a nearby tree.

"Yeah?" Malcolm asked, begrudgingly intrigued since this information was coming from Jason.

"Yeah, they got all the old classics, pinball machines and everything and some cool new stuff too!" Jason described excitedly.

"Where's it at?" For the first time during this conversation, Malcolm began to relax.

"Right off the highway, a few miles south of downtown." Jason pointed far off beyond the tree line.

"Okay, that's not too far from where I'm staying." Malcolm nodded.

"Oh yeah? Me too. I live on a farm off the Northwood Exit."

"Me too."

"The south side of the highway? We must be neighbors!" Jason exclaimed.

"No, the north side," Malcolm responded flatly, remembering what Aunt Carol had said about how the neighborhoods were divided.

"Oh, there's not too much farmland on that side of the highway," Jason commented.

"Not anymore, but don't worry. We won't be there long." Malcolm scoffed.

"Why?" Jason inquired.

"Never mind," Malcolm said, sucking his teeth as he attempted to end the conversation. Just like that, he felt his temple pulse and his fist clench up again.

"No, why?" Jason persisted. "Y'all selling?"

"Yeah, but not by choice," Malcolm said, immediately regretting saying anything. *How can the world be so unfair to some while allowing others to live in blissful ignorance of their privileges?* he wondered.

"What do you mean?" Jason asked.

"Man, don't even worry about it." Malcolm shook his head. He stood up and made his way toward the community center's doors, hoping Jasmine was ready.

"Wait, for real, why?" Jason asked following him.

Malcolm let out a long sigh. "'Cause the state is taking my family's land, *again*, so they can expand the highway," he reluctantly admitted, turning around to face Jason.

"What?" Jason asked. "They can't do that!"

"Maybe not to your family," Malcolm said under his breath. At this point, Malcolm almost wished he had never drawn Snoopy for Jeremy. Malcolm barely understood what was happening himself, or how he was going to fight it. There was no way he was about to explain all this to Jason.

"That's not right, man. Is there anything I can do to help?" Jason offered, surprising Malcolm.

Malcolm laughed out loud, before responding, "Naw man, you good." *Like we'd even want his help.*

Just then, Jasmine emerged through the doors and stopped dead in her tracks when she saw who Malcolm was talking to. "Malcolm, you ready to go?" she asked anxiously, not wanting to have to break up another fight.

"Yeah." Malcolm turned abruptly and headed toward Jasmine's truck without saying another word.

● ● ●

Malcolm was quiet for most of the ride back to Aunt Carol's.

"You okay?" Jasmine asked as she pulled off the highway at his exit.

"Yeah. I tried to put what happened at the fair behind me, but seeing that dude brought it all back. And it just seems like everywhere I look, my family is dealing with stuff White people don't even have to think about. Like my uncle just got out of prison after sixteen years over some bull that White kids get community service for, and now he's struggling to find a job. My family is about to get kicked off our land, and I can't even go to a fair without getting beat up and then blamed for it. And don't even get me started on what my homies are going through back in D.C.," Malcolm said, shaking his head. *Oh, and yeah, there's also a ghost in the house who sent me back to the 1800s,* Malcolm thought, fuming.

Jasmine reached over and squeezed his hand encouragingly. "I'm sorry, Malcolm. I didn't know your family was going through all that. Maybe it sounds too simple, but my dad always says, 'Life's a struggle, but winners never quit and quitters never win.' We just got to keep fighting to make things right."

Jasmine turned onto the gravel drive leading up to Aunt Carol's house. When she pulled to a stop, Malcolm looked over at Jasmine and asked, "What happens when you're too tired to fight?"

Shrugging her shoulders sympathetically, she replied, "I just don't think that's an option."

Malcolm returned a weak smile and then leaned over and gave her a kiss on the cheek.

Jasmine's face lit up. Malcolm got out of the truck and shut the door. As Jasmine rounded the drive, he gave a small wave and watched her pull onto to the main road.

He was still angry and his mind felt heavy. He dragged himself inside the front door, through the living room to the kitchen. It looked like Aunt Carol had just stepped out. Fresh shrimp were sitting on some butcher paper by the sink. He went on up the stairway to his room and crashed on his bed, staring at the ceiling.

He could see his dad's posters taunting him from the corners of his eyes. How come after all the amazing things he saw Black people do more than a hundred years ago, things hadn't ended up any better? Uncle Leroy still grew up sharecropping, Uncle Corey spent half his life in prison, and the state was about to take the rest of Aunt Carol's land, continuing an injustice from decades ago. It was stupid to think things would ever get better. What was Cedric thinking asking him to save the farm? He'd had enough. Malcolm rose swiftly from the bed and ripped the Martin Luther King Jr. poster off the wall. Then he felt it. That same cool breeze. Malcolm froze.

"Tsk, tsk," the voice said disapprovingly. "So that's it? You're giving up?" Cedric asked, sitting on the edge of the second twin bed.

Malcolm turned to address the ghost, more annoyed than afraid this time. "Ugh. Not you again." Malcolm groaned as he lay back on his bed and buried his head under a pillow. "Why can't you leave me alone?" he screamed.

"Because you are clearly not receiving the message I'm sending. You think we got this far by giving up every time an obstacle was thrown in

our path? Black people have had to fight for every inch we got—and not just for us but for our children."

"But—" Malcolm said in protest, and then he felt the now familiar sensation.

He was falling into black.

23

Malcolm landed gently in a heap at the foot of a bed in a dark, moist room. It took a moment for his eyes to adjust to the darkness before he saw the wood-burning stove and a brown suit jacket splayed over the back of a wicker chair. He knew instantly what he was dreading to be true—he was back in Cedric's basement apartment on Capitol Hill.

There was a faint early-morning light just appearing outside the window. Malcolm jumped up but his knees buckled beneath him, and he fell to the floor. The last time he'd been here, it took days to get home. How long would he be stuck this time? Even worse, no one at the farm ever noticed he was gone. He could be here for years, unable to get back to his life, and no one would even care. What if he never returned? Would his family just forget he existed? He felt short of breath.

No, Cedric wouldn't let that happen. I'm here for a reason. Maybe there were just some things Malcolm needed to see or do, like last time, before Cedric returned him home. "Okay," Malcolm said as he began to catch his breath and calm down. Whatever he had to do to get home again—even if that meant living as Cedric for a little while—was what he'd do. But where to start? How much time had passed since the last time he was in stuck in the past? Was it still 1870?

The diary, Malcolm thought. Cedric had his diary in D.C. Maybe it could tell him what was going on in Cedric's life right now. He found a match on the nightstand, lit a candle, and looked around the room. The dresser was the most likely place. He walked over and rummaged through the drawers. A small jewelry box caught his eye. Inside was a shiny, gold, heart-shaped locket. A photograph of Cedric was on one side and one of a beautiful woman with long, charcoal plaits and almond-shaped eyes was on the other. He was well acquainted with what Cedric looked like, but it was nice to see Isabel's face as well. Beneath the jewelry box was the diary. Malcolm pulled it out of the drawer and brought it to the wicker chair, throwing the suit over to the bed, so he could sit down and have a look. He quickly skimmed the pages. The last entry was dated March 8, 1871.

March 8, 1871

A couple of weeks ago, Senator Revels shocked me with the announcement that he was returning to Natchez at the end of his one-year Senate appointment. He simply missed his wife, daughters, and life there too much to stay in Washington any longer. I also miss Isabel with all my heart, but I'm just not ready to return to Mississippi yet. I can't shake the feeling that there is so much more I can do here to help my people.

Just this week, there was a shoot-out in a courtroom in Meridian, Mississippi, where the judge and a negro policeman were killed. Then a faceless band of criminals that calls itself the Ku Klux Klan went on a wild rampage, murdering nearly all the leading negro men in town. Any negroes that they placed under arrest were later found murdered in their cells. As soon as the riots started, the governor reached out to the federal government for assistance, but just like with the Mechanics' Institute massacre, the response was too little, too late. By the time federal troops arrived days later, more than thirty negroes had been brutally murdered and the mayor had been run out of town.

If there is any hope to create a safer world for negroes, it lies here in Washington. Fortunately, six new negro representatives were elected to Congress this term: three from South Carolina—Joseph Rainey, Robert De Large, and Robert Elliott; Jefferson Long of Georgia; Benjamin Turner of Alabama; and Josiah Walls of Florida. I'd be lucky to land a job with any of them, but I have decided to focus my attention on Congressman Elliott. I have been a great admirer of his ever since I got ahold of his weekly newspaper, the *Missionary Record*, my favorite periodical after my own paper the *New Orleans Tribune* went out of business.

I went to the Capitol early this morning hoping to spot Congressman Elliott as soon as he arrived for the first day of Congress. Good thing I did, because Capitol Hill was a madhouse with hundreds of new arrivals scurrying through the halls trying to find out their committee assignments. I saluted Mr. Downing in the House dining room and sat down to enjoy my biscuits and coffee. One of my favorite pastimes is testing whether I can accurately detect the state, if not district, of a congressman by their accent and attire. Enjoying my game, I spotted Congressman Elliott the moment he walked into the room. He stood out as a tall man of the deepest brown hue with close-cut hair and a well-groomed mustache. I couldn't help but see the Lord's hand at work in this moment.

Doing my best to hide my nervousness, I congratulated the congressman on his impressive victory and told him what a fan I was of the *Missionary Record*. He smiled at me cautiously and extended a wary hand before asking who I was. I was so nervous I barely got out my name, but once I told him I was also a journalist, I began to relax. It turned out, he was also a fan of my paper! Finally having the courage to reveal my true purpose, I told him that my previous boss, Senator Revels, had returned to Mississippi, and I was looking for work. Curious as to why Senator Revels would leave Washington after only a year, he asked whether I had any dirt on him. Sensing he was laying a trap, I said, "We all have dirt, but we don't all have friends." My answer must have been satisfactory because he tossed me his jacket and said, "Let's get to work." I assume that means I'm hired.

"So I—I mean, Cedric works for Congressman Elliott now," Malcolm reflected, scanning back up to the list of names. "Congressman . . . *Robert Elliot.*" He got up and returned the diary to the dresser drawer. "I'll find him first thing in the morning," Malcolm said, and yawned. He climbed into the bed, dozing off to catch a few more hours of sleep.

● ● ●

When Malcolm approached Capitol security, the same officer was there. But this time, when Malcolm asked if he knew where he could find Congressman Elliott, he didn't ask if Malcolm was looking for "the Negro congressman." With six new Black congressmen that wouldn't be as helpful a descriptor.

Malcolm set off in the direction indicated by the security officer, scanning the hallway for Congressman Elliot.

"Cedric, you lost?" a voice called from behind.

Malcolm looked around and saw a poised Black man with a neat mustache approaching. "Congressman Elliott?" he asked hopefully.

"Yes, yes. Look, Cedric, I need your help," Congressman Elliott said, handing Malcolm a giant stack of papers without so much as a *good morning.* "We have a very important hearing coming up next week about the wave of violence plaguing Negroes in the South. We must show Congress that the federal government needs greater authority to stamp it out."

"What do you need me to do?" Malcolm asked as he followed him into a barren meeting room. A single table and two leather chairs sat in the center of the room. Atop the table was a large pile of envelopes. He was surprised at how seamlessly he'd slipped back into his role as Cedric.

"You see all this mail?" Congressman Elliott said pointing at the table. "It's from my constituents in South Carolina begging for federal protection."

Malcolm hung Cedric's suit jacket on the back of a chair and sat down.

"The United States freed us from slavery and owes it to us to make sure we stay free," Congressman Elliott continued. "Meanwhile, former Confederates are doing everything in their power to ensure White supremacy, not equality, remains the law of the land. The local governments are largely in cahoots with them, leaving poor Negroes defenseless. We need to bring witnesses to Washington to prove that state and local governments are failing to protect Negroes from murder and mayhem. And if the states won't do their job, then the federal government must. Somewhere in this heap are our witnesses."

Malcolm looked at the overflowing pile of mail and gulped. "Sure, I'll get right on it," he said, trying to project confidence as he started flipping through the mail. Congressman Elliott sat down in the chair across from him.

"So here's what we're going to do, Cedric. I'm sure you're aware of the two Ku Klux Klan Enforcement Acts that Congress passed in the last term to protect Negroes' voting rights," Congressman Elliott explained. "Because of those laws, for the first time ever, federal prosecutors can bring criminal charges against people for violating Black people's civil rights. That's a good start but it doesn't do a lot of good if Klan members are able to kill all the witnesses before trial. I'm working with some congressmen on a bill that would allow the president to order the military to suppress insurrections and suspend the writ of habeas corpus."

"What does that mean?"

"It means," Congressman Elliott said, smiling as he leaned back in his chair, interlacing his fingers, "that the federal government could arrest and imprison people without having to justify their actions to a court first. This way, prosecutors can lock up Klan members *before* they have the chance to kill the witnesses or intimidate them into silence. Then the justice system would finally have a chance to work."

"Keeping people alive is good," Malcolm responded, taking one of the envelopes from atop the pile.

"Indeed it is," Congressman Elliot affirmed, grabbing one for himself.

Just as Malcolm and the congressman were making headway on their task, a distinguished-looking Black man with a chubby face and long sideburns that poofed out just under his cheeks walked into the meeting room. He was followed by a young Black man, who was tall and lean with short, curly hair and a mustache. He looked to be around

Cedric's age, but was wearing a much finer pin-striped three-piece suit and polished loafers.

"Congressman Rainey!" Congressman Elliott exclaimed jumping up to greet them. "Always a pleasure to see you! And in Washington of all places? Whoever would've thought the two of us would meet again here!"

"We've come a long way, brother!" Congressman Rainey responded, grinning back.

"Cedric, meet one of the finest men South Carolina has ever produced!" Congressman Elliott said, motioning him over.

"Pleasure to meet you, sir," Malcolm said, getting up from the table to shake the congressman's hand.

"Likewise. Cedric, meet my assistant Nathaniel."

"Hello," they greeted each other. Malcolm was surprised and somewhat excited to meet another young Black aide.

"Excuse us, gentlemen, while Congressman Rainey and I have a word in private," Congressman Elliott said, as they stepped outside of the room, laughing on their way out.

"I guess they're pretty close?" Malcolm asked.

"Yes, the Negro politicians in South Carolina tend to all know each other and stick together. Although Congressman Elliott is slightly different. As we say, he's not quite homegrown."

"What do you mean?"

"Well, I heard one rumor that he was born in England, became a lawyer, and only moved to South Carolina after the war."

Malcolm's jaw dropped open. "Why would a Black person leave a free place like England to move to the United States, and South Carolina of all places?"

"Exactly. I also heard that he was born in Jamaica and raised in Boston and became a lawyer up there. Who knows what's true? All I know is he seems to know every inch of South Carolina like the back of his hand and every person in the state that matters," Nathaniel said, shrugging his shoulders. "I don't know. Maybe he was a runaway slave who managed to create a new identity for himself?"

Malcolm shook his head in confusion realizing there was more to

Cedric's boss than met the eye. Congressmen Elliott and Rainey returned a few minutes later smiling, each holding a celebratory cigar in hand.

"I got to get back to business. Nice to meet you, Cedric," Congressman Rainey said on his way out the door. Nathaniel waved and followed him out.

Congressman Elliott grabbed his hat, "I'm headed out for a quick errand, Cedric, but I'll be back shortly. I trust you have what you need to get started?"

"Yes, sir," Malcolm said, glancing down at the envelopes. Seconds later the room was quiet. Malcolm returned to the stack of mail before him. How could he possibly figure out who would make a good witness? If only he could enter a few search terms on the Internet to pull up their bio or hit Ctrl F to find key words in the letters like he would when researching a school project, but no such luck. He was going to have to do this the old-fashioned way.

Malcolm let out a long sigh as he opened the first letter. He could hardly read the handwriting, so he set it aside. That happened a dozen more times before he finally came across a letter from a man named Joshua Wardlaw, whose tale of bravery and defiance led Malcolm to believe he wouldn't be easily intimidated. Malcolm placed him into the "yes" stack and kept going.

24

Day after day, Malcolm returned to the Capitol and performed his best imitation of a legislative aide—all the while wondering when Cedric was going to send him back home. It was weird to report to a job instead of school, but Malcolm was beginning to get used to it. The biggest difference was he didn't have a schedule and a bell to tell him where he was supposed to be every second of the day. He had to figure out on his own how to fill his time in a way that was helpful. He also didn't have anyone to answer to, except for the congressman. He had never had such independence.

Gradually, he developed a routine. He began each morning by reading the newspaper, which was a lot more congested and less colorful than the ones back home. Not that he regularly read the newspaper at home, but every now and then his mom would leave the sports section out for him. Thankfully as an aide, Malcolm didn't have to read the whole thing. He just skimmed it for stories about what was happening to Black people in the South, which was all Congressman Elliott was really interested in, and those stories were few and far between. He also tried to help the congressman prepare for the upcoming hearing on the Third Ku Klux Klan Enforcement bill. Everything took way longer than he expected since there were no computers or internet to rely on. No Google. No Wikipedia. He was amazed that anybody was able to get anything done in the 1800s.

Finally, a week after contacting the witnesses, Joshua Wardlaw arrived in Washington to testify before Congress, along with a few other witnesses. Malcolm was just as impressed with Mr. Wardlaw in person as when he read his letter. He was a humble man, but stood proud, reminding him a little of Uncle Leroy.

"You sure all these White people gonna care what happened to me?" Mr. Wardlaw asked Congressman Elliott timidly. He sat on the couch in a waiting room wearing a navy-blue suit that hung a little loose, a black bowler hat in hand.

"When you don't have to look people in the eye, it's real easy to think their pain isn't real. You're here to show them it is. We'll make them care." Congressman Elliott approached Mr. Wardlaw with a twinkle in his eye and offered his hand to help him up. Then they all walked over to a small but ornately decorated hearing room where vibrant reliefs of swooning angels graced the ceiling.

Malcolm grabbed a chair on the perimeter of the room in between a couple of reporters, who were eager to hear firsthand about the ongoing terror plaguing Black people in the South. Five congressmen each sat on opposite sides of a long rectangular oak table with an empty seat at the head. Congressman Elliott directed Mr. Wardlaw to a row of chairs behind the empty seat where a few other witnesses were waiting to testify.

"Good morning, sir. Please state your name for the record," Congressman Elliott asked as he confidently strode up to the witness chair after Mr. Wardlaw had been seated and sworn in.

"My name is Joshua Wardlaw."

Malcolm pulled out his graphite pencil and some paper to take meticulous notes.

"Do you know of any outrages or any means of intimidation or threats used to keep persons from voting in the last general election?" He interlaced his fingers and stared intently at Mr. Wardlaw to draw everyone's attention to him.

"Yes. I was tortured for refusing to vote the Democratic ticket." Mr. Wardlaw paused and looked down at his hands. Congressman Elliott nodded supportively. Mr. Wardlaw continued. "A group of White men dragged me and my brother-in-law from our homes in the middle of the night, forced us to lie on the ground, stripped us naked, and beat us.

I managed to escape, but I was so frightened that I hid in the woods naked all night, shivering from the cold, but I survived. My brother-in-law was not so lucky. When I made it back to town, I learned that several other Negroes had also been kidnapped from their homes and nearly beaten to death that same night."

"Is there anything you did to justify this treatment?" Congressman Elliott asked skeptically.

"No sir. Before that night, I had no quarrels with the men that beat me. A few weeks before this happened, a couple of those scoundrels pulled me aside on the street to ask whether I was a Radical or a Democrat. I didn't want no trouble, so I told them what they wanted to hear. Well, when I went to vote on Election Day, I refused to vote the way they wanted, and they threw me out of the polling place, but not before threatening to take my life before six months. And they nearly did."

"Was anyone prosecuted for this heinous act?"

"No sir. The only Klan trial I ever heard of was for a Negro who reported the Klan had whipped him and set his house on fire. That Negro was charged with perjury and thrown in jail."

The crowd let out a mix of gasps and laughter.

Congressman Elliott threw a curt glance in their direction, which silenced the crowd. "Mr. Wardlaw, thank you for coming to tell your story today. It is most informative," Congressman Elliott said, excusing him from the witness chair so he could return to his seat.

One Black person after another testified about similar horrors they had faced, confirming that Mr. Wardlaw's experience was not an aberration in the South, but the norm. A part of Malcolm could relate to their fear. A tremor went down his body whenever a cop was near, and he hoped he wouldn't end up dead like his dad or locked up like Uncle Corey. But he could hardly imagine living under the constant threat of death for how he voted—when he was able to vote. Even after everything these people had experienced, they were still brave enough to come to Washington to testify. Malcolm hoped Congressman Elliott was right and that this hearing would make people care.

When the hearing was over, Congressman Elliott walked over to

Malcolm and patted him on the shoulder. "You found an excellent witness. I knew you would," he said appreciatively. Malcolm felt a rush of pride at the compliment.

While they were talking, a bald White man with a full mustache and droopy eyes tapped Congressman Elliott on the shoulder.

"Mighty fine job you did there, son," he remarked.

"Thank you, Congressman Butler. I appreciate everything that you're doing to push this bill through."

As soon as the man walked away, Malcolm asked who he was.

"Oh, that's Congressman Butler from Massachusetts," Congressman Elliott answered matter-of-factly. "He's the chairman of the House Committee on Reconstruction. I thought you would have recognized him from when he served as the military governor of New Orleans during the war," he continued eyeing Malcolm suspiciously.

"Oh yes, of course. That's what I thought. It's just he's aged a lot since then, and I almost didn't recognize him," Malcolm explained, trying to justify his gaffe and hoping he hadn't blown his cover.

● ● ●

Barely a week after the hearing, the Third Ku Klux Klan bill was scheduled for a debate. Malcolm found Congressman Elliott pacing the cloak room with the kinetic energy of a boxer getting ready to enter the ring.

"How are you feeling, boss?" Malcolm asked, vibing off his energy.

Shaking his shoulders up and down excitedly, the congressman replied, "I feel great! I've been waiting for this day for a long time."

Malcolm believed him.

Together they walked over to the floor of the House of Representatives. Malcolm held the large oak doors open as Congressman Elliott brashly walked through and strolled down the center aisle to claim a seat in the very first row. Malcolm sat directly behind him and had the congressman's notes handy in the unlikely event he needed them. As it was when Senator Revels was sworn in to the Senate, the gallery above the House floor was packed with everyone in rapt attention. *Glad all these people think it's cool to hear a Black congressman speak*, Malcolm mused optimistically. *Maybe that means they care about what he has to say.*

His optimism was short-lived as the debate opened with several White congressmen actually defending the Klan. One even went so far as to say the Klan was necessary to punish Negro vagabonds who roamed the country in idleness, depending upon theft instead of labor and organizing themselves into bands for the perpetration of robbery, arson, and murder. *Am I hearing them right? Are they really trying to say terrorists like the Klan are a good thing?* Malcolm wondered in disbelief.

When it was Congressman Elliott's turn to speak, Malcolm moved to the edge of his seat, hoping his words would be powerful enough to repel the avalanche of hate. But Malcolm had no need to fear. In a booming voice, Congressman Elliott quickly reset the terms of the debate by reminding everyone what the American experiment was supposed to be about.

"If a republican form of government means anything, it means it is a government for the people and by the people. But how can a republican form of government exist, when most of the electorate is put in terror and subjected to murder, exile, and the lash, through domestic violence organized and operated by the minority for the sole purpose of acquiring a political domination in the state?" Malcolm noticed some of the congressmen looked away guiltily as Congressman Elliott spoke, while others looked inspired. A few of the Black onlookers in the gallery wiped away tears from their eyes. Malcolm knew he was witnessing something historic based on their reactions and tried to sketch the scene on some loose paper in his notes, his sturdy pencil collecting his thoughts.

He tried to imagine using his voice to move people so persuasively, but words didn't always come easily for Malcolm. Drawing, however, was where he was most comfortable. He could take his time to get the picture right. The eraser was his friend, or he could always start fresh, but there were no do-overs in public speaking. *But I can't always draw a solution to the problem*, Malcolm thought. Then again, he had had so many firsts these past few weeks, who knew what the future held in store. He was still only sixteen after all.

By the time Congressman Elliott finished his speech, neither the constitutionality nor the necessity of the bill remained in doubt. Doubt was for those without hope.

HON. ROBERT B. ELLIOTT
of South Carolina
ADDRESSING THE HOUSE OF REPRESENTATIVES

A week later, the Third Ku Klux Klan Enforcement Act was up for a vote. Malcolm had been living as Cedric for three weeks now, which was more than twice as long as the last time Cedric brought him to the past. He was getting antsy and feeling ready to go home, but at the same time, he really wanted to know if the bill he had been working so hard on was going to pass. It had to pass!

In the morning light, Congressman Elliott and Malcolm anxiously approached the Capitol, leery of how the vote might go. A familiar face stopped them on their way in. Buddy.

"Congressman Elliott, suh, I'd love to give you a quick polish, if you have a moment," Buddy said, ushering the congressman to his chair.

"Sure, but can you make it fast? They are going to vote any minute," Congressman Elliott responded nervously as he took a seat. Malcolm grinned at Buddy and stepped to the side to wait.

"Yes suh. I hear that was a mighty fine speech you gave in support of the Third KKK Enforcement Act the other day. I could hear the applause all the way out here. Quite an impression you made on folks. I also hear things are gonna work out just fine today," Buddy said, rubbing his cloth back and forth over Congressman Elliott's shoes.

"Is that so? Folks have been tight-lipped. I am not sure we have the votes." The congressman sighed.

"Don't you worry, suh. The Lord has his thumbprints all over this one," Buddy said, reassuringly squeezing Congressman Elliott's shoulder. Malcolm chuckled, knowing he'd been right before.

25

For the second time in a row, Buddy had been right. The House and Senate voted to pass the bill. Next thing Malcolm knew, he was swept up by a crowd of congressmen and aides into a room in the Capitol that was more extravagant than anything he had ever seen in his life. Every inch of the walls was engraved in gold—two huge, gold-framed wall mirrors, gold-framed portraits of some important-looking White men, a gold-embossed ceiling adorned with paintings that would rival Michelangelo's best work, and a gold chandelier. Malcolm thought some of the hip-hop artists' homes he'd seen on TV were gaudy, but this was crazy!

"What is this room?" Malcolm whispered to Congressman Elliott, who was seated beside him.

Before the congressman could answer, the doors swung open and President Grant walked in. Everyone jumped to attention. President Grant sat down at a long green oval table where a stack of official papers awaited next to a black fountain pen with a golden-tipped nib. Congressman Elliott whispered back, "The President's Room."

With a dramatic flourish, President Grant signed the Third Ku Klux Klan Enforcement Act into law. Bypassing the throngs of legislators who were hoping to get his attention, President Grant walked over to Congressman Elliott and said admiringly, "Your people owe you a tremendous debt of gratitude."

Congressman Elliott stood up to shake the president's hand, and Malcolm instinctively jumped up as well. Congressman Elliott shook his head, deflecting the praise. "With this law, the federal government can finally hold White supremacy groups like the Klan accountable for the terror they've unleashed across the South, thereby giving Negroes the chance to live a life of peace as full members of this democracy. All Americans should be grateful and proud to have a president as honorable and committed to justice as you."

Malcolm edged closer as President Grant leaned forward and whispered into the congressman's ear, "We have a busy agenda ahead. I need you with me on other items."

Congressman Elliott nodded knowingly and whispered back, "Mr. President, you show me you are with my people by implementing this law to the fullest, and I'll show you how much I'm with you."

President Grant nodded before moving on to greet other legislators eagerly awaiting his attention.

Afterward, Malcolm and Congressman Elliott followed a few other congressmen and their aides from the Capitol over to a newly opened hotel and restaurant across the street from the White House to celebrate. Malcolm was happy to see Congressman Rainey and Nathaniel again, but didn't really know the others in the group. "Do you know what the president wants from you?" Malcolm asked Congressman Elliott as they crossed the street.

"Not exactly, but he still has to follow through on what we accomplished today before he has my ear to the fullest."

Malcolm was impressed the second they stepped inside the hotel. The dark mahogany walls, rich leather seating, and crystal chandeliers screamed elegance and class. White customers were comfortably dining next to Black ones, and everyone seemed to be enjoying themselves. A pretty young hostess led them to a booth, where a waiter immediately appeared to recite the menu and take their order. Before the waiter could write anything down, a nicely dressed, middle-aged Black man swooped in and said he would handle their table.

"James, my good man," Congressman Elliott greeted the interloper.

"What brings my favorite congressmen to the Wormley on this fine evening?" he asked.

"President Grant just signed the Third KKK Enforcement Act today, and I couldn't think of a better place to celebrate than your restaurant."

"A Black person owns this restaurant?" Malcolm gasped in shock. "I mean," Malcolm said, trying to correct himself as the other congressmen at the table eyed him disapprovingly. "What a nice restaurant you have. What inspired you to open it?"

"Well"—Mr. Wormley smiled, stretching taller and adjusting his tie— "I have always loved the finer things in life," he said with a wink. "And it was my great honor and privilege to work as a caterer to one of President Buchanan's foreign ministers. I traveled with him to England for a year and learned firsthand from the royal staff how to provide service fit for a king. How do you like the china you are about to dine on?" Mr. Wormley asked the group.

Everyone nodded their approval, with Congressman Rainey picking up his plate for closer inspection.

"I purchased the linen and the china while I was in England, knowing that one day I would use them in my very own establishment. But I never imagined in my wildest dreams that my hotel would be across the street from the White House, and I'd have the pleasure of serving the first Negro members of Congress. It is quite a fortuitous confluence of events."

Malcolm was truly impressed.

"Please know that you are always welcome here, and I will do whatever I can to make your visits most comfortable," Mr. Wormley said with a nod, and politely excused himself from their table.

Malcolm half listened to the congressmen discussing the day's events. He wondered whether the Wormley still existed in his own time. Maybe he could take his mom there for her birthday, or maybe he'd take Jasmine there one day if she decided to visit D.C. Malcolm couldn't help but feel a little homesick.

As the first round of drinks arrived, Malcolm returned his attention to the table. "A ginger ale with a sugar cube, please," he ordered. He was finally adjusting to the acerbic taste and was proud of inventing his own way to make it more palatable.

Congressman Rainey pulled a letter from his coat pocket.

"What's that, Joe?" Congressman Elliott asked.

"It's a letter I received," Congressman Rainey said, opening it and placing it on the table for all to see.

The letter, written in red ink made to look like blood, with a skull and crossbones stamped on top, read:

> BLOOD.
> ### K. K. K.
> BEWARE! BEWARE! BEWARE!
> Your doom is sealed in blood.
> Forbearance has ceased to be a virtue.
> SPECIAL ORDER,
> HEADQUARTERS 17TH DIVISION,
> CYCLOPIAN CYCLOP COMMANDERY.
> No 54.
> First—At a regular meeting of this post on Saturday night, it was unanimously resolved that due notice be given to J. H. Rainey, W. H. Jones, J. H. Bowley, S. R. Carr and H. F. Heriot, to prepare to meet their God. Take heed, stay not. Here the climate is too hot for you. Legal cap scoundrels, leave once forever. We warn you to flee. Each and every one of you are watched each hour. K.K.K. We warn you to go, go, go. The auditor we trust. On motion of O.R.F.L, the lodge adjourned to meet at 7. O.L.A.A.G., Sec. V.M.R.V., Colonel Commanding, Valorous Democracy.

The congressmen exchanged concerned looks, likely wondering whether the KKK had placed a similar mark on their heads.

"What you gonna do about that, Joe?" someone asked.

"Not much I can do. I represent the people of South Carolina in the United States Congress, so fleeing ain't an option for me. I'm gonna keep doing what I've been doing. Meeting with my constituents to understand their needs and representing their interests in Washington. I can't let no cowards in sheets keep me from what I was put on earth to do," he said, slamming his whiskey glass on the table.

Malcolm jumped in his seat, startled by the man's intensity.

"I spent the first fifteen years of my life as a slave until my pa saved enough to purchase my freedom. And in those fifteen years, I was afraid every day. I was afraid I wasn't gonna make count and the overseer was gonna whip me. I was afraid somebody would accuse me of taking something I hadn't and cut off my hand. I was afraid I'd be sold away from my ma and pa and never see them again. The day my pa bought my freedom, I made a promise to myself." Congressman Rainey suddenly rose up, banged his fist on the table, and shouted, "I ain't spending another goddamn day being afraid. To hell with those crackers!"

Congressman Rainey sat back down, but the steam was still rising from his ears. For a moment, everyone at their table was silent, until Congressman Elliott raised his whiskey glass up high and repeated, "To hell with 'em."

"Hear! Hear!" everyone echoed, clinking their glasses.

Malcolm couldn't believe Congressman Rainey's bravery. Even with people threatening his life, threats that had been carried out countless times before, he was just going to march on undeterred? These congressmen must really believe in what they were doing and the difference they could make. After everything Congressman Rainey had experienced during slavery, it didn't sound like there was much that could scare him. Malcolm thought back to his brushes with death, remembering the fear that gripped his body when bullets rang out on the basketball court. He was even more terrified staring into the gun barrel of the cop who couldn't seem to tell a victim from a perp. Perhaps you could only look death in the eye so many times before you would no longer blink.

When the meal was wrapping up and the gentlemen rose to leave, Nathaniel asked Malcolm if he wanted to try to find a bar nearby that he had heard people went to when they really wanted to let loose. Curious, Malcolm said, "Sure," and followed him out.

Malcolm and Nathaniel walked down the alley behind the Wormley for a few minutes searching for the spot, but without any luck.

"Maybe it's the next block over," Nathaniel said, leading the way toward the corner.

"Wait," Malcolm said. He listened and heard the creak of a door opening, followed by the faint sound of music wafting into the night. "Did you hear that?" Malcolm asked, but Nathaniel hadn't.

Malcolm walked toward the sound, and the closer he got, the stronger the aroma of cigars filled the air, but he still didn't see anything. He approached what appeared to be a solid brick wall and noticed a sliver of light on the ground. He traced its path until he came upon a door that had been painted to blend in with the surrounding brick wall, making it almost invisible.

Malcolm smiled back at Nathaniel, stepped forward, and knocked. When the door opened, it became readily apparent why it was hidden. Through the fog of the smoke, he could see a dozen scantily clad women of the most beautiful shades of brown, from crème to espresso, milling about, slow dancing on tables, sitting in the laps of men, and carrying drinks back and forth from the bar. Through dim candlelight, he could see a group of musicians playing sensuous music to complement the mood. Malcolm straightened his back to look as tall and old as possible, but as soon as he crossed the door's threshold, everything went black.

26

"**N**ooooooo!!!" Malcolm screamed as he landed back on his bed at Aunt Carol's. "That was foul, Cedric!" Malcolm called out, mad that he didn't get to spend any time on the other side of that door, but Cedric was nowhere to be found.

Malcolm's irritation quickly passed. It felt so good to be home. Aromas from Aunt Carol's cooking wafted up to his bedroom providing a momentary distraction. From the smell, he knew it was dinnertime and exactly what Aunt Carol had made—that distinctive medley of meat, seafood, and rice. Jambalaya.

His stomach growled. *What? How can I be hungry? I just ate at the—*. Remembering he was no longer Cedric, he tried to get his head together. First, he had to remember what day it was. He had been so long in the past, on Capitol Hill, weeks—although he knew no time had passed at the farm while he was gone. The last thing he remembered was going to the Boys & Girls Club with Jasmine. *Right*, Malcolm thought. *Jasmine dropped me off just a while ago*. He looked at his phone: 6:58 p.m. His stomach growled again. Time to eat.

As Malcolm rose from the bed, he noticed the Martin Luther King Jr. poster was hanging halfway off the wall. He couldn't leave it like that. Malcolm fumbled around in his dad's desk for a few minutes before finding some tape to put on the corner. "Good to see you guys again," he said, taping the poster properly on the wall before heading downstairs.

"Aunt Carol, you made my favorite. What's the occasion?" Malcolm asked, taking a seat at the table and noticing a beautiful bouquet of red, orange, and yellow flowers in a vase at the center. He wanted to give her a giant hug, but that would seem suspicious. A single plate was waiting for him, and he helped himself to more than his stomach could hold. Everyone else seemed to have eaten already and Aunt Carol sat across from him playing solitaire. Uncle Leroy and Uncle Corey were in the living room watching a baseball game.

"Nothing special," Aunt Carol replied, concentrating on her cards. "Leroy brought these begonias in from the garden. He knows they're my favorite." She nodded at the vase. "Also, I spoke to your mother today, and she told me how much you love jambalaya. I realized I hadn't made it in a while, so I decided to whip some up."

"It's delicious," Malcolm said after taking his first bite. "It tastes just like my mom's." He closed his eyes and savored the flavors as long as he could. He felt like he hadn't been home in so long, but this hit the spot.

"Mama Lucille taught me and your grandma Evelyn how to make it when we were little girls. After that, Evelyn and I always made it together, and we showed your momma how. It feels a little different making it without Evelyn, so I don't fix it as often, but hopefully it tastes just as good." Aunt Carol picked up the cards to shuffle the deck.

"It's great," Malcolm reassured her. It had never dawned on him as odd that his family was from Mississippi but made such delicious jambalaya, a traditional Louisiana dish. Malcolm wondered if this was the same recipe that Cedric wrote about Isabel making in his journal.

"How's my mom?" Malcolm asked in between bites.

"She's good. She was mostly worried about you. Wanted to make sure you were getting along all right and weren't too shaken up by what happened at the fair. I told her you seemed to bounce back just fine and had already been off gallivanting with Jasmine again." She smiled mischievously, laying her final solitaire hand on the table.

Malcolm's eyes bulged in embarrassment, knowing they had been gossiping about him. He shook his head. "What you guys getting into tonight?" he asked, attempting to change the subject of conversation as quickly as possible.

"Oh, nothing much, unless you feel like getting your butt whipped with these cards," Aunt Carol teased playfully.

"What?" Malcolm asked, feigning shock. "What you playing?"

"I could deal up a hand of bid whist. But you and Corey wouldn't stand a chance against me and Leroy." Aunt Carol chuckled.

"What's bid whist?" Malcolm asked.

"Spades for grown-ups. Pull up a chair. I'll teach you. Corey, Leroy, come in here. Class is in session, and we got a new student." She beckoned the rest of the family into the kitchen for game night and reshuffled the cards.

Malcolm's heart swelled. He hadn't realized how much he missed his family. He was happy to just be in the kitchen with them all, playing cards.

"What you say, Carol?" Uncle Leroy asked, poking his head in.

"Malcolm asked me what bid whist is," Aunt Carol explained as she cut the deck in four. Malcolm knew then she was getting serious.

"Deal me in!" Uncle Leroy said, pulling a chair up to the table with Uncle Corey close behind. Uncle Leroy cracked his knuckles and popped the bones in his neck, ready for the competition.

"So basically, it's just like spades only the person who wins the book gets to name which suit is trump. Got it?" Uncle Leroy asked as he organized his cards in his hand.

"Sure." Malcolm nodded nervously. He had no idea what most of the words in his Uncle Leroy's sentence meant.

"Don't worry, Nephew. I got you. Just follow my lead," Uncle Corey reassured him.

It didn't take Malcolm long to get the hang of it; he was always a quick learner—especially when it came to reading people, which was what most card games came down to. After winning a few books, he started to loosen up.

"So Aunt Carol, what was that about schoolin' me? Looks like I'm ready to graduate," Malcolm boasted, collecting the last book. It felt good to win at something, even if it was something small. He hadn't realized until this moment how much he needed these simple, precious moments with his relatives. He smiled deeply until his aunt Carol interrupted his thoughts with her playful teasing.

"That's because I'm a damn good teacher," she said, laughing and reshuffling the cards. "I didn't teach for forty years in public schools for no reason!"

"What did you teach again?" Malcolm asked. Uncle Corey stood up and left the table in between games. Not wanting to interrupt the conversation, he gave a signal to Uncle Leroy, who responded with a nod. Malcolm wondered what they were up to.

"Well, I started as an English teacher at the colored primary school in town. Your grandma and I shared a classroom. She handled the little kids while I whipped the big ones into shape. Then after integration, I became a library assistant at the high school your daddy and Corey ended up going to. Then your grandma left teaching so she could focus on having a family. It was a blessing she could have children at the age she was then. Anyway, you come from a long, proud line of teachers." She looked around to see where Uncle Corey went. He reappeared in the doorway with two rummers.

"Oh man, it wasn't no fun having Aunt Carol at school. Believe that! Anytime I wanted to sneak a girlfriend into the library to, ahem, study, I had to think twice 'cause there Aunt Carol was, peering at us over a stack of books!" He opened up one of the highest cabinets in the room and pulled out a glass milk jug with a crimson liquid swirling inside.

"Ha, I had to keep you boys on your toes! Couldn't let one of those hussies trap my handsome nephews!" Aunt Carol said, laughing.

"Was it real different?" Malcolm asked hesitantly.

"Was what real different, sweetie?" Aunt Carol replied.

"Teaching at the different schools—the Black school and the integrated one," Malcolm clarified.

"Night and day. As different as black and white." She laughed. "When we were at the Black school, we didn't have much—just an old building where all the kids, from six to sixteen, were taught in the same room. The older kids helped teach the younger ones how to read and do math. We never had a textbook that didn't already have ten kids' names in it before we got it. But what we lacked in resources, we made up with love. We were like a family. Shoot, most of us were family long as we've been living in this part of Mississippi. Half the time, my students' parents knew how their kids did in school before they made it home."

"Oh yeah," Uncle Leroy chimed in. "Word traveled real fast back then. But them kids didn't cause too much trouble, huh, Carol? I know I would've rather be in that schoolhouse learnin' than out in them fields any damn day."

At first Malcolm had a hard time imagining kids wanting to be in school, but after remembering how tired he was after helping out Uncle Leroy, he started to see the appeal.

"Sho you right. But everything changed with integration. It was great that we got new books and the children had access to better classes, but we lost our sense of community. And worse, the White folks didn't want us there and never missed a chance to let us know it." Malcolm's brow furrowed as he contemplated how once again a law intended to improve Black people's lives fell short of the goal.

"So why'd you switch to being a library assistant?" Malcolm asked, studying the cards in his hand. If he was playing poker, he would've won the hand, but this game had more to do with partners and strategy than luck.

"I wasn't given a teaching position—they already had enough English teachers, and I think the White parents would have had a fit if their children had to learn English from a Black lady." She laughed again. "But at the end of the day, integration needed to happen. This country has got to get over its obsession with race and what better way to do it than to have kids growing up beside each other so they can see for themselves that race is only skin-deep. I'm not sure how much of a difference it ended up making though, since most of the White families either moved out of the city or put their kids in private school." Aunt Carol reached over and pulled out Uncle Corey's chair as he returned with two drink glasses about a quarter full. He handed one to Uncle Leroy and sat back down.

Malcolm could smell a vague scent of plum coming from the glass. "Can I have some?"

"No!" Uncle Leroy and Uncle Corey shouted in unison.

"Okay . . . Yeah, my school in D.C. is almost all Black, with a couple of Latino kids. I don't think that integration thing worked out so well," he said, resuming his conversation with Aunt Carol.

"No, probably not," Aunt Carol said. She did a little dance in her seat while collecting the first book of the round off the table. Then she lightly fist-bumped Uncle Leroy and smiled smugly at the rest of her cards.

"So I was wondering, about the house—?" Malcolm started.

"Not again," Aunt Carol interrupted. Her eyes warned him that she was having a great night and wasn't in the mood for him to rain on her parade.

"Have you thought about contacting your city councillor or a state rep?" Malcolm asked, undeterred.

Uncle Leroy cleared his throat to get Malcolm's attention and answered him dryly. "They gerrymander our votes by either crowding all the Black folks into a few districts or spreading us out so thin that there aren't enough of us in a district for our candidate to win. This state is almost 40 percent Black, but that don't matter. Either way, nobody with power answers to us. They don't care what we think."

"Y'all ever think about reaching out to your White neighbors, tell them what's going on and see if they'll talk to their representatives?" Malcolm suggested.

"Boy, I don't know what cotton-picking ideas you brought down from D.C., but these White folks don't give a rat's ass about us." Uncle Leroy snorted. He scratched the back of his head and let out a loud yawn, as if this wasn't something that needed explaining.

"Maybe all of them don't feel that way. Maybe they just don't know what's really going on in Black communities so they don't do anything to help, but if they understood how unjust things were, they would do something." Malcolm was surprised he was defending people who continuously wronged him, but he didn't want to believe that all White people were the same.

"You find me a White person that really cares about Black people, I'll give you a hundred dollars." Uncle Leroy chuckled.

Uncle Corey started laughing. "I'll throw in a hundred too, and I don't even got a job. That's how confident I am!" They clinked their glasses together, cracking up at the ridiculousness of the proposition.

"But—" Malcolm started as he played his next card. *What about Senator Sumner?* he thought.

"Leave it alone, Malcolm. It's been hard enough preparing for our move," Aunt Carol said waving her hand dismissively. "Now what's that you were saying about being ready to graduate? 'Cause it looks to me like you might need to repeat a grade!" She smacked her final card down on the table and collected the last book of the game. She and Uncle Leroy exchanged high fives to celebrate their win.

"Speaking of graduating, young man, my church planned a Black college tour for the teenagers in the congregation. They are wrapping up on Wednesday at Alcorn State, my alma mater, just up the street. Want to join them?" Aunt Carol asked, putting the cards away. Uncle Corey and Uncle Leroy got up from the table to return to their baseball game in the living room.

"Better say yes, Nephew," Uncle Corey said on his way out. "She's got her teaching voice on."

"What are you tryin' to say?" Aunt Carol put her hand on her hip, giving Uncle Corey the eye, then turning that eye on Malcolm.

Malcolm hesitated for a moment before answering. If his mom had suggested this a few months ago, he would have tried to get out of it. Not too many kids from his high school went to college. When school let out, he hadn't really imagined himself doing more over the summer than hanging out and playing video games with his boy Damian.

But things were different now.

He'd visited Howard University as Cedric with John Mercer Langston. It had felt really good to be surrounded by so much positivity and hope, especially coming from people only a few years older than he was. Plus, it sure beat brushing a horse named Sally. He was in!

"Sure," he answered.

"Okay. See! The boy wants to go. I'll drop you off in the church parking lot Wednesday morning around eleven, and you can ride up with them." She grabbed her water glass, gulped what remained, and motioned for him to tidy up his place at the table.

"Cool. Thanks, Auntie," Malcolm said. He picked up his plate and carried it over to the sink. "I'm gonna get some sleep, but before I go, can you tell me what's in that milk jug Uncle Corey poured drinks from?" Malcolm asked in his sweetest voice.

Aunt Carol turned around with just as sweet a smile and answered, "It's our family's plum brandy, passed down from generations. I'll teach you how to make it if you come back next summer."

Malcolm's eyes lit up as he walked over to give her a kiss on the cheek before heading upstairs for the night.

27

"What?" Malcolm called out groggily to whoever was knocking on his door while he was sleeping. He was completely worn down from everything that had happened the last couple of days—or was it weeks now?—and was starting to completely lose track of time. He happily slept right through the rooster's crow and checked his phone: 9:00 a.m.

"Hey Nephew," Uncle Corey said, poking his head in at the door. "Want to run with me to the barbershop? I used to visit your dad at Alcorn every now and then, and there are some fine honeys on campus. I can't have you going on a college tour looking like a busta. I got a reputation to uphold!"

Malcolm laughed as he sat up and looked in the mirror at his hair. "Yeah. I could probably use a little edge up."

"Cool. Me and your pops been going to this barbershop in town, Kenny's, since we were kids. Aunt Carol said she'd drive us. Meet me downstairs in ten? We need to be quick so you don't miss the tour bus at eleven." Malcolm waited until he heard Uncle Corey at the bottom of the stairs before forcing himself out of bed.

Half an hour later Aunt Carol was dropping Malcolm and Uncle Corey off in front of a little strip mall with a 7-Eleven and a chicken wing spot on one end and Kenny's Barbershop on the other. From the outside it looked like any old barbershop with a weathered barber pole sitting next to a neon OPEN sign. There were hardly any cars in the parking lot, except for the ones parked in front of Kenny's.

As soon as Uncle Corey walked into the barbershop, he was greeted like a returning war hero. A handful of Black men of different ages and hairstyles sat in chairs along the wall, leading to the man they were all waiting to see.

"My man!" a big guy in a black smock said, as he put down his clippers and bounced over to give Uncle Corey a hug. "How long's it been? You put on a little weight since I seen you last," he teased gingerly.

"Yeah. It's been a while. Sixteen years," he said, nodding reflectively.

"Ahh, man. That's too damn long. I'm glad you out, brother."

"Thanks, man. It feels good to be out." Uncle Corey looked up in the air while saying this as if speaking directly to God and then reached his arm around Malcolm, pulling him close. "This is my nephew, Malcolm, Michael's boy."

"You don't say?" the big guy asked, peering into Malcolm's eyes. "I can see it. He's got those same piercing eyes, like he knows what's going on out here even if all you other fools don't! Nice to meet you, little brother. I'm Kenny."

Malcolm extended his hand, and Kenny pulled him in for a hug. "This is a hugging shop right here, little brother. Folks come up in here for two things: the freshest cuts, dare I say in all of Mississippi, and some brotherly love." Kenny was such a large man that Malcolm was almost swallowed in the embrace.

"That's right!" Uncle Corey said, laughing and watching Malcolm turn purple as Kenny gave him one more big squeeze.

A middle-aged Black man in a suit sitting along the wall didn't seem to be as enthused with their exchange. Malcolm noticed him roll his eyes and shuffle uncomfortably in his seat. Uncle Corey noticed as well and asked Kenny, "What's the deal with your customer over there?"

"I don't know, he's new," Kenny replied dismissively.

Uncle Corey turned to the man. "You got a problem with me, bruh?"

"No, none at all," the man said aloofly before quickly changing his mind. "Actually, I'm just sick of these thugs getting out of prison thinking the world owes them something. Don't like the time, don't do the crime." He fluffed the old *JET* magazine he was reading in front of his face to block his view of the miscreants.

"What did you say?" Uncle Corey exclaimed, his eyes flying open. "First of all, you don't know me, bruh!" Uncle Corey walked over to the man and pushed the magazine down so that he could see his eyes, and then tried in a calmer voice. "Second, you ain't never made a mistake, made a wrong choice, been at the wrong place at the wrong time? If not, good for you. Congratulations! But the rest of us out here ain't perfect, and we shouldn't have to pay for one mistake for the rest of our life."

"Must've been a pretty bad mistake for them to put you away for sixteen years. You kill somebody?" he taunted, probably hoping Uncle Corey would lose his temper and snap, proving that he hadn't misjudged him.

Malcolm moved a step closer to Uncle Corey defensively. The only thing separating Uncle Corey and this man was Drake's picture on the magazine cover, but Malcolm didn't think that would be nearly enough to help the man if Uncle Corey lost control.

Uncle Corey inhaled deeply. He looked over at Malcolm who was watching him intently, waiting to see how his uncle handled himself. Uncle Corey spoke clearly. "Naw, I didn't kill nobody. All I did is what most White boys are out here doing—smoking a little weed—and now that I spent half my life in prison, it's legal in half the country. Go figure."

"Hmph," the man scoffed. He had made up his mind the moment he saw Uncle Corey walk in and didn't care to sympathize over the details surrounding his case.

"Look, man, I'm really not feeling your energy. I think you need to get your cut somewhere else," Kenny piped in, ready to defuse the situation before it got out of hand.

"Gladly. Maybe I can find a barbershop without a criminal clientele." He eyed the other men in the room condescendingly while he grabbed his coat and marched toward the exit.

"Don't let the door hit ya," Kenny said, ushering the man out.

"Man, you didn't have to do that. I didn't mean to come in here and cost you business," Uncle Corey apologized as he sat down in Kenny's chair for his cut. Malcolm took a seat nearby, relieved to avoid another fight. Last thing he needed was two trips to a Mississippi jail.

"Please, I don't need a dollar that bad." Kenny shook out his smock and snapped it around Uncle Corey's neck.

"People are probably going to always see me differently now. They either gonna judge me or wonder if they should be afraid of me," Uncle Corey said, staring at his reflection in the mirror—like all the time behind bars had made the man staring back unrecognizable.

"Don't worry about what other people think. Long as you know who you are, and that you're always welcome here," Kenny reassured him as he lined up Uncle Corey's fade.

Another customer in a suit piped in, "Yeah man, don't even let that fool get to you. He clearly hates himself, so he's gotta put you down to convince himself how different y'all are. I hope, for his sake, life doesn't prove otherwise."

"Thanks, man," Uncle Corey responded with a weak smile. "I wouldn't wish what I've been through on nobody, not even his punk ass," he said as all the customers in the barbershop burst out laughing.

Malcolm felt bad for Uncle Corey. He had done his time, much longer than he deserved, but it seemed like the label *criminal* was going to follow him wherever he went—from job interviews to voting booths and even to the barbershop. It was like his freedom came with an asterisk, and he had to read the fine print to learn all the ways he still wasn't free.

* * *

Uncle Corey and Malcolm rode silently in the car as Aunt Carol drove Malcolm over from the barbershop to the church parking lot. Aunt Carol looked at them suspiciously. "Y'all are awfully quiet. What's goin' on?"

"We're all good, Auntie," Uncle Corey said from the front seat. The car stayed quiet.

"Uh-huh, well, if you two gonna sit there, did I mention I went to Alcorn State?" she asked Malcolm.

"Yeah. Didn't my grandma go there too?" Malcolm recalled.

"Yep, she sure did!" Aunt Carol answered proudly.

"What was it like?" Malcolm asked, always happy to hear memories involving his grandma.

"Oh, we had the most wonderful time. It was very different back then, and the school was sort of a safe haven for us."

"What do you mean?"

"Well, I graduated in the class of '58 and segregation was just beginning to show cracks in its foundation, but it wasn't going to give way without a fight. First, the NAACP came to town and then SNCC and—"

"What's SNCC?" Malcolm interrupted.

"Boy, don't they teach you anything in them schools?" Aunt Carol asked incredulously.

Apparently not, Malcolm stewed.

"Student Nonviolent Coordinating Committee," Uncle Corey answered. "Even I know that much." He laughed.

Aunt Carol nodded. "Not long after I graduated, SNCC came to town and started trying to help register Black folks to vote, and that's when things turned ugly. White folks started doing drive-by shootings, throwing pipe bombs at people's homes, killing folks, just brazen in their attempts to keep Black people down. My classmates and I, we participated in sit-ins and boycotts and voter registration drives. We had all kinds of nasty things said to us, thrown at us, folks spat in our faces. It was a real ugly time." Malcolm could see the sadness reflected in her eyes through the rearview mirror, but just as he was about to say something to try to comfort her, she jumped back into her story, her familiar fierceness having returned.

"That's when they killed Medgar Evers in front of his house, with his wife and children inside. Didn't even matter that he was a World War II vet," she said, shaking her head in disgust. "He graduated from Alcorn State a couple of years ahead of me and went on to become the Mississippi field director for the NAACP," she nodded proudly.

"Well, the summer after they shot Medgar, the local police helped the Klan ambush three civil rights workers down here who were registering people to vote, a Black fella from Mississippi and two Jewish boys from New York. The Klan beat the Black boy senseless, shot all three of them, and then left them for dead. All 'cause Black folks wanted to vote. But it got the country's attention and sure enough some laws were passed to protect us. 'Course, just as soon as we got 'em, folks started trying to take 'em away." She paused reflexively. "Fighting these same battles over and over again gets real tiring. Like my girl Fannie Lou Hamer said, 'I'm sick and tired of being sick and tired.'"

Malcolm let the moment sink in, unsure of exactly how to respond.

"Fannie Lou Hamer said that?" Uncle Corey questioned breaking the silence. "I always thought it was the rapper Mystikal."

"You know there ain't nothing new under the sun, Corey!" Aunt Carol teased, her mood lightening up again.

"You got that right, Auntie." Uncle Corey chuckled knowingly.

"Wow, Aunt Carol, you lived through a lot." Malcolm mentally added Fannie Lou Hamer to the long list of people he'd have to look up later.

"But to answer your original question," Aunt Carol said, pulling into the church parking lot. "Alcorn State was a wonderful, loving community where I felt supported and safe, made lifelong friends and found my voice as a young woman. You'll have a nice visit."

"Thanks, Auntie," Malcolm said. He reached through the seats to give Uncle Corey dap and then headed out toward the group of teenagers congregating around a bus in front of the church.

28

Malcolm was getting settled on the bus when a familiar face stepped aboard. "Hey Kliff!" Malcolm called out, recognizing his cousin from the family reunion. "Aunt Carol didn't tell me you were on this trip." Kliff moseyed aboard the bus, taking his time to get to Malcolm's seat in the back. He motioned for Malcolm to scoot over and make room for him.

"Yeah man. I've been on this tour the last two weeks. We've been all over. We went to Morehouse, Spelman, North Carolina A&T, South Carolina State, then hit FAMU, Tuskegee, and Southern in Baton Rouge. Man, I'm spent," Kliff said, swinging into the seat.

"Yeah, that sounds like a lot. So what did you think?" Malcolm asked. In a way, he had gotten a taste of his own mini-Black college tour on his trip to Howard without ever leaving the farm.

"It was cool. I've never seen so many fine sistas in my life. Good God!" Kliff laughed, putting his backpack under the seat. "The schools were cool too. I'm kinda nasty with numbers, so I'm focusing on schools that have strong science or engineering programs," he boasted. "I could definitely see myself at one of them. We'll see who's trying to come up with some scrilla for your boy!"

Malcolm was surprised that Kliff already knew what he wanted to do after high school. Half the kids at his school didn't graduate on time, and he only knew a handful that went to college. He hadn't the slightest idea what he wanted to do—not yet. He'd only really focused on basketball and drawing back in D.C. Cedric had sparked his interest in history, though. Maybe he could study that.

Time passed quickly as Malcolm and Kliff chatted about the hottest songs out that summer, with Kliff letting him listen to some new hits on his iPod. Malcolm was surprised by how easily they clicked, as if something in their souls knew they were connected. Before Malcolm knew it, they were at Alcorn State.

The moment Malcolm stepped off the bus, he was overwhelmed by the flurry of activity. Kliff wasn't lying about the campuses. There were beautiful sisters everywhere: tall, short, thick, skinny, some with braids, some with natural curls, some with fades, some with long straight hair. Not that he hadn't been surrounded by all types of Black girls in D.C., but here they appeared more at ease. That was a good thing, because Malcolm didn't realize that he had been standing in the same place, gawking, since he got off the bus. *Cedric, you better not show up now*, Malcolm thought, not wanting to miss a moment of the tour.

"Yo, Mal, you all right? Can you move?" Kliff asked as he playfully nudged him out the way.

Regaining his composure, Malcolm announced, "I'm good," and took a few steps farther toward the center of the lush green campus. Once everyone from the bus had assembled on a sidewalk near the parking lot in front of a classic brick building, a student guide wearing khaki shorts and a bright purple polo and with hair twisted in short locks came up to greet them.

"Welcome to Alcorn. My name is Justin, and I am going to be your tour guide today. Alcorn State was founded in 1871 to provide higher education for freedmen after the Civil War. We have the distinction of being the first Black land-grant college established in the United States." With that introduction, Justin turned and began escorting the group past a small pond and toward a cluster of school buildings surrounding an open lawn where more students had gathered.

"What's a land-grant college?" someone asked.

Justin paused to face the group. "It's a school that was initially funded by a federal grant of land to the states and is designed to focus on more practical studies like agriculture, science, or engineering. In most states, these institutions are the flagship public universities for the state. Most Northern states typically have one land-grant college, while most Southern states have at least two, a predominantly White one and a historically Black one. A lot of states out West also have ones for Native Americans," Justin carefully explained.

As great as it was that Black people had this community, Malcolm couldn't help but be reminded of when he was helping Senator Sumner and John Mercer Langston draft their Civil Rights Act. They had both been adamant that the bill needed to prohibit cities from separating Black and White children into different schools, and they had agreed that segregation was no way to come together as a country and make sure all Americans had a fair shot. *Maybe all the racial tension still around today would be gone if people had just listened to them way back then.* Malcolm sighed.

Malcolm had a hard time focusing completely on what Justin was saying because there were so many sights to take in. On one side of the lawn was a group of men in purple jackets and army pants jumping around and swinging their arms with military precision. On the other side was a group of students in actual fatigues, who he assumed were part of ROTC, marching down the sidewalk in single file. Malcolm jumped out of the way of some guy in athletic gear rushing past with a tennis racket in hand and watched bemused as a cluster of students carrying band instruments frantically ran in and out of some tall building. Then his eyes landed on a group of friends hanging out underneath a tree a few feet away, laughing with their books casually opened in front of them.

"As you can see, we have a very robust summer program," Justin said, motioning toward the bustling campus. "It's part of our commitment to help students graduate within four years."

The tour passed in front of a group of young women, all dressed in red, who were seated at a table on the side of the lawn trying to get students to sign a petition. Malcolm lingered long enough to read the heading: *End the School-to-Prison Pipeline Now,* before he had to quickly move on to catch up with the group.

It was a lot to take in, and he marveled at all the different ways these students had found to express themselves and pursue their passions. It was like he was seeing the world in color for the first time, instead of the black-and-white or shades of gray that he was used to back home in D.C.

From the rear of the group, Malcolm overheard Justin mention a name that made him stop in his tracks. "Excuse me, what did you say?" Malcolm asked as he edged his way forward to where Justin was standing.

"I said this is Hiram Revels Hall, an all-male honors dorm named after the university's first president."

Malcolm looked around, wondering if anyone was as shocked as he was to hear Hiram Revels's name aloud, but no one else seemed to grasp the significance. To them, this was just another building named after someone long dead and gone.

Stepping away from the others, Malcolm moved closer to a plaque on a stand in front of the dormitory that read:

Alcorn Agricultural and Mechanical College
Established May 13, 1871, as Alcorn Univ. of Miss
on site of Oakland College. Hiram Revels, first president.
Reorganized 1878 and Alcorn A.&M.
Oldest land-grant college for Negroes in the United States.

Malcolm smiled and felt a tear well in the corner of his eye as he recalled the immense pride he had felt watching Revels get sworn in as the country's first Black senator. But why had he never heard of him or any of the first Black congressmen before? Why had they been erased from history? At least Alcorn State stood as proof that Senator Revels had existed. All the students that graduated from here, including his grandma, his aunt Carol, and his dad, were a part of that legacy. Hiram Revels not only made a difference in Cedric's time—he'd also laid the groundwork for something that continued to provide opportunities for Cedric's entire family for generations. And here was Malcolm, walking on the campus grounds almost 150 years later.

Malcolm trailed behind as the group made its way back to the entrance. He did a double take as he passed a man in business clothes who looked familiar before realizing it was Jasmine's dad.

"Mr. Rogers!" Malcolm called out.

Mr. Rogers turned in his direction. It took him a second to recognize Malcolm. "Malcolm, son. Good to see you, and in a much better setting, dare I say. What brings you here?" he said, smiling warmly.

"I was just wrapping up a college tour. This place is incredible. What are you doing here?" Malcolm asked.

Mr. Rogers waved hello to a couple of students passing by him and then said, "I teach here. I'm an American history professor."

"Oh wow. That's cool!" Malcolm responded enthusiastically.

Mr. Rogers raised his eyebrows in surprise at Malcolm's apparent interest. "Well, if you like history, you are welcome to sit in on one of my classes anytime you like," he offered.

"For real? Even though I'm only a junior in high school?" Before this summer, Malcolm hadn't even thought of what his life would look like after graduation, and now he was being invited to observe a class on a college campus.

"Of course. There's nothing you can't learn if you have the will to learn it. Just let me know when you feel like stopping by," Professor Rogers encouraged.

"All right. I appreciate that. I'll have to check you out," Malcolm answered excitedly, as he shook the professor's hand.

"You do that. You know how to find me." Mr. Rogers looked at his watch. "I have to get to my next class. Enjoy yourself and take care, son," he said and then walked purposefully toward a nearby building.

"Thanks!" Malcolm replied.

By the time Malcolm made it to the front gates, his group was gone. Justin spotted him looking around. "They're all back on the bus," he said pointing at the parking lot.

"Thanks, man, and thanks for the tour," he said, waving as he walked past him.

"No problem," Justin said, smiling.

Malcolm returned to the bus and squeezed into his seat next to Kliff, who was already knocked out. Malcolm rested his head on the back of his seat, closed his eyes, and thought about what he had seen that day. He was still stunned to have seen proof that Hiram Revels wasn't just a figment of his imagination. The realness of it all set in, bringing a flood of memories of all the other fascinating people he'd met in Cedric's body.

Today, he'd also seen students who weren't too much older than him and who were educated, engaged, and hopeful—attending a college where the first Black senator served as their school's first president. *Maybe Cedric's right*, Malcolm thought. *Maybe there's reason to believe that we can change things for the better, as long as we don't give up.* Ever so slowly, Malcolm began to hope.

29

When Malcolm arrived back at Aunt Carol's, he was itching to draw some images from his visit to Alcorn State, but he was also starving. Aunt Carol had outdone herself once again, and the family gathered together for smothered pork chops and green bean casserole. Aunt Carol was happy to see how much he loved Alcorn State.

"Now I'm not saying you *have* to go to my alma mater, I'm just sayin' it would be nice, that's all. You know, family traditions," she teased.

After Uncle Leroy and Uncle Corey headed to the living room for their nightly TV fix, Malcolm kissed Aunt Carol on the cheek. "Thank you, Auntie," he said, and went on upstairs.

Up in his room he grabbed his sketch pad and pen and kicked back on his bed to draw. Strangely, he found himself missing Cedric, wishing he could share his experience of the day and ask more questions.

"Cedric?" he whispered, sitting up and looking around. "Cedric, you here?" He hadn't been up to the attic in a while. Maybe Cedric would appear to him again up there. After all, that's where he'd first shown himself. Malcolm headed out of his room with his sketch pad in hand to go check it out.

"Cedric?" he called from the top of the attic stairs, but no luck. The room was empty. Malcolm walked over to the desk and pulled out the diary. He began fingering through the pages, smiling when he came across entries he recognized, like President Grant signing the Third Ku Klux Klan Enforcement Act on April 20, 1871, and the celebratory dinner at the Wormley. *Whatever happened to that bar Cedric and*

Nathaniel were about to check out? Malcolm wondered as he scanned to the end of that entry.

"Hey now!" Cedric popped up near the desk and slammed the diary closed. "Some things need to remain private."

Malcolm jumped back. "You're here!" Malcolm exclaimed.

"Were you expecting someone else?" Cedric asked facetiously.

Malcolm chuckled as he walked over to the beanbag chair and sat down. "I don't know how you're making all of this work, but I know you mean well. You still freak me out, but I know you're doing right by me," he said.

Cedric smiled back at him approvingly.

"So look," Malcolm said, leaning forward with his elbows on knees. "I've been thinking a lot about what's happening with the state taking the family farm, and all that you've been showing me, and I want to help. I really do, but I have no idea how."

"Modern problems call for modern solutions. I'm sorry, but I don't have the answer for you. All I can do is show you how we worked to overcome insurmountable obstacles in my time and hope something resonates with you." Cedric perched on the edge of the desk before continuing. "When I was growing up, death and slavery were all I knew for our people. I never thought this many years after the Civil War, my descendants would be facing the same battles. And yet we persevere. Malcolm, my boy, now it's time for you to understand the power of your community. In it, you'll find your voice and the strength to fight injustice and set things right."

And with that, Malcolm felt a familiar pull and began falling.

• • •

Malcolm came to with his head resting on a table in what was now a familiar room at the Capitol.

"Catching a little catnap?" Congressman Elliott asked, entering the room and taking a seat. "I know we've had some long days lately, and I appreciate how hard you've been working."

Malcolm nodded as he adjusted himself in his chair and tried to get his bearings straight. No matter how many times he made the trip, it was still disorienting. At least now he knew that when he returned to his family, no time would have passed there. The notion helped him relax a little. Still, he hoped Cedric wouldn't keep him too long.

"Cedric, I have another tough assignment for you," Congressman Elliott announced.

"What's up? I mean, how can I help, boss?" Malcolm said, shaking his head to clear the cobwebs—and his modern dialect—out of his mind.

Congressman Elliott looked up at the ceiling. Confused and not understanding what Malcolm was referring to, the congressman went on with explaining the assignment. "Well, the situation in South Carolina with the Klan is only getting more and more out of hand. They've committed at least eleven murders and whipped more than six hundred Negroes around the state. President Grant has finally decided it's time to use that new tool Congress gave him last spring and suspend habeas corpus in South Carolina."

"Are you serious?" Malcolm asked in disbelief. "So the federal government is just gonna start rounding up thugs left and right and throw them in jail? A White president is willing to go that far to protect Black people?" Malcolm asked, flabbergasted.

"Yes, it's about time the government is willing to stand up for us."

"So what can I do?"

"President Grant is sending his attorney general Amos Akerman down to South Carolina to oversee the first set of trials under the Third KKK Enforcement Act. Mr. Akerman is going to have all the resources of the newly created US Department of Justice at his disposal to crush the Klan, but I'm not sure if I can trust him because he used to serve in the Confederate army. I want you to accompany me to South Carolina so we can watch him and see our law at work."

"All right," Malcolm said hesitantly, slightly afraid of venturing into the real South so close to the end of slavery. With all of Washington, D.C.,'s anti-segregation laws, it didn't feel all that different from home— if you replaced the cars with carriages and the jeans and white tees with suits and suspenders—but South Carolina was a whole different beast.

Nevertheless, Malcolm agreed to board a train to South Carolina that afternoon with Congressman Elliott and Attorney General Akerman, as well as two US attorneys and a marshal, who was armed and ready for action.

● ● ●

"Congressman Elliott, I'm so glad you could join me. And this must be your aide, Cedric," Attorney General Akerman said, reaching up to shake Malcolm's and Congressman Elliot's hands. They sat down across from the attorney general and waited for the train to get underway.

"Well, you are headed to my home state to go after my number one enemy. I wouldn't miss it for the world," Congressmen Elliott responded brashly, eyeing the attorney general suspiciously.

"Yes. And go after them we will. This Ku-Kluxery has got to come to an end. This is a nation of laws. I will not sit idly by while vigilante justice and lawlessness consumes our streets."

Congressman Elliott sat up straighter in his seat, looking surprised by Akerman's conviction.

"Already, the marshals have arrested fifteen hundred suspected Klansmen in South Carolina. If we have to, we'll arrest fifteen hundred more," Attorney General Akerman continued. "I know these hooded figures are used to doing whatever they want and getting away with it, but those days are over. Mark my word."

Congressman Elliott nodded and gave Malcolm a side glance. Malcolm was sure his face looked shocked by what he'd heard, especially from this White attorney general. He wondered if the man was just telling them what he thought they wanted to hear, or if he was sincere.

"You see this magazine here?" Attorney General Akerman asked, holding up a beat-up copy of *Harper's Weekly*. He flipped to an illustration of two Klansmen in their infamous white hoods, sporting weapons.

"This image has forced Northerners to recognize that the Klan, and the atrocities they commit, are not just figments of Negroes' imaginations," he continued, "and now there is at least some interest

in reinstating the rule of law to keep the South from descending into a rogue state controlled by a violent mob."

"Why is it the ones calling for law and order are always at the head of a mob?" Congressman Elliott mused aloud. "I was surprised that picture got as much attention as it did. Of course the Klan is real! Negroes have been warning about the danger they pose to law-abiding citizens for years," Congressman Elliott shouted with exasperation, momentarily losing his temper.

Malcolm shook his head as he realized cell phone videos of police shooting unarmed Black people had the same effect in his time. People just refused to believe the brutality Black people describe was real, until they saw it for themselves.

"Well, it was more convenient to pretend it wasn't," Akerman replied. "This nation has been at war with itself for so long, people have grown tired of fighting. Now, enforcing these laws is not without risk," he said with a sigh. "Several of my US attorneys have been killed trying to do what's right in holding the Klan accountable. In the last few months in Mississippi alone, one US attorney was poisoned, another killed by a sniper, and yet another shot while sleeping. Many more have been arrested by local police on baseless charges, but we can't give in. It really boils down to who we are as a people, as a nation. I believe in my heart justice will prevail."

Malcolm wished he felt more hopeful, but considering what he knew of his own time, it was difficult. The day passed slowly on the train. Malcolm stared out the window, mesmerized as the terrain transformed from sluggish marshes to gushing rivers and, finally, lush rolling hills. He asked Akerman if he could borrow a couple of sheets of paper and doodled the changing scenery until he drifted off to sleep.

Later that evening, as their train pulled into the Columbia, South Carolina train station, a dozen White men were waiting for them on the platform in the rain.

"Do you think this is an ambush?" Malcolm asked, looking out the window, concerned.

Attorney General Akerman turned to the US marshal on his security detail and asked, "Johnny, would you mind going on ahead of us and checking out the situation?"

The marshal stepped down from the train with his gun cocked while the rest of them remained in the train car.

"State your business here!" he ordered.

The men immediately put their hands up and dropped to their knees. They were all soaking wet.

"Please don't shoot," the eldest among them said. "We are here to surrender. We heard about all of these charges, and while yes, it's true, I have on occasion donned a white robe, I swear before God, I ain't never kilt no nigger. I don't want no parts in that foolishness. I told them boys I'm done and gave my robe back. I brought my boys with me, and I want you to know that none of them ain't kilt no niggers either. We just want this whole mess to be over with so we can go back to working our farm in peace."

The other men with him all nodded in agreement, some more begrudgingly than others.

Congressman Elliott and Malcolm finally descended from the train with Attorney General Akerman. Akerman motioned for one of his accompanying attorneys to join him. "Write down each of these men's names and addresses," he instructed, and then turned to the men on their knees. "We'll give you the amnesty you're looking for, but not for free. I, or one of my men, will be calling on you to deliver your testimony when needed."

Congressman Elliott and Malcolm smiled at each other, pleased that within five minutes of arriving in South Carolina they had already witnessed the power of the Third KKK Enforcement Act at work.

From the station, Congressman Elliott brought Malcolm to his home, a small bungalow not far from Columbia, to spend the night. His wife, Grace, a beautiful woman whose jet-black ringlets formed a loose bun on top of her head, was waiting for them with a hearty pot of gumbo on the stove. After taking a short time to clean up after the long journey, Malcolm sat down at the table with the congressman and his wife and dove into the gumbo as if he hadn't eaten in weeks.

"I can't tell you how good this is!" he said, stuffing his mouth with gumbo-soaked French bread. "I needed this like medicine. Thank you, Mrs. Elliott!"

"It's my pleasure, shugah. I know they starving you in Washington. No good food, no ladies up there to look after you helpless fellas. Just a bunch of men, running around, yapping your jaws, trying to save the world," she teased good-naturedly.

"You make it worth saving, doll," Congressman Elliott said, as he pulled her in by the waist to kiss her.

"Oh stop it!" she said, swatting him away. Malcolm laughed at their tender display of affection.

There was a knock at the door, and Congressman Elliott went to answer it.

"You made it! I'm so glad you could come!" he said excitedly as he welcomed someone into the house. "Grace, you remember my good friend Robert Smalls from Beaufort?"

"Of course. He's a South Carolinian state senator now. How could I

forget? Please come in and enjoy some gumbo," she said as Congressman
Elliott took the newcomer's hat and coat and ushered him to the table.

"Cedric, meet my buddy Senator Smalls, and when you shake his
hand, know that you are meeting a real live American hero."

"Oh, Robert, stop!" State Senator Smalls said.

"No, it's true! I'm talking a one-man revolutionary machine. Everywhere he goes, systems of oppression crumble!" Congressman Elliott
said, waving his arms in the air dramatically.

"You're ridiculous, Robert!" State Senator Smalls said, cracking up
laughing. He turned to Malcolm and shook his hand. "Heard good things
about you, Cedric."

"Thank you, sir," Malcolm said, grinning at the rapport between
the men.

As Mrs. Elliott grabbed another bowl from a nearby shelf and
spooned up some gumbo for their new guest, Congressman Elliott
recounted Smalls's most famous adventures. "You might have heard how
he won his freedom from slavery by stealing a Confederate artillery
ship, the *Planter*, and delivering it to the Union? Or maybe you heard
about the time he met with President Lincoln and convinced him to let
Negroes fight for the Union and their own freedom? Or how about as a
delegate to South Carolina's 1868 Constitutional Convention. He introduced free, compulsory public education into the state's constitution,
a first for a Southern state."

"That's incredible! You did all that?" Malcolm asked in between
spoonfuls of gumbo.

State Senator Smalls smiled bashfully while blowing his bowlful
to cool it.

"That's right!" Congressman Elliott said, answering for him. "So
when your kids and grandkids have the chance to go to school to better
themselves instead of slaving away in some field making somebody else
rich, you have Senator Smalls to thank. But did you think I was done?
Have you ever been to Philadelphia and had the pleasure of riding on
an integrated streetcar? Well, Senator Smalls here is the reason for that!
He refused to move to the colored section and ended up inspiring a protest that got Pennsylvania to pass a bill outlawing segregation in public

transportation! The list goes on and on," Congressman Elliott said, beaming proudly at his friend.

"A few of those things might have been mildly exaggerated, but yes, you got me," State Senator Smalls said, smiling with his hands opened wide.

"Wow," Malcolm said, humbled. "It's a real honor to meet you. How did you do all those things?"

"I just did what needed to be done in the moment. I'm sure you'll do the same when your time comes. Now, enough about me. Let's focus on the task at hand, making sure tomorrow's trial goes well."

"Who are the men on trial tomorrow?" Malcolm asked, picking up his bowl to slurp the last drop.

"It's South Carolina's first trial of not just one White man, but five, who stand accused of interfering with a Black family's civil rights. The stakes couldn't be higher," State Senator Smalls explained. "These men led a Klan raid on the home of a mulatto man named Amzi Rainey for professing his allegiance to the Republican Party. Looks like we'll get the chance to see how well this law of yours works," State Senator Smalls said, winking at Congressman Elliott.

* * *

They arrived at the tiny courthouse that looked like a converted barn right as the bailiff was opening the doors at 8:30 a.m. There was already a line around the building of spectators waiting to get in. White folks sauntered in as if they owned the place—spitting tobacco on the floor, loudly telling crass jokes, laughing, and glaring with contempt at the Black folks who dared attend the trial. As Black townspeople filled out the periphery of the courtroom, Malcolm followed Congressman Elliott and State Senator Smalls through the center aisle past several rows of bench seating to claim a row directly behind the prosecutor's table. The local district attorney David Corbin and Attorney General Akerman leaned on the table whispering in hushed tones over a tall stack of legal documents. The judge sat in an elevated chair at the front of the room behind a desk, eyeing the entire affair suspiciously.

One by one the jurors entered the room and took their seats in the jury box along the wall on the right-hand side of the room. A White man entered first, and then another, followed by a Black man, and then another. When the final juror was seated, it became apparent that there were slightly more Blacks than Whites in the jury box.

"Have you ever seen such a thing?" people whispered through hushed voices as shock slowly registered on the faces of nearly everyone in the courtroom.

Suddenly, the White men on trial were no longer laughing as the seriousness of the occasion settled over them. Malcolm reached into his jacket pocket and found a spare piece of paper he had tucked away on the train trip. He began capturing the shock on the defendants' faces as they realized this was going to be a real trial, as opposed to the sham proceeding they'd been expecting.

District Attorney Corbin called Mr. Rainey to the stand and began his line of questioning.

"Will you tell the jury whether the Ku Klux Klan raided on you, and, if so, what they said and did to you?"

"Well, on a Saturday night in the last of March, as near as I can recollect, I was laying down by the fire. About ten o'clock, my little daughter called me. I got up, and turned around, I looked out of the window, and I see some four or five disguised men coming up, and I ran up in the loft, and they came to the door and commenced beating and knocking on both doors to my house. 'God damn you, open the door!' —My wife run to one of the doors, and they knocked the top hinges off of the doors—and when they come in, they struck her four or five licks before they said a word—They asked her who lived here. She said, 'Rainey—Amzi Rainey,' and he struck her another lick, and says: 'Where is he? God damn him, where is he?' And one said: 'Oh. I smell him, God damn him; he has gone up in the loft.'

"'We'll kill him, too,' he said, and they come up then. And the other says: 'Don't kill him yet'; and they took me down. This man that struck my wife first, ran back to her and says: 'God damn her, I will kill her now; I will kill her out'; and the one that went after me, he says: 'Don't kill her'; and he commenced beating her and then run back and struck me;

he run back to her then, and drawed his pistol, and says: 'Now, I am going to blow your damn brains out' and the one by me threw the pistol up, and says: 'Don't kill her.' He aimed to strike me over the head, and struck me over the back, and sunk me right down. Then, after he had done that, my little daughter—she was back in the room with the other little children—he says: 'I am going to kill him'; and she run out of the room, and says: 'Don't kill my pappy; please don't kill my pappy!' He shoved her back, and says; 'You go back in the room, you God damned little bitch; I'll blow your brains out!' and fired and shot her, sure enough—"

"Did he hit her?"

"Yes sir; the ball glanced off from her head. Then they took me right off up the road, about one hundred and fifty yards; and they wanted to kill me up there, and one said, 'Stop, don't kill him, let's talk a little to him first.' Then, he asked me which way did I voted. I told him I voted the Radical ticket. He says, 'Now you raise your hand and swear that you will never vote another Radical ticket, and I will not let them kill you.' And he made me stand and raise my hand before him and my God, that I never would vote another Radical ticket, against my principle."

"Did you swear so?"

"I did raise my hand and swear. Then he took me out among the rest of them, and wouldn't let them shoot me, and told me to go back home."

"How many of the Ku Klux Klan were there?"

"It looked to me like there was about twenty-five."

"How were they dressed?"

"Some of them had on white gowns, and some of them had on red ones, and some had on false faces and something over their heads."

"Do you know what they did to your daughter in the other room?"

"Yes sir."

"Did you see it yourself?"

"I didn't see it; have only her word for it."

"I won't ask you that then. Are any of the men who assaulted you in this courtroom today? If so, could you point them out?"

Mr. Rainey slowly raised his hand and pointed at each of the defendants who stared back without any remorse in their eyes.

"You may have the witness," the prosecutor said, concluding his interrogation, but the defense counsel declined to question Mr. Rainey.

Other witnesses took the stand and testified that after the Klan left Mr. Rainey's house, unquenched in their thirst for blood, they went on a rampage, whipping and torturing any Black person they could find.

As soon as the trial came to a close, a group of Black onlookers swarmed Congressman Elliott and State Senator Smalls in the atrium just outside the courtroom to pay their respects.

"Things have gotten real bad here," an elderly man said. "Sometimes it feels like the Yankees forgot to tell the White folks here in South Carolina that the war is over 'cause they still attacking us every day."

"Yes sir," a middle-aged lady piped in. "Some cracker dragged my son out of his house in the middle of the night and whooped him with a lash, claiming that he was an uppity nigger. Just 'cause he tried to open his own shop at the edge of town. Junior didn't mean no harm, but these White folks don't want us to do nothin' if it ain't workin' for them."

Malcolm watched the scene unfold, impressed with how intently Congressman Elliot and State Senator Smalls listened to everyone's concerns.

"What's the point of not being a slave if we still ain't free to do as we please?" asked a young man around Malcolm's age with a nasty scar under his eye. Malcolm knew this feeling all too well. It was the same disappointment he felt every time he looked at his dad's civil rights posters and felt like they were mocking him.

"I know you're suffering," Congressman Elliott empathized. "We've come a long way, but we still have a long way to go. Today's trial is an important step towards letting the White man know that their cherished refrain 'all men are created equal' now includes the Negro. Whites will no longer be allowed to disrespect, denigrate, and destroy us, without consequences at least. You have spoken and the folks in Washington have heard you. Washington now recognizes that if America is to succeed, all her citizens must have the freedom to thrive. As long as I have breath in my body, I will push for laws that secure that right."

"Those of you who testified today are so brave. You put your own life on the line by speaking up," State Senator Smalls added appreciatively.

"Shucks, our lives were on the line whether we spoke up or not. At least today gave us a chance to fight back," another replied defiantly. Something moved within Malcolm hearing these words, reminding him of how frustrated he'd felt after running into Jason at the Boys & Girls Club. He was so tired of fighting for the right to live in peace, but he couldn't be more tired than these people standing in front of him, or more tired than Aunt Carol, Uncle Leroy, Uncle Corey, or his mom even. Jasmine was right—giving up wasn't an option. Not even death threats could stop this community from coming together to make sure their truth was heard. *We've been fighting too long to give up now*, he resolved.

A woman in a floor-length black dress whose face was covered with a black veil loomed at the back of the crowd. Finally, she stepped forward and through tears whispered, "Thank you, Congressman Elliott and Senator Smalls. I can't tell you how much your support means to my family. Nothing will erase the pain that we carry from that night, but it would absolutely tear me to pieces if these monsters get away with what they did. I pray to God that your law works."

Everyone huddled together, sharing her prayer, until they were interrupted by a booming voice.

"Hear ye, hear ye. Take your seats. The court is back in session. The jury has returned with a verdict," the bailiff announced from the front of the courtroom as the judge ascended to his chair. Malcolm scrambled back to his seat from the atrium and waited breathlessly for the foreman to speak.

Turning to the jury, the judge asked briskly, "Has the jury reached a verdict?"

"We have, your honor," a tall White man grumbled.

"And?"

Reading from a piece of paper in a monotone voice as if he were reading a hostage statement, he continued, "'The defendants are hereby found guilty of using terror and force to deprive citizens of their civil rights, interfering with the right to vote and engaging in a conspiracy to do the same.'"

The room went wild.

"Order," the judge shouted, pounding his gavel forcefully. His face was flushed red. He didn't look pleased with the result, but he refused to let his courtroom descend into chaos. One by one, the judge asked the defendants to rise.

"Defendant number one, the judgment of the court, in your case, is that you be fined one thousand dollars and imprisoned for five years."

Audible gasps rang out and shock reverberated around the room at this unprecedented outcome. Malcolm couldn't even hear the sentences of the other defendants over the racket, but watched as the defendants hung their heads in disbelief and shame as they were led out of the courtroom in restraints.

Malcolm sat frozen in his seat, hardly able to believe that the Third KKK Enforcement Act actually worked. Even in his day, it was a rare sight to see a White person convicted of committing a crime against a Black person, especially if that White person had power. But here, in a South Carolina courtroom in 1871, justice was served.

"Mr. Akerman," Congressman Elliott whispered, leaning forward and tapping him on the shoulder as he wiped a tear from his eye, "I have to admit I was wrong about you. To be honest, I was suspicious of your commitment to equal justice under the law due to your prior service in the Confederate army, but you proved me wrong today. Maybe there is such a thing as a reconstructed rebel! Let the Klan everywhere take notice. Thank you."

"No need to thank me," he said, grinning back. "My job is to uphold the law, and that's exactly what we did here. Today was a good day for Lady Justice."

Malcolm floated through the throng of excited spectators on his way out of the courthouse as if he was riding a cloud. Justice felt good.

31

The train moved quickly through the South Carolinian landscape, back around the rolling hills, over the rivers, and past the swamps. Malcolm sat across from Congressman Elliott and State Senator Smalls. He was glad Congressman Elliott had suggested they escort State Senator Smalls back to Charleston. They planned to attend a celebratory prayer vigil that their good friend Richard "Daddy" Cain was holding at his church. Malcolm wanted to celebrate as much as the two men in front of him, and he was also glad for the chance to ask some burning questions.

Leaning forward, Malcolm whispered, "So how did you do it?"

Without looking up from the newspaper he was reading, State Senator Smalls casually replied with a smirk, "Do what?"

Congressman Elliott grinned. "Come on, Cedric. You gonna have to do better than that. I told you how many exploits this man has engineered. Try to be a little more specific."

"Okay. The *Planter*, sir. Could you tell me about the night you stole the *Planter*?"

"I see you're not going to let this go," State Senator Smalls said, smiling as he folded his newspaper up. The candles lighting the inside of the train car flickered a little, as if they too wanted to muster all their energy to hear this tale.

"I was born a slave in Beaufort, South Carolina, in the Sea Islands. My master, who also happened to be my pa, gave me permission to work in Charleston as a seafarer, so long as I gave a portion of my proceeds to him. When the war broke out, I was conscripted into the Confederate army to help navigate ships around the treacherous South Carolina coastline. At the end of each night, the White captain and crew would go stay in comfortable lodgings onshore and would leave me and the rest of the slaves behind to sleep on the ship. One day about a year into the war, we were aboard the *Planter* and had picked up a heavy load of artillery, which we were supposed to deliver to a Confederate fort the next morning. As usual, at the end of the day, the White crew got off the ship and left us behind. But that night, we had other plans.

"From Charleston, where our boat was stationed, we could see the Union blockade not too far in the distance behind a line of Confederate ships that were protecting Charleston from attack. During our many voyages, I studied the *Planter's* captain closely to learn how to signal to Confederate ships that we were a friendly vessel so that they would allow us to sail along the blockade line. I had also learned how to mimic the captain's gait and mannerisms to perfection." State Senator Smalls kissed the tips of his fingers and then dramatically waved his hand open as if concluding the bunny-in-the-hat magic trick.

"We waited until just before dawn, and then slowly, carefully, we raised the anchor on the *Planter* and allowed her to drift away from the dock. Once we were a safe distance away, we fired up the engine and made a quick pre-planned stop to pick up our loved ones, knowing that if we did not get them then, we would likely never see them again.

"Once everyone was on board, I had the entire Negro crew and our families hide belowdecks and then we set out for the Confederate blockade line. The captain always wore a wide-brimmed hat, which he thankfully left behind on the ship. I put his hat on to hide my face and, as we approached the blockade, I began imitating the captain's walk and issued the appropriate signals, as I had seen him do a hundred times before. To my great relief, they let us pass.

"We followed the path we were expected to take until we were just out of reach of the Confederate ship's cannons, and then we made a hard-right turn towards the Union vessels, hoisting white sheets, towels, and shirts from every part of the ship. By the time the Confederates realized their mistake, it was too late. We were gone, and welcomed into the Union's fold as heroes and freemen. And they didn't mind that we brought a ship full of Confederate artillery with us either!"

By the time State Senator Smalls finished telling his story, Malcolm was smiling from ear to ear. It was an incredible tale of heroism, right up there with Paul Revere. But this time, he was no longer surprised he hadn't learned about it at school. There had just been too many missing stories. "Thank you," he said, still smiling.

*　*　*

"Welcome to Emanuel African Methodist Episcopal Church, which we fondly refer to as Mother Emanuel," Pastor Cain greeted warmly as they arrived on the church's front steps at dusk. "Please watch your step as our new church home is currently under construction."

Upon entering, Malcolm looked around the large, cavernous space in awe. Through exposed wooden beams and hanging canvas tarps that extended from the outline of the pews all the way up to the pitch of the cathedral ceiling, Malcolm could see the beauty in the church's potential. After stepping over tools on the floor and around some scaffolding, Pastor Cain paused in front of a Black man kneeling over blueprints with a protractor in hand.

"I'd like to introduce you to Robert Vesey, our head architect," Pastor Cain said.

Mr. Vesey nodded in their direction in polite acknowledgment. He gathered his tools, placing them in a small leather bag. "Good night, Pastor Cain. See you bright and early tomorrow morning," he said, and then waved on his way out.

"Robert's daddy founded this church in 1818," Pastor Cain explained proudly as he watched him leave. "You may have heard of him—Denmark Vesey? He was a freeman who organized one of the largest attempted slave revolts in the South."

"Yes, indeed," Congressman Elliott said, taking off his hat.

"Unfortunately, his plot was discovered, and he was hung along with dozens of other so-called co-conspirators. In their fury, the White townspeople burned our church to the ground and our congregation was forced to meet in secret until the end of the war. But now we are free," Pastor Cain said, spreading his arms wide as if to embrace the spirit of the Lord, "and our church will rise again from the ashes."

Malcolm felt a palpable sense of liberation in the air, as if all those poor murdered souls from long ago finally had a place to rest in peace.

The group then made their way down from the church to the oceanfront where the congregation gathered. Malcolm walked along with Pastor Cain, Congressman Elliott, and State Senator Smalls. The men's company felt so familiar to Malcolm, like he was hanging around ordinary Black men from his time—even though these men did such extraordinary things in anything but ordinary times. Malcolm listened as Pastor Cain and Congressman Elliott reminisced about the good times working together on the *Missionary Record*. State Senator Smalls chimed in as well with his memories of launching the Enterprise Railroad with Pastor Cain.

"What is the Enterprise Railroad?" Malcolm asked.

"Oh you should see it! It's something special. It's a horse-drawn railway line we chartered a few years ago to move cargo and passengers in and out of Charleston to the surrounding wharves and depots. We laid eighteen miles of track. Our board is almost all Black, and Pastor Cain here is our first president!" State Senator Smalls explained excitedly.

"That sounds cool—er, great! I'd love to see it," Malcolm replied enthusiastically.

Malcolm knew they had arrived at their destination as soon as he saw dozens of women draped in long white flowy gowns and men in their finest Sunday suits swaying from side to side on the beach illuminated by candlelight. Pastor Cain walked swiftly through the crowd of parishioners to the ocean's shoreline and then turned to face eeveryone. He then lit a long, white candle and held it in his hands.

"Lord, we are gathered here today to praise you and give glory and thanks for delivering us from the evils of slavery. But Lord, even though that evil was temporarily subdued, it hasn't disappeared. And so we humbly look to you, Lord, because we know this isn't an enemy we can defeat on our own, and we pray for your protection, your benevolence, and your grace. Bless our church, Lord, and give us the strength we need to stand together, strong in the face of tyranny with the peace of knowing that our Lord is a just God and his divine will *will* be done. Amen."

The congregation echoed a chorus of enthusiastic amens in response to Pastor Cain's prayer. Malcolm prayed intently alongside them, silently hoping the prayer was powerful enough to reach his own time, nearly 150 years in the future.

The glow of the vigil's candlelight washed over Malcolm's body, as the ocean water lapped his feet, cleansing and renewing his spirit. Standing on the shores of the Atlantic Ocean—where countless Black people had once landed after being kidnapped in Africa, only to be enslaved for centuries—was powerful. But being there with the Mother Emanuel congregation to bless their church, which had been destroyed fifty years prior for resisting slavery, was more magical than anything Malcolm had ever experienced. As they all swayed together in the moonlight, Malcolm felt his soul merge with theirs, and the demarcations of time from Africa to slavery, from revolts to freedom, melted away. Malcolm was them, and they were him, just like he was Cedric and Cedric was him.

Malcolm was so caught up in the moment, he almost didn't recognize the falling sensation creeping up from beneath his feet as everything went black. In a blink, he was back on the yellow beanbag chair in Aunt Carol's attic.

Malcolm was in no hurry to get up. He lay there continuing to savor the peacefulness of the moment. Despite what he had been told or not told about his history, he now knew he was part of a proud, strong, resilient, and beautiful legacy. Each generation, from his mother, father, and Uncle Corey, to Grandma Evelyn, Aunt Carol, and Uncle Leroy, to Mama Lucille, to Cedric and Isabel, to countless others whose names he would never know, had found its own unique way to resist oppression and overcome the obstacles set in their path. He would do no less.

He looked out the attic window. It was dark outside. He remembered now. He'd come up to the attic after dinner, after his tour of Alcorn State. He leaned his head back and drifted into a peaceful sleep.

32

Sunlight streamed through the attic window, waking Malcolm. He'd been in the beanbag chair all night. He pulled himself up and out of the chair and made his way down to his room. He changed his clothes and decided he'd go on down to surprise Uncle Leroy and help him with some chores, since he was sure he'd already be out there. He sat on the side of the bed to pull on the work boots. *Would have never thought I'd be doing this.* He chuckled.

"Noooooooooo!" A bloodcurdling wail rang out, lurching Malcolm from the bed. He took off racing downstairs.

"What is it? Are you okay? Did you fall? Are you hurt?" he asked when he found Aunt Carol crumpled in a heap on the floor in the living room. Uncle Leroy was standing behind her, with his hand on her shoulder. The smell of breakfast still being prepared lingered in the air. Aunt Carol couldn't get a word out between her sobs and instead silently pointed at the TV.

Malcolm stared at the screen transfixed as he read the headline: "Massacre at Mother Emanuel." Horrified, he grabbed the arm of the couch to steady himself before lowering down to the floor to watch the news coverage. An anchor reported on the terrible event:

"Last night, a white supremacist entered the sanctuary of Emanuel African Methodist Episcopal Church in Charleston, South Carolina, affectionately called Mother Emanuel, in the middle of Bible study. Although the parishioners did not know the stranger, they welcomed him into their

fold. This man sat with them for over an hour, pretending to be engaged in their Bible reading before standing up to unleash a torrent of death with a Glock semiautomatic handgun. He killed nine African American parishioners ranging in age from twenty-six to eighty-seven. One woman and her five-year-old grandchild survived the incident by pretending to be dead. Another was spared by the gunman, who said it was because she was to tell people what happened. This massacre is tied for the largest mass shooting at a house of worship that this country has ever seen, and we are still trying to understand why this happened.

"The selection of Mother Emanuel as the site of this massacre was no coincidence. This is the oldest African Methodist Episcopal church in the South, and one of the oldest Black churches in the country. The founder of this church, Denmark Vesey, planned what ultimately proved to be a failed slave rebellion in the summer of 1822. Once his plot was discovered, he was hung, along with thirty-four other Black men, and the church was burned to the ground. Coincidentally, the date of last night's massacre, June 17, 2015, was also the 193rd anniversary of Denmark Vesey's thwarted slave rebellion."

Malcolm stared at the TV stunned in disbelief. He was just there! Uncle Corey entered the living room, rubbing sleep from his eyes. "What's going on?" Then he turned to the TV where everyone had fixed their attention. A civil rights expert was now speaking to the news anchor.

"Long after the Civil War, this church continued to hold signifi-cance for the African American community with many legendary leaders paying homage there, including Booker T. Washington and Dr. Martin Luther King Jr. In 1969, Coretta Scott King led a march to Mother Emanuel to support striking hospital workers. When they arrived at the church, bayonet-wielding members of the South Carolina National Guard con-fronted them and arrested nine hundred demonstrators, including the church's pastor. Again, the church is forced to confront the scourge of racism and legacy of bigotry. Sadly, now its name will forever be remem-bered as the site of this horrific crime."

"How could something so horrible happen at such a beautiful place?" Malcolm bemoaned. "All these people did was sit in their church and welcome in a soulless stranger."

"It's happening. All over again. It's happening. I just don't understand why they hate us so much," Aunt Carol whimpered as tears streaked down her face. Uncle Leroy whispered something in Aunt Carol's ear and went into the kitchen and out the back door.

Malcolm was at a loss for words. With tears falling from his eyes, he placed his arms around Aunt Carol's shoulders and squeezed her tight.

After catching her breath, she continued. "I just thought we were past this! I haven't felt this type of pain since those four little Black girls were killed at their church in Birmingham on their way to choir practice. That was before your time, so you may not even have a frame of reference for this type of cruelty."

"Oh, but I do," Malcolm whispered.

The smell of burning bread was coming from the kitchen. "I'm going to go check the oven," Uncle Corey said. Malcolm nodded.

"I just never imagined I would live to see something like this happen again. The more things change, the more they stay the same," she said, shaking her head in defeat.

As Mother Emanuel receded from view, the news camera switched to the South Carolina State House where a Confederate flag waved prominently as usual in front.

"This country has been fighting these same demons since its beginning," Malcolm fumed, suddenly needing to stand up to clear his head. "I gotta get some fresh air. Need anything, Aunt Carol?"

"Just some peace." She sighed, lifting the bottom of her apron to wipe the tears from her eyes.

33

Malcolm stormed outside letting the kitchen door slam behind him. He paced around the backyard kicking up dirt wherever he went.

"Cedric played me," he mumbled to himself. "He tricked me into thinking things were getting better when he knew good and well things are the same or worse! Why would he let me get my hopes up like that?"

"Boy, my yard do something to you? Kicking it around like that? Talking to yourself? You feelin' all right?" Uncle Leroy called out from his perch on the tractor in front of the barn where he was smoking one of his hand-rolled cigarettes.

Malcolm shielded his eyes so he could see him through the glare of the sun. "Naw, Unc. I'm not," Malcolm said, walking out of the backyard and over to him. "You saw all those innocent people were murdered at Mother Emanuel by some racist kid."

"Yep. I saw," Uncle Leroy said, taking a long drag of his cigarette.

"Well?" Malcolm challenged him. "Aren't you pissed? Don't you want to just go fight somebody right now?"

Uncle Leroy chuckled. "Sure, I'm pissed. I'm an eighty-year-old Black man. I've *been* pissed. But after you've lived long enough and seen as much as I have, eventually, you gotta decide how much power you're gonna give other people over you. And my threshold is none."

"So what does that mean? You just stop caring?" Malcolm asked, pacing back and forth.

"Oh, I care plenty. But I'm wise enough to know there are some things I can change, and some things I can't. America's been showing me who she is my whole life, and I choose to believe her. Once you accept that, it's hard to be surprised when these sorts of things happen. Instead I pay attention to the things I can control, like keepin' Carol safe and makin' sure she's provided for. Everybody's gotta find their purpose," Uncle Leroy said, putting his cigarette out on the sole of his boot.

Malcolm stopped pacing and turned to confront him directly. "So you just hide out here on the farm?"

"Ain't nobody hiding!" Uncle Leroy answered testily sitting up straighter in his tractor seat. "I just choose to mind my own business. But I tell you what, if somebody comes on my property looking for trouble, they damn sure gonna find it."

Malcolm nodded, respecting Uncle Leroy's gangsta, and resumed pacing. "I'm just tired of not feeling welcome in my own country."

"You tired?" Uncle Leroy asked, raising his eyebrows as he slowly lowered himself from the tractor. "How old you is? Twelve? Thirteen? Boy, get in line."

"I'm sixteen, Uncle Leroy." Malcolm tried to cool down, but his mind jumped from one injustice to another. "What are you gonna do when y'all have to leave the farm?"

"I ain't tryin' to think about that right now," Uncle Leroy said, furrowing his brow. "God'll work something out. Always has. But you know what I *am* thinking about?" he said, quickly changing the subject. "I got a real hankering for a fish dinner tonight. How you feel about that?"

"Yeah," Malcolm said, shrugging his shoulders. "I like fish."

"All right then. Why don't you go'on over to the barn and grab two fishing poles and some hooks hanging on the back wall."

Malcolm stopped dead in his tracks. "What? Why?" he exclaimed, fearing he had already gotten himself into more trouble than it was worth.

"Didn't you just hear me say I was getting hungry? We goin' fishing," he said, clapping his hands for emphasis.

"But can't we just pick up some at the supermarket?" Malcolm asked.

"A supermarket?" Uncle Leroy scoffed, looking at Malcolm like he'd lost his mind. "Didn't I tell you we got everything we need on this here farm? Now go'on and do what I said." He pointed adamantly in the direction of the barn.

Now it was Malcolm's turn to look at Uncle Leroy like his marbles were missing. He hadn't seen a pond or stream anywhere on the farm, but he had learned better than to question the old man, so he went and got the poles.

When Malcolm got back from the barn, Uncle Leroy was holding a small ice chest. Poles in hand, they set off for the dense tree line behind the family cemetery.

Malcolm had no idea how thick the woods were past the cemetery, and he was also surprised that the property included them. The land the farm sat on must be much larger than he had envisioned—not that he had ever thought about the size of acres before that summer.

Even though it was only midmorning, the dense foliage of the trees blocked out most of the sunlight, allowing sparse isolated rays to penetrate the darkness. Malcolm carefully walked along the forest floor, stepping over fallen logs, and keeping an eye out for anything that might attack—like snakes or spiders or who knew what. A melodious chorus of birds chirped back and forth overhead as if playing a game of Marco Polo.

"Um—um, say, Unc," Malcolm stammered, feeling completely out of his element, "so, ah, what do I do if like, a snake drops out of a tree on top of me, or like a bear tries to get us."

Uncle Leroy laughed. "Well, son, not sure what *you* should do, but I got a jackknife on me, and I pity the snake or bear that tries to make a move on me. He just might find himself on the wrong end of my dinner plate." Uncle Leroy made a quick sidestep-and-jab motion, surprisingly agile for such an old man. "You ever had snake soup? De-licious!"

Uncle Leroy was clearly getting a kick out of Malcolm's discomfort. Malcolm rolled his eyes. *This is the reason why we have supermarkets!* he thought, remaining silent for the remainder of their trek. His eyes darted around on high alert for any sign of a threat. He nearly took off running when he saw a pile of leaves quickly shift beside him, only to feel foolish when a harmless brown rabbit emerged.

After hiking for about ten minutes, Malcolm was relieved to see a sunny patch of land in the distance. As they neared the clearing, the sound of gurgling water became increasingly louder. Uncle Leroy led them closer to the sound until Malcolm found himself on the bank of a wide river, slowly flowing with muddy red water.

"The Mighty Mississippi," Uncle Leroy said, bending down to the river's edge and wiggling his hand in the red earth of its bank. A few seconds later, he'd unearthed a handful of worms. Soon he had the worms pierced on the hooks hanging from the ends of the fishing lines. He rose and handed Malcolm a pole.

Malcolm took the pole but his face was filled with confusion.

Uncle Leroy smiled. "You see, son, it's simple. You just wind your line tight, swing the pole back behind you, and then fling the end of your pole forward and release the line as your pole glides toward the water. Then you sit and wait for a tug. If you get that far, I'll let you know what to do next." Uncle Leroy demonstrated how it was done and then sat down a few feet away.

It sounds simple enough, Malcolm thought. He wound his line tight and swung it back, as Uncle Leroy instructed, but when he released it, the hook and worm came straight for his head!

Malcolm jumped out of the soaring projectile's way.

Uncle Leroy fell out laughing. "Now, son, you're here to catch fish! Not yourself! You cast too soon! Go'on and grab the pole and try again."

Malcolm looked at the pole hesitantly, having no desire to come face-to-face with a worm or lose an eye to a hook.

"Go'on now," Uncle Leroy prodded him, not taking no for an answer.

Reluctantly, Malcolm grabbed the pole and prepared to try again.

"Now this time, hold your line and don't release it until your pole is at about a forty-five-degree angle. That'll give her a nice arc."

He did as he was told and watched his worm soar high in the sky before landing in the water. Malcolm smiled, feeling pleased with himself. He sat next to Uncle Leroy and looked out at his line in the river.

"Want a beer?" Uncle Leroy asked, while lighting another one of his cigarettes.

Wondering if this was a test, Malcolm responded, "I just told you I'm sixteen, right?"

"That was about the drinking age when I was young," Uncle Leroy said, handing him an opened can of brew.

All right, Malcolm thought, nodding. *Fishing ain't so bad*. Being out in nature, he began to feel more clearheaded and relaxed. Sitting on the river's edge brought his thoughts back to the oceanfront and Mother Emanuel's dedication. For Malcolm, that was just yesterday. He couldn't shake how much the recent mass shooting reminded him of how long Black people had been terrorized in America.

"Hey Unc, I was wondering if I could ask you something," Malcolm said as he drew a slightly tepid sip of beer. It didn't taste great, but was still refreshing on such a hot morning.

"Shoot."

"So I've been reading up on the history of this area, this part of the country, and I keep coming across things I never heard of. You ever heard of Hiram Revels?"

"Naw, don't reckon I have. That fella from around here?"

Malcolm nodded quickly and decided to move on. "I've also read about different massacres of Black people after the Civil War that I had never heard of before. I was wondering if the reason I hadn't heard about them was because I go to school up in D.C. Is that something they teach down here?"

For the second time that day, Uncle Leroy looked at Malcolm like he'd lost his mind.

"You askin' me if in the South, in the former Confederate States of America, if they teach a version of history in school that is anywhere close to the truth about how badly White folks have treated Black folks in this country?"

Based on Uncle Leroy's tone, Malcolm was almost positive he was about to finish with *Negro, please,* but he really wanted to understand where Uncle Leroy was coming from.

"Did you ever hear about things yourself? Take, for instance, the Mechanics' Institute massacre or the Meridian massacre after the Civil War was over. Did you ever hear of them?" Malcolm asked.

Malcolm watched his uncle's eyes narrow and then close for a few seconds. He dragged his dark, sun-wrinkled hand from his brow down to his chin. His lips were pursed tight when he opened his eyes. He took a deep breath and then slowly let it out in a long heavy sigh.

"To be honest, no. I was born in 1935, so that's a good bit after the Civil War, but as I told you, I've seen enough in my day that I don't have to look too far back to know what White folks are capable of. The Tulsa Riots wasn't that long before I was born, when they burned that well-to-do Black community in Oklahoma to the ground. The Klan was still hanging Black folks from trees when I was growin' up—if you stepped out of line. And it wasn't just a few bad apples involved," Uncle Leroy said as he fished around the ice chest for another beer. "Nope, all the White folks in town would come out to cheer 'em on, bring they chir'en too, to teach them the ways of the world. Whites on top. Blacks on bottom."

Uncle Leroy paused for a second to open a beer and take a long drag of his cigarette. He then inhaled deeply, as if the fresh air could block out his painful memories. Malcolm followed suit. He took in the pungent smells of swamp water mixed with the sweet smells of birch and listened closely to a rare splash from a turtle. A gray heron made a dash under the water in pursuit. Uncle Leroy let time sit still for another moment, then continued his melancholy recount.

"One time, they tried to get my little brother, Rodney, when we were about your age. Said he was too uppity and friendly with the White gals around town. Couple of White boys chased him to the far side of town and surrounded him, noose all ready, before me and my other brothers caught wind of what was happening. They liked to do him like they did that boy Emmett Till, you know the boy around your age from Chicago who was down here visiting his family? They messed that boy up so bad his momma couldn't hardly recognize him.

"Well, we gathered all the guns we had and rode over to where they was holding Rodney and fired some warning shots to scare 'em off. We outnumbered them that day, and Rodney made sure to never be caught alone for the rest of the school year. He moved to California after that, went to stay with some family, and ain't been back since. I know what they capable of. I ain't gotta read no history book. Ha!" Uncle Leroy said, laughing suddenly, "and they say we the monsters." He took another long slug of his beer while staring out at the water.

Malcolm fell silent as he tried to process the weight of Uncle Leroy's experiences. While Malcolm didn't live in constant fear of Klansmen and lynchings, he was terrified every time the police came around, afraid that he would end up a statistic like his dad. Uncle Leroy was right. America had done a good job convincing itself that Black people were violent monsters, but rarely did it look at its own reflection in the mirror.

Suddenly, Malcolm felt a pull on his line. "Unc, what do I do? My line got tight," he asked excitedly.

That snapped Uncle Leroy out of his daze. "All right, son, you gonna reel her in slow. No fast or jerky motions that might set her free. Just turn the reel, slowly, slowly. Lift her easy, easy."

Malcolm felt his pole bending with the weight of his catch as he did exactly as Uncle Leroy instructed. When it finally came to the surface, Uncle Leroy fell over cackling.

"Looks like you caught yourself a sock!" He laughed, slapping Malcolm on the back. "Don't worry, son. You don't always catch a fish the first time you cast your pole, but if you stay at it long enough, sooner or later, something real will bite."

Malcolm's face burned with embarrassment.

"Ahhhhh, I'm gonna miss this," Uncle Leroy said, suddenly getting misty-eyed.

Malcolm had never seen his uncle's tender side before and was at a loss for words.

34

That evening, Aunt Carol fried up some of the tastiest catfish Malcolm had ever had with her famous mac and cheese, collard greens, and honey-buttered cornbread. He could tell her energy was still off from what she'd seen on the news, but cooking and being told how good it was brought a small smile back to her lips.

After inhaling his dinner and lavishing Aunt Carol with praise, Malcolm went upstairs to decompress. So much had occurred over just a matter of days—or hundreds of years if he was to count where Cedric took him. Malcolm wondered if he was losing touch with reality, and that scared him. He needed some time, maybe spend time with Jasmine or see what Kliff was up to. Because everything just felt like too much.

When he entered his room, Malcolm noticed his pen and sketch pad on the floor next to his bed and stared at them for a moment. The Mother Emanuel massacre was still lingering in his mind, but he didn't want to remember the church that way. Instead, he picked up his pen and began drawing the beautiful gathering by the Charleston Harbor. As he sketched the crow's-feet around the eyes of an old lady, holding hands with a barefoot young child and illuminated by the glow of candlelight, the peace he'd felt at the vigil descended over him again.

Malcolm felt the familiar cool gust of air blow past. "You *are* quite talented," a deep baritone voice said as Cedric appeared, looming overhead.

Without looking up, Malcolm shook his head and continued to focus on his drawing. "Not now, Cedric. I'm not in the mood," he replied tersely.

"Today was hard. My heart breaks too, but now's not the time to give up." Cedric walked around to the foot of the bed and sat down, as Malcolm turned his body in the opposite direction.

"Look, I don't need a pep talk. You lied to me!" Malcolm shouted. "You showed me that by coming together, pushing for change, things would get better. But all we've done is fight. All we do is fight. We've stood, we've sat, we've marched, we've pleaded. And then something like this still happens?" Malcolm shook his head in disbelief. "I don't need you giving me any more false hope."

"I never told you progress would be a straight line. We have made progress, little by little," Cedric insisted. "But I'm not going to lie. We've had setbacks. We've always had setbacks. We get swept back, like a river carrying us downstream no matter what we do. But if we support one another, keep pushing for what we know is right, eventually, we'll make it back to shore and continue the good work."

Malcolm got up and stood directly in front of him. "Yeah? What about all that Black progress made after the Civil War? How was that progress? You showed me how good we had it—with Black senators and congressmen and business owners. That the law actually protected us and locked up White people when they killed us. We had a *Black bank* for Christ's sake! And what difference did it really make? My momma's broke, and the cop that killed my dad still walks free."

For the first time since they met, Cedric was speechless and shrank back uncomfortably. "It took a lot more than a war to defeat the Confederacy," he finally admitted reluctantly.

"Yeah, well, sometimes it seems like we are still fighting that war," Malcolm said, turning away from Cedric and sitting back on his bed.

"Yes, and we'll get to why it's like that, but not yet. It's important you learn how to take stock in your wins, to savor the good, share the good with others, encourage one another. You need to see us at our best. But I can tell you need some time. I'll leave you to get some rest tonight." And with that, Cedric vanished.

"Good!" Malcolm shouted after him, but later, lying in bed and turning out the light, he couldn't help but wonder what "wins" he'd been referring to.

• • •

So far a week had passed without any sign of Cedric. Malcolm was glad he kept his word. He needed time to grieve what had happened and just take a break from all that he'd seen. He played hoops with Uncle Corey and helped him fill out some job applications. He helped Aunt Carol around the house with some chores. It wasn't exactly normal, because he knew that a ghost could show up any minute, but it was as normal as it could get. On Friday afternoon, Malcolm decided to give Jasmine a call to see what she was up to.

Jasmine picked up the phone on the first ring and must've recognized the number because Malcolm barely had put the phone to his ear when he heard her electric voice say, "Hey Malcolm!"

"Hey," he responded, smiling reflexively. He hadn't expected how soothing hearing her voice on the other side of the line would feel and was looking forward to seeing her again soon.

"I thought you might've been over hanging out with me. Seems like every time we get together, something wild happens."

"Naw girl. I just been busy trying to help out around here and stuff. What you up to?"

"Nothing much. I was getting ready to run to the mall to return something. Want to roll with me?"

Malcolm was hesitant to go on a date in another public place with her, since the past few times had each gone awry. However, he quickly flashed through his options in his head—which weren't many—and responded, "Yeah. I'm not doing anything today."

"Okay. Cool. I'll pick you up in thirty," she said and hung up.

Exactly thirty minutes later, Jasmine pulled up in front of Aunt Carol's house in her dad's pickup truck. Malcolm ran out the front door and hopped into the passenger side, giving Jasmine a small smile.

"You ready?" she asked.

"Yep, it's good to get out and about."

At the end of the gravel driveway, Jasmine pointed down the country road. "Our farm is that way," she said as she turned toward the opposite direction. A few minutes later, she merged onto the highway.

My highway, Malcolm thought defiantly.

"So when you say mall . . . ?" Malcolm asked, turning his attention back to the moment.

"Don't get your hopes up. This ain't too special. We got a department store and a couple of other shops, but it'll do when you don't feel like driving two hours to Jackson."

Jasmine was right. Twenty minutes later, Malcolm realized that there wasn't too much to see at this "mall." They parked the truck and went through a small parking lot and into a long, one-story concrete building. The second they stepped inside, text messages began streaming into his phone. He finally had cell service again! While Jasmine was returning her dresses, he took his phone over to the watch counter and leaned on the glass to check his messages. He overheard some giggling and glanced up. Standing a few feet away were a handful of White teenage girls trying on designer sunglasses.

"Can I help you find something?" an elderly man who appeared out of nowhere asked curtly.

"Naw, I'm just waitin' on my girl to finish up," Malcolm responded, barely glancing up from his phone as he pointed to Jasmine at a nearby register. He caught himself off guard by referring to Jasmine as his girl, but he liked the way it sounded.

"We don't offer layaway plans here, just so you know," the obtrusive store clerk continued, lingering behind him like a mosquito on a hot summer day.

"What?" Malcolm asked, taken aback. "Look, I'll let you know if I need some help."

Malcolm turned away from the man just in time to see the White girls walking right behind the clerk and leaving the store—wearing the sunglasses they'd been trying on without paying for them.

"You ready?" Jasmine asked, walking up.

"Yeah. Let's go," Malcolm said, as he tucked his phone in his back pocket and walked briskly out of the store, heading to the truck.

"Everything okay?" Jasmine asked, struggling to walk fast enough to keep up with him.

"Yeah man, just the usual. The rent-a-cop clerk in there was so busy harassing me, he didn't notice the cheerleading squad walk out with all his stuff. Typical." Malcolm snorted.

Jasmine sighed, shook her head, and reached for his hand to comfort him. "Want to go somewhere where we don't have to deal with any people?" she suggested, squeezing his hand tightly. He didn't respond. "We could catch a show?" she proposed.

"There's a movie theater in this place?" Malcolm asked, surprised. Jasmine nodded.

"Yeah! What's out?" Malcolm let the situation with the girls drift from his mind.

"There's a new Marvel movie, as always, *Jurassic World*, *Poltergeist*. Ohhh, the '80s version of that movie was so good. I love scary movies. Let's do *Poltergeist!*" Jasmine suggested excitedly.

Malcolm wasn't so sure. He had seen more than enough ghosts already this summer, but he didn't want to disappoint Jasmine. "Sure," he replied with a half shrug as they walked back into the mall, through the store, and over to the theater on the other side of the building.

Malcolm bought two tickets for *Poltergeist*, silently thanking Aunt Carol for putting a bit of cash in his hands before he'd headed out. Jasmine bought the popcorn. They were lucky that the show was starting in about twenty minutes. They could sit and chill in the theater lobby, out of the heat.

When it was time, they walked down a carpeted hall and entered a dark theater, but stopped short when they saw a black-and-white movie was already playing.

"Do you think this is a preview?" Jasmine whispered.

"I'm not sure," Malcolm answered, confused by the strange old-timey feel of the movie.

They hung back near the door while figuring it out. The film was silent, except for a musical score, and you had to read the words at the bottom of the screen to know what was happening. Black and White people were in the movie, but the Black people looked strange— almost unnaturally black with exaggerated lips and straw-like hair. The White people looked panicked and frenzied every time a Black character entered the scene. The Black people stuffed ballot boxes, while

White people were turned away from a voting booth. Then the camera cut to Black politicians in the Capitol acting a fool, putting their bare feet on the desk, getting drunk, and eating fried chicken. Malcolm stood there stunned as he tried to wrap his mind around what he was seeing. A roar of laughter came from the audience—loud, raucous laughter. Malcolm looked around and realized the theater was packed.

"I don't think this is our show," Malcolm snapped as he grabbed Jasmine's hand and stormed out.

Back in the hallway, he realized their mistake. They had accidentally gone into theater three, instead of five. They hadn't seen the poster on a small stand by the entrance that read: THE CONCERNED CITIZENS' COUNCIL CELEBRATES 100 YEARS OF THE CLASSIC FILM *BIRTH OF A NATION*.

"That movie was weird," Jasmine observed, looking around for theater five.

"It wasn't weird. It was a lie!" Malcolm bellowed. "I can't believe people are sitting in there celebrating a movie full of ugly and false images of what they think Black people were like after the Civil War. Especially the Black politicians!" Malcolm consciously began raising his voice louder in case any of the viewers or anyone else in the building, for that matter, was listening in. "Do you know how amazing those men were? Do you know what they lived through and overcame, and how despite all of those obstacles, they *still* represented their people with dignity and poise and grace?" he asked, nearly shouting at Jasmine.

"Whoa, Malcolm," Jasmine responded, taken aback. "I agree it was offensive, but it's just an old movie. You seem to be taking this personally."

Malcolm closed his eyes and took a deep breath to try to regain his composure, but it wasn't working. He wished he could tell her that he'd been there, seen it for himself, but he knew that was not possible. It wasn't like it was something he could make people understand. "It's not just a movie. It's rewriting history with lies," he shouted at his loudest, hoping that the people inside the theater might be shamed by his outburst.

An usher looked in their direction from the end of the hallway.

"Keep your voice down or I'm going to have to ask you to leave," he huffed.

Malcolm rolled his eyes. "Oh, now you're offended," he said under his breath.

"Look, things are getting better now," Jasmine whispered. "Did you hear they took the Confederate flag down from the South Carolina Capitol after the Mother Emanuel massacre?"

"What year is it again?" he asked rhetorically.

Jasmine gave him a blank stare, unappreciative of the sarcasm and replied, "It's 2015."

"Right. Only 150 years after they lost the war. About damn time. Come on, let's find our movie," he said, angrily marching away.

Jasmine quickly followed Malcolm into theater five to watch a far less scary film: *Poltergeist*. They settled in their seats just as the previews were wrapping. Malcolm tried to relax but he was still so heated he couldn't see straight. He tried to focus on what was happening in the movie. A little blonde girl with bangs was talking to a fuzzy TV screen. He looked over at Jasmine. She was already chuckling at the scene. He closed his eyes for a moment hoping that when he opened them, he could leave his anger behind, but instead his eyelids became too heavy to lift—and he was falling.

35

"Welcome, my brothers! Welcome!" was the first thing Malcolm heard when he woke. He was sitting at an oval walnut table with his head in his hands. Out of the corner of his eye, he saw a chandelier above his head and dozens of people, both Black and White, were sitting around in booths enjoying their meals. He quickly realized he was at the Wormley.

Congressman Elliott stood at the front of the table raising a whiskey glass high, beaming with pride. Congressman Rainey, his aide Nathaniel, Pastor Cain from Emanuel AME Church, and Josiah Walls, the congressman from Florida, stared at him attentively. As soon as he spotted Pastor Cain, he wanted to tell him how sorry he was about the tragedy at his church, but then remembered that it wouldn't happen for almost 150 years. A few other Black men Malcolm didn't recognize also sat at the table smiling radiantly.

"Cedric, I didn't know you were such a lightweight," Nathaniel ribbed him. "You had one shot of whiskey and were out!" He laughed.

Malcolm smiled and sat up taller in his chair.

"And so I raise this glass in a toast to the newly elected members of Congress, John Roy Lynch of Mississippi and James Rapier of Alabama. I'm especially pleased to welcome the newest members of Congress from South Carolina, my dearest friends Pastor Richard 'Daddy' Cain and Alonzo Ransier. Together, we worked tirelessly to bring our baby, the *Missionary Record*, to life. From writing news stories to writing laws, here we are!" Congressman Elliott enthused. "Let's toast! But Cedric, I think you've had enough to drink," he teased as everyone at the table fell out laughing.

Malcolm looked down sheepishly, but chuckled along. He was glad to see real Black congressmen in front of him, instead of the grotesque images from the movie theater.

Congressman Rainey stood to congratulate them as well. "The 1872 election was marred by voter suppression, intimidation, and violence against Negroes at unprecedented levels. It only speaks to how resounding your victories were that you are sitting here with us today."

As they raised their glasses, a White man with a full salt-and-pepper beard and straight black hair, wearing a colorful plaid, three-piece suit and a top hat, strolled over to their table.

"I know y'all aren't celebrating without me?" he asked in feigned dismay.

"P.B.S. Pinchback, we are so glad you're able to join us! We weren't sure if you were going to make it. We heard the election results in Louisiana were a sizable mess," Congressman Elliott said, jumping up and smacking the man on the back. "Someone get this man a seat and a glass!"

A waiter came by with an extra chair and everyone made room. Congressman Elliott grabbed the bottle of whiskey off the table and filled Pinchback's glass to the brim. Based on Congressman Elliott's reaction, Malcolm realized that despite the man's appearance, he was actually Black.

"A mess would be an understatement," Pinchback rebuffed. "Neither the Republican nor Democratic gubernatorial candidate is willing to concede defeat! And most of the down ballot elections are also being contested. While I was serving as Louisiana's lieutenant governor, I ran for a seat in the US House of Representatives. I think it was pretty clear I won that election, even though the scoundrels down there are doing everything in their power to challenge my win. But . . . the joke is on them! The Louisiana Senate has chosen me to represent Louisiana in the US Senate!" he said, tipping his hat with a flourish and bowing slightly as if awaiting applause.

"You'll be sworn into the Senate tomorrow?" Congressman Rainey asked, nearly falling out of his seat in shock. "We haven't had any representation in the Senate since Hiram left two years ago, and boy, is having a voice in that chamber missed!"

"It sure is!" Malcolm agreed. "When I worked for Senator Revels in the Senate, there weren't any Negro members in the House, and that made it harder to get bills passed. So it's great that you're here! We now have representation in both chambers!" Malcolm surprised himself by how much he'd learned about how Washington worked.

"If only it were that simple." Pinchback sighed. "The governor has to certify the State Senate's choice of senator, but since the governor's race is still in dispute, *both* gubernatorial candidates have sent their preferred senator to Washington. Unfortunately, I have to wait for the US Senate to decide which governor's certification to accept before I can be seated. I've given up my claim to the House seat I won, but I'm ready to fight tooth and nail for my seat in the Senate."

"Good. This ain't a town for sheep," Congressman Elliott said, nodding in approval.

"You know what they say, play to win. So I'm placing my strongest hand on the table and praying it works out," Pinchback bellowed, chugging his shot, then setting his glass down for a refill.

"Glad you're back, Governor Pinchback." Congressman Ransier toasted him from across the table, smiling broadly. "Who would've thought two men of such humble origins would rise to serve as lieutenant governors of their states and meet again in Congress. And you went even further than I did. When Louisiana Governor Warmoth was forced to resign, you stepped in as governor until the end of his term. First Negro governor in the history of the United States! Even if it only lasted for a few weeks. You make us proud!"

"Hear! Hear!" everyone said, toasting his accomplishment.

"You're too kind, my dear brother. Fortune placed me at the right place at the right time. Let's hope she strikes again!" Pinchback smiled. "And let us not forget the other accomplishments of the men at this table. Congressman Lynch, congratulations on successfully completing your term as Mississippi's Speaker of the House. And Congressman

Rapier, thank you for your service as vice president of the National Negro Labor Union. I couldn't ask for better company! This country may yet become a place we can call home."

"Hear! Hear!" everyone said again, raising their glasses. Malcolm did his best to join in with his glass of water since everyone refused to pour him any of the good stuff.

After another round of drinks, Congressman Elliott cleared his throat. "Gentlemen, I'd like to invite you to join me at my home tomorrow night to celebrate President Grant's reelection. We can head to the inauguration ball from there. I'll arrange for transportation."

"Looking forward to it!" the men at the table echoed before gathering their things to leave.

* * *

While Malcolm was having dinner in Cedric's apartment later that evening, a loud knock rapped at the door. Malcolm set down his plate that he had picked up from the landlady and went to the door. Upon opening it, he was dumbfounded to see Governor Pinchback standing in the doorway.

"Good evening, Governor," he greeted. "How can I help you?"

"What's that I smell? Fried fish? Yams? You in here frying, and you didn't offer your favorite senator from Louisiana some?" he joked.

"Excuse me, sir?" Malcolm asked, still confused about why and how Governor Pinchback had come to be on his doorstep. "How did you know where I live?"

"I told Robert that I needed someone to help me get around town, and he volunteered you. Now look, son, I've come all this way to Washington, and I know there are some people with money in this town, and I intend to help them lose it."

"Sir, are you looking for a place to gamble?" Malcolm asked, bewildered.

Governor Pinchback looked from left to right and then signaled Malcolm to lean in. He whispered, "I heard about this place in Georgetown where the high rollers, dice throwers, and card sharks hang. I'm new to town and don't want to go on my own. Care to be my second set of eyes?"

That sounded a heck of a lot more interesting than lying in bed staring at the ceiling all night. Malcolm grabbed Cedric's jacket and followed him out.

A carriage was waiting for them on the street in front of the apartment. Malcolm eyed it warily—still scarred from his last D.C. carriage ride, which had ended disastrously. Yet there were no other options: no metro to ride or cab to hail.

Malcolm was quiet on the way to the saloon.

"You doing all right over there, Cedric?" Pinchback asked. Malcolm realized he was gripping his seat.

"Not a fan of carriages," he responded.

Pinchback laughed. "I'm sure there's a story there. Now son, I don't want you to take offense to this, but after we arrive and go in to the saloon, you don't know me and I don't know you."

Malcolm looked at him with confusion, wondering why the governor had invited him along if he didn't want to be seen with him.

"I know that might sound rash, but I have my reasons, and I would appreciate it if you would just indulge me, this one time," he said with a wink. "But if anything, shall I say, goes awry, I hope you'll have my back."

Malcolm nodded but still felt the sting of embarrassment. He thought of turning around and going back to the apartment, but then he figured that since Pinchback had already interrupted his dinner, it wouldn't hurt to see what he was being dragged across town for.

When the carriage pulled away from the saloon, Malcolm remained a few paces behind as he followed Governor Pinchback through the entrance. Inside, there were a dozen or so round tables each surrounded by finely dressed men smoking cigars and drinking whiskey. Malcolm headed to the bar in the center of the room to wait for Governor Pinchback, and—to not raise suspicions—ordered a ginger ale with a sugar cube.

As Malcolm sat on a stool at the bar taking in his surroundings, he realized that he had lost sight of Pinchback. Although the saloon was integrated, the tables were evenly divided by race: Black players and dealers, and White players and dealers. He scanned the face of every man seated at the Black tables, with no sign of Pinchback. Then, a few tables over, a top hat caught his eye. Pinchback was seated at an all-White table and had completely blended in.

Malcolm thought he recognized two US Senators and a congressman at the table. What was Pinchback doing? Did he know he was playing with fire? Malcolm moved down a couple of stools so that he could be within earshot of the table.

"So that's when I told that nigger," he overheard the congressman say, "don't get too big for your britches, son. We ain't that far from Virginia, and we still know how to take care of our niggers down there."

Malcolm felt his skin crawl with discomfort while the table erupted in laughter, including Pinchback, who, to his horror, laughed the hardest.

"So what'd that nigger say back?" one of the senators asked.

"He didn't say nothing. He knew better and just did what he was told. Every now and then, you just gotta put them darkies in their place," he said, tossing a chip up in the air and catching it with the same hand. "Some are taking this whole freedom thing a bit too far. They may live here, but it's still our country."

The hairs on the back of Malcolm's neck rose in anger. He turned away from the table in disgust. He couldn't believe Pinchback would sit in the company of men who talked like this, and drag him there to listen!

Malcolm rose from his stool. As he looked for Cedric's wallet in his pocket to pay and leave, his eyes locked with Pinchback's. Malcolm was about to give him his strongest evil eye, but Pinchback returned his gaze with an almost imperceptible wink and a hint of a smile. Malcolm looked at the chips in front of Pinchback. In the time Malcolm had drunk his sugar cube–ginger ale concoction, Pinchback had amassed nearly double the chips of every other man at his table. Maybe he did know what he was doing after all.

Malcolm sat back down on the stool and tried to blend in.

Suddenly, the other men at Pinchback's table grew less chatty and began to regard the newcomer with unease.

"Where did you say you were from again?" one of the senators asked Pinchback.

"I didn't," Pinchback replied, placing his chips on the table. "All in," he announced.

"Now, sir, don't forget you're a guest at our table. We play by house rules and abide by a gentleman's code. You can't just sit down here and bluff your way to a win. You betta be able to back up a bet like that," said the congressman.

Smiling broadly with his hands outstretched before him, Pinchback responded, "I am a gentleman above all else. If you doubt me, call my bet."

The congressman moved his few remaining chips around the table nervously, before saying, "I call," and pushed the remainder of his chips into the center.

"Gentlemen, show your cards," declared the dealer, to which Pinchback turned over an ace, king, queen, jack, and ten of spades.

"You cheated!" the congressman shouted, standing up and slapping the table, nearly turning it over.

Every head in the room whipped over to see the commotion.

Pinchback stood and declared, "Gentlemen, it appears I have outworn my welcome. I best be on my way," at which point he tipped his top hat and purposefully exposed a head of tight black curls instead of the slicked-back hairstyle he'd worn the first time Malcolm saw him.

The congressman's jaw dropped, as did that of every other person at the table and in the room. "He's a nigger!" the congressman shouted, pointing at Pinchback's hair. "This is a Whites only table. You can't play at this table. That voids your win. Give me back my chips!" Pinchback cocked his head and smirked at the congressman before stating, "I was under the impression that D.C. law forbade segregation in all places open to the public. Looks to me like this saloon is open to the public and is therefore subject to that law."

Both men looked at the dealer, who clearly did not relish being placed in the uncomfortable position.

"I'm sorry, Congressman, but the scoundrel is right. For the comfort of our guests, we allow patrons to choose to socialize with whom they please, and this may create the appearance that certain tables are for Whites and other tables are for Negroes, but enforcing such a seating arrangement would be a violation of the law. Sir," the dealer said, turning to Pinchback, "I think it would best if you take your winnings and leave. And for good measure, don't show your face around here again."

"Gladly," Pinchback said while cleaning his pile of chips off the table, but not before tossing one chip in the air and cockily catching it with one hand, as the congressman had done earlier.

Malcolm waited at the bar for Pinchback to cash in his chips and make it safely out of the saloon, before following him out.

"What in the world was that?" Malcolm asked, joining Pinchback outside.

"Just a friendly card game amongst some new friends," Pinchback said, laughing. "Let's hurry up and get out of here," he added, hailing his carriage, which was waiting for him at the corner.

Malcolm had too many questions to be nervous about a carriage ride now. "Where did you learn to play like that?" Malcolm asked once they had settled inside. He had to admit he was starstruck. Pinchback had game—literally.

"On a riverboat in Ohio. I worked on one as a cabin boy from a young age."

"Why? Where were your parents?"

"Well, my pa was the owner of the Mississippi plantation where I grew up, but he died when I was eleven. Good thing for us, he freed my mother before I was born, so me and my brother were born free. Unfortunately, when he died, no one else in his family recognized our freedom or our claim to the money he left us. My mother was terrified we'd be kidnapped and forced into slavery, so we fled for Ohio. We had our freedom, but little else."

Malcolm's curiosity grew. "How did you get by?"

"We were dirt poor, so my brother and I had no choice but to learn how to hustle. I began working on the riverboat and learned the craft from some of the meanest card sharks on the Ohio River. They took me under their wing, feeling sorry for a fellow who had to figure out how to make his own way in the world at such a young age. They showed me the tricks of the trade, the art of diversion, how to get people to see only what you want them to see." Pinchback twirled his hand in the air like a magician until the five-dollar chip he'd tossed earlier reappeared.

Malcolm laughed and eyed the former governor suspiciously. "I gotta ask, did you cheat back there?"

Pinchback smiled mischievously and said, "Son, haven't you learned by now, the whole game is rigged?" As Malcolm stepped out onto the street in front of Cedric's apartment, Pinchback tossed him the five-dollar chip and winked, making the late-night jaunt all the more worthwhile—not that Malcolm wanted to go back to the saloon to cash it.

As Pinchback's carriage pulled away from the apartment, Malcolm, for the first time since his journeys began, hoped he could stay in the past a little longer. He was looking forward to the inauguration party at Congressman Elliott's house. He'd lived in D.C. his whole life, but he'd never seen a president's inauguration up close. D.C. was strange in that way. You were always so close to, yet so far from, the seat of power.

36

Malcolm woke up to the sound of someone persistently knocking. He grudgingly opened his eyes and through the sunbeams streaming in from the window, confirmed he was still in Cedric's apartment. He smiled, happy his wish had been granted. The knocking began again.

If Governor Pinchback was back wanting someone to show him where to find breakfast, he'd tell him to kick rocks. He hadn't signed up to be that dude's full-time concierge. Malcolm climbed out of bed and shuffled over to the door. He cracked it open, looking out suspiciously. A radiant woman stood on the other side with a small duffel bag in hand.

"Cedric, did you forget about me and oversleep?"

Malcolm woke up instantly.

"You didn't pick me up at the train station like you said you would. Good thing I had your address from your letters or I would just be walking around stranded," she said, rolling her eyes.

The woman's face was familiar. *Wait. Cedric's locket! This is Isabel!*

"Isabel, you're here!" Malcolm replied, plastering a huge grin on his face.

"Of course, I'm here. Today is Inauguration Day, and you asked me to be your date to the ball."

"I'm so sorry. Please, come in, come in." Malcolm apologized. "I've been working so hard, the days all started to blend together. I'm so glad you found me. Here, let me take your bag. How can I make it up to you?"

Isabel sighed. "Could you please just get my other suitcase? I left it at the top of the stairs on the sidewalk. And would it be okay if I take a quick nap? I've had such a long journey and I'm exhausted."

"Yes, of course. I'll be right back," Malcolm said as he ran upstairs to get her trunk of clothes and a few other bags. When he returned, Isabel was fast asleep.

While Isabel slept, Malcolm prepared for the inauguration. As he was freshening himself up, he spotted a glass container filled with crimson liquid under Cedric's sink. Remembering the concoction he wasn't allowed to drink at Aunt Carol's house, his eyes lit up. He picked up the bottle, uncorked it, and gave it a sniff. A fruity whiff of spiced plums filled his nostrils, followed quickly by a lightening bolt that made his nose hairs stand on end. He recorked the bottle and put it back under the sink. Malcolm chuckled. He couldn't believe his family was still making the stuff.

After cleaning up, he found the tickets to the ceremony in Cedric's dresser and gathered two blankets to take with them to keep warm in the January weather.

A couple of hours later, he woke Isabel in time to dress warmly for the occasion. Thankfully, it was a quick walk to the nearby Capitol grounds. She was in a much better mood after resting and didn't seem to hold a grudge about being left at the train station earlier. Malcolm was relieved because the last thing he needed was to be the reason Cedric and Isabel broke up!

They found great seats at the eastern end of the National Mall, which did little to shelter them from the cold. Buried deep under layers of coats and blankets and hats, they could hardly see or hear the event, but the freezing temperatures could not dampen the crowd's joyful spirit. Champagne flowed freely from one hand to the next among the crowd and probably did more to keep them warm than any of their outer garments. Blacks and Whites alike were in attendance, and everyone—which admittedly was a self-selected bunch—was enthusiastic about Grant's second term. A sense of hope that Americans could finally put their differences aside and come together as a nation permeated the air.

• • •

After the Inauguration ceremony, Malcolm and Isabel returned to Cedric's apartment to dress for the ball. Noticing a bouquet of flowers on the dresser, Isabel happily exclaimed, "Oh, you got my favorite flowers, begonias. You shouldn't have!"

Malcolm gulped. Cedric must have asked the landlady to bring them before he arrived. They were pretty and looked just like the ones Uncle Leroy had given Aunt Carol.

Malcolm put on the nicest suit he could find in Cedric's collection, which was marginally better than what Cedric owned when he first arrived in D.C., and then left to thank the landlady for the flowers and to give Isabel some privacy. When he returned, Isabel was wearing a stunning burgundy taffeta ball gown with her hair pinned in a beautiful array of curls. A short carriage ride later, they were at Congressman Elliott's home. The congressman's striking wife, Grace, greeted them at the door. "Cedric! It's so nice to see you again. We don't have gumbo for you tonight, but I am sure you won't be disappointed."

"Thank you," he said, making room for Isabel to meet Grace more properly. "I'd like to introduce you to Isabel Davis."

"It's so very nice to meet you, Mrs. Elliott," Isabel said.

"Please, call me Grace!"

After Grace showed them inside, she returned to the door to greet other guests. Isabel's eyes popped open wide as they entered the main room. Standing inside such a beautiful home, impeccably decorated with rich, chocolate-colored velvet curtains adorning the windows and intricate handwoven rugs accenting the floor, she was astonished.

"I just can't believe Negroes live like this anywhere," she whispered, amazed. "In Mississippi, you can be lynched for even dreaming of such a life." Malcolm remembered how impressed he was the first time he went to the Downings' house and also couldn't believe Black people lived like that in Washington, D.C.—right after the Civil War, no less. Of course, that wasn't how most Black people lived, but the fact that even a few did was awe-inspiring.

As they made their way through the home, they passed a sitting room where the newly elected congressmen were gathered around a fireplace enjoying cigars. To the crowd's delight, Governor Pinchback dramatically recounted the gambling escapade from the previous night. Malcolm pointed out each man and shared key background details.

"I can't believe you work with such impressive people!"

"Me neither!" Malcolm agreed as he spotted his boss walking by.

"Congressman Elliott," Malcolm called out. "I'd like to introduce you to Isabel, who came all the way from Natchez to be my date to the ball."

"*The* Isabel? Why, it is so nice to finally meet you! Cedric talks about you constantly. Every morning I'm afraid he's going to tell me he's moving back to Mississippi to be with you. Please convince him to stay a little longer. We have so much good work left to do."

Isabel smiled bashfully, pleased that the congressman knew her by name. "Cedric's cause is my cause, so I'm happy to lend him to Washington for a little while longer. If it wasn't for my sick grandmother, I'd be up here seeing what I could do myself."

"You're a teacher, correct?" Congressman Elliott asked.

"Yes sir."

"There's no more important work than that. Just make sure the next generation is ready to defend these rights we're getting for them. Nice to meet you, Miss Isabel," he said as he excused himself with a wink and a smile.

Always a man of class, Congressman Elliott had carriages waiting outside to transport his guests to the ball, which was being held at the Treasury Department, right next to the White House. Malcolm helped Isabel down from the carriage. Seeing the White House all lit up at night, Isabel squealed with glee. He laughed but shared her excitement as they followed Congressman Elliot and his wife through the Treasury doors.

As the four made their way through the ballroom, Malcolm and Isabel overheard a couple of men snickering in a foreign language and pointing in Congressman Elliott's direction. Without a moment's hesitation, Congressman Elliott faced them and issued a sharp rebuke in their language.

"What was that about?" Malcolm asked, shocked.

"Those simpletons joked that they didn't know monkeys had been invited to the ball, else they would have brought their pets along too. I told them this so-called monkey is a United States congressman and will have their respect or they can get the hell out of my country."

"Your boss speaks French?" Isabel whispered skeptically, before smiling innocently in the congressman's direction.

Malcolm shrugged, remembering what Nathaniel had told him about the murkiness of Congressman Elliott's past. "Well, that seemed to shut them up. I wasn't aware that you spoke French, boss. Are there many French speakers in South Carolina?" Malcolm asked.

"I picked up a little French and Spanish here and there, enough to embarrass any idiot who dares to insult me on my own soil," Congressman Elliott said, avoiding answering the question directly. "I'm going to see if I can find Pinchback. Miss Isabel, keep an eye on this one. He can't hold his whiskey." And with that he left them to their own fun.

Malcolm threw his hands up at Isabel and shrugged again.

Apart from the snide remarks that the congressman had swiftly addressed, Malcolm and Isabel had a great time at the ball. President Grant had spared no expense in celebrating his reelection. A brass band played while people danced and mingled. The food in the ballroom stretched farther than the eye could see with turkey, ham, chicken, pot roast, casseroles, squash, greens, and desserts on tables lining the entire perimeter of the room.

After filling themselves at the food tables, Malcolm and Isabel made their way onto the dance floor. Congressman Butler was already there, gleefully spinning his wife around in circles, and Mrs. Elliott was dancing with a West Point graduate in full military regalia. A few people stared in their direction having probably never seen a White man dance with a Black woman before, but to Malcolm's surprise, most people just minded their business and kept dancing. Malcolm was glad he was able to spend this time getting to know Isabel. After all, she was family.

A short while later, President Grant made his grand entrance, with all the pomp of a king coming to claim his throne. The band momentarily switched to "Hail to the Chief," but immediately went back to playing the livelier songs that energized the crowd. The revelry continued until sunrise. At the end of the magical evening, each guest was given a little brass bell to signify that liberty for all would continue to ring in the Grant era. Malcolm turned the bell over in his hand, wondering why it looked so familiar.

"Cedric, I have to confess, I'm a little nervous about socializing with women of this caliber," Isabel said as she and Malcolm made their way by carriage over a bridge crossing the Potomac River on their way to the beautiful Syphax estate. Mrs. Syphax, Cedric's volunteer social attaché, had been so delighted to meet Isabel during the previous night's celebration that she invited her to a women's suffrage tea meeting at her home the next day. "And didn't you say they are a part of George Washington's family?" Isabel asked, wringing her hands.

"Yes, but the more time I spend with these types of people, the more I see they aren't all that different from us," Malcolm reassured her, doing his best to speak like Cedric. It was late afternoon, and Malcolm felt each and every bump on the road. He had slept in Cedric's wicker chair the night before so that Isabel could have the bed to herself—and he was paying for it. But really, he didn't mind. "Sure, they have more possessions and privileges than we ever dreamed of, but they pray for the safety of their husbands and children every time they leave the house, just as our family does for us. All you have to do is relax and be yourself, and you will be fine."

"Okay." She nodded meekly.

As their carriage arrived at the estate, a valet met them in the middle of a circular pebbled driveway in front of a beautifully maintained, but modestly proportioned, solid redbrick home. The valet escorted Isabel to the front door, and Malcolm attempted to follow her inside, but was stopped by Mrs. Syphax herself.

"Hello, Cedric. Lovely to see you again. Thank you for bringing Isabel. I'm sorry, honey, but this is a ladies' only affair, so ta-ta," she said, shooing him off.

As she shut the door in his face, Malcolm was fairly certain that he saw someone drinking tea in the formal living room who looked like a picture he'd once seen of Harriet Tubman—but he couldn't be sure.

The valet standing by the door instructed him to return in an hour and a half, at 5:00 p.m. on the dot, to retrieve Isabel. Rather than return to Cedric's apartment, Malcolm decided to pass the time admiring the Syphaxes' extensive grounds overlooking the Potomac River. Only a few minutes into his self-guided tour, he ran into Mr. Syphax, who was wandering aimlessly along a gravel pathway alongside the house, biding his time away from the ladies.

"Mr. Syphax, pleasure to see you again, sir," Malcolm said, greeting him warmly.

"Why, yes, hello. And how did you manage to score an invitation to Abbie's famous 'tumult and tea,' as I like to call it?" he asked with a snicker.

"My lady friend is visiting from Mississippi, and Mrs. Syphax was kind enough to include her."

"Oh. Lucky her," Mr. Syphax retorted dryly. "Care to walk with me, Cedric? I find we are both in similar boats, cast out by the petticoats."

"I would be honored, sir," Malcolm replied. He really felt like he was getting the hang of how people spoke in the 1870s. He hadn't heard anyone mention his "dialect" in a while.

"Did you know that you are walking on hallowed ground, Cedric?"

"What do you mean, sir?"

"This land used to belong to George Washington's family. Martha Washington's grandson, George Washington Parke Custis, left most of his property to his White daughter, the one who married General Lee. But, he also gave seventeen acres to his mulatto daughter, my grandmother Mariah. General Lee lived a little farther up the property in the Arlington House. So for a while the two families were neighbors, albeit on opposite sides of the cause. To spit in the face of General Lee, the Union decided to bury their soldiers on Lee's land during the war and renamed his property Arlington Cemetery."

Malcolm looked out in awe at another D.C. landmark that he was familiar with but that was completely unrecognizable at the moment.

"Wow," Malcolm whispered, dumbfounded.

Mr. Syphax let out a half snort, somewhere between laughter and derision.

They walked across a green pasture sprinkled with flowering magnolia and dogwood trees, which gave off the most delightful fragrance, until they reached a clearing. Malcolm stopped in his tracks when he noticed a cluster of buildings emerging in the distance, as if they were coming upon a small town, tucked within this vast estate. Rows of small, white wooden homes dotted a well-trodden path, as Black men, women, and children bustled about in every direction.

"What is this?" he asked, surprised, as he marveled at all the activity.

"This, my boy, is Freedman's Village. It was created after the start of the war when former slaves started flooding Washington by the hundreds and needed a place to stay. Again, General Lee's land came in handy."

"I've seen some of the tent villages in Washington, but this looks like a real town. Is that a church?" Malcolm asked pointing at a steeple in the distance.

"Yes. Freedman's Village has a hospital, a mess hall, a schoolhouse, an old people's home, a laundry, everything you need to live a full and free life. And these people are earning their keep, working for a living."

"How many people live here?"

"Around a thousand. Miss Sojourner Truth herself resided here for a year or so in its early days. She was one of the biggest champions of the village. Helped the residents advocate for themselves and got the government to clean this place up and do right by the people."

"It looks nice!" Malcolm gawked, thinking it looked a lot better than the projects some of his friends lived in.

"Yes, which is what is going to make it all the more painful when folks have to leave."

"Why would they leave? They're doing better than most Black people I've seen," *including the ones in 2015*, Malcolm added silently.

"They aren't still living on their old master's plantation, and it beats sleeping outside in a tent!"

"Well, some of these folks *are* living on their old master's plantation. Plenty of them used to work for the Washington and Lee families, but you're right. At least they have jobs that pay money and aren't share-cropping for their old master."

"My bad. I mean, er, of course," Malcolm slipped again. So much for not using his "dialect." *I was doing so well!*

"Lots of folks came here looking for a better life. A fresh start. It's by no means perfect. The government keeps raising their rent and the residents have had to work hard to improve the conditions themselves, but the vultures are circling. They're eyeing this prime real estate on the Potomac and thinking about how they can use it for a better purpose than housing a bunch of, as they see it, worthless Negroes. These people are gonna fight eviction with every ounce of their being, I'll tell you that."

Malcolm had never even heard of Freedman's Village, so he knew it mustn't have lasted into modern times, but once the village closed, where would all these people go? *Are my neighbors in southeast D.C. descendants of the people who lived here?* he wondered.

As the winter sun began to set, they returned to the house. After all, he'd promised the valet he'd be there at 5:00 p.m. sharp. Malcolm thanked Mr. Syphax for the tour as he spotted Isabel outside mingling with the other ladies, chatting with them as if they were old friends. He'd had a feeling she would fit in naturally, and he was proven right. When she caught his eye, Isabel said her goodbyes and politely excused herself, meeting Malcolm at the waiting carriage.

Malcolm held the door open as Isabel climbed in and sat next to him. She was beaming from ear to ear and had a distinct glow about her.

"How was it?" Malcolm asked, intrigued.

"Oh Cedric, it was just wonderful. Those women, they are so smart and informed about issues, and organized, and connected, and powerful. And you will never guess who was there. Never in a million years!" Isabel taunted.

"Harriet Tubman?" Malcolm asked. Isabel's face fell momentarily, and he immediately regretted stealing her thunder. But her gorgeous smile returned.

"How did you know, you devil? Did you see her?" Isabel pounced.

"Yes. When I was dropping you off, I thought I saw Mrs. Tubman inside, but I wasn't completely sure. I wondered if I was seeing things."

"Well, you weren't. I met Mrs. Harriet Tubman today. I had tea with Moses, and she was just as wise and wonderful as I imagined her to be. She talked about what it felt like to be a slave, where she grew up like a neglected weed, ignorant of liberty, never happy or contented, and afraid of being carried away every time she saw a White man. But she said she decided that there was one of two things she had a right to, liberty or death. If she could not have one, she would have the other, for no man would take her alive.

"Now that slavery is over, she said that she no longer lives in constant fear for her life, but as a woman, she still yearns to be truly free, and for that, she needs the right to vote. She said she's going to keep fighting for that freedom so long as her strength lasts, and when the time comes for her to go, the good Lord will take her. Oh Cedric, I yearn to live my life with such unbridled passion and conviction."

Her enthusiasm was contagious. "That's wonderful. It sounds like you've been bitten by the activist bug. I wish I could have been there, but, you know, no boys allowed," Malcolm teased.

"You men have enough. One afternoon for the ladies won't kill ya, and if it does, that's one less man we have to knock down to get our rights!" she shot back playfully.

Malcolm laughed along. He suddenly realized where so many of the strong women in his family had inherited their fight from—even if they didn't know it. Malcolm looked over at Isabel with a deep appreciation for his family. He was proud, smiling at her. Suddenly Isabel was leaning in to kiss him. Malcolm's eyes widened.

38

Malcolm felt a punch on the arm. He stirred in the movie theater chair, thankful to be back in the present. "Close one, Cedric," Malcolm whispered sleepily under his breath.

"Malcolm, who are you talking to? Are you even going to watch this movie? Some date you are!" Jasmine exclaimed, exasperated.

Malcolm opened his eyes and looked about the room. The movie was still only in the first few scenes. The little blond girl with bangs was still talking to the ghostly television screen. "I'm sorry. I didn't realize I was so tired," Malcolm apologized, looking over at Jasmine. "Can you forgive me?" he asked with his best puppy-dog eyes. He tried not to chuckle, thinking he was getting good at groveling for a lady's forgiveness.

Jasmine rolled her eyes and looked away. Feeling emboldened by his recent adventures, Malcolm gently pulled her chin toward him and planted a gentle kiss on her lips. He could taste the salt and butter from the popcorn.

Jasmine blushed and smiled at Malcolm as they settled back in to watch the movie. "Don't think you won't have to make this up to me," she whispered, teasing.

"Oh I won't," Malcolm whispered back, letting Jasmine's soft hand rest in his.

• • •

Malcolm couldn't believe it was already the Fourth of July. The Fourth was one of his favorite holidays. He loved the ribs, the burgers, the hot dogs, and the potato salad that usually came with it. He loved hanging out with friends all day back in D.C., even better if it was at a pool, and he loved watching the fireworks at night. Every year, he and Damian would scale a fence—ignoring a NO TRESPASSING sign—to get to the perfect spot on a hill in his neighborhood that had a clear view of the National Mall.

"Hey, Aunt Carol," Malcolm asked while fixing himself a plate of grits and bacon that she'd made for breakfast. "What do you all usually do on the Fourth?"

Aunt Carol was putting a large wooden spoon to good use, softly stirring a bowl of potato salad for later in the day. "Oh, it's different every year, but we still eat good!" she said, chuckling. "I'm gonna finish making this potato salad, then start prepping the burgers. A few girl-friends are gonna swing by later for a little bid whist game. You could join in if you want, but these girlfriends are fierce. Don't expect you'd get one book," she teased, putting the spoon in the sink and reaching for a lid to cover her finished bowl of potato salad.

"What about you, Uncle Leroy? What's the plan?" Malcolm asked, sitting at the table with Uncle Leroy and Uncle Corey to eat.

Uncle Leroy slowly placed his cup of coffee on the table and looked up from his newspaper. "Well, I reckon I'm gonna eat some of that potato salad and have a burger with my beer. I'm not big on going out these days, but there is a nice spot along the river where you can catch some fireworks and avoid the crowds. Corey, you remember where it is?"

"Yeah, I remember," Uncle Corey nodded, engrossed in this week's crossword challenge.

"Good to know. What about you, Uncle Corey? Excited to celebrate your first Fourth of July since you got out?"

"Ehh." He shrugged. He tapped his pen several times on the table as he racked his brain for the final answer. "I don't know. Want to shoot some hoops this morning?"

"Bet," Malcolm said. His day was coming together. Even if Cedric did show up to send him to the past, he knew the festivities would be waiting for him as soon as he got back. "You ready, Uncle Corey?"

"Yup. Lemme get changed. Gimme five minutes." Malcolm knew that five minutes could easily grow to fifty if Uncle Corey didn't finish his puzzle soon. But suddenly Uncle Corey looked up as if an invisible light bulb was going off in his head and then scribbled the answer down with a proud smile. Challenge completed.

"Malcolm, while Corey's finishing up, can you grab me a couple platters from my buffet cabinet?" Aunt Carol asked.

Malcolm nodded and headed to the living room. As soon as he opened the cabinet doors, he knew why the party favor at President Grant's inauguration looked so familiar. *The bells!* Both of them were sitting together on a shelf. He pulled one of them out to inspect it and could faintly make out its inscription: *G . . . a . . . t l . . . 73.* Malcolm could hardly believing what he was holding. He smiled as he fondly remembered ringing them at the end of that extraordinary night.

"Aunt Carol, do you know what these are?" Malcolm asked excitedly as he returned to the kitchen holding up the bells.

Aunt Carol arched an eyebrow and pursed her lips. "Boy, do you take me for a fool? Asking me stupid questions like that. What's wrong with you?" she asked.

"Aunt Carol, I'm serious. I know you know these are bells, but do you know where they're from or why they're here?" Malcolm pushed on, undeterred.

As she walked toward the laundry room to grab her dustrag, she continued the absurd conversation from over her shoulder. "No, Malcolm. I told you our family has had this house a real long time, so no, I don't know where every plate, cup, piece of furniture, or bell came from. And weren't you supposed to bring me my platters? Frankly, I have better things to concern myself with, as do you! My guests will be here soon," she exclaimed anxiously, before muttering to herself, "Send a boy for platters, and he brings back bells."

"Yes ma'am. I'll get them. Um . . . Aunt Carol, would you mind if I held on to these bells for a little bit?" Malcolm asked, wanting to have a souvenir from his travels.

Aunt Carol looked at him quizzically, as if she was starting to worry about his mental health. "Sure, baby. You can play with the bells, but just remember to put them back. My mother was always fussin' about the contents of her cabinets and didn't want nothing messed with. I guess whatever is in there holds some value, even if it is only sentimental."

"Thanks, Aunt Carol," Malcolm said, quickly returning to the kitchen with the platters she'd requested. "You have a lot going on inside that buffet cabinet."

"Yes." She laughed, calming down a little. "We've had that cabinet in the family forever and things tend to just pile up over the years. Oh well. I guess the move is as good a time as any to declutter. How about I give you a box to start putting some of these things in? We might as well get a head start on packing. Lord knows how long it's gonna take with how many people have lived in this house over the years," Aunt Carol said, taking a seat at the table to dust off her platters.

"Sure, Auntie." He nodded, while internally refusing to concede they were moving.

"You ready, Nephew?" Uncle Corey asked, coming out of his room dressed and ready to play.

"You good, Aunt Carol?"

"I'm fine, baby. Thanks for your help. Y'all enjoy yourselves," she said, getting up from the table and grabbing some more ingredients out of the refrigerator for the dish she was making.

◆ ◆ ◆

"Is the fireworks spot far?" Malcolm asked Uncle Corey on their way to the milk crate on the back of the barn. Malcolm looked up at the cloudless sky. It was a sunny summer day, hot but with a slight breeze. "Want to go check it out together after dinner?"

"Ehhh," Uncle Corey deflected as they reached their hoop spot. He dribbled a couple of times and prepared to shoot.

"You got something against fireworks?" Malcolm asked, sensing his lack of enthusiasm.

He threw the ball up in the air and watched it bang off the barn wall above the crate. "I'm just not feeling all that patriotic right now," Uncle Corey answered flatly, walking nonchalantly over to retrieve the ball. "It's like, what? Am I supposed to be grateful to this country for letting me out of prison a few years early after stealing my life away? I was locked in a cell for half my life because I was friends with dudes that sold weed. Living in a box smaller than this square of ground we're playin' on—with no freedom, no privacy." He dribbled the ball between his legs as he walked up to the faded three-point line.

"Always having to watch my back from inmates and guards. You know how many people I saw get taken out in body bags over the years—some from suicide, some made to look like suicide, and some from old age. Imagine dying in a cage." Uncle Corey winced as he took his next shot, a haunted expression hanging over his face.

"At least you're out now," Malcolm said, trying to offer words of encouragement.

Uncle Corey passed the ball to Malcolm with an unintentional amount of force, almost knocking Malcolm off his feet. "And? What kind of life I got? I'm a grown man and ain't got nothing of my own. No wife, no kids, no job. Most of my friends are locked up. My brother is dead. What's the point of all this? Sometimes I wonder why I'm even here."

Malcolm took a shot and watched the ball patiently bounce around the rim of the crate while he tried to find the right thing to say. "Don't say that, Uncle. You're here because you matter. You survived prison for a reason. I don't know the whole reason, but getting to know my dad through you has meant everything to me. And we can change things. We can make things better." The ball hooked back out of the rim of the crate, and Malcolm ran in for the rebound to make a layup. Then he tossed the ball back over to his uncle.

Uncle Corey gripped the ball with one hand and held it out directly in front of him as he pondered out loud, "How? How we gonna do that? The system has been crushing us forever."

"Well, we can vote. We can vote to change the system," Malcolm said, waving his hands dramatically for emphasis.

Uncle Corey threw his head back in laughter.

"What's so funny?" Malcolm challenged him.

Uncle Corey tossed the ball in the air and spun it on his finger, smirking at his nephew's naivete. "Ex-cons can't vote. I ain't never voted, and I probably never will. I was too young when I got locked up and now it's too late. You know my daddy only got to vote in a couple of elections before he died. My granddaddy couldn't vote most of his life because of Jim Crow. Probably my great-granddaddy couldn't vote either. And before that we were slaves." Uncle Corey tapped the ball still balanced on his pointer finger to keep it spinning. "Nobody in our family has ever had a say in how this country is run. Maybe that's why it keeps chewing us up and spitting us out." He looked down sullenly and let the ball teeter off his finger until it fell to the ground and rolled off a few feet away.

"It wasn't always this way," Malcolm said as he walked over and placed his hand on his uncle's shoulder.

Uncle Corey flashed Malcolm a *What you talkin' 'bout?* look.

"It wasn't, man. There was a time when we counted—we voted, we were elected to office, we passed laws to protect ourselves." Malcolm wondered whether people would be inspired like he was and have reason to hope if they knew all the amazing things Black people had done after the Civil War.

"Yeah, well, I don't know what fantasy world you're talking about, but they sure put an end to any of that real quick," Uncle Corey said, walking over to pick up the ball and sinking a shot. "For most Americans, this country is their paradise because their ancestors chose to come here, but for the millions of us who descend from Africans that were ripped from their homes, transported under decks of disease-infested ships and forced to toil for centuries with only brutality as their pay, this land has been our hell."

Even after all Malcolm had seen, he couldn't come up with a counter-argument to that and instead snatched the ball from under the net to take a shot.

Uncle Corey stole the ball back from Malcolm before it even left his hands and then dribbled to the top of the court before pausing to reflect on an exchange between him and his brother. "You know, you're starting to sound like your pops. One time I was messing around at school and got a detention. When I made it home that night, your dad looked up from the book he was reading and asked me, what was I doing with my freedom and was I using it to set others free. I thought he was talking crazy, as usual. I was like, 'Nigga, what you talkin' about? Ain't nobody a slave 'round here. You don't see no chains on me.'" Uncle Corey held up his wrists to demonstrate his point and then took another shot.

The ball hit the rim and went flying into the air. Preoccupied with his thoughts, Uncle Corey didn't even attempt to rebound the ball, but instead continued to muse. "But when I was sitting in my cell a couple years later, I started hearing his words echoing in my head over and over again. Because in there, more than anywhere else, when you look around and see Black men in cages as far as the eye can see, you realize freedom ain't guaranteed for us. Never has been. It's more like we got freedom on lease or maybe on layaway. After enough payments, maybe you get to sample that sweet nectar but don't get greedy because they're always ready to repo your shit.

"So I went to the prison library and got my hands on some of those books your pop was always reading and, all of a sudden, the world around me started to come into focus. Eventually, I had to accept the answer that I didn't want to admit. What did I do with my freedom? I squandered it. Who did I help set free?" Uncle Corey snorted. "Not a damn soul. I was so caught up in my own struggles, I didn't even realize I was a pawn in somebody else's game just playing the part they wrote for me."

Malcolm walked over to collect the ball and placed it in his uncle's hands. "Look, I get it, Unc. We all out here playin' parts. The game is rigged, designed so that most of us don't stand a chance," Malcolm said, suddenly remembering Pinchback's words. "That doesn't mean we can't win. We just gotta be smarter about how we play our hand."

"I was right." Uncle Corey grinned fondly. "You are just like your dad."

"How's that?" Malcolm asked, pleased by the comparison.

"You're smarter than you look," he said, laughing. "But you're right, most of us don't make it. The ones that do usually feel so lucky, they never look back." He threw the ball over his shoulder in a lucky attempt to make a blind shot but missed completely.

"Like the dude in the barbershop?" Malcolm asked trying to make sure he and his uncle were still on the same page.

"Yeah. Exactly. But what he don't realize is ain't none of us free till we all free. Until then, every one of us is just a dice throw away from a bullet in the head or a life wasted behind bars. And if not you, then somebody you love." Uncle Corey shook his head in frustration. "We gotta wake up 'cause what we're doing ain't working. It might be working according to plan, but it damn sure ain't our plan." He walked over to the ball lying still in a thick patch of grass and kicked it back over to Malcolm.

"How do you think we get out of this cycle?" Malcolm probed. He picked up the ball and tried to imitate his uncle's trick where he spun the ball on the tip of his finger, but it wobbled off immediately.

"Man, I don't know. Each one, teach one? Soon as you get free, start freeing others."

"Like Harriet Tubman?" Malcolm suggested.

"Yeah," Uncle Corey said, nodding in reflection. "Just like Harriet. Once folks know better, they can do better. We gotta stop playing these tired parts that White people wrote for us centuries ago. We ain't slaves. We kings. Real freedom starts in the mind." Uncle Corey walked closer to Malcolm and placed the ball back on his finger so Malcolm could get a close-up view of the trick.

"I like how you talking now, Unc," Malcolm said, smiling, still mesmerized by the basketball's resistance to gravity.

"Okay, Nephew. I see what you doin'." He chuckled, handing the ball back to Malcolm for another try. "Yeah, first I gotta finish getting myself free. I might be outta prison, but I still gotta check in with massa—I mean my parole officer—every week, but God as my witness, I'm gonna make sure you don't repeat my mistakes. And maybe I can get involved in some program that talks to kids about how to make better choices. I don't know just yet but there must be something I can do. I'll find it. Better question is, what *you* gonna do?"

Malcolm carefully placed the ball back on his finger and spun three rotations this time. "I don't know yet. I'm still trying to figure that out."

Uncle Corey watched patiently as Malcolm attempted the trick again and again. "You're a quick learner and more importantly, you ain't a quitter. I ain't worried about you. You keep thinkin' on it, and it'll come to you."

Malcolm smiled playfully. "What I'm thinking 'bout right now is how I'm gonna embarrass an old man on the court," he said as he took a break from the trick and swept past Uncle Corey while he was distracted to sink a shot from the makeshift half-court line.

"That was a sucka shot. It don't count," Uncle Corey protested, laughing, grabbing the rebound and putting the game back into high gear.

After a couple of hours, they wore themselves out on the court and went inside to grab a bite to eat. Aunt Carol and her friends were deep into their card game in the kitchen. After greeting everyone, Malcolm piled his plate high with all his favorites and set up a TV tray in the living room. He looked down at his plate—filled with all the love Aunt Carol poured into her cooking. She couldn't make these kinds of meals at some old folks' home. She needed her kitchen, her garden, her memories. He had to find a way to help her save the farm. He just had to.

He picked up the remote control and began flipping channels. There wasn't much on. He finally landed on *SportsCenter*, picked up his fork, and was out cold.

39

Malcolm found himself with his head leaning against a panoramic window, the bright sun warming the pane. He felt vaguely nauseated as his body bobbed up and then down. His skin felt sticky, as if covered in a mist.

Malcolm sat up, alarmed, as he saw choppy water streaming past, suddenly realizing he was on a boat. A middle-aged White man with slicked-back blond hair, deep-set eyes, and a fuzzy mustache, in a blue-and-white seersucker suit was seated across a table from him reading a newspaper. The man looked up.

"Good, Cedric. You're awake. I was hoping we'd get a chance to talk before we arrived in Colfax," he said, peering at him over a pair of bifocals.

Malcolm rubbed the sleep from his eyes and tried to figure what was going on and where he was going.

"Here, have some coffee," the man said, offering him a cup.

Malcolm had one sip of the bitter, gritty black drink and nearly spit it out. It was worse than drinking dirt, although that was the closest thing he could compare it to. Starbucks this was not. But at least he was fully awake now, so he guessed it served its purpose.

"Yes, let's talk," Malcolm said, fully intending to only listen.

"I appreciate Congressman Elliott sending you to accompany me on this investigation. With Louisiana still not having any Negro representation in Congress, even though Negroes outnumber Whites in parishes throughout the state, your ties to Louisiana and your understanding of the people and culture will prove quite helpful. I'm not sure if you've done an investigation like this before, but it can be brutal. Some of the things you'll see here, you may never be able to unsee."

What has Cedric gotten me into? Malcolm wondered as the hairs on his neck started to rise.

"Our main goal while we're down there is to find eyewitnesses, to the extent there are any survivors," the man continued. "Even better if the witness can identify the assailants. That's the only chance we have of getting a conviction."

Malcolm wasn't sure that would be possible. Whenever things went wrong in his hood and the police started knocking on doors, folks knew better than to talk. Snitches get stitches. "What if people are too afraid to talk to us?" Malcolm asked, even though he didn't know exactly what they were investigating.

"Well, as representatives of the federal government, we are their last and best hope for justice. We have to convince them to trust us so we can help them. Here," the man said, handing Malcolm a badge with US *Department of Justice* inscribed around a star. "I got a loaner badge for you. If anybody asks, you tell them you're here on behalf of the United States under the supervision of me, US Attorney James Beckwith. Hopefully, this will help put folks at ease since it was local law enforcement that led the raid on their community."

"Thanks, Mr. Beckwith," Malcolm said, glad to finally know who he was speaking with.

"Call me James," he said, kindness emanating from his eyes.

"Umm, thanks, James," Malcolm said hesitantly, afraid to completely let his guard down. "Just so I'm fully prepared, are there any background materials I should read?"

"Good question," the man said as he rustled in his briefcase and pulled out a newspaper. "There's some good coverage of the incident in here."

"Thanks," Malcolm said, unfolding the paper. He gulped upon seeing the horrifying image on the front page. *Not again*, he thought as he was reminded of the unrivaled horrors he'd seen at the Mechanics' Institute in New Orleans. Why would Cedric send him back to a place like this? Witnessing one massacre was enough for a lifetime.

THE LOUISIANA MURDERS—GATHERING THE DEAD AND WOUNDED.—[See Page 398.]

RIOT IN COLFAX, LOUISIANA, LEAVES HUNDREDS DEAD

Grant Parish, Louisiana — In the small town of Colfax, a riot broke out at a courthouse leaving hundreds dead on Easter Sunday, April 13, 1873. The dispute stemmed from the long-awaited and fervently disputed results of the 1872 election in Louisiana, with both the Democratic candidate, John McEnery, and the Republican candidate, William Kellogg, declaring victory. With neither candidate willing to concede defeat, the men established parallel governments and issued commissions for their down-ballot slate of candidates, including the sheriff and parish judge of Grant County.

A federal court in New Orleans recently declared Kellogg the rightful Governor of Louisiana, and he wasted no time installing his down-ballot candidates into office. To ensure the judge he selected was able to take his seat, Governor Kellogg ordered a negro militia to guard the Grant Parish courthouse.

Unwilling to concede defeat, the Democrat-commissioned sheriff recruited white men from nearby parishes and as far as Texas to retake the Grant Parish courthouse. When those recruits arrived, the negro militia began firing unprovoked shots. After allowing the women and children to leave, the sheriff and his troops were left with no choice but to retaliate and in doing so thwarted the negro militia's plans to go on a rampage of raping and pillaging the good white people in the neighboring town. Ultimately, somewhere between 150 and 300 negroes and 3 whites were killed.

What?! Malcolm thought, his eyes bulging out of his head as he read how many Black people died and how few Whites. Yet the article implied that the massacre was all the Black people's fault—and that they'd intended to harm people. Something definitely smelled fishy. Malcolm rubbed his hands together, salivating at the chance to get to the bottom of it.

A few hours later, the boat arrived at a dock on the outskirts of Colfax, Louisiana. Malcolm and James walked about a mile into the town center, past a cluster of small shotgun homes. It was early dusk. There were no people around—no sounds of laughter, no pots banging, no children squealing. Just empty, desolate silence. As soon as they entered the field in front of the courthouse, the overpowering smell of death and charred flesh filled Malcolm's nostrils, leaving him gagging. *Get it together*, Malcolm, he thought.

The closer they came to the courthouse, the stronger the stench grew. In the distance, a pack of wild wolves circled, waiting for their opportunity to feast on the remains. He could barely see what remained of the courthouse in the distance. It was burnt to a crisp, with the roof destroyed so badly, one couldn't be certain it had ever had one.

Part of Malcolm wanted Cedric to pull him back home right then and there, but another part of him knew that Cedric would have the courage to do the work. He had to as well. "It looks like a war was fought here," Malcolm observed morosely.

"We have to find out what really happened." James nodded in agreement. "Let's come back in the morning when there's better light. Hard to know what we're seeing here."

"Yes," Malcolm agreed, but as he circled back, his foot bumped something and he tripped, bringing him face-to-face with not one, but two corpses. "Ahhhh!!!" Malcolm screamed, jumping up as quickly as he could, but in the process of scrambling up, he turned the bodies over. Peeking out from underneath one of the men was something white.

Malcolm took a deep breath. He'd seen the dead before, but never touched them, or really observed one up close. *I'm Cedric. Cedric.* He pulled his shirt collar up over his nose and bent down to get a closer look. He lifted the man's body slightly, trying not to look at his face, afraid the body would come to life like in a zombie movie. Underneath, Malcolm found a tattered piece of white fabric tied to a stick. "What's this?" he asked, picking it up.

"White flag," James noted alarmingly.

As Malcolm's eyes adjusted to the darkness, he noticed several other white cloths poking out from under bodies, several of which were stacked one on top of the other on the ground, like the men he'd tripped over. "Don't white flags mean surrender?" Malcolm asked. "If these men were killed while surrendering—"

"Then this atrocity was nothing short of cold-blooded murder," James said, finishing Malcolm's sentence.

Anger and disgust rose within Malcolm as he followed James off the field to the boardinghouse where they were staying. Now he was more determined than ever to figure out what had happened at that courthouse.

* * *

From house to house, Malcolm and James searched for anyone who could tell them what had happened, but the Black residents met them with silence, fear, and slammed doors. Understandably, no one wanted to talk. The poor community had just suffered an almost complete annihilation of its men—its fathers, husbands, sons, grandfathers, brothers, preachers, teachers, and students. There was no one around to offer comfort, cook a meal or help them cope because nearly every household was affected. The government had failed to protect them before, and the townspeople did not intend to give Malcolm and James the chance to let them down again.

As Malcolm and James walked down another dirt path between a row of houses, they saw a boy who looked to be about twelve years old carrying a bucket of water. As soon as the boy realized they were watching him, he began limping away as fast as he could, but given his uneven gait, Malcolm caught up with him quickly.

"Can I help you carry that bucket?" Malcolm asked, approaching slowly so as not to scare him away.

"No suh," he said without looking up.

"You mind if I ask how you got that limp?" Malcolm inquired.

"Yes suh. I mean, I got it 'cause I—I was helping break a horse, and I fell off and landed bad on my leg," he stammered, looking around nervously. "My ma says I can't be talking to you folks, so I best be on my way," he said, attempting to shuffle off.

"Look, you don't know me, but I know you," Malcolm said, moving in front of the kid to block his exit. The boy looked back nervously at James, who was standing behind him, and then trained his eyes on the ground. From looking at him, Malcolm could tell he'd probably got injured on that field and if he had, it probably also meant he'd lost someone he loved. "White folks killed my dad for no reason," Malcolm said softly, getting wistful as he thought about the senseless murder of both his and Cedric's dads before pivoting to Cedric's more relatable story. "They killed my pa at the Mechanics' Institute massacre in New Orleans, and I barely escaped myself, except my pa made sacrifices that saved my life." Malcolm paused to allow his words to sink in while empathizing with how fresh this kid's pain must be. He knew how long it would last. Forever. The kid refused to make eye contact with Malcolm, but Malcolm knew he was listening. The kid began shifting his feet nervously in the dirt, so Malcolm continued before he made a break for it.

"I've seen so many good men die for no good reason and not a damn thing was ever done about it. But I had the chance to go to Washington and work on laws to make sure that there were consequences for taking a Negro's life, just as there are for taking White people's lives. So that the next time a White man decides he wants to kill a Negro, he'll have to ask himself something he never had to ask before: is it worth it?" Malcolm could sense he had finally piqued the kid's interest by raising the possibility of avenging his loved one's murder. The kid glanced up for a quick second before diverting his eyes back to the ground.

"What you want from me?" he whispered nervously.

"We can send the murderers who killed all those people at the courthouse to jail, but we're gonna need your help to do it. We need you to tell us what happened, what you saw. So that another boy like you and another community like this one doesn't have to learn how to go on

without their husbands, fathers, grandfathers, brothers, and sons. Will
you help us?"

The boy finally looked Malcolm in the eye. "My pa died tryin' to
protect our freedoms. No matter what my ma says, I can't let his death
be for nothin'. If you meet me by the red barn half a mile north of here
at sundown, I'll tell you."

* * *

That evening Malcolm and James met the boy as he requested in an abandoned barn on the edge of town. Thomas, as he introduced himself, was
the son of a preacher who was active in the Black militia.

After taking a deep breath and looking around nervously, Thomas
told them what had happened. "My pa had a militia. The governor asked
them to go guard the courthouse so that the new judge could take his
seat. When we got there, we was puttin' up barriers and digging trenches
so that we'd be safe. That's what we was doin' when we heard the hootin'
and hollerin' of the White folks riding up on dey horses, swinging dey
whips and shootin' all in da air.

"We all ran to the courthouse to hide, but then those devils set fire to
it while we were inside. We knew we was trapped and tried to surrender.
My pa told us to hold white cloths out the window for dem to see. Then
dey said, 'All right, come out wit cha hands up,' so that's what a bunch of
fellas did, but soon as they got outside, dem devils shot 'em dead.

"After that, the rest of us knew dem doggone White folks couldn't be
trusted, so we stayed put in the courthouse, even though it was burnin'
all around us. Next thing you know, those White folks burst through the
front door, pulled guns on us, and said we all best come out now. Dey
blamed what happened to the dead on a couple of folks who was riled up
and got out of hand, but say dey accepted our surrender and was gonna
take us to a safe place." Thomas suddenly started pacing around the barn
appearing to be reliving what happened.

"Dey had us line up with a guard between e'ery two men. I was
with my pa near the back of the line. Then I heard one fella say, 'Hey
boss, I think I'm running low on ammunition.' And then he took his

gun and fired it straight in the back of the head of a Negro. Both that Negro and the one in front of him fell to the ground, dead. That White man started laughing and said, 'Look at that, I killed two niggers with one shot. I ain't even got to waste two bullets.' Then other men started firing and shots were ringin' out all around. Before I knew it, they had shot my pa in the back and he fell on top of me, pinnin' me to the ground. I lay real still with my eyes closed and pretended I was dead too. I lay like that until nightfall, and when I was sure wasn't no one else around, I whispered goodbye to my pa. I crept off and have been trying to be as invisible as a ghost ever since. After all, I'm supposed to be dead."

Malcolm and James thanked the boy for coming forward to talk to them. He shook both of their hands and stood tall, looking older than he was—and then he disappeared into the night.

Heading back to the boardinghouse, Malcolm reflected on how Thomas had played dead in order to stay alive. It reminded him of how he'd lain flat on the basketball court until he knew the shooters were gone, hoping they couldn't smell the terror pulsing through his veins. Or how two of the survivors of the Mother Emanuel church massacre played dead to survive the slaughter. Malcolm thought of Aunt Carol. He wondered if she was playing dead too, in her own way. By giving up the farm without a fight. Constantly fighting was draining, but playing dead took a toll as well.

Before Malcolm spoke with Thomas, he'd appeared a shadow of himself, but once Malcolm planted the seeds of hope, encouraged him, it was as if a light inside of Thomas had flickered back on—something bright enough to let him see hope on the other side of a river of despair. *If you play dead for long enough, does a part of you actually die?* Malcolm wondered.

● ● ●

It took several weeks to gather the evidence, even with the help of a few more investigators who joined them, but in the end, Malcolm felt it was all worth it. He sat transfixed in a small country courthouse on a row next to Thomas and watched as James secured federal indictments against ninety-seven White men, many of whom were former Confederate soldiers. The Third KKK Enforcement Act had worked again to put bad guys where they belonged, behind bars.

Malcolm heard a sniffle beside him and looked over. Thomas was weeping cathartically into his mother's bosom. She held him close, her tears soaking into his hair. Malcolm's heart filled with pride at the role he'd played in bringing these murderers to justice.

The next day, James and Malcolm boarded the boat back to New Orleans. Now that the truth was out, Malcolm enjoyed reading the revised news coverage in the newspaper that rightfully exposed the heinous acts of barbarity that had occurred in Colfax. He was glad it no longer mentioned the Black militia's supposed plans to rape and pillage the town to justify their being slaughtered. The humanity of Black Americans was being recognized. Malcolm looked out at the water rushing past the boat. Feeling satisfied that he had done his part, Malcolm was ready to go home. He closed his eyes and whispered, "Cedric, I'm ready."

When Malcolm opened his eyes, Uncle Corey was standing over him laughing. "Damn, Mal. I must've really wore you out on that court. Most people don't get the 'itis until after they eat!" Uncle Corey said, pointing at Malcolm's full plate of food still on the TV tray.

Laughing awkwardly, Malcolm got up to reheat his food, making sure no one saw as he wiped away a tear from the corner of his eye. He was so glad to be home.

40

"Malcolm, you got company," Aunt Carol called from downstairs. It had been a week since the Fourth of July and his last sojourn to the past, and he had spent a good deal of it hanging out in his room or in the attic drawing, which was what he was doing just then. He'd grown quite fond of the beanbag chair. He had even been helping Uncle Leroy with chores— almost happy to do them. He was glad for the rest, to be in his Jordans again and out of Cedric's tight leather boots. He'd needed time to think and process all he had seen and experienced.

When Malcolm arrived downstairs, he was surprised to see Jasmine sitting at the kitchen table across from Aunt Carol with a picnic basket in front of her.

"What's this?" he asked.

"I wanted to see if I could finally take you on that picnic I promised." Jasmine beamed, briefly opening up the top of her basket so a few of the delicious scents could escape.

"Awww, yeah! Let's do it," he said, reaching toward the basket to carry it for her. "Where are we going on this picnic, exactly?"

Jasmine happily handed over the heavy basket and pulled out her phone to show him a few pictures, explaining, "There's a nice park near downtown. I was thinking we could go there and then maybe get some ice cream afterward."

"Cool," he agreed, grinning.

"Be home around dinnertime," Aunt Carol said from the kitchen table. She was deep into a game of solitaire.

"See you later, Aunt Carol," Malcolm called on his way out the front door.

"Uh-huh. Have fun," Aunt Carol said, distracted by her game.

"So what you got for us to eat?" Malcolm asked once they were in Jasmine's truck. He tried to sneak a peek into the picnic basket.

Jasmine reached over and slammed it shut. "You'll have to wait and see."

"All right. All right," Malcolm said, chuckling.

When they arrived at the park, Jasmine parked the truck and gave Malcolm a few things to carry. She led him to a nice area under a tree in the shade and pulled out a checkered blanket from a bag and laid it on the ground. Then she pulled out a small orange speaker and began playing a chill playlist with soulful artists Malcolm hadn't heard before. Finally, when they were all settled, she opened the picnic basket and pulled out a two-liter bottle of grape soda, red plastic cups, a couple of ham-and-cheddar sandwiches, some chips, a fruit salad, and a mini-pecan pie.

"Nice spread!" Malcolm complimented her, impressed with her taste.

"Why, thank you! The pie is my granny's secret recipe." She beamed as she filled their cups. "Cheers!"

"Cheers," Malcolm toasted before sticking his fork into the pie to taste it first. "Ohmygod," he said, his eyes rolling back in his head. "You keep this up, I might never leave Mississippi."

"That's the plan." Jasmine winked. "So for real, am I ever going to see you again after this summer?" Jasmine asked, getting serious for a moment.

"Of course. Now that I know what I'm missing, I'll definitely be back," Malcolm said, nodding.

"Cool," she said, lighting up and blushing a little bit.

After Malcolm decimated the pie, sandwiches, and fruit, he felt full and content. He lay down on the blanket and stared up through the trees at the clear blue sky, allowing a sense of peace to wash over him. Jasmine lay back as well next to him. He reached over and grabbed Jasmine's hand and gave it a squeeze. She squeezed back.

"So, how you been?" he asked.

Jasmine interlocked her fingers between his as she answered his question. "I've been good. Same ole, same ole. Slow summer. My older brother is heading off to the army in a little bit, so we are getting ready for that, but that's about it. You doing okay?"

The palm of Malcolm's hand started sweating as he debated whether she could handle the wild truth about seeing and being Cedric. "I'm mostly good. I've been doing a little . . . reading," Malcolm said, at least ready to tell someone about the diary.

"Reading? I didn't know you like to read. I love books! I love mysteries and dramas, mostly. What are you reading?" Jasmine asked excitedly, seemingly surprised to be hanging out with a teenage boy who enjoyed books as much as she did.

"*The Diary of Cedric Johnson.*" Malcolm paused to let this sink in.

Jasmine racked her brain for the title, hoping they shared another thing in common, but couldn't seem to place it. "I've never heard of that one. Who wrote it?"

"Cedric Johnson." Malcolm was already having second thoughts about mentioning it. How could he explain the author's identity and how he'd got ahold of the book?

"Who?" Jasmine asked, looking confused.

Malcolm decided the simplest explanation was the best as he began opening up. "Cedric Johnson," he repeated confidently. "He was one of my ancestors. He was born a slave and ended up working in Washington for some of the first Black members of Congress."

"What?" She squinted.

"I know this sounds crazy, but I found this diary, Cedric's diary, in Aunt Carol's attic. I've been reading what life was like for Black people right after the Civil War, after slavery ended," Malcolm confessed aloud for the first time.

Jasmine's eyes opened wide in shock. "That's unbelievable. What does he say it was like?" she asked.

Malcolm was grateful for her interest and began to share freely. "For the most part, it was pretty horrible. Once slavery ended, Black folks wanted to be treated equally, but White people across the South weren't having it, and they kept killing Black people when they tried to stand up for their rights. But there were also Black leaders during that time—like Black senators and congressmen and lawyers and doctors and business owners—plenty of folks you've probably never heard of, who were fighting so that Black people could be truly free." Malcolm stared up at the clouds, hoping Jasmine wouldn't think he sounded foolish, until her sweet voice interrupted his thoughts.

"Wait, are you talking about Reconstruction?" Jasmine clarified, her eyes lighting up.

"You know about this?" Malcolm asked, dumbfounded.

Jasmine smiled. She rubbed her thumb on the back of his hand as she thought out loud. "A little. We barely covered it in school, but I've heard my dad talk about it. He said it was a time after slavery when Black people had a lot of hope that life would get better for them, but things didn't really work out that way."

"Yeah," Malcolm agreed, feeling relieved that he finally had someone to share his new knowledge with. "You wouldn't believe how much Black people today have in common with Black folks back then. We still have the worst schools, the worst housing, the worst jobs, we're the poorest, the most likely to be locked up, and we still live in fear of the law. On the surface, things may look different, but not that much has changed for ordinary Black folk—not enough anyway." His words trailed off as memories of his visions began to replay in his head.

"Wow, Malcolm. Are all dudes from D.C. this woke?" Jasmine teased affectionately, turning over and sitting up on her elbows.

Malcolm let out a hearty laugh, feeling a great weight lifted by this exchange. He may not have shared all that he'd experienced—all that he'd seen—but it was something and it felt good.

"Seriously though, you should talk to my dad. He loves history—I mean, he teaches it even—and he would love to hear about this diary."

"Yeah," Malcolm said, his eyes growing wide. "I forgot to tell you I ran into him when I went to visit Alcorn. He invited me to sit in on one of his classes."

"See! You should totally do it," Jasmine said, grinning.

After they finished eating, they packed up and put their picnic items in the truck so they could take a stroll through the park. A ways down a path they came to a beautiful, multi-tiered stone fountain and a tall pilaster topped with a statue of a man in military uniform carrying a rifle. Malcolm stopped to read the inscription at the base of the monument.

IN MEMORY OF THE CONFEDERATE DEAD
FROM NATCHEZ AND ADAMS COUNTY, MISSISSIPPI.

Then he walked around the memorial to read the inscription on the back.

ERECTED BY THE CONFEDERATE MEMORIAL
ASSOCIATION OF NATCHEZ AND
ADAMS COUNTY MISS. 1890.

Malcolm looked skeptically around the park for any statutes dedicated to the Black people killed all over the state of Mississippi during and after the Civil War.

"You okay?" Jasmine asked, noticing how his mood had darkened.

Malcolm let out a heavy sigh. "Yeah, I guess. Just seeing a statue dedicated to slaveholders and traitors in the middle of the park has thrown me a little bit. I wonder if Germany has monuments in its parks dedicated to Nazi soldiers. And how come I've never seen a memorial for any Black victims of racial terrorism. It just feels like wherever I look, I see a twisted version of history," he said his voice growing louder and sharper with each word he spoke.

"Malcolm, calm down," Jasmine interjected, refusing to lose another good date to things she had no control over. "I don't even pay attention to these things anymore. I see 'em, but I don't see 'em. Like, if they want to honor some old dead White dudes, whatever."

"They sure put a lot of effort into telling a lie. I guess if everybody believes the same lie, it becomes the truth," Malcolm said snarkily. "Just like what they tried to do in Colfax and like they did with that stupid *Birth of a Nation* movie. When is *our* story gonna get told?"

"What? I don't even know what you're talking about," Jasmine said, tears beginning to form in her eyes. "Look, I get it. We're in the South, and everywhere you look there are reminders of a really painful history, but for the people that actually live here, you can't spend your whole life angry. You just have to accept some things are the way they are." Jasmine turned and headed back toward her truck.

"Hey wait," Malcolm said, chasing after her. He grabbed her hand when he caught up. "I'm sorry, Jas," Malcolm apologized, realizing that he had hurt her feelings after she had put all this effort into their date. "I'm just dealing with a lot right now. Honestly, ever since I found Cedric's diary, I feel like I've been living two lives—one in the 1870s and one in 2015. And they have so many things in common that I'm confusing the two. It feels like we've been sweeping history under the rug for so long, we're about to drown in all the garbage." He held on to her hand, hoping she would understand.

Without pulling away, she responded tensely, "You're right. The world is messed up, but do we have to solve all its problems today?"

"Naw," Malcolm said, taking a deep breath. "How about we finish our walk?"

Jasmine gently wrapped her arms around his chest and whispered in his ear, "I have a better idea to help you relax." Malcolm looked down at her and smiled broadly as she let go and headed back toward the truck.

"Where are we going?" Malcolm asked, excitedly following her.

Jasmine smiled and said slyly, as if she was hinting at something, "Back to my house."

41

Malcolm stood in front of a sprawling, Spanish-style villa with a red tile roof and a wide front porch adorned with a set of wooden rocking chairs. Jasmine tugged his hand and led him around the back of her house toward a red metal barn that was much bigger and newer looking than Uncle Leroy's.

"Jasmine, where are you taking me?" Malcolm asked, getting a little annoyed by her secretiveness. He was starting to think maybe he'd misread her when she suggested bringing him home.

Out of excitement, Jasmine dropped Malcolm's hand and walked ahead by a few paces.

"I want you to meet Destiny," she called back to him as she continued toward the barn.

"What?" he asked, even more confused as he followed her into a stable. *This can't be right*, Malcolm thought, *I must've had this all wrong.*

"Not what. Who! This is Destiny," Jasmine said proudly, going into a large stall and caressing the jet-black mane of a muscular chocolate mare.

"She's beautiful," Malcolm noted, even though he was a little let down at the surprise. "You know Uncle Leroy has horses, right?"

Jasmine giggled at his awkwardness and hoped he would appreciate what she said next. "I know, Mal, but have you gotten the chance to ride one yet?"

Malcolm put his hands in the air and took three steps back before exclaiming, "What? I'm not getting on that thing! It's huge! It would kill me!"

Jasmine fell out laughing. "I've been riding since I was five. You'll be fine. Horses vibe off your energy so if you're relaxed, she'll be relaxed. I'll be right back," she said, walking out and leaving Malcolm alone with Destiny in her stall.

Malcolm and Destiny stood looking at each other. Malcolm hoped he wouldn't upset her or frighten her. She was a good bit bigger than Sally, and he knew what horses were like when they got spooked. "Jasmine," Malcolm hollered out from the stall, "for real. I'm not riding no horse."

Jasmine returned with a leather saddle and bridle and began outfitting her girl. "That's your problem, Mal. You're too uptight and don't know how to relax."

Malcolm rolled his eyes and sighed.

Once everything was latched and buckled, Jasmine led Destiny out of the stable and into a large fenced-in pasture. "Could you please just trust me?" she asked, as Malcolm hung back at the fence. "Destiny is as gentle as a kitten. Come pet her so she can get used to you," she invited him. He sighed again and walked over. Jasmine took his hand and used it to stroke Destiny's mane and nose. The horse turned its head to the side and nuzzled in their direction.

"See! She likes you already. Now you see this stirrup here. I want you to put one foot in it and then grab this handle on the saddle and swing your other leg over Destiny's back. I'm going to hold her reins so you don't need to worry. She's not going anywhere."

Without moving, Malcolm looked at her with extreme hesitation until Jasmine whispered, "Trust me."

He shook his head, hardly able to believe he was doing this. He put his left foot in the stirrup, pulled himself up, and swung his right leg over the horse and across the saddle.

"Jas, this is really high up," he said, looking down at her. "One sudden move, and I could break my neck, for real."

Jasmine snorted and tried her best to be supportive of her friend, but couldn't help teasing him a bit in between. "Fool, you are not going to break your neck! Just chill. You're making Destiny nervous. Now look, we're just going to slow-walk around the yard, okay. I want you to push your butt back and lean forward and use your thigh muscles to hold on to the saddle. You've been swimming, right? Just think of it like you're riding a wave. Let your body just respond and adjust to her movements." Jasmine began leading Destiny around the yard. "See, that's not so bad," Jasmine said, trying to calm Malcolm down. He was gritting his teeth and holding on to the saddle with a death grip. "Okay, now I'm going to hand you the reins," Jasmine said slowly.

"You're going to hand me the what?" Malcolm shouted, looking terrified, barely able to take his eyes off the saddle horn.

"Shhh. Easy. Easy," she said soothingly to Destiny who appeared startled. "Just take this rope here, so you can guide her." Jasmine displayed the reins in front of Malcolm making sure he saw what she was referring to this time. "If you want her to go left, just pull gently on the left rein. If you want her to go right, pull gently on the right. If you want her to go faster kick softly with your heel. And if you want her to stop, pull both reins back evenly. Got it?" She handed him the reins without waiting for his answer.

"No," Malcolm muttered.

"Great! Off you go," she said, smacking Destiny on the rear.

"Where are you going?" Malcolm shouted out as Destiny trotted off.

"Don't worry. I'm right here," Jasmine shouted from behind him as she waved him off. "Why don't you give her a slight kick? Just remember, hold the reins, lean forward, and squeeze your thighs. Trust me, Mal. You're going to love it."

Malcolm shook his head in disbelief certain that the last thing he wanted to do was give Destiny a kick. He trotted around the fenced-in pasture a few times, holding on for dear life. He looked up wondering where Jasmine was off to and noticed the setting sun turning the horizon into a deep blood orange. Stunned by its beauty, Malcolm finally began to relax.

"Jas, do you see this sunset?" he called out, but she didn't respond. Just when he was about to freak out about being alone with the horse with Jasmine nowhere in sight, Jasmine emerged from the stable on top of a jet-black stallion looking as steady and confident as Clint Eastwood in an old western.

"You're looking good, Mal! Now are you ready to have some fun?" she proposed, winking at him as she caught up with his horse.

"Fun?" Malcolm asked skeptically, knowing he would regret saying yes to anything she suggested right now.

"You remember everything I taught you?" she confirmed, answering his question with a question.

"No! What did you tell me? I don't remember anything. Get me off this thing," Malcolm said, trying to figure out how hard it would be for him to jump off a moving horse.

"Malcolm, relax! Trust me. Hold the reins. Lean forward. Squeeze your thighs," Jasmine instructed as she moved her horse in front of Destiny. Then she clicked her tongue, quickly dug in her heels, and immediately, her horse started trotting faster with Destiny right behind. They passed through a wide opening in the fence that led to a larger pasture.

"It's getting really bumpy, Jasmine," Malcolm yelled. "Can we slow down?"

"The faster we go, the smoother the ride," she shouted back, ignoring his request as she made her horse go faster and faster.

Malcolm was terrified and continued to hold on with all his might, but after a few moments, the bumpiness stopped and the ride became smooth and exhilarating! He felt like he was flying, sailing with the wind into the mesmerizing horizon. Every thought or worry flew out of his head and all he felt was free and one with Destiny.

"This is incredible!" he shouted.

"I knew you would love it!" she shouted back.

They galloped across the wide expanse of pasture until the sun finished setting, signaling them to return to the stables.

As they made their way back into the smaller pasture next to the stables, Malcolm looked over at Jasmine. "I never did anything like that before," he confessed.

"Now you'll always have something to remember me by," she said, smiling and hopping down off her horse. She reached up to help Malcolm down, but as he pulled his right leg over to dismount, he missed his footing on the ground and felt the all-to-familiar fall into the abyss.

42

Malcolm came to standing at the foot of the US Capitol with Congressman Elliott ascending the steps in front of him. *Why am I back? Haven't I seen enough?* he thought, trying to shake off the dizziness.

A newspaper had been discarded on the side of the steps. Malcolm picked it up to check the date: January 6, 1874. Nearly a year had passed since the Colfax massacre. He almost lost sight of Congressman Elliott while skimming the front page of the paper and quickly took off after him into the Capitol. He finally found him in a meeting room speaking with another congressman. Seeing Malcolm at the door, he motioned him inside.

"So the House has finally scheduled a floor debate on Senator Sumner's civil rights bill, nearly four years after he first introduced it in the Senate," Congressman Elliott observed wryly.

Malcolm's head was still spinning from the sudden trip to the past. He quickly sat down on a couch in the room to stop the blood from rushing to his head and tried to figure out who Congressman Elliott was speaking to. It took him a moment, but he eventually recognized it was Congressman Butler, the White man who was so complimentary of Congressman Elliott after his speech in support of the Third KKK Enforcement Act.

"I just can't stand these Southern hypocrites," Congressman Butler said standing near a side table, pouring glasses of whiskey for himself and his guests. "They didn't have any problem socializing with Negroes when they were their slaves. They let their children play together, rode first class on trains with Negro servants by their side, let their babies suckle off Negro breasts, and plenty of times, laid with Negro women and fathered their babies. But now that Negroes are free, they can no longer stand the sight of them. Ain't that something? They embrace the company of the slave and shun the free man. Which has a higher station? What kind of sense does that make?"

Congressman Butler handed Congressman Elliott and Malcolm their glasses. Malcolm took his glass of whiskey but didn't drink it. The last thing he needed was to feel more light-headed.

"None," Congressman Elliott retorted. "But that's exactly why this bill is so important. By prohibiting discrimination in places open to the public, this bill is the great equalizer that will break down the final barriers that neither the war, the abolishment of slavery, nor the Reconstruction Amendments could: a reversal of the presumption of the inferiority of Negroes. This bill will make clear once and for all that Negroes are full citizens with rights equal to any."

"I just hope you're ready," Congressman Butler warned. "Mark my words, Robert, they are going to do everything they can to sink this bill."

"I was born ready," Congressman Elliott said, draining the last sip of his whiskey. "I'm just glad I have the chance to prove it."

Congressman Butler patted him on the back as they left their glasses behind and departed for the House floor. Still groggy, Malcolm set his glass down as well on a nearby table and followed them out the door. He was glad the bill Sumner and Langston drafted all those years ago was finally getting some traction, but it was hard to be hopeful about it when he knew Black people were still struggling with these issues more than a century later. Why would Cedric bring him back here just to watch these men try and fail? *And how is this going to help me save the farm?*

Once again, the galleries were full. It was even more packed than the last time he was here, with the press and the public, Black and White, gathered to soak in every word of the debate. It was as if their lives depended on the outcome, and for many, it did. Malcolm squeezed through a row and found a seat next to his buddy Nathaniel.

He watched aghast as some of the congressmen recycled their now-familiar racist rants—with the greatest of all coming from Georgia congressman Alexander Stephens. After entering the Chamber, he spewed racist bile in a loud, monotone voice for nearly an hour while banging on his wheelchair.

"Isn't that the former vice president of the Confederacy?" Nathaniel whispered to Malcolm. "I can't believe he has the nerve to appear on this House floor and tell these lies after betraying his country like he did!"

"Nothing angers these men more than having to share seats in Congress with Black people. I'm sure he'd love to put an end to that," Malcolm retorted.

Finally, it was Congressman Elliott's turn, and he dissected each of Congressman Stephens's arguments point by point, ripping them to shreds. He began his attack by laying waste to Stephens's claim that the bill was unconstitutional, when, in fact, the Supreme Court had recently encouraged Congress to pass legislation under the Fourteenth Amendment, if necessary, to protect Black people's civil rights.

Then he went on to decimate the old Georgian's character by reminding the public that, "It is scarcely twelve years since that gentleman shocked the civilized world by announcing the birth of a separate government, which rested on human slavery as its cornerstone. The progress of events since then has swept away that pseudo-government, which rested on greed, pride, and tyranny. And today, the race whom he then ruthlessly spurned and trampled on are here to meet him in debate. They demand that the rights which are enjoyed by their former oppressors—who vainly sought to overthrow a government which refused to prostitute itself to the base uses of slavery—be accorded to those who, even in slavery's darkness, kept their allegiance true to freedom and the Union."

Applause filled the chambers and overshadowed the isolated boos and hisses. Unabated, Congressman Elliott continued, pounding on the podium for emphasis. "The gentleman from Georgia has learned much since 1861, but he is still a laggard. Let him put away entirely the false and fatal theories, which have so greatly marred an otherwise enviable record. Let him accept, in its fullness and goodness, the great doctrine that American citizenship carries with it every civil and political right manhood can confer.

"Let him lend his influence, with all his masterly ability, to complete the proud structure of legislation which makes this nation worthy of the great declaration which heralded its birth. And by doing so, he will most nearly redeem his reputation in the eyes of the world, and best vindicate the wisdom of that policy which has permitted him to regain his seat on this floor."

The room fell silent. Mouths hung agape. Malcolm wondered whether there had ever been a time before or since when a member of Congress so thoroughly excoriated another on the House floor. Visually, the contrast between Congressmen Stephens and Elliott couldn't have been starker. Congressman Stephens was old and weak, pale and frail, and filled to the brim with hatred for Black people. Congressman Elliott, on the other hand, was tall, strong, full of vitality, and didn't look like he had a drop of European blood flowing through his veins, which probably made the rebuke sting all the more.

"If Negroes are so inferior, why is Congressman Stephens getting his butt kicked by one now," Nathaniel asked as he and Malcolm fell out laughing.

But Congressman Elliott still wasn't finished and continued to press the case for the urgency of the bill. "Mr. Speaker, the results of the war, as seen in Reconstruction, have settled forever the political status of my race. The passage of this bill will determine the civil status, not only of the Negro, but of any other class of citizens who may feel themselves discriminated against. It will form the capstone of liberty, begun on this continent under discouraging circumstances and carried on in spite of the sneers of monarchists and the cavils of pretended friends of freedom, until at last it stands in all its beautiful symmetry and proportions, a building as grand as the world has ever seen, realizing the most sanguine expectations and the highest hopes of those who, in the name of equal, impartial, and universal liberty, laid the foundation stones."

Congressman Elliott paused for effect and took a deep breath, wiping the sweat from his brow. In a low growl, he concluded, "The rights contended for in this bill are among the sacred rights of mankind, which are not to be rummaged for among old parchments or musty records, because they are written as with a sunbeam in the whole volume of human nature, by the hand of the Divinity itself, and can never be erased or obscured by mortal power."

Malcolm's heart swelled with immense pride. Congressman Elliott had done it. His words painted a vivid picture of the inherent tension in the American experiment—founded with the cries of liberty and justice for all on the backs of the enslaved—all while showing the path forward. Malcolm understood that what Black people wanted in the 1870s as they emerged from slavery was the same thing Black people wanted in his day. They wanted to be treated fairly and with dignity. They wanted to live with safety and security. They wanted access to opportunities so they could achieve their dreams and reach their potential. They wanted to be treated as fully and undeniably human. Was that so much to ask?

Malcolm rose to his feet, letting out a slow, dignified clap. Nearly every person in the House Chamber followed suit until the clapping crescendoed into a roar. Some wiped tears from their eyes. Others looked on in stunned disbelief, having never seen a Black person so eloquently represent their cause and at the same time rout a White man as venerable as the former vice president of the Confederacy. Malcolm almost felt sorry for Congressman Stephens, almost, but not quite. He had that and plenty more coming to him for all the evils he had inflicted on the world.

But not everyone enjoyed Congressman Elliott's performance. Malcolm watched amused as several of the former Confederate congressmen stared sheepishly at their shoes and hurriedly pushed their way out of the Capitol through the crowds of jubilant people that had lined up to shake Congressman Elliott's hand. Based on their reaction, it was safe to assume that they too knew who had won the debate.

That evening was one of pure revelry at Congressman Elliott's house with friends from all over gathered to drink and celebrate, as an impromptu brass band played outside in the streets. The crowd was effusive in its praise of both the genius of the congressman's remarks and the eloquence of his delivery. Malcolm looked at the community that surrounded him with pride, grateful that he'd returned to the past in time to witness that speech. He finally understood what Cedric

had meant when he said Malcolm hadn't "seen us at our best yet." Now he had.

Malcolm felt himself being pulled back to his time. Before he knew it, he was lying in a small pasture with Jasmine leaning over him.

"I'm so sorry!" Jasmine apologized. "I thought I had a solid grip on your hand and then you just tumbled down. Are you okay?" she asked.

"Ahhhh," Malcolm said as he sat up, made a couple of neck circles, and stretched his arms above his head. "I'm fine. I just can't believe I didn't fall until I was getting *off* the horse."

Jasmine laughed and helped him up. "All right, it's getting late. Let me get you back home."

43

When Malcolm made it downstairs the next morning, Uncle Corey was finishing up his breakfast sporting a suit and a cleaned-up fade. A huge stack of blueberry muffins was sitting in the middle of the table.

"Hey, looking sharp, Uncle! Where you headed?" Malcolm asked as he entered the kitchen, grabbing a muffin.

"Thanks! I got a job interview to be an office assistant at a small construction company. It'd be a good look. They got benefits, and with some training, maybe I could work my way up. Start meeting with clients," he said excitedly, chewing quickly and stuffing another big bite of muffin in his mouth. "Aunt Carol left these for us. She had some errands to run this morning but she said she'll be back soon to pick me up so I can get there a few minutes early," Uncle Corey said, making sure not to get crumbs on his shirt.

This was the first time Malcolm had seen a spark in Uncle Corey's eyes since they picked him up from prison.

"That sounds great! With your personality, you'd kill at that!" Malcolm encouraged him as he sat down next to his uncle.

"Thanks man! I'll let you know how it goes. Where you headed?" Uncle Corey asked, eyeing Malcolm's old, baggy jeans and Tupac concert T-shirt.

"I'm gonna help Uncle Leroy for a little bit outside and then Jasmine and I are gonna check out an arcade in town," Malcolm said, peeling the cupcake liner off his muffin.

"Word? Y'all going to Comets? That place is still around?" Uncle

Corey asked, laughing. He pushed his empty plate away and dabbed the corners of his mouth.

"You know it?" Malcolm said with a mouth full of food. He was in a rush too. Uncle Leroy would be done with morning chores in no time.

"Yeah man. I ain't been there in a minute, but your dad and I used to pass some long afternoons in that spot. Looks like you've been spending a lot of time with Miss Jasmine," Uncle Corey observed slyly.

"Yeah, she's real cool," Malcolm responded, trying his best to keep from grinning ear to ear and refusing to say any more on the matter.

"Uh-huh. Y'all kids have fun," Uncle Corey said as he stood up to head back to his room and finish getting ready.

Malcolm finally broke into a grin as he got up from the table. "Thanks, and good luck, Unc!" he called out, licking the rest of the blueberry juices off his fingertips and then heading outside.

At first Malcolm couldn't figure out where Uncle Leroy was on the farm. He checked all the usual places, but all he found were half smoked cigarettes here and there. Right when Malcolm was about to give up and go back inside, he heard someone whistling from behind the barn. *Wasn't I just over there?* he wondered, before spotting Uncle Leroy coming from the woods with a bundle of firewood tucked under one arm and an ax in the other. He looked surprised when he saw Malcolm walking toward him.

"Carol send you out here?" he asked skeptically. Malcolm had been helping him with things around the farm for weeks now, but Uncle Leroy still seemed surprised he was willing.

"Naw, I just wanted to see if you needed some help."

"Okay, yeah. Could you grab that hose over there and fill up the trough? Not the one with feed, but the one next to it." Uncle Leroy pointed to a long green hose curled up in a knotted mess on the ground near the corner of the barn.

"Sure," Malcolm said agreeably, wondering why there were no simple chores on the farm. He walked over to the heavy hose and detangled it before filling the empty trough with water. After finishing that task, he came back to ask what he could do next.

Uncle Leroy looked at his great-nephew with skepticism after he accomplished the task faster than expected, but Malcolm brushed off the look. After all the years of wear and tear, he was sure Uncle Leroy was feeling his age through his joints and muscles and could use some help. Still eyeing Malcolm suspiciously, Uncle Leroy began rolling another cigarette.

"For starters, you can tell me what you're up to lately. I know you ain't too keen on country life. You don't like the bugs, it's too hot, too dirty for you. So what you got up your sleeve?" Through squinted eyes, he sized Malcolm up again and then smirked. "Need some extra cash for that lady friend you been courtin'?" Uncle Leroy waggled his eyebrows up and down.

Malcolm chortled and shrugged his shoulders. "Honestly, nothing's up. Sometimes it's good to get some fresh air. Even though I don't exactly love farm life, it does feel awfully free out here." He filled his lungs with the crisp outside air and took a moment to feel the cool breeze.

"Yeah," Uncle Leroy agreed, smiling. "The hogs don't boss you, the horses mind they business, and the chickens keep from speaking they mind. My kind of company!" He laughed, lighting his freshly rolled cigarette. "Might be the freest place in Mississippi."

"So what can I do next?" Malcolm asked, eager to finish the remaining chores.

"You can grab some hay from the shed and move it over to the barn for the horses. I 'preciate your help," he said in between puffs, tipping his cowboy hat in Malcolm's direction.

● ● ●

After helping Uncle Leroy out in the heat of the morning, Malcolm found himself happily inside a cool, air-conditioned, dark room filled with neon-colored video games. Before he and Jasmine even had a chance to trade his money for tokens, a small White boy with strawberry-blond hair ran toward them and threw himself into Jasmine's arms. She looked down surprised to see Jeremy from the Boys & Girls Club.

"Jeremy, what are you doing here?" she exclaimed happily.

"My brother brought me," he said, pointing at Jason across the room who waved at them for a second before quickly stuffing his hands into his pockets.

"Come on!" Jeremy said, taking Jasmine's hand and leading them across the room. As they approached Jason, Malcolm felt his jaw tighten and his body tense up all over again.

"Hey," Jason greeted them when they reached him.

Malcolm nodded back, maintaining as much distance as he could. If he was being honest with himself, Malcolm knew there wasn't much holding him back from getting even with Jason. However, with Jasmine and Jeremy around, he continued to keep his cool.

"So you remembered to check out the arcade?" Jason asked, trying to make things less awkward.

"Yeah, my uncle told me about this place," Malcolm lied, not wanting to give Jason any credit for mentioning it earlier.

"Cool. It's got some nice retro games in here: a couple pinball machines, *PAC-MAN*, *Space Invaders*, but it also has a sick new virtual reality game." Jason pointed to the different games in the arcade as he listed them out.

"Pinball is my favorite," Jeremy volunteered.

"Which new VR game y'all got?" Malcolm asked, finally interested in something Jason was saying.

Jason brightened, looking hopeful he had found a way to make peace with Malcolm. "Man, you ever played *Valkyrie*? It's sick. I got some tokens left, if you want to check it out." Jason held out his hand to show Malcolm his extra tokens, waiting to see if he would accept the olive branch.

Malcolm shrugged nonchalantly and followed Jason over to the game.

"I'll play some pinball with you, Jeremy," Jasmine offered.

Malcolm sat down next to Jason in a pretend cockpit and they put on virtual reality headsets. Instantly, Malcolm was transported to a high-tech ship in outer space with Jason as his copilot. The ship tilted and wound its way through space around asteroids and meteors. Then the cockpit began shaking violently as they were hit once, then twice with enemy fire.

"We gotta hit back," Jason resolved as he turned the ship around to face their attackers.

Together, they bombarded their enemy with fire and fury while explosions detonated all around them.

"Watch out on your right!" Malcolm shouted when he saw an enemy vessel approaching from the side. Jason turned his artillery and fired. Soon they were able to carve out an escape route and return to their mission.

"We gotta hit the target at the end of that long trench on that ship," Jason explained.

"Like *Star Wars?*"

"Yep. Just like *Star Wars.*"

"Let's do it."

They huddled down and began planning their approach.

"If we come in from this side, we might be able to avoid detection from those fighter ships," Malcolm suggested.

"All right, you navigate. I'll hold off enemy fire."

Malcolm began easing the ship into view of the target, and as expected, a slew of attacker ships began to swarm. Jason immediately began firing back, swinging his firearm from left to right, taking out ship after ship.

"We're almost there!" Malcolm shouted. Just then, he felt another jolt. "Everything okay?" he checked.

"We've been hit, it's fine. Just stay focused on getting the target. I got your back," Jason confirmed.

The ship started rattling, as if it were on its last leg, just as Malcolm closed in on the target and released the missile.

"That's right, Damian!" Malcolm shouted before quickly correcting himself. "I mean Jason. Good defense." He couldn't believe he'd accidentally called Jason his best friend's name, but somehow being on the same team made his walls come down, just a little.

"My pops always said the best defense is a good offense," Jason said, extending his hand as they removed their helmets. Malcolm hesitated for a second, but then decided to bury the hatchet and shake his hand.

As they walked back to where Jasmine and Jeremy were sitting,

Malcolm noticed Jeremy was looking at several charcoal drawings, his drawings.

"Where'd you get those?" Malcolm asked angrily.

"Calm down, Mal. They fell out of your jacket pocket when you headed over to play the VR game. Jeremy was just admiring your work," Jasmine explained.

"What is this?" Jeremy asked, pointing to a building that was on fire with a sea of Black people running away and screaming in horror. Other Black people lay on the ground dead with White people standing over them grinning, pistols in hand.

"Yo, you drew this horror show? Why?" Jason asked, pissed off as he looked at the drawing Jeremy was holding. "Jeremy, you don't need to see this," he said, picking up the papers still on the floor. He quickly flipped through the images before handing them all back to Malcolm. "Is this what you fantasize about? White people hunting Black people? Are you crazy or something?"

Malcolm took in a long deep breath with his eyes closed and exhaled before responding.

"I'm not crazy. I'm just drawing historical events—things that really happened. Just because nobody remembers it or ever talks about it, doesn't mean we should forget the thousands of Black people who were murdered by White people all over the South after the Civil War. This is a picture of a massacre that took place in Colfax, Louisiana, a couple hours from here, in 1873."

"You say it happened," Jason interjected defensively, eyeing him warily. "Even if it did, that was like hundreds of years ago. Why are you dwelling on it now and drawing about it? That's weird, dude."

Malcolm wasn't sure if Jason was more upset about the drawings or that his little brother had seen them. He decided to give Jason the benefit of the doubt. He took a deep breath to gain his composure and began explaining. "Because it was a part of a campaign of terror that White supremacists used to crush the spirit of Black people. And it's not like the work of White supremacists is over and done. Sometimes it's obvious, like beating up a Black kid at a fair or shooting up a Black church, but other times it's subtle, like giving a Black man a harsher prison sentence, or a cop shooting a Black person first and asking questions later, or taking the land of a Black family because you can. I drew this picture to remind myself what White supremacy looks like so I recognize it when it shows up in my life."

Jason stood there dumbfounded for a minute. Malcolm couldn't tell what he was thinking. Maybe he felt like Malcolm was accusing him of everything everyone had done in the past, or maybe he was just tired of the conversation, or maybe he just didn't believe him. No matter, Malcolm didn't care. Finally, Jason recovered and grabbed Jeremy's hand. "Give him his picture back. It's time to go," he snapped before storming out of the arcade.

44

Malcolm couldn't shake the afternoon. That night, he paced around the attic pissed about his argument with Jason. "White people don't even see what's right in front of their faces because they don't have to. They just walk around thinking things are the way they are and never questioning why," Malcolm muttered to himself.

"Don't blame Jason. It's not all his fault," Cedric said, suddenly appearing alongside Malcolm.

"Are you defending him?" Malcolm asked, shocked by Cedric's opinion, but not by his presence. "He saw a fragment of the Black experience and freaked out and called me either a liar or a lunatic!"

"Yes, well, that's not the version of history he's been taught. All around him are monuments to White men's unquestionable greatness. Everything he's learned in school has reinforced that narrative. You can't expect people to shift their worldview overnight."

"Why not, if their worldview is wrong?"

"Well, if folks are taught that the reason their lives are better than other people's—like Black people's—is because they're smarter or worked harder or are morally superior, then what happens when they learn the truth? How will they see themselves when they realize that the only reason they are 'winning' is because the game was permanently rigged in their favor?" Cedric queried, watching Malcolm pace around the room.

"So is it hopeless? Are we too far in the hole to ever get out?"

"Achieving a just society will be hard, but it's not hopeless, especially if we're working with allies who want to help make things right. Know any potential allies?"

"No," Malcolm said stubbornly.

Cedric let out a long sigh. Malcolm realized that Cedric was about to send him off again, so he surrendered into the yellow beanbag chair and closed his eyes before the room and everything in it disappeared.

• • •

Malcolm was momentarily blinded by the light reflecting off the gold adorning every inch of a room's walls. Immediately, he knew where he was: the President's Room in the US Capitol. He came to just in time, because right then President Grant entered the room and everyone jumped to their feet.

Every eye in the room watched as President Grant sat behind the green oval desk and picked up a pen. Without much fanfare, he signed the bill and held it up for all to see. Malcolm was close enough to read: *The Civil Rights Act of 1875.*

1875? Wow, Malcolm thought. That meant it had been over a year since his last trip to the past, when he saw Congressman Elliott mop the floor with Congressman Stephens in a debate. He couldn't believe the bill was finally getting signed into law or that it had taken so long. Malcolm looked around for Senator Sumner or Congressman Elliott and was surprised he didn't see them. He couldn't imagine either of them missing an event like this.

After the signing ceremony, he knew exactly where everyone was heading to celebrate: the Wormley. As their large, jubilant group took over the restaurant, Malcolm looked around to see who was there: Congressmen Rainey, Cain, and Butler, as well as Nathaniel and John Mercer Langston. Even Robert Smalls was there, which was surprising since the last time he'd seen him, he was a South Carolina state senator. Several other people that he didn't recognize were also hanging out around their table.

John Mercer Langston lifted his glass high and tapped it gently to make a toast. With tears glistening in the corners of his eyes, he said,

"I would like to toast our great friend, the relentless, intractable, stubborn as all hell, visionary the world knew as Senator Charles Sumner. He was the truest of patriots, who took this country's monumental values at their word and would not rest until all who lived on this country's soil could enjoy its bounty. We love you, we cherish you, and we miss you. Moreover, we would not be here today without you, so we thank you."

"Hear! Hear! Hear! Hear!" the chorus resounded. "To Charles."

"Oh no," Malcolm whispered, realizing Senator Sumner must have died. He fervently hoped that wasn't the reason for Congressman Elliott's absence. A tear came to Malcolm's eye as he fondly remembered one of his earliest trips to the past, when he'd helped Senator Sumner and John Mercer Langston review an early version of the Civil Rights Act that they were drafting. Their hope and optimism that America could be transformed into a safe place for Black people to call home was contagious. "You did it, Senator Sumner," Malcolm whispered, saddened that he hadn't lived to see this moment.

"And we can't forget the valiant efforts of Congressman Benjamin Butler, who relentlessly shepherded this bill through the House over these many, many years. You're one of a kind. Thank you!" Mr. Langston continued, raising his glass high again.

Congressman Butler's face turned beet red at the attention, and he quickly downed his double shot of whiskey before speaking. "I'd just like to say, nearly five years after the late, great Senator Charles Sumner first introduced this monumental Civil Rights Act in Congress, I am happy to see it finally get signed into law. Today, with the stroke of President Grant's pen, Negroes will no longer wear the badge of inferiority that has cursed them since they arrived on these shores."

"It's about time this bill was passed," another White man cried out. "You know how many times I've been told since the end of the war that by doing justice to the Negro we shall pull down the pillars of our political temple and bury ourselves in the ruins? When we were abolishing slavery by adopting the Thirteenth Amendment, we were warned that we were bringing measureless calamity upon the Republic. Did it come? When the Fourteenth Amendment was passed, the same wail of the fearfulness and unbelieving was heard. Again, when it was proposed to elevate the Negro to citizenship, to give him the ballot as his weapon of self-defense, we were told the cup of our destruction was filled to its brim." The man laughed out loud at the absurdity. "Well, thankfully, I have lived long enough to learn that in the long run it is safest for a nation, a political party, or an individual man to dare to do right, and let consequences take care of themselves, for he that loseth his life for the truth's sake, shall find it."

Applause rang out as folks lifted their glasses in a toast.

Allies, thought Malcolm. *Cedric wants me to see allies.*

"Good ole Congressman Garfield," Nathaniel said as he turned to Malcolm smiling. Malcolm vaguely remembered the name President Garfield from history class, like the cartoon cat, and wondered if this was the same guy.

"Can you believe President Grant signed this bill with just one day left in the Congressional session?" Nathaniel asked in disbelief.

"No," Malcolm said, shaking his head and unsure what else to say.

"I mean, the bill ain't perfect, don't get me wrong. It's been watered down a lot since Senator Sumner first introduced it, but with the House turning over to the Democrats tomorrow, this was our last chance to get something through. We had to sacrifice the prohibition against segregation in schools, but at least it still makes it illegal to discriminate in jury service and places open to the public. That's something. Better than nothing."

"I couldn't bring myself to vote for it," Congressman Walls conceded, overhearing their conversation. "If I still gotta send my kids to an inferior school, what difference does it make if I can go see a play and sit next to a White person?"

"It's better than nothing," Nathaniel repeated, shrugging.

Congressman Rainey cleared his throat to commandeer the room's attention. "As the most senior member of this delegation, I want to welcome the newest Negroes who will be sworn into Congress tomorrow. I'll start with Jeremiah Haralson, who is joining us from Alabama and most recently served as a representative in both the Alabama State House and Senate. Welcome!" Congressman Rainey said, holding up his glass in salute.

"Next we have John Hyman, our very first Negro representative from North Carolina. I'm so glad the lesser Carolina finally came to its senses and sent a suitable representative of the people," he said, lightly teasing. "Congressman Hyman is also joining us from his State Senate.

"I'd also like to welcome Charles Nash, the first Negro representative from the great state of Louisiana. To be clear, he's not the first Negro to be elected because John Willis Menard and P.B.S. Pinchback also won seats in Congress to represent Louisiana, but you will be the first to actually be seated, which is a feat within itself. Hats off to you!" he said as applause broke out. "It's been two years, and we're still holding out hope that the Senate will do the right thing and accept Pinchback's credentials. Only time will tell," he said, shaking his head in annoyance.

Smiling again, Congressman Rainey jumped back into his hype-man speech. "Next, my buddy who needs no introduction at all, Robert Smalls. 'Bout time you made it here, Robert! I'm sure the South Carolina Senate is very happy to be rid of you!" Congressman Smalls got the biggest applause of all, along with some hoots and whistles.

"And last, but certainly not least"—Congressman Rainey paused as he looked on with pride—"finally, after four long years, we have another Negro joining the Senate. Everybody, please put your hands together to welcome Senator Blanche Bruce from Mississippi!" With that introduction, everyone in the Wormley rose to their feet and gave a deafening applause that lasted no less than five minutes.

Malcolm decided to get up and make his rounds, saying hello to the people he knew. He walked over to Congressman Smalls first.

"Congressman Smalls, it's great to see you again! Congratulations on your election!" Malcolm said, extending his hand.

"Cedric, great to see you too! Can you believe your old boss is running things in South Carolina as Speaker of the House! Ha! I said, 'Shoot for the moon, Robert!' He took me up on it! I'm so proud of him."

Malcolm let out a sigh of relief upon hearing that Congressman Elliott was alive, well, and doing great by the sounds of it.

"Yeah, me too! It's unbelievable!" Malcolm said, playing along.

"Have you found another job yet?" Congressman Smalls inquired.

Malcolm didn't know how to answer the question, but seeing how all these new members had only recently arrived in town for their swearing in, he figured it was unlikely Cedric had already lined something up. He managed to squeak out an equivocal, "No."

"Well, what are you waiting for. You worked for Senator Revels, didn't you? That means you're about the only Negro in Washington who has any Senate experience. Follow me," he said, leading Malcolm over to Senator Bruce, a heavyset man with a commanding presence and curly black hair.

"Senator Bruce," Congressman Smalls said, tapping him lightly on the shoulder.

"Congressman Smalls! Pleasure to make your acquaintance! You know you're a legend where I come from."

Congressman Smalls chuckled, seemingly used to that reaction. "It's a pleasure to meet you too. Congratulations on your appointment to the Senate. It's been far too long since we've had someone who speaks for us in that Chamber, which is what brings me over to you. I'd like to introduce you to Cedric Johnson. He was Senator Revels's aide and most recently worked for my good friend Congressman Elliott."

"You don't say?" Senator Bruce said, turning to Malcolm and looking him up and down. "Very impressive. Obviously, both of those jobs are in the past tense. Who do you work for now?" he asked, his interest noticeably piqued.

"I am actually in between jobs at the moment," Malcolm improvised. "Congressman Elliott is currently serving as South Carolina's Speaker of the House, and I stayed in Washington to help different congressmen out on an as-needed basis."

"You appear far too talented of a fellow for that. Would you care to join my staff? If you're good enough for Hiram, you're good enough for me."

"Thank you, sir. I'd be happy to. I promise you won't regret this decision," Malcolm said as professionally as possible. He was excited for the chance to work in the Senate again. It definitely felt like the right move for Cedric, since it would give him more opportunities to visit Mississippi and Isabel.

"I'm sure I won't. Life is too short for regrets. See you bright and early Monday morning," he said, smiling.

That evening, as Malcolm ate the dinner brought up by Cedric's landlady, he thought about how long it took for the Civil Rights Act to finally pass—five years was a long time. All the people who had worked to push it over the finish line faced countless setbacks, but through persistence, Black and White people had worked together to win a huge victory.

"Okay, Cedric, I've seen your allies. Maybe it's time I find my own Sumner or Butler—or even a James Beckwith."

45

"It's good to have allies," Malcolm overheard Cedric say as Aunt Carol's attic came back into focus from his spot on the yellow beanbag chair.

Malcolm rubbed his eyes. Cedric was sitting in the wooden chair with his feet kicked up on the old oak desk.

"Hi Cedric," Malcolm said, smiling, actually glad to see him again. "Yeah, you had some good ones too. But I still feel like I'm missing something." Malcolm stood up to stretch his arms and legs.

"What's that?" Cedric asked, swinging his feet to the floor.

"Well, it just seems like things were finally starting to go well for us. More and more Black people were joining Congress, the laws were holding Klansmen accountable, the Civil Rights Act finally passed. I just feel like we should be further along today if all those things happened 150 years ago." Malcolm walked over and sat on the edge of the desk so he could look Cedric directly in the eye, but Cedric's gaze hit the floor.

"It was like domino pieces falling one into another, until the whole chain collapsed." Cedric's eyes brimmed with tears.

"Show me what happened," Malcolm entreated. It was the first time Malcolm had actually wanted Cedric to whisk him off somewhere, even if what he was about to see might be terrible. He walked over to the beanbag chair, leaned his head back, and closed his eyes.

● ● ●

The next second Malcolm found himself walking out the door of Cedric's apartment into the morning light. He shook the disorientation from his head and tried to focus on where Cedric must have been going. He snagged a newspaper from the regular paperboy on the corner and checked the date: March 8, 1876. That was almost exactly a full year after his last visit. *Maybe Cedric is on his way to meet with Senator Bruce, if he still works there?* Malcolm wondered. He decided to take a chance and headed to the Capitol.

When Malcolm arrived at the Capitol, he went first to the Senate floor. Luckily, he found Senator Bruce huddling at a table and sharing a glass of whiskey with another familiar character, P.B.S. Pinchback, only this time his normal smirk was missing and in its place was a scowl. Malcolm pulled up a chair next to them, but the men barely glanced up to acknowledge him.

"How could they refuse to seat me? I jumped through all their hoops. I had valid papers from the recognized governor of the State of Louisiana. I met with everyone who asked to meet with me. Even the Senate Committee on Privileges and Elections approved my appointment, for God's sake! What right do they have to reject me?" Governor Pinchback fumed, throwing back a shot of whiskey. "I should've seen it coming. They did me just like they did Menard, all those years ago. You know in all this time, there has only been one Negro representative from Louisiana, and the state is more than half Negro!"

"It is unconscionable," Senator Bruce replied. "You know I did everything I could to get them to do the right thing. I even threatened to give up my own seat if the Senate failed to treat you fairly. I told my Republican colleagues that they were a bunch of hypocrites for thinking Negroes were good enough to elect White men to office but not good enough to hold office with them. I guess they decided one Negro in the Senate was enough. They released the shackles of slavery only to step on our necks," Senator Bruce retorted in disgust.

Malcolm was also surprised that the Senate had never seated Pinchback, but then he remembered their adventure at the Georgetown saloon. Trying to lighten the mood, he cracked a joke, "Maybe they were just tired of you taking their money at the poker table." Upon seeing the glares that Senator Bruce and Governor Pinchback shot in his direction, he immediately regretted what he'd said and quickly changed the subject "What's next for you, Governor? I don't doubt you already have a plan?" He cleared his throat, hoping he had made up for his gaffe.

"All the time I spent up here . . . and for what? I guess I should be grateful they decided to give me the full salary I would have earned as a Senator. Some consolation. Now I gotta uproot my family again."

"But truth be told," Pinchback continued, getting up from his seat and collecting his hat and coat, "the missus has been ready to trade this northern swamp for the ones she knows and loves in Louisiana for a while now. So don't you worry about me, kid. I'm the liveliest corpse in the old dead South." Pinchback drained the last sip of whiskey from his glass. He then tipped his hat at Malcolm and Senator Bruce, and exited the floor with his characteristic saunter.

"I need to get some fresh air," Senator Bruce remarked, standing up abruptly to leave.

"Absolutely, sir," Malcolm said.

Malcolm felt bad for Governor Pinchback—and for Senator Bruce now that he was forced to remain the lone voice for Black Americans in the Senate. Malcolm couldn't quite put his finger on it, but he felt a shift in the state of things. The air in the halls of the Capitol felt different— heavier, stiffer, bleaker—and he didn't like it. This must be what Cedric had meant when he said he knew when things were changing.

● ● ●

For the next two and a half weeks, Malcolm thought he'd be whisked back to the farm at any minute, but that minute never came. Each day Malcolm reported to the Capitol and did whatever Senator Bruce needed. Nothing big was really happening, and Malcolm began to wonder why Cedric was keeping him there. Thankfully, his answer finally came. The headline on the front page of the morning paper dated March 27, 1876, read:

U.S. SUPREME COURT TO RENDER DECISION TODAY

IN *U.S. v. CRUIKSHANK*, AN APPEAL FROM MEN CONVICTED OF CONSPIRACY
TO DENY THE CONSTITUTIONAL RIGHTS OF NEGROES IN COLFAX, LOUISIANA

The horrors he'd seen in Colfax instantly flooded his mind, alongside his immense pride at being able to find witnesses to bring the murderers to justice. He couldn't imagine the sentence ever being repealed. He made a beeline straight to the Supreme Court Chamber in the US Capitol, hoping he hadn't missed any part of the deliberations. By the time he arrived, several Black congressmen and their aides were already seated in chairs on the periphery of the room, but all were too tense to exchange their normal pleasantries. The Supreme Court met in the Old Senate Chamber, a semicircle-shaped room decorated in crimson and gold with a domed ceiling from which a brass chandelier hung. Crimson carpet with gold stars covered the floor, crimson drapes hung on each side of the justices' seating area at the front of the room below a golden eagle and shield, and crimson valences hung from the ceiling along the walls. Malcolm tried not to be overwhelmed by the gaudiness as he looked for an empty seat in the back of the room.

Reminiscent of the attitudes at the Amzi Rainey trial in South Carolina, the men convicted of killing hundreds of innocent people in Colfax, Louisiana, sat confidently at the front of the courtroom cracking jokes with their lawyers. But unlike in South Carolina, Malcolm knew there were no Black justices on the Supreme Court to make sure these men were held accountable.

Finally, Senator Bruce entered the room and made his way down the aisle toward the seating section reserved for senators. "Good morning, Senator Bruce," Malcolm called out as the senator passed him, but he was in a zone and only half-nodded in response.

Nathaniel grabbed the seat next to Malcolm and whispered wistfully, "It's too bad John Rock isn't here to argue the case."

Malcolm remembered Sojourner Truth mentioning this person during her meeting with Senator Revels, but he still didn't know who John Rock was.

"Who is that?" Malcolm asked.

"You don't know about John Rock? Man, he was special. He was the first Negro allowed to argue before the Supreme Court," Nathaniel whispered, leaning closer to Malcolm. "After the Supreme Court issued its shameful *Dred Scott* decision, with the bastard Chief Justice Taney proclaiming that Negroes 'had no rights which White men were bound to respect,' John Rock became a lawyer to prove him wrong. Senator Sumner moved for his admission to the bar of the Supreme Court the day after Lincoln signed the Thirteenth Amendment abolishing slavery. Rock was a genius. He wasn't just a lawyer. He was a doctor, a dentist, and a teacher."

"Why isn't he here now? We could sure use him," Malcolm asked, flabbergasted.

"He died before his time, ten years ago, but isn't it amazing what Negroes can achieve when their potential is unleashed?"

Malcolm managed a weak smile and added John Rock to the long list of people he should have learned about in school. "Maybe one day a Black person will even sit on the Supreme Court," Malcolm said, wanting to offer a word of hope, but instead Nathaniel looked at him like he'd sprouted a second head.

"Hear ye. Hear ye. All rise. The court is now in session," the bailiff announced. Nine robed White men entered the room, immediately silencing all noise. Everyone rose to their feet while the justices took their seats.

Chief Justice Morrison Waite began reading the court's opinion. He started with some garble about how one's rights as a citizen of the United States were distinct from the rights that came from being a citizen of a state, and the United States only had the power to protect the rights that existed as a result of being a United States citizen. Then he said that all the rights listed in the Bill of Rights—the right to peaceful assembly, freedom of speech, the right to bear arms, et cetera—were not actually rights that came as a result of being a United States citizen, so the federal government had no business protecting them.

Malcolm felt his heart drop.

"The very highest duty of the states, when they entered into the Union under the Constitution, was to protect all persons within their boundaries in the enjoyment of these unalienable rights with which they were endowed by their Creator. Sovereignty, for this purpose, rests alone with the states. It is no more the duty or within the power of the United States to punish for a conspiracy to falsely imprison or murder within a state, than it would be to punish for false imprisonment or murder itself."

"But that's the problem," Malcolm whispered to Nathaniel. "The states weren't doing their job. Until the KKK Acts were passed, Black people's lives were left entirely in the hands of their oppressors."

Then, Chief Justice Waite went a step further and added, "The Fourteenth Amendment prohibits a state from denying to any person within its jurisdiction the equal protection of the laws; but this provision does not add anything to the rights which one citizen has under the Constitution against another."

Malcolm couldn't believe what he was hearing. In the midst of all this legalese justifying the murderers' release, Justice Waite didn't even mention the nearly two hundred innocent Black people who were murdered in Colfax. It was like their lives didn't even matter. One by one, Malcolm stared into the face of each justice on the bench, searching for empathy or at least a recognition of Black people's humanity, but only stone-cold stares were reflected back.

Smiles broke out on the faces of the convicted killers as they realized they had won their appeal. Malcolm thought back to how hard it had been to get the KKK Acts passed through Congress and how difficult it had been to find witnesses willing to testify at trial. He felt sick. The Supreme Court had undone all that effort with a flick of a pen.

It suddenly sank in that no one would ever be punished for what had happened in Colfax, Louisiana, just like no one was ever punished for the Mechanics' Institute massacre where Cedric's father died, or for Malcolm's own father's murder for that matter. Malcolm was too disgusted to keep listening and stood up and walked out of the courtroom in the middle of Justice Waite's recitation. He walked past Congressman Butler, whose beet-red face was pulsing with anger, the jugular vein in his neck looking like it was about to pop. Malcolm was starting to understand what Cedric needed him to see.

46

Malcolm hardly wanted to get out of bed the next morning. He pulled Cedric's blanket up over his head and sighed. After hearing the Supreme Court's decision overturning the convictions in the Colfax massacre case, any motivation to do anything had left him. Plus, not waking up at Aunt Carol's meant there must be more Cedric wanted him to see before he could go home and he didn't expect it to be good. But what he was seeing had already happened. There was nothing he could do about it, so Malcolm got dressed and dragged himself back to the Capitol.

Malcolm decided to make his first stop the mailroom. He picked up a stack of envelopes addressed to Senator Bruce and then went to a library where the senator regularly frequented, but he was nowhere to be found. Having nothing else to do, Malcolm sat down at a desk facing the wall full of books and began opening and reading the mail. One letter after another spoke about the dire straits the sender was in since the collapse of Freedman's Savings Bank and how the government's mismanagement of the bank had left them penniless. *Wait. What happened to the bank?*

Each story was more heartbreaking than the last: widows who deposited their husband's entire war pension in the bank were left broke with ten children to feed; small business owners who kept all their money at Freedman's Bank now had to fire all of their employees; an elderly couple who lost all of their hard-earned savings barely had enough to afford their next meal.

Malcolm didn't understand. When he'd visited Freedman's Bank, it seemed like such an impressive institution. What could have caused it to collapse in just a few short years and led to all this devastation? He remembered Senator Revels telling him that the bank had the backing of the US government, so why wouldn't the government just reimburse these people for their loss?

One of the letters in the pile was from a state legislator. Hoping it could provide him with some additional insight into what had happened, Malcolm spread the pages flat on the desk and read intently.

March 20, 1876
Dear Senator Bruce,

Let me start by saying how delighted I am that you hold this seat of utmost importance in the United States Senate. As you are the lone voice for negroes in the Senate, I and my constituents, on whose behalf I'm writing, request that you demand an investigation into the collapse of Freedman's Bank and seek reimbursement for the thousands of negroes who have lost their life savings in this calamity.

Despite assurances from Congress that our deposits in Freedman's Savings Bank were safe, protected, and secure, they were not. After five years, and at the behest of white investors, Congress changed the bank's original charter, signed by Lincoln, which provided the utmost security to depositors, to suddenly allow lending for speculative investments. This change, combined with the unscrupulous actions of the all-white board, who used the bank's funds to finance their own risky ventures, placed the financial security of this bank, and by extension, the financial future of untold negroes in jeopardy.

When we heard a few years back that Freedman's Bank was experiencing financial trouble, we took great relief in learning that no less than the esteemed Frederick Douglass had agreed to take over as the bank's president to try to get it back on track. Through no fault of his own, and despite doing everything he could to save the bank, including lending it tens of thousands of his own personal funds, the bank collapsed. Finally, Mr. Douglass realized that he "was married to a corpse," and there was nothing he could do to bring her back to life. Rendered completely insolvent, Freedman's Bank owes nearly $3 million to more than 61,000 negro depositors, which it has no means to pay.

We humbly request that you introduce a bill in Congress that authorizes the Treasury Department to disburse funds to compensate depositors for their loss. For a community that is only on the precipice of emerging from nearly three hundred years under the yoke of slavery, to have whatever we managed to scrape together in our first years of freedom be wiped out by mismanagement, greed, and criminal negligence is a tragedy beyond measure. We ask that you do whatever is in your power to ensure that our faith in the federal government has not once again been misplaced.

Most Sincerely,
Albert T. Williams

Malcolm couldn't believe what he had read. He was devastated. Out of all the calamities Black people endured, this had to be among the worst. Needing some fresh air, Malcolm decided to go for a walk, but as soon as he stood up to leave, Senator Bruce stormed in with Congressman Butler and another White man that Malcolm didn't recognize right behind him. They plopped down onto a set of couches surrounding a low table in the center of the library.

"Goddamn it, Blanche, they were coming for my head!" the stranger shouted.

Malcolm walked over to make sure everything was okay and tried to shift his attention from the tragic collapse of Freedman's Bank to whatever current travesty the men were discussing. Senator Bruce met Malcolm's eyes and motioned for him to sit down beside him.

"Gentlemen, this is my aide, Cedric Johnson. Cedric, you already know Congressman Butler, I presume. This is his son-in-law and the governor of Mississippi Adelbert Ames."

"Nice to meet you," Malcolm said.

"Could we get you gentlemen a drink of some kind?" Senator Bruce asked.

"Don't worry about me. I got what I need already," Congressman Butler said, pulling a flask from his coat pocket and calmly taking a sip.

"The Mississippi legislature just impeached our fine Negro lieutenant governor, Alexander Davis, and they came for me next," Governor Ames said heatedly. "You heard they shot a cannon at my governor's mansion? A goddamn cannon! I had no choice but to resign. Their object is to restore the Confederacy and reduce the colored people to a state of serfdom, and I was in their way."

"I told you hardly a one of them has any damn sense down there and that you needed to watch your back," Congressman Butler chimed in unhelpfully.

Governor Ames began rolling a cigarette, ignoring the comment. "Those rebels are still pissed as hell that I armed the Negro militia and told them to defend themselves. I told you what they did to Charles Caldwell? You know him, one of the Negroes in the State Senate?"

Senator Bruce nodded.

"Well, these rebels never got over the fact that Charles had been acquitted by an all-White jury of killing a White man in self-defense way back in 1868," he said, lighting his freshly rolled cigarette. "He might be the first and only Negro to ever get away with that defense, which tells you how good his case must've been. Well, they ain't never forgot it 'cause they been looking for revenge ever since. They harassed his nephew in Clinton just to get a rise out of him, and when Charles asked why they were messin' with his nephew, one of the White fellas invited him over to his store for a drink so they could talk about the 'misunderstanding.' Don't you know, soon as he sat down, someone shot him in the back!" Governor Ames suddenly jumped up in anger and began to pace the room, puffing up smoke.

Malcolm's mind began to drift. He was tired of hearing one bad thing after another and tried to think of an excuse to take that walk he was about to take a few minutes ago.

Governor Ames continued. "They brought that man there for the sole purpose of murdering him. But I heard ole Charles got the last word. I heard he told them, 'Remember, when you kill me, you kill a gentleman and a brave man. Never say you killed a coward. I want you to remember it when I am gone.' Then those bastards filled his body with bullets and drug him into the street for everybody to see. He was a goddamn state senator. I knew right then I had to get the hell out of Mississippi. Ain't hardly a decent man left."

"They've got a single-minded preoccupation with destroying the

Negro. No other way around it," Congressman Butler murmured to himself in between sips of his flask.

"I heard about that and still can't believe Charles is gone," Senator Bruce bemoaned. "Negro lives are worth less than the bullets used to kill us."

Congressman Butler let out a long sigh. "As much as it pains me to admit it"—he paused to take a long swig from his flask—"I used to believe some of those same horrible things."

Senator Bruce and Malcolm swung their heads toward Congressman Butler in shock.

"Really?" Malcolm asked, leaning forward, surprised by that revelation. "But you are such a strong supporter of Negroes' rights. What made you change?"

"My experience in the War of the Rebellion. I used to believe Negro men were but half men, unwilling to fight, defend themselves, unworthy of the dignity owed to White men, but then I had the privilege of organizing and leading a regiment of Negro soldiers and realized they were some of the bravest men I had ever known. As I passed by the remains of hundreds of my colored comrades, slain in defense of their country, who willingly laid down their lives to uphold its flag—a flag that had only been to them a flag of stripes on which no star of glory had ever shone—I swore a solemn oath to myself, 'May my right hand forget its cunning and my tongue cleave to the roof of my mouth if I ever fail to defend the rights of these men who have given their blood for me and my country this day and for their race forever,'" Congressman Butler said as he lifted his right hand in the air to reenact his oath.

"From that moment, all prejudice was gone, and an old time states-rights Democrat became a lover of the Negro race. As long as their rights are not equal to the rights of others, I am with them against all comers. But when their rights are finally assured, we shall at last have a united country—North and South, White and Black—under one glorious flag, for which we and our fathers have fought with an equal, and not to be distinguished, valor."

"If more White people thought the way you do, this country would be a far better place," Malcolm said, nodding appreciatively. "But I'm afraid after the Supreme Court let the Colfax murderers go free, things are only going to get worse. These people down South don't fear the law. They know everybody with power is on their side, and now the federal government is powerless to stop them."

Senator Bruce nodded in agreement. "Listen, Governor Ames, you're in Washington now. You've got to tell Congress what is going on in Mississippi. White folks don't always believe the stories when they come from us, but they will listen to you. Cedric's right. The *Cruikshank* decision was a huge step backwards. Congress needs to act swiftly to pass new legislation that the Supreme Court cannot undermine. Otherwise, what is the point of the Reconstruction Amendments if there is no mechanism to enforce them?"

"I'll do what I can, Blanche, but I honestly think the country's appetite to address these issues has waned. Election Day may find our voters fleeing before rebel bullets rather than balloting for their rights," Governor Ames predicted as he sat back down on the couch and took a final drag of his cigarette before stubbing it out in an ashtray on the table. "I fear Negroes are to be returned to a condition of serfdom—an era of a second slavery—in the South. It is the Negroes' fault, not mine, that this fate is before them. They refused to prepare for war when in a time of peace. Now it is too late. The nation should have acted but it was, as Attorney General Pierrepont informed me when I requested the assistance of federal troops to quell the violence, 'tired of the annual autumnal outbreaks in the South.' The political death of the Negro will forever release the nation of its weariness from such 'political outbreaks.' You may think I exaggerate. Time will show you how accurate my statements are. I'm sorry, Blanche. I tried. I really did, but it appears that your people are on their own."

Everyone in the room was crestfallen as his words sank in. Malcolm sat there stunned, trying to separate his anger from his grief, but in his heart, he knew better than any of them how right Governor Ames was, at least about the part of Black people being on their own. Malcolm leaned his head back, closed his eyes, and took a deep breath. Suddenly, he felt the floor give way, and he was falling.

47

Malcolm expected the fall would return him to Aunt Carol's house, but it didn't. Instead, he was in a small dark room sitting at a table across from Cedric's old boss Robert Elliott and next to Congressmen Rainey and Smalls. Sunlight streamed in through linen curtains casting a shadow from the bed onto the other side of the room. *I must be in a hotel room, but where?* he wondered. He was happy to see Robert Elliott again, but as soon as he saw his tightly drawn face, he knew that something terrible had happened.

"Glad to have you gentlemen in Charleston. I hope you can help us with this situation."

"Happy to help the best Speaker of South Carolina's House of Representatives ever to hold office," Congressman Smalls said encouragingly.

"You're too kind, old friend. I ordered some ham sandwiches for lunch in case you're hungry after your long trip," Speaker Elliot said, smiling weakly. Malcolm noticed new wrinkles around his tired, bloodshot eyes. It looked as if serving as the Speaker had aged the man.

"Have you seen this cartoon in the paper?" Congressman Rainey asked, laying the newspaper on the table for everyone to see.

"Who's the man on the right?" Malcolm asked.

"Looks like Sam Tilden," Congressman Rainey said, eyeing the illustration. "He's running for President on the Democratic ticket."

"We'd rather Rutherford Hayes, the Republican candidate, but neither one of them really give a hill of beans about us," Speaker Elliott quipped.

After quickly noting the date on the newspaper was July 1876, Malcolm glanced at the images of slain Black people surrounded by words racists had used to justify murder at a celebration: "impudent," "reformed in cold blood." He shook his head in disgust.

"At least the country is paying attention to what's happening to us again," Malcolm offered, trying to find the silver lining. "Was it as bad as it looks in this cartoon?"

"Worse," Speaker Elliott answered flatly.

"What happened?" Malcolm asked nervously.

Speaker Elliott rubbed his eyes and then dove into explaining why they were there. "A few weeks ago, during America's centennial anniversary, a Negro militia paraded through Hamburg in celebration."

"Where is Hamburg?" Malcolm asked, not recognizing the name.

"It's a mostly Negro town on the western side of South Carolina, near the Georgia border. While the militia was marching through the streets, a group of White folks walked up and told them to disperse so that they could pass. At first, the leader of the militia, a fellow named Dock Adams, ordered his militia to resist, but then he relented and let the White men pass to avoid a confrontation. Thinking the incident was over, Dock was surprised to find out a few days later that the White folks had filed a complaint in court accusing him of blocking a public highway. When Dock and his militia showed up at court for the hearing, the plaintiffs' lawyer, who some of y'all might remember as Confederate

General Matthew Butler, was waiting for them outside the courthouse with a slew of armed men."

I know where this story is headed, Malcolm predicted morosely.

"They already got their court date. What else did the White folks want?" asked Congressman Rainey, annoyed.

"They wanted to humiliate them. General Butler demanded Dock Adams apologize and insisted that Dock's militia disarm and surrender their weapons to him. Dock offered to send his militia's weapons to the governor of South Carolina, but General Butler rejected that offer and replied, 'Damn the governor—I am not here to consult him; this won't stop until November,' threatening that his harassment of Negroes would not cease until after the 1876 election."

"I wouldn't have surrendered nothing," Congressman Smalls said, his eyes narrowing in contempt.

"Well, Dock tried to make peace," Speaker Elliott continued. "He asked General Butler if he would guarantee that if the arms were surrendered, no one would be hurt, but Butler replied, 'I guarantee nothing.' With no promise of safety, Dock and his men retreated to a local armory for protection."

"But they weren't safe there, were they?" Malcolm asked, looking at the cartoon of Black bodies piled on top of one another.

"No, they weren't. Hundreds of armed White men quickly surrounded the armory and launched an attack, shooting at them with pistols and even an old cannon. Dock's militia fired back, hitting and killing one of the White fellas, which only angered the Whites more. Realizing they were trapped, Dock's men tried to escape out the back of the armory but were easily captured."

Thinking back to the Colfax Massacre, Malcolm already knew what happened next.

"They were brought before a kangaroo court, where each man was tried and quickly found guilty before being sentenced to death. After executing about six men from Dock's militia and wounding several more, the wild fiends went on a riotous rampage through town, destroying businesses, stealing property, looting prominent Negroes' homes, mutilating the bodies of the dead, and grotesquely taunting children with the flesh of dead bodies. They even shot the Negro sheriff to death and bashed his head in with muskets."

Malcolm dropped his head into his hand. "It wasn't enough to murder the militiamen? They had to terrorize the townspeople and destroy their town too? All this for blocking a highway?"

"So what's the plan?" Congressman Smalls asked, shaking his head in disgust.

"I'm heading to a rally in Charleston's Citadel Square now. Why don't y'all come along?" Congressman Elliott invited them.

Malcolm jumped up ready to go. He knew there was a chance this rally would attract the same vile actors that had terrorized the people in Hamburg, but he didn't care. He needed to be around people who were as outraged as him.

They walked a block from the hotel to a wide-open park where hundreds of Black people had gathered in front of a stage platform. Malcolm could feel the tension and anger in the air as he squeezed through the crowd to find a place to stand near the stage.

Speaker Elliott hopped onto the stage and wasted no time laying the blame for the Hamburg massacre squarely where it belonged: at the feet of "Matthew Butler and the lawless men, the ex-Confederate soldiers, the outlaws and barbarians who, ever since the war, have practiced wrong and outrage upon the helpless, unoffending colored people because of their emancipation by the war."

Malcolm immediately recognized the next speaker who stepped onto on the platform. Former congressman Cain, Pastor Cain once again, energetically asked the crowd, "Do you think Whites would stand for Negroes insisting they give up their arms, as Butler had demanded of Negroes at Hamburg?"

"No!" the crowd shouted in response. Malcolm realized he was shouting too.

"The Whites know their rights, but the Negroes are learning from them rapidly," Pastor Cain continued. "Remember, there are eighty thousand Negro men in this state who can bear Winchester rifles and know how to use them, and there are two hundred thousand Negro women who can light a torch and use the knife, and that there are one hundred thousand boys and girls who have not known the lash of a White master, who have tasted freedom once and forever, and that there is a deep determination never, so help them God, to submit to be shot down by lawless regulators for no crimes committed against society and law."

A White instigator tried to interrupt the rally, but the crowd shouted him down with protests of, "This is not Hamburg! This is not Hamburg!"

"Yeah!" Malcolm shouted, feeling even more fired up by the crowd's resolve. A young boy pushing the wheelchair of a man in a dark blue suit with gold buttons down the front and a blue cap with a gold buckle tried to pass in front of him, and Malcolm took a step back to let them through. As they passed, Malcolm noticed both of the man's legs were missing. He watched as the man was wheeled out of the crowd and, with his head hanging low, left the rally.

After a few hours of fiery speeches, the crowd began to disperse.

"Mother Emanuel is only a block from here. Would you gentlemen care to join me there to discuss next steps?" Pastor Cain invited. His former colleagues eagerly accepted.

They made it quickly to the church, but as soon as Malcolm stepped over the threshold into the sanctuary, he felt a wave of panic hit him. The last time he'd been there, the church was still under construction. He remembered walking down the aisle in awe of the church's history and purpose, but that was before the church became the scene of another bloody massacre of innocent Black people.

BANG!

Startled, Malcolm leaped a few inches in the air and looked around for where the sound came from. It was only a door slamming as it opened. No one else looked up.

CRASH!

Malcolm's head jerked toward the sound. A lady carrying a tray of glasses had tripped on the carpet and dropped everything. Pastor Cain walked over to help the lady up, while Malcolm stood there frozen.

WHOOSH!

Malcolm felt something whiz by. He fell to his knees and covered his head. When nothing else happened, he peeked through his fingers and saw a bird sitting on one of the rafters.

Speaker Elliott knelt down beside Malcolm and placed a hand on his back. "Are you okay, son?" he asked.

Malcolm tried his best to slow his breathing. "I'm not sure, sir. I think, um, I think I just need a moment."

"Why don't you have a seat over there," Speaker Elliott, said pointing to a pew. "I'll have someone bring you some water."

Malcolm nodded, pulled himself up, and took a seat with his head buried between his knees, trying to regain his breath. A moment later, he felt a tap on his shoulder. He looked up to see the man in the wheelchair from the rally holding a glass of water out to him.

"Thank you," Malcolm said. He took a sip and instantly felt better.

"You were looking a little jumpy over there," the man observed.

"Yeah," Malcolm agreed. "I don't know what got into me."

"You seen some things."

Malcolm didn't know if the man was asking him or telling him.

"I seen some things too," the man continued. "Out there on the battlefield, I seen plenty things I wish I could unsee."

"You were a soldier?" Malcolm asked, intrigued.

"Sure was," the man said, proudly puffing out his chest. "I fought for the Union as a part of the 33rd Regiment, United States Colored Infantry. You seem a little young to have fought in the War of the Rebellion."

"What?" Malcolm asked. "No sir. I haven't gone to war. I'm not a soldier."

"Oh really? I swore I recognized how skittish you were back there," he said, looking at where Malcolm had fallen to the floor a few moments before. "You looked just like some of my friends coming out of battle."

Malcolm paused for a moment, caught off guard by the suggestion. He wondered if everything he had seen in the past and the present was starting to affect him in ways he didn't realize. "Why did you leave the rally earlier?" Malcolm asked.

The soldier thought for a second before answering. "Don't you ever just get tired of it all?" he asked, sighing. "War been over more than ten years, and the Confederates are still killing us for sport. Where's the country that we gave our lives for? That I gave my legs for?" the man said, looking down at the stumps poking out from underneath his blanket. "I just got the feeling out there today that we've been abandoned behind enemy lines and no amount of hollering gonna do anything to change that, so I just as soon save my breath."

Malcolm knew exactly how the man felt; he had earned every drop of his disillusionment. A few months ago, Malcolm would've just nodded in agreement, but after all he'd seen, he wasn't willing to give up without a fight. Maybe he was a soldier after all.

"Do you know where the men I came here with went?" Malcolm asked, feeling better now that he'd had a chance to cool off and have some water.

"There's an office round back. They're probably in there."

"Thank you for the water," Malcolm said, standing up. "And for your service."

"My pleasure. Take care of yourself, son."

Malcolm walked around to the back of the church and found the men sitting at a large oval table in an office that was dimly lit by candlelight, discussing the events at hand. He took a seat in the last empty chair just as Speaker Elliott was pounding on the table for emphasis.

"We need to make an unequivocal statement to the American people about the barbarism that Negroes are subjected to daily," Speaker Elliott demanded. "After the War of the Rebellion nearly ripped this country in half, how can folks sit on the sidelines while American citizens, color notwithstanding, are hunted down and slaughtered like hogs? I thought this was supposed to be a country of laws, of order, of reason, but when are those principles ever applied in our favor?"

Everyone nodded in agreement.

"There used to be twelve thousand federal troops stationed throughout the South," Pastor Cain pointed out. "Now there are fewer than three thousand. They've moved all the troops out West to go kill Indians, while they've left us for dead. We need those troops back!" Pastor Cain shouted.

"I received a letter from an eyewitness that is willing to step forward to tell his story," Congressman Smalls reported. "We can let the American people know exactly what happened in Hamburg, every grotesque detail."

"Cedric," Speaker Elliott said, sliding a leather-bound notebook across the table to him that also contained a graphite pencil inside. "We're going to draft an address to President Grant and the people of the United States. We have to appeal to the decency and morality of our fellow man to enforce the law of the land and not let these murders go unanswered. Can you keep track of what we want to say?"

"Sure, boss," Malcolm agreed, happy to contribute.

"I think the main point we need to get across is that this country is founded on the principal of equal justice under the law. Write this down," Congressman Smalls said, turning to Malcolm. "In the just administration of our government, there is none so low as to be beneath the protection of the law, and none so high as to be beyond the reach of its authority."

Malcolm wrote down Congressman Small's words as neatly as possible in his best cursive. He hoped that when they sent the final address, President Grant would be moved to send federal troops back to South Carolina to stamp out the violence, like he had done at the beginning of his presidency. But that hope was a thin one. Malcolm didn't think it was likely, but they had to try. In his heart, Malcolm knew Governor Ames's prediction with Senator Bruce back in D.C. had been right. For now, at least, Black people were on their own.

After sending off the address, Malcolm offered to travel to Hamburg to observe the court hearing where a judge was going to decide whether to allow murder and conspiracy charges to go forward against Matthew Butler and his gang. A local Black pastor met Malcolm at the train station when he arrived and brought him to his home to spend the night.

The next morning, the pastor loaned Malcolm a horse and pointed him in the direction of the courthouse. Malcolm would have to remember to thank Jasmine for the horseback riding lesson when he got back. He still barely knew what he was doing, but at least he wasn't terrified of riding anymore.

As Malcolm rode up to the courthouse, he quickly realized that everything was in turmoil. He stopped under a tree a couple of hundred feet away and watched in terror as a gang of White men wearing red shirts, which looked as though they were soaked in blood, surrounded the courthouse.

The men hollered loudly while brandishing their rifles and pistols until people slowly emerged from the courthouse to find out what was causing all the ruckus. Pointing at a one-eyed bandit who was leading the charge, an elderly Black lady exclaimed in fear, "It's Benjamin Tillman!"

Malcolm was terrified the men were going to open fire on the crowd. More and more Black people started pouring out of the courthouse and rushed to get as far away from Tillman's gang as possible. He overheard one person fleeing the courthouse say the judge had hastily announced that there would be no indictments against Confederate General Butler or his men and that court was adjourned. Malcolm was dismayed, but no longer surprised by these routine miscarriages of justice. He was ready to get back to D.C. anyway—in either 1876 or 2015. He turned the horse around and began riding back to the pastor's house.

Halfway there, a small cavalry of White men surrounded him and ordered him to stop. A tremor ran down Malcolm's body, as he hoped today wasn't the day he got Cedric killed.

"What you doing in these parts, nigger?" one of the men asked.

Malcolm felt his heart skip a beat as he was reminded of his many encounters of being stopped and questioned by the police for no reason, and tried to remain calm.

"You don't look like you's from around here," said another. "'Cause I don't recognize your ugly face."

"Yeah, and you dressed mighty fine for a nigger 'round here. What is you? Some type of city boy or sumthin'? You got yo'self a office job?" the first one asked, chuckling. "Imagine that, a nigger, in a office. Y'all ever heard something so dumb."

"You heard what we do down here to niggers that be in places they ain't supposed to be and ain't mindin' their bidness?" the largest one asked.

Malcolm quickly ran through his options in his head. He could try to outrun them, but they'd probably shoot him in the back. He could tell them that they better leave him alone because he worked for a powerful US Senator, but then they'd probably shoot him in the face. He could feel his breath getting shallow. He wiped the sweat accumulating on his brow as he tried to figure out how to get out of this situation. Thinking back to everything he'd learned from Congressman Elliott about what was going on in South Carolina, Malcolm remembered hearing about Wade Hampton, a former slave owner and Confederate general turned Democrat candidate for governor. Congressman Elliott had said that he was rising star in South Carolina politics. Malcolm decided aligning himself with him might be his best chance at survival.

"I's an errand boy for Wade Hampton, the soon-to-be Democratic governor. He asked me to bring a message to the judge. I did and now I's

leavin'," Malcolm said, trying his best to
sound at least as ignorant as his harassers.

"You expect us to believe that Wade Hampton, the
former Confederate general, would trust a nigger to deliver a
message for him," one of the men said, cocking his pistol and
twirling it around his thumb in disbelief.

"Suh, how could I lie? South Carolina is too small. If I lied,
I know what would happen the next time you seen me. My family been
wit Massa Hampton since before the War of Northern Aggression. Even
after the war, we didn't leave. He treat us well, and we's real loyal to the
Hampton family and Massa Hampton knows it. Now you don't wanna
cause no harm to one of Massa Hampton's boys, would you? I don't
think he'd take too kindly to that," Malcolm said, hoping his impression
of slave talk hadn't gone too far.

The ringleader looked around at his gang and lowered his gun, but
not before hurling a spitball at Malcolm's feet. "Lookee here, nigger,

you better hurry back to yo massa and don't let me catch you round here after sundown. It won't turn out so good for you. You can count on that."

"Thank you kindly, suh. I's best be on my way." Tears stung Malcolm's eyes as he rode off, coming to terms with the fact that he'd only survived the encounter by turning himself into the one thing they wanted to see him as: a slave. He rode as fast as he could, trying to create as much distance as possible from those thugs and allowing his mind to drift to how liberating it had felt to gallop on horseback into the sunset with Jasmine. He kept kicking the horse's side until he felt like he was flying and, the next thing he knew, he really was flying, then falling, falling. The horse disappeared. The world went dark. Malcolm reached out his hands. Something smooth, cool, and soft rose up underneath him.

It was the yellow beanbag chair.

49

Malcolm stared out his bedroom window at Uncle Leroy working the land his family had called home for generations. It was no longer lost on him how truly special it was for Black people in America to have something of their own. As long as his family owned this land, they would have shelter and food and a way to provide for themselves. In essence, they had freedom; the kind of freedom Sojourner Truth and so many others wanted all former slaves and their descendants to have. He wouldn't let the state take that away, but he knew he needed some guidance—in 2015.

Malcolm had been meaning to talk to Professor Rogers for a while. Maybe he could help him understand everything Cedric had shown him and put the final missing pieces of the puzzle together. He quickly got dressed and headed downstairs.

"Good morning, Uncle Corey," Malcolm said when he entered the kitchen and saw him at the table eating a bowl of cornbread and milk.

"Mornin'. How'd you sleep?" Uncle Corey asked, staring at the circles under Malcolm's eyes.

"Ehhhh. Not so great. I've been having some wild dreams lately, but I'll be all right. I'm not sure if I mentioned it, but congratulations on getting your driver's license back!" Malcolm said, smiling a little too broadly.

"Sounds like you need a ride somewhere." Uncle Corey smirked.

"How'd you guess? Think you could swing me by Alcorn State today?" he asked, cheesing like a Cheshire cat.

"Sure, I have some résumés I want to drop off this afternoon in that direction," Uncle Corey said, getting up to put his bowl in the sink.

He turned the water on high and let the sink fill up with warm water and soap.

"That should work! I owe you one," Malcolm answered, still grinning. Just as he was about to clear the doorway, Uncle Corey cleared his throat to get his attention.

"How about you pay me back by getting these morning dishes done?" Uncle Corey proposed, returning the broad smile to Malcolm.

Malcolm and Uncle Corey headed north on the highway in Aunt Carol's car. Malcolm was happy to not be on a horse, a carriage, or a train, but in a car with AC and radio again. He was also glad Jasmine had been home earlier to let her dad know Malcolm was heading by his office that afternoon.

"How did that office interview go?" Malcolm asked his uncle.

Uncle Corey batted the steering wheel with his hands for a few beats, then opened up. "Ahhhh, interview went well. They seemed to like me, but they said they were gonna do a background check, so I don't know," he confessed, looking dejected.

"Well, they haven't said no yet, right?" Malcolm persisted hopefully.

Uncle Corey passed a few cars, weaving effortlessly through some light traffic, taking his sweet time to respond. "Naw, not yet. It's all good. Your daddy used to always say nothing good comes easy, so I guess at some point I oughta be in store for a whole lotta good 'cause nothing in my life ever came easy," Uncle Corey said, laughing.

After driving for a little while, Uncle Corey pulled off the highway to get some gas. They pulled up to a stoplight and waited for the arrow to turn green. Uncle Corey rolled the windows down for a little fresh air. When they maneuvered back onto the highway, they passed a group of Black people working in the fields. "Those fields used to be plantations," Uncle Corey said when he saw what Malcolm was looking at. "Some of the folks working out there come from families that have been working these same fields for hundreds of years."

Malcolm rolled down his window as well and sullenly agreed,

"Yeah. I know. As slaves."

"Not just slaves," Uncle Corey corrected. "Even after slavery ended, prisoners were forced to work the fields for free." He hung his hand out the window and drove a little under the speed limit, taking in the view of towering oak trees that lined the highway for miles.

Malcolm shook his head in confusion. "I don't understand. Why do Black people stay? Why don't they move North or something?"

Uncle Corey placed one hand on the steering wheel and reclined his seat slightly, then he scratched the top of his head until he landed on the right way to explain it. "This is home to them . . . to us! This is where our family is, our church, our communities. They might not have much, but plenty of folks take comfort in the familiar. And moving is expensive. Not just getting there, but living up North ain't cheap. Some of these plantations—I mean farms—used to only pay their workers in scrip."

"What's scrip?" Malcolm asked.

Uncle Corey pressed play on Aunt Carol's car radio. An Isley Brother's began playing, with Ron Isley delivering his trademark velvety falsetto. "That man just never seems to age, huh? How you gonna make hits for Aunt Carol's generation, for my generation, and still be on the radio in 2015? Timeless," Uncle Corey said, chuckling as he turned the radio down low to focus on Malcolm's question. "It's useless mostly," he finally answered. "It's like money, but you can't use it nowhere but at the company store. So you can't save it or invest it or do nothing with it besides stay put." Then he raised the volume up as he let his nephew soak in this new information.

"Wow. I never heard of anything like that."

"Yeah man. Not too long before I was born, there were still farms around here that paid people like that. We been through some shit. Don't ever forget it," Uncle Corey said reflectively, as he decelerated to exit the highway.

You have no idea, Malcolm thought. What he'd seen so far that summer would be in his mind for the rest of his life. A few minutes later they pulled up to the campus. "Think you'll be finished in about an hour?"

"Yeah, I think so. Thanks, Unc," Malcolm said, giving him dap on the way out of the car.

Being back on the campus, Malcolm felt a rush of positive energy. He wasn't afraid of being shot, or harassed, or surveilled or anything—he could just be. He entered the main campus building and checked the directory for Professor Rogers's office number. As he walked down a hallway filled with pictures of Black deans and distinguished professors, he couldn't help but stop. It made him feel so proud. But not wanting to miss his window with Professor Rogers, he quickly got back to counting office numbers: 279 . . . 277 . . . 275. *Here it is.* Malcolm knocked on the door.

"Come in," Professor Rogers called.

"Hi sir. It's me, Malcolm," he said, poking his head inside a small office overflowing with books—books in shelves along the walls, books scattered across the professor's large desk, a stack of books piled high on the floor next to the desk.

"Malcolm, I'm so glad you made it back to campus! Have a seat," Professor Rogers invited with a big smile on his face.

"Thank you. I've been wanting to come check you out. You're a history teacher, right?" Malcolm asked, moving an encyclopedia-size text from the chair to Professor Rogers's desk so he could sit down.

"Pardon the mess," he excused himself sheepishly. "Yes. I teach American history with a focus on the civil rights movement."

"Which civil rights movement?" Malcolm asked provocatively.

Professor Rogers leaned forward in his seat and laced his fingers together. "What exactly are you referring to?" he probed.

Malcolm confidently clarified his question, like a scholar who had spent many years in the field. "Well, it seems to me like a lot of people talk about the civil rights movement in the 1960s, you know the one with Martin Luther King and Rosa Parks, but there was another one, wasn't there?"

"Are you talking about Reconstruction?" Professor Rogers asked flabbergasted, echoing Jasmine's surprise when Malcolm had also raised the topic with her.

Malcolm pulled the now empty chair out farther from Professor Rogers's desk and sat down to make himself comfortable. He figured this conversation could take a while. "Yeah. I, uh, recently learned about a time after the Civil War when Black people had all sorts of rights. They were voting and holding office and had money and businesses, and it looked like maybe Black people were going to be all right in this country, but something happened because—" Malcolm paused. "Well, just look at us," he said, throwing his hands up in the air.

"Yeah, you're talking about Reconstruction," Professor Rogers said, leaning back in his chair. "Most people don't know about that triumphant period. History books pretty much ignore it. Plenty folks are convinced that Black people are bad off because we're lazy and stupid, not because whatever we built was taken and destroyed at every turn. How did you learn about this?"

Malcolm paused, still feeling awkward about telling people about Cedric's diary, but if anyone would understand, it would be Professor Rogers.

"I found an old diary at my aunt's house. It's from one of my ancestors who started writing it right after the Civil War," Malcolm revealed.

Professor Rogers's mouth dropped open. It took him a few moments to collect himself.

"You found what? I have to see this. Who wrote it? Are you sure it's authentic?" Professor Rogers rambled, caught up in his own scholarly excitement.

Malcolm laughed and put his hands up to slow down the onslaught. When Professor Rogers had composed himself, Malcolm attempted to answer as many of the questions as he could. "Yeah, I'm sure. I found it in the attic a couple of months ago. His name was Cedric Johnson. He worked as an aide for Senator Hiram Revels and other Black members of Congress."

"That is an amazing find, Malcolm. Not many records exist from during that time that describe the era from a personal standpoint. Would you be willing to bring it to me to look at?" he asked excitedly from the edge of his seat.

"Sure. As soon as I'm done reading it," Malcolm agreed without any hesitancy.

Professor Rogers shook Malcolm's hand in thanks and continued speaking, but primarily to himself: "This is wonderful news. After it's properly logged, this diary could be placed on display in museums and libraries or at least preserved in the university vault for posterity."

"What's the vault?" Malcolm asked, interrupting Professor Rogers's monologue.

"Hmm?" Professor Rogers mused, distracted.

"What's in the vault?"

"Oh, sorry. I was getting carried away. It's our school archives, where we keep old records, retired faculty papers, memorabilia," the professor said, rising and walking over to his bookshelf as if he was looking for something.

Malcolm smiled. He liked the idea that Cedric and his work would be remembered in a bigger way. "That would be cool. I think Cedric would like that," Malcolm said. He grabbed a bright red stress ball from the corner of the desk, gave it a quick squeeze, and began tossing it from one hand to the other. He looked up at Professor Rogers. "One thing that's been bothering me is how quickly everything fell apart. Like, one minute it looked like things were going to be fine for Black folks and then the next, it all came crashing down. And then it's like that whole period got washed away like it never happened. Nobody talks about it or even remembers it."

"Ahh, yes. To the victor go the spoils, right?" Professor Rogers asked as he turned around with an old book in his hand. He sat back down and placed the book in front of him. "One of the best books on Reconstruction," he said, tapping it.

Malcolm peered over the desk and read *Black Reconstruction in America* by W.E.B. Du Bois on the cover.

"Nice," he whispered. "So, um, what do you mean about the spoils?" Malcolm asked. "The Confederates didn't win the Civil War. The Union did."

"Did they though?" He blew the dust off the worn cover, which was barely holding together by its threads and flipped past the first few pages before giving his response.

"The old Confederate soldiers rebranded as the KKK or red shirts or whatever they wanted to call themselves on any given day and led a campaign of terror and violence that vanquished all hope for equality and fair treatment for Blacks." He turned the book around so Malcolm could see a few interior pictures reflecting what he was describing. "Once the federal troops pulled out of the South, we didn't stand a chance. We were outmanned and outgunned. And once the Confederates regained control of state governments, they rigged their state constitutions to reduce or eliminate the power of our votes to make sure we never regained power again. Then they rewrote history to make sure no one ever questioned why."

"So is that what's up with all these Confederate monuments and school names everywhere and films like *Birth of a Nation* being played?"

A grimace swept over the professor's face. "Yep. In their telling of history, the terrorists become the heroes and the true heroes are forgotten at best, maligned at worse. Some of the vilest among them even went on to hold higher government offices, like Matthew Butler and Benjamin Tillman, who both became US Senators from South Carolina."

"Matthew Butler from the Hamburg massacre?" Malcolm asked, shocked.

"Wow, you really do know your history," Professor Rogers replied, equally shocked. He closed the book and looked Malcolm directly in the eye. "The one and only. Meanwhile, not a single Black person from the South was elected to the House of Representatives for almost a hundred years after Reconstruction ended or to the Senate for nearly a hundred and fifty, despite the large numbers of Black people that continued to live in that region. Some democracy. Imagine if former Confederate soldiers and Confederate sympathizers are writing the laws that govern your life? You think Black people stood a chance in hell at getting fair treatment?"

"Nope." Remembering Governor Ames's dire prediction, Malcolm continued, "I would expect Blacks to be returned to an era of second slavery."

Professor Rogers eyebrows shot up. "How old did you say you were again?" he teased incredulously.

Chuckling, Malcolm answered, "Sixteen," to which Professor Rogers nodded approvingly, then turned back around to his copious library in search of another book.

"The Supreme Court also did it's damnedest to stand in the way of progress and unwind all of the gains made during Reconstruction. They issued rulings that significantly weakened the equal protection clause of the Fourteenth Amendment," he said. "When Congress passed the Civil Rights Act in 1875, making segregation illegal in places open to the public, the Supreme Court struck it down only a few years after it passed."

"They did?" Malcolm gasped, nearly leaping out of his seat.

"Yes," Professor Rogers responded, turning around and looking at Malcolm, concerned. He sat back down at his desk and took a sip of coffee from his thermal mug, seeming to savor the flavors for a moment. "You've got me giving you a lecture from my introductory course," he noted, his eyes twinkling as he spoke.

"Go ahead." Malcolm smiled.

"It took almost a hundred years for Congress to pass another civil rights bill like that again. Those Supreme Court decisions are what set the stage for the terror that followed: like the decimation of numerous prosperous Black towns, the lynchings of thousands of Black men, women, and children, all the Black people who were forced into the convict leasing system, and the millions who are incarcerated today. Not to mention the dehumanizing legacy of Jim Crow. So while it's been one hundred and fifty years since the end of the Civil War, we can't be all that surprised that vast inequalities between Blacks and Whites still exist."

Malcolm took a moment to let it all sink in and regain his composure before asking, "So if this country has basically been stuck in a holding pattern since the Civil War, how do we get out of it?"

Professor Rogers's eyes lit up with hope. "The answer is both extremely simple and incredibly complicated. First, we, as a country, have to *want* to get out of it. Enough people have to look at the status quo and recognize that it is not okay and things need to change. Then, to bring about that change, we—Blacks, Whites, everyone—must educate ourselves on how these systems that lock Black people into a permanent underclass came to be and do an honest assessment of the damage that's been done. Lastly, and this is the hardest part, we have to work together to repair that damage and heal the wounds. Is it possible? Yes," he said, nodding. "But is it likely?" Professor Rogers concluded by shaking his head. Fatigue and cynicism peppered his voice. "Don't hold your breath."

"Thanks, Professor Rogers," Malcolm said as he looked at the clock and realized how quickly the hour had flown by. Uncle Corey was probably outside waiting. "You've given me a lot to think about." He stood up and placed the stress ball back on the professor's desk and then shook his hand one more time.

"You are quite welcome, Malcolm. Please feel free to stop by anytime," Professor Rogers offered, smiling fondly. "And consider that offer about the diary. I'm sure the university would love to preserve it properly for you."

"I will, and I'll talk to my Aunt Carol about it," Malcolm said, nodding, and then made his way to the door.

Malcolm smiled as he walked past the center of campus where a group of students had gathered on the lawn to soak up the summer sun; he felt more at home on a college campus than ever before. He paused in front of Revels Hall once more. "All right, Cedric. I'm ready to see how it all ended," he said quietly. "I know that just because it all fell apart in your time doesn't mean we can't make it right today. Better late than never." He gave a nod to the Hiram Revels memorial plaque and went on to meet Uncle Corey.

He spotted Uncle Corey waiting inside Aunt Carol's car at the edge of campus keeping an eye out. He waved at him and headed over to the passenger-side door. "Hey Unc," he said, opening the door. As soon as he sat in the seat, he was falling.

In an instant, Malcolm was seated in the dining room of the Wormley Hotel surrounded by all the regular congressmen and their aides. Even Pastor Cain was there. *Is he a congressman again?* Malcolm wondered.

"I can't believe it's been two months since the election, and we still don't know who the next president is!" Congressman Lynch exclaimed.

"We're at a standstill. Neither Tilden nor Hayes is willing to budge. Now Congress has created a bipartisan electoral commission to choose the winner," said Senator Bruce. "As with all things political, the outcome will be determined less by the merits of the arguments and more by who is making the decision."

"Who's on the commission?" Malcolm asked, quickly recovering from his trip.

"It's a mix of Democrats and Republicans with five members coming from the Senate, five from the House of Representatives, and five from the Supreme Court—fifteen in all. Whatever the commission decides will be final unless both houses of Congress vote to override it," Senator Bruce explained.

"The only person on the commission that I have any faith in is James Garfield, who has time and again stood up for Negroes in the name of righteousness. I can only pray that he has the strength and ability to convince the rest of the commission to do what is right," Congressman Rainey hoped solemnly.

"I heard the Tilden supporters said that they would never support a

Hayes presidency, and they're planning to storm Washington if Hayes is declared the winner," said Congressman Nash, throwing his hands up in exasperation.

"Yeah, and I heard President Grant ordered additional troops to Washington to fortify the city," reported Congressman Haralson.

Malcolm had never heard of an election being this tense or it taking so long to know who the winner was. He couldn't imagine how it could be resolved peacefully if neither side was willing to accept defeat.

"Gentlemen, it's going to be what it's going to be," Senator Bruce said, trying to calm the tension. "Until then, we just have to focus on what we can do to make a difference in the lives of our people. What kind of bills can we draft to help address the rise in mob violence, reverse the effects of voter suppression, or help these poor people who lost all their savings at Freedman's Bank get their money back?"

"How are we gonna do any of that, Blanche? We don't have the votes!" Congressman Lynch shouted, frustrated.

"We'll have to convince folks it's the right thing to do. It's patriotic to uphold the rule of law while making sure fellow citizens have an equal say in our democracy. If our country no longer believes that, then what was the point of the war?"

The congressmen sitting around the table shrugged their shoulders in defeat, unsure how to answer his question.

While the congressmen were deep in thought, a door to one of the meeting rooms behind the hotel dining area opened, and one of the Supreme Court justices that Malcolm recognized from the Colfax case walked out and then another. Then came a handful of senators and congressmen. Suddenly, it dawned on everyone at their table that the Electoral Commission had been meeting at the Wormley right then. The faces of the people leaving the room were stern and not a single person smiled or acknowledged their table as they walked by.

Malcolm scanned the group for Congressman Garfield, but as soon as their eyes locked, the congressman quickly looked down and away. In that moment, Malcolm knew all hope was lost. Whatever deal was struck behind those walls did not account for the well-being of Black people.

"'Father, forgive them, for they know not what they do,'" Congressman Cain whispered as they walked past.

"Maybe God will forgive them, but I sure as shit can't," Congressman Smalls growled as he slammed his mug down. As soon as his cup hit the table, Malcolm felt a quick pull and was jolted back into Aunt Carol's car.

♦ ♦ ♦

When Uncle Corey parked the car back at the farmhouse, Malcolm hopped out and dashed up to the attic. He was desperate to tell Cedric that he finally understood how the progress Black people had begun to achieve during Reconstruction had been reversed. But, Cedric was nowhere to be found. Instead, his diary lay open on the desk expectantly. Malcolm picked it up and began reading the last entry.

May 1, 1877

President Hayes wasted no time withdrawing the last of the federal troops from the South. The three states with contested elections, Louisiana, South Carolina, and Florida, are all in Democratic hands now. God help us all. I knew right then my time in Washington was up. Thankfully, my old boss Senator Revels, who is now the university president of Alcorn State invited me to come teach a course on American history.

This reminded me of the time I visited Howard University with John Mercer Langston, and he said I needed to pass on what I learned in Washington to the next generation. Immediately, I knew that my answer was yes. I am looking forward to starting my teaching job in the fall. I pray the innocence of the youth will rejuvenate me and help me channel my frustrations from my time in Washington in a positive direction.

My last fond memory in Washington was running into Buddy as I was leaving the Capitol. I thanked him for being our eyes and ears on the ground and asked him what he was going to do with so much change in the air. With a sharpness in his eyes that I had never seen before, he said, 'Don't worry about me. I'll be right here. When you make it back, I'll be right here.' I knew right then, however long it took for us to make it back to the seats of power, he'd be there waiting, minding the shop, so to speak.

Since returning to Mississippi, Isabel and I have been eagerly making up for lost time. We got married right away and are already expecting our first child. With every dollar I managed to save after losing it all in the collapse of Freedman's Bank, I bought a farm in Natchez and had a nice little house built for us to raise our family. One of our neighbors was kind enough to build me a sturdy desk in the attic where I can work in the evenings.

All those years ago, my pa encouraged me to find a way to tell the world we were here and what we stood for. That's what led me to keep a diary in the first place. Now this diary may come in handy as I try to teach my students about what really happened during Reconstruction in the face of the lies that our enemies will undoubtedly spread in order to hide the truth about all the good that was done when negroes and whites governed as one. The better we understand how we got to where we are, the more prepared we will be to shape the course of our future.

Malcolm sat there staring at the last page of the diary for a moment and then felt a cool breeze on his neck.

"One last thing?" Cedric's deep baritone voice bellowed out.

"Yes?" Malcolm asked, looking around for Cedric but not finding him.

"It's time. Save *our* farm." And with that, Cedric was gone.

51

"So I have to ask," Jasmine said when they were hanging out the next day having just ordered sno-balls from a little stand, "what did you say to my dad? He's in love with you. 'When is Malcolm going to come see me again?'" Jasmine pleaded in a fake whiny voice. "I was like, 'who's dating him, Dad, me or you?' That shut him up real quick." Jasmine laughed.

Malcolm laughed back while reaching for her hand. "I'm gonna miss you, girl. I'm definitely coming back to visit Mississippi. Think you might have a chance to visit me in D.C.?"

"Yeah." Jasmine nodded. "Maybe I can convince my dad to take me on an East Coast college tour this fall."

"That would be dope. Let me know if I can come!"

Malcolm was glad he and Jasmine had gotten together to do something lighthearted. He had seen so much, learned so much. They sat at some metal picnic tables in a parking lot, next to the sno-ball stand. Malcolm looked around and noticed how downtrodden things were in the part of town they were in. It reminded him of his own neighborhood in D.C.

"I've been doing a lot of thinking about how bad things are for Black people all over the country and how, in some ways, we were better off right after the Civil War," Malcolm reflected as he took a lick of his sno-ball that was already starting to melt.

"That's crazy. Why would you say that?" Jasmine asked, bewildered.

Malcolm paused for a second, trying to figure out how to explain his thought process to her. "Well, for one thing, we used to have hope that things would get better. Back when slavery ended, Black people were busy trying to do all the things that we couldn't do as slaves, like vote, run for office, open businesses, get an education, get married and raise our own family, save for our future, buy land, go to church. All that stuff. I guess when freedom rang hollow and started looking just like slavery, people just gave up. Also, we did a better job lifting each other up instead of trying to destroy one another."

"What do you mean?" Jasmine asked, licking her sno-ball as well. She offered Malcolm a taste, but he liked his own better.

Malcolm got up and started pacing in a circle in front of the picnic bench. "I mean, there's enough people out there that hate us and want to see us dead, but why do we have to help them? Like, just a couple of months ago, I almost got shot by some gangbangers on a basketball court and then five minutes later I almost got shot by the cops."

"What! Are you okay?" Jasmine asked, her eyes flying open in surprise. She swung around to face him so fast, a big piece of her sno-ball fell off and landed in a puddle in the parking lot. They both looked at it for a second and then started laughing.

Malcolm walked over to Jasmine with a half smirk on his face. "Yeah. *Now* I'm all right. I was real shook when it happened, but being down here away from everything has helped me clear my head. As a young Black man, I feel like I should be put on the endangered species list. Then maybe people would care if I lived or died." Malcolm shrugged, sitting back down on the picnic table bench.

"Wow. That's real." Jasmine nodded and then paused pensively. "Maybe after all those years of being treated like we were nothing and lied to about our history, we forgot our greatness. If we destroy ourselves and our communities, then White supremacists don't have to work as hard. That's pretty genius if you think about it. The racists barely have to get their hands dirty anymore."

"I have an idea!" he announced, his eyes suddenly lighting up.

Jasmine looked at him expectantly.

"Remember when we went to that park with the Confederate

monuments? That park, those monuments, they are historical markers, right?" Malcolm asked suddenly, jumping up in excitement and putting his sno-ball cup on the table.

"Yeah, I think so." She glanced down and grabbed a napkin out of the dispenser to wipe off the sugary syrup from her fingertips.

"So that means they can't be destroyed, right? The city can't just get rid of them without going through some process. They can't just turn the park into a mall or something," he said, flinging his hands dramatically in the air.

"That sounds right, I guess." She shrugged taking a lick of Malcolm's sno-ball.

"Well, if racists can use historic designations to write their own version of history, why can't we use the same tools to write our own? What if we got Aunt Carol's house designated as a historic place?" He turned to face her head-on, a smile slowly spreading across his lips.

"That sounds interesting, but how?" Jasmine asked.

Looking at her, he held his palms open. "I don't know." He paused, shaking his head. "But her house has more significance than all these made-up Confederate statutes combined. My ancestor Cedric was an amazing person who made a difference in the lives of Black people and tried to make this country better. That makes his house sound pretty historic to me. And if it's a historic place, it shouldn't be torn down to expand some highway. It should be preserved so people can remember his life and learn from it," he said, pointing his index finger forcefully in the air.

"You might be on to something." She nodded.

"Think your dad could help?" he asked, reaching over to grab his sno-ball cup back.

"Yeah. I think he actually helped Alcorn do something similar once. Let me call him," she said, pulling out her cell phone. "Dad, how do we get a house added to the list of historic places?" She grabbed her purse and pulled a pen out to take a few notes on a clean napkin. "Okay, got it, got it, okay. Thanks, Daddy!" Jasmine said.

"Okay," she said as she hung up the phone. "There's a form we need to fill out that asks a bunch of questions like why is the property historically significant and is it endangered. Then, after you submit the form, the Mississippi National Register of Historic Places Review Board will call a hearing and you can present your case." She handed Malcolm the napkin so that he could read the notes for himself.

"Let's do it," Malcolm said, smiling, "Like right now," he said, chugging the icy remains of his sno-ball.

"Sure, but can I finish *my* sno-ball?" Jasmine asked, taking a sip of the melted slush.

"Nope," Malcolm teased.

"Whatever, fool," Jasmine said, laughing.

52

On their way home from having their sno-balls, Malcolm and Jasmine were excited about what they were about to do to try to save the farm. They stopped by the library to print and fill out the form and then returned to Aunt Carol's to take pictures of the house to submit with their application. Just before the post office closed, the two mailed it off. Malcolm was on cloud nine. It just had to work.

It was hard keeping their ploy a secret from Aunt Carol during dinner, but Malcolm knew it would be worth it. If Aunt Carol got to stay in her house, and Uncle Leroy got to stay on his farm, and Uncle Corey had a place to live while he got back on his feet, it would be worth it.

After dinner, Malcolm offered to do the dishes. Aunt Carol grabbed her favorite deck of cards and sat down to play some solitaire.

"You've been mighty helpful 'round the house lately, Malcolm. In a good mood. Smiling all the time," Aunt Carol observed slyly, clicking her tongue. "Not half the hoodlum you were when you got here." She cackled.

Malcolm stopped mid-dish wipe and looked over at her, startled.

"I don't suppose Ms. Jasmine has anything to do with that," she asked, letting her question hang in the air.

Malcolm laughed and shook his head. "Nice try, Aunt Carol."

She shrugged and went back to playing her game.

Right when Malcolm was putting away the last dish, the phone rang. Aunt Carol got up from her game and answered it. "Who is this?" she asked. "Sure, just a second," she said, sitting back down at the table and handing the phone over toward Malcolm. "It's for you, shugah," she said.

"Hey, Malcolm?"

Malcolm was surprised to hear a guy's voice on the line. "Who's this?" he asked suspiciously.

"It's Jason."

Malcolm paused for a moment before asking, "How did you get my number?"

"From the phone book. It's a landline."

He paused again, confused why this boy went through the trouble of looking up his Aunt's number in the phone book. "Well, what do you want?" Malcolm demanded.

Jason's voice dipped in volume as he started speaking, "I just wanted to say . . . I looked up some of the things you were talking about at the arcade, like the Colfax massacre. I'm sorry I didn't believe you. I just couldn't believe something like that happened right here in my own backyard, and I never even heard about it. I'm sorry, man."

Surprised, Malcolm's heart softened a bit. "Okay," he said. "Thanks." Unsure of what else to say, he waited for Jason to continue or bring something else up.

Jason's voice came through the phone stronger this time, sounding less surprised and more disgusted. "Dude, what I read kind of freaked me out. It wasn't just the massacres, and those were bad enough, but all the lynchings of Black people too. I saw this one picture where it was like the whole town was out celebrating this Black man being hung from a tree. Children picked off pieces of his burnt skin for sport." Jason was quiet for a moment. "My grandparents could've been kids at something like that. It's not that long ago."

"No, it's not." Malcolm could tell that Jason was having a hard time coming to terms with all the history that had been hidden from him, and decided to let Jason get it all out.

"It just made me sick, man," Jason continued. "I don't want to be one of those people that sits back and watches while horrible things happen anymore. Listen, I know you said something was going on with your family's land, and I just want you to know that if you need anything, you know, if there is something I can do, I want to help however I can. I got your back."

Malcolm paused for a long moment while he thought about all of Cedric's White allies: Senator Sumner, President Grant, Attorney General Akerman, Congressman Butler, James Beckwith, and many more. None of the successes of Reconstruction would have been possible without people from different backgrounds working together to advance the cause of justice. *If Congressman Butler's eyes could be opened, maybe there's hope for others,* Malcolm thought optimistically.

"All right, man. I'm gonna take you up on that. Thank you. For real," Malcolm said solemnly as he said goodbye and hung up the phone.

◆ ◆ ◆

A couple of days later, Malcolm was finally ready to tell Aunt Carol about the diary. He grabbed the diary from the attic and Grant's celebratory bells from his dresser and headed downstairs. He found her watching *Family Feud* in the living room. Uncle Leroy sat in his favorite chair, out cold.

"Aunt Carol. You got a second?" Malcolm asked.

"Sure, these folks don't have *any* answers tonight. Ain't nobody gonna win," she said, turning her attention to Malcolm.

Malcolm sat on the couch next to her. "Thanks for letting me hold on to these bells for a little while," Malcolm said.

"Sure thing, baby. No problem," she responded as she patted his knee and again looked concerned about why a boy his age would be so interested in some old bells.

"Do you know where they're from?" Malcolm asked. He placed the bells on the coffee table in front of them.

Aunt Carol groaned, a bit exasperated by her great-nephew's obsession. "Malcolm, jeez, what is up with you and these bells? I already told you I don't know where they're from. Why are you asking me about it again?"

Malcolm smiled patiently before responding. "Because *I* do. They are from President Ulysses S. Grant's second inaugural ball."

She grabbed the remote to mute the TV and picked up one of the bells. With a placid smile that one might use to patronize a toddler's fancy, she needled, "Now Malcolm, how could you possibly know that? Even if that was true, what would they be doing in this house so far from Washington?"

Malcolm pulled out the diary and began to show it to her, turning each page delicately, careful not to damage the artifact. "Aunt Carol, I found this diary in the desk in the attic. It's a diary from one of your ancestors, one of my ancestors, Cedric Johnson. He worked for Black congressmen after the Civil War and wrote down everything that he saw. After Reconstruction ended, he came back here and bought this farm, and this is where his diary has been ever since."

Aunt Carol grabbed the diary from Malcolm and began flipping through the pages, her eyes wide with disbelief.

"Malcolm," she said as her eyes filled with tears, "Malcolm, when did you . . . how did you . . . You know how much family means to me." Since arriving in Mississippi that summer, Malcolm had never seen his great aunt speechless, but in this moment, she couldn't find the words. She pulled a handkerchief out of her apron pocket and wiped away a tear. She then patted his hand, giving it a firm squeeze without taking her eyes off the newly discovered family heirloom. "Thank you for this," she finally got out.

"No, thank you, Aunt Carol. This trip has changed my life," Malcolm said, reaching over and squeezing her hand back. "I was just wondering if it would be okay for me to keep the bells?"

"Sure, darling. Whatever you like," Aunt Carol said as she ran her fingers down the page, noting the delicate texture and the elegant cursive. Malcolm was pretty sure he knew what she'd be doing for the next couple of days. "Unbelievable," Aunt Carol said as she inspected every inch of the diary. "Did you say his name was Cedric?" she asked with a hint of recognition in her eyes.

"Yes." Malcolm nodded.

"He was my grandfather," she said, glancing up with a twinkle in her eye. "I didn't know him, but he's buried in our cemetery out back. He's on our family tree in our Bible," Aunt Carol said, getting up and walking over to the bookshelf. She pulled over a footstool and stepped up on it to pull down a large dusty tome from the highest shelf.

Malcolm scooted over a few inches on the couch to make room for her and the large book.

Aunt Carol sat back down with the book in her lap and continued, "I remember I was looking in the family Bible once when I was younger and saw his name listed inside. I asked my mother about him, but she completely clammed up. Turned white as a ghost and said she didn't want to talk about it. I didn't want to upset her so I didn't bring him up again."

Aunt Carol then placed the Bible down between them and opened it to the first page. There, staring back at them was the family tree with the names *Cedric Johnson* and *Isabel Johnson* listed as parents to Mama Lucille and a few others. Now Malcolm finally understood the relationship: Cedric was his great-great-grandfather.

Sticking halfway out of the Bible was an obituary with a black-and-white photo of a man and woman sitting in rocking chairs holding hands on the back porch of Aunt Carol's house, with several children on the ground in front of them. Malcolm instantly recognized Cedric and Isabel and opened the obituary to read it.

OBITUARY

CEDRIC JOHNSON (CIRCA 1851—OCTOBER 19, 1902)

Brother Cedric Johnson was a pillar of the Natchez community. For the last 20 years, he served as a dedicated professor of government and political affairs at Alcorn State University. Brother Johnson also worked tirelessly in secret to register people to vote and help legions of Natchez residents prepare for Mississippi's unjust literacy exams.

One fateful night, October 19, 1902, the Ku Klux Klan discovered his secret and decided to put an end to his work. Brother Johnson received word that the Klan was on its way and thus concealed his beloved wife, Isabel, and their children in the attic. From his bedroom, he fired shots in an attempt to fend off the attack but he was overrun. The Klan broke into his house, found him, and dragged him from his home. They hung him from a tree behind his barn and riddled his body with bullets. While his mortal body is no longer with us, his spirit is undoubtedly with the Lord above, watching over us and protecting us from evil.

Brother Johnson is survived by his wife, Isabel, who serves as the Head Teacher of the local colored primary school, as well as his children, Ethel, Junior, Chester, and Lucille, who all need the prayers and support of our community at this time.

Brother Johnson will be buried with full Masonic rites as a member of a Prince Hall Grand Lodge.

"No!" Malcolm shouted, as he threw the obituary to the floor. He leaped off the couch and made a mad dash out the kitchen door. He was running to the graveyard before he even realized it, his shadow trailing behind him in the moonlight.

When he reached Cedric and Isabel's grave, he collapsed in front of it and began to cry uncontrollably. How could he have been so naive to think Cedric's fate would be any different than that of so many other Black leaders during his time? Of course an intelligent Black man trying to help his community wouldn't be safe in Mississippi after the collapse of Reconstruction. Eventually, Malcolm gained enough composure to speak.

"Cedric, if you can hear me, and I'm pretty sure you can, just know I've got a plan to save the farm. It's a long shot, but it just might work. I'm not gonna let your life or death be in vain. You did your part," Malcolm said as he wiped a tear from his eye. "And you opened my eyes when I didn't even know they were closed. Thank you." Malcolm stood up, laying his palm on Cedric's grave once more before turning to walk away.

When Malcolm got back to the house, he saw Aunt Carol sitting at the kitchen table with a bloodshot eyes and knew that she had read the obituary too. Malcolm walked over to her, gave her a hug, and said, "I guess now we know why Mama Lucille never allowed anyone in the attic."

Aunt Carol nodded sadly in agreement. The obituary lay open inside the crease of the Bible on the kitchen table in front of her. "It held her final treasured memories of her murdered father, my grandfather." She touched the edge of the obituary and ran her hands down the pages of the Good Book. She began to close it, but changed her mind, pulling it closer to her. "Makes sense that she didn't really like to talk about the past. She would just as soon leave it behind her. Whenever I asked questions about our family, it seemed to cause her so much pain that I usually let it go. There is so much I never knew and didn't dare ask."

Aunt Carol held up a heart-shaped locket she was wearing and opened it. "My mother gave this to me before she died. She didn't tell me whose it was, but she said it was special to our family, so I always wear it." As soon as Malcolm saw it, he knew it was the locket he'd found in Cedric's basement apartment.

Aunt Carol looked down at the obituary again. "Cedric looks a little like you. You even have the same chin dimple," Aunt Carol pointed out, amused.

Malcolm laughed nervously. He looked at Aunt Carol with her family memories lying in front of her and couldn't keep the information to himself any longer. He had to tell her about his plans to protect their family's land. "Aunt Carol, I think I might have found a way to save the farm."

"What are you talking about?" she asked, perplexed.

He pulled out the chair next to her and sat with her so she could take in what followed. "Last week, I submitted an application for this farm to be added to the National Register of Historic Places. If it works, then it'll be harder for the state to take the farm from you."

Aunt Carol's eyes flew wide open in shock. "You did this without talking to me?" she asked, taken aback.

Malcolm, worried he had offended his aunt, explained himself. "Yes ma'am. I know how much this farm means to you and the family, and I didn't want to get your hopes up if nothing was going to come of it. I didn't mean any disrespect."

"Come here, baby," Aunt Carol said, filled with anything but disappointment. She stood up from the kitchen table and wrapped her arms around him in a loving embrace. "You did good. Where'd you get that fighter spirit from?"

"It's in our blood," Malcolm answered, squeezing her back.

I t only took two weeks for the family to receive a letter announcing a date for a hearing to determine if the house would become registered as a historic place, and Malcolm was pumped.

Standing tall and proud in one of his dad's navy suits that Aunt Carol had tailored to fit him perfectly, Malcolm walked boldly into the Mississippi National Register of Historic Places Review Board hearing room. He took a seat in the first row of benches with Aunt Carol, Uncle Leroy, Uncle Corey, Jasmine, and Professor Rogers filling up the row. Just as the Review Board members were taking their seats on an elevated row of black leather chairs, Jason walked in with a couple of White people Malcolm didn't recognize.

"I'd like to call this hearing to order," one of the women on the Review Board announced, banging her gavel. "Can Mr. Malcolm Williams approach the podium?"

Malcolm nervously stood up and stepped forward suddenly feeling the weight of the moment upon him. How did he think he could stand alone in a courtroom and present his case in front of all these people? What if he didn't make any sense or the Review Board didn't think Cedric was important enough to add his home to the registry?

If he failed, he'd be the reason his family lost their farm and everyone would know it, including Cedric. Malcolm's vision began to blur and his legs started to shake as he walked toward the podium. Then he remembered Senator Revels's calming technique and closed his eyes, took a deep breath in, and held it.

With his eyes closed, he pictured Congressman Robert Elliott full of confidence and poise delivering one of his masterful speeches before Congress. He heard Congressman Smalls tell him that all he did was what needed to be done in the moment, and that when it was Malcolm's turn, he had no doubt he would do the same. Cedric had believed in him enough to share some of the most important parts of his life with him. He had told Malcolm that it was time for him to find his voice to set things right. With this knowledge firmly in his mind, Malcolm slowly let out his breath and stepped behind the podium.

He was ready to present his case, and he wasn't alone.

"You're Malcolm Williams?" the woman asked, surprised to see a teenager at the microphone.

"Yes ma'am."

"Okay," she said straightening her glasses. "And why do you think the farm you designated in your application should be added to the National Register of Historic Places?"

Malcolm took a final look at his notes and then dove into his prepared speech. "This land has been in my family for over a hundred years. It was purchased by my great-great-grandfather Cedric Johnson in the late 1870s. Although you have probably never heard of him, Cedric represents the best this country has to offer. Cedric was born on a plantation in Louisiana and was enslaved there until the end of the Civil War when he gained his freedom as a teenager. ¯Later, Cedric followed his soon-to-be wife to Mississippi and began working for her uncle Hiram Revels, who was the first African American member of Congress as a US Senator from Mississippi."

Malcolm became more relaxed as he spoke and slowly released his death grip on the sides of the podium.

"When Senator Revels returned to Mississippi to serve as the first president of Alcorn State University, Cedric remained in Washington to continue serving his country. He went on to work for the distinguished Congressman Robert Elliott from South Carolina, as well as the second Black senator, Blanche Bruce, also from Mississippi. During this time, he helped write, pass, and enforce significant pieces of legislation, which were signed into law by President Ulysses S. Grant. This legislation helped our country live up to its founding principle that all men are created equal.

"After the period known as Reconstruction came to a close, Cedric returned to Mississippi and became a history professor at Alcorn State. He married, purchased land, and built the farmhouse we're talking about today. He left a diary documenting all of this." Malcolm held up Cedric's diary for dramatic effect.

"Cedric was a man who refused to accept the inferior status that White supremacists assigned to him and other Black people in his community. He believed in a vibrant democracy where all citizens were represented in government, so he helped his community prepare for the impossible literacy tests that the State of Mississippi gave Black people to prevent them from voting. Because of these efforts, the Klan targeted him and dragged him from his house to his death, hanging him from a tree in his yard."

Malcolm paused to let that point marinate for a moment before continuing.

"This farm and the land it sits on are historically significant because it is where a great American and Mississippian lived, and sadly, where he died. The state has already taken part of my family's land to build the highway, and now they are attempting to take the rest. If they are allowed to succeed, all landmarks related to Cedric's distinguished and inspiring life will be lost. We can't allow that to happen to a notable historical figure. This land means a lot to my family, Alcorn State University, and the greater Natchez community. Thank you for hearing our case." Malcolm let out a huge sigh of relief, hoping he'd made his heroes proud.

"Thank you. Does anyone else want to speak regarding this application?"

"I'd like to say something," Jason said, raising his hand.

"Please step up to the podium," the Review Board woman said, looking further mystified by the interest of another teenager.

Jason nervously approached the stand, fingers trembling as he adjusted the microphone. "Thank you, ma'am. My name is Jason." His voice squeaked. He shuffled his feet, cleared his throat, and then continued evenly, holding on to the microphone for support. "I just want to say that a lot of our history, America's history, Mississippi's history, has been lost and buried, and that's not good. I never heard of Cedric Johnson, or Hiram Revels, or any of the other Mississippians that were just mentioned, but I should have. Their history is my history too. And you know what they say: when people don't learn from their history, they are doomed to repeat it. I'd much rather know our history, good and bad, so we can move toward a brighter future together instead of repeating the mistakes of our past. So I believe it's important that this house, my neighbor's house, stay put so people can learn from Cedric's story and hopefully this time, never forget our community's history. That's all. Thank you." Jason looked over at Malcolm while returning to his seat, and gave him a nod.

"Thank you both for your presentations," the Review Board woman said. "The hearing will recess for deliberations and will resume in approximately thirty minutes."

As soon as the Review Board members left the room, everyone let out a collective sigh, although Aunt Carol and Uncle Leroy still looked pretty nervous. Aunt Carol smiled proudly at Malcolm and then grabbed Uncle Leroy's hand and bowed her head in prayer.

"I knew you had it in you, Nephew. Chip off the old block," Uncle Corey said wistfully.

"You did so good!" Jasmine said, turning to Malcolm to give him a big hug.

"You hit it out of the park, Malcolm!" Professor Rogers said, patting him on the shoulder. "Did you say Cedric was a professor at Alcorn State?"

Malcolm nodded, feeling relieved his speech was over, but still extremely anxious about the result.

"Then there's a chance we might have some records for him in the vault. Could you swing by tomorrow so we can check it out?" Professor Rogers proposed cheerfully.

Malcolm nervously picked at a few loose threads at the bottom of his jacket. Part of him was still in the past, mixing images of his presentation with Cedric's memories, praying he had said enough.

"Absolutely," he responded absentmindedly, before bringing his attention back to the present. "Jas, do you think you could give me a ride tomorrow?"

"Sure!" she agreed, excited to help Malcolm see all of this through.

After a few minutes of silence, Aunt Carol opened her eyes and, appearing at peace, asked, "Who's the other young man who spoke in support of our family's farm?"

Malcolm piped up to Jason a few feet away: "Jason, come meet my family." Malcolm motioned him over and then turned back to Aunt Carol. "He's a friend I met down here who wanted to help set things right."

"Told ya I got your back," Jason whispered out of the side of his mouth to Malcolm.

Remembering Jason's pledge while playing their VR game and later on the phone, Malcolm smiled back. He had finally seen enough to believe Jason was sincere.

Jason put his hand out and shook Aunt Carol's hand. "Hi ma'am. Pleasure to meet you. These are my parents." Jason introduced his mom and dad. "And you might know Miss Madeline who organizes the bake sale at the county fair. She's my neighbor and when she heard one of Jasmine's friends was in trouble, she insisted on coming." Miss Madeline offered Aunt Carol and Malcolm a hug instead of a handshake.

"It's so nice to finally meet y'all," she said, releasing them.

"Hi Miss Madeline," Jasmine said, coming over to give her a hug as well.

"Hey shugah!" she fondly greeted Jasmine as she tightened her arms around her.

Malcolm looked around at the people who'd come to support him and his family, noting that he had only met most of them this summer. "Thanks everybody," Malcolm said gratefully to his new friends. "We really appreciate you being here."

After everyone visited for a little while, they began to meander back to their seats still chatting with one another. Aunt Carol seemed to be in a deep conversation with Jason's parents, and Miss Madeline was laughing wholeheartedly at something Professor Rogers had just said.

"Gotdammit. Looks like I owe Malcolm a hundred dollars," Uncle Leroy said under his breath to Uncle Corey, referencing the bet they'd made during their bid whist game about White folks not caring what happened to them.

"Don't remind him," Uncle Corey whispered, giving him a nudge in the side.

Just then the Review Board reentered the room. Silence weighed heavily in the air, as no one dared to move and affect the board's decision.

"Please be seated," the woman with the gavel announced. Immediately, tension filled the room as everyone returned to their seats.

"I just have one more question," the woman announced. The silence in the room became deafening. "How do we know the things you said about Cedric are real?" she asked, peering over the frames of her glasses. She stared intensely at Malcolm waiting on him to provide proof to his story.

Malcolm pulled out Cedric's diary again, walking closer to the woman so that she could witness the age of the book and its tattered cover with her own eyes. "Everything Cedric wrote in this diary can be independently verified. It's not a history that a lot of people know, but it doesn't make it any less real." Malcolm presented the book to her assertively, knowing that if the case rested on the legitimacy of the diary entries, he alone knew just how real they were.

The woman squinted her eyes, carefully choosing her next words, fully aware of the impact of her decision. "After considering the testimony of the witnesses and the historic record, the board and I have decided to *conditionally* grant your request for the Johnson farm to be added to Mississippi's list on the National Register of Historic Places. We would like to verify some of the historic events you mentioned today, before issuing final approval."

"Yay!" everyone hollered, rejoicing loudly before the woman banged her gavel to restore order. Malcolm was confident that their research would confirm that everything he'd said was true. All of his friends and family continued to embrace each other as they lowered their voices and tried to contain their excitement, waiting patiently for the woman to finish speaking.

"Please take a form to request a plaque be placed on the front of the house and take this pamphlet encouraging you to allow public visitation. This hearing is adjourned." She got up and walked over to where Malcolm was in the front row. "Congratulations," she said, handing him the paperwork and smiling warmly.

Malcolm looked around the room. It was abuzz with excitement. "It worked," Malcolm said under his breath, looking at everyone smiling and reveling in their win. "We did it."

Everyone grabbed their belongings and moved out into the hallway. Malcolm's head was still spinning, and all he could hear were joyous sounds of laughter and glee. He waited for everyone else to file out of the courtroom and then paused in the doorway, closing his eyes to savor the moment. "We did it, Cedric. We saved our farm," he whispered before calmly exiting the room. He walked straight over to Aunt Carol, who was beaming at him with proud eyes and open arms.

"I can't thank you all enough for your support today," Aunt Carol said, taking Malcolm under her wing, looking around at everyone misty-eyed. "Y'all are all welcome back at my house for some celebratory dessert. I got some cakes from Jasmine's grandma, just in case things went well today or for a pick-me-up if they didn't." She smiled radiantly as she wiped a tear of joy from her eye.

"Um, did you happen to get a rum cake?" Miss Madeline asked, her eyes lighting up in anticipation.

"Sure did. Two of 'em. And even better, I fixed some homemade peach cobbler," she added to the announcement, ensuring no one could possibly stay away.

Malcolm's eyes lit up as he remembered how delicious Grandma Evelyn's cobbler tasted. Aunt Carol's was surely every bit as tasty. "And vanilla ice cream?" he asked, hoping the dessert would be exactly like in his memories.

Aunt Carol winked and planted a big kiss on his forehead.

"Then what are we waiting for!" Miss Madeline exclaimed excitedly, and began ushering everyone out the front door.

55

Malcolm was so excited the next morning to find out if the vault might have more information about Cedric's life, he had hardly slept the night before. Saving the family farm was a huge win, but Malcolm was still distraught by how tragically Cedric's life had ended and felt he needed closure. He didn't want the obituary to be the last thing he remembered about him.

After waiting until a respectable hour, Malcolm dashed downstairs and punched Jasmine's number into the phone. "Hey Jasmine, what time you gonna be ready to go to Alcorn?" he asked breathlessly.

"Malcolm, it's only 9:00 a.m.!" Jasmine retorted, still half asleep.

"I know. I waited a couple of hours before calling," Malcolm clarified, waiting expectantly on the other line for her to get a move on.

"Jeez, Mal." She sighed. "Today's my day to sleep in. But you were very brave at the hearing yesterday," she said coyly, then laughed. "All right. I'll pick you up around eleven."

"Bet!" Malcolm agreed eagerly, and then mindlessly hung up the phone without saying bye.

By 11:45 a.m., Malcolm and Jasmine were already on campus making a beeline for Professor Rogers's office. Malcolm reached for the door handle only to find it locked and that he wasn't there. Malcolm could hardly contain himself. "He knows we're coming, right?" He knocked on the door a few times in case he was inside reading.

"Yes, of course he knows. But I don't know his morning schedule," Jasmine said. "Don't worry, he's here somewhere." Jasmine grabbed his hand and led him up a flight of stairs to a hallway of classrooms, only a few of them being occupied at the time.

Finally, they made it to the end of the hall and found Professor Rogers giving a lecture to a class of about twenty students. They quietly entered and sat down in the back row of seats, trying their best not to disturb the class.

Professor Rogers's voice echoed throughout the classroom. "And so you see here the various barriers that the state has erected over the years to keep Black people from being able to fully participate in the voting franchise. From outright denials of citizenship during the slavery period to grandfather clauses, poll taxes, literacy tests, and rampant violence and intimidation in the Jim Crow era to felony disenfranchisement, gerrymandering, and voter ID laws today," he stated boldly.

On the projector screen, Professor Rogers clicked through a variety of pictures illuminating each of the concepts he discussed, making a point to stop in between each slide so that the images could marinate in his students' minds. "As recently as two years ago, in June 2013, the Supreme Court in *Shelby County v. Holder* struck down a key protection in the Voting Rights Act, the preclearance requirement, which for the past fifty years has limited Southern states' ability to implement discriminatory schemes to further disenfranchise Blacks. What does the elimination of that protection mean for the fragile state of our democracy? Only time will tell, but if past is prologue, one has reason to be concerned." He powered off the projector and gathered his papers and then turned his full attention to the class to conclude his lecture.

"Okay, your assignment, due in a week, is to write an essay on the threat that the disenfranchisement of a segment of a population poses to the viability and validity of a democracy. Don't forget to take into account examples from other countries throughout history. Class is dismissed." The classroom began to fill with noise as students made their way toward the doors.

When the classroom cleared, Jasmine and Malcolm walked down the steps to greet Professor Rogers. They stood off in a corner behind a few students who lingered around to pick the professor's brain. As soon as the final student receded from the podium, Jasmine skipped up to her dad.

"Hi Daddy!" Jasmine said, giving him a hug.

Professor Rogers's face lit up when he saw them. "I'm glad you two could make it," he said. "And perfect timing too. That was my last class for the day. Shall we go check out the vault?" Professor Rogers wasted no time in getting right to the point.

"Yes sir!" Malcolm said, sharing Professor Rogers's excitement.

Fifteen minutes later and on the other side of campus, Malcolm stood in front of a stately brick building framed by two large white marble columns. Professor Rogers presented his faculty badge to the head librarian, and then led them past the front desk and down two flights of stairs. They entered a basement with spotty fluorescent lighting that had aisles of cardboard boxes on metal shelves from wall to wall.

"How do you find anything in here?" Malcolm asked, feeling daunted. He touched one of the boxes leaving a finger trail in the accumulated dust, and then sneezed from the few dust particles that had lifted into the air.

"Bless you. Well, the faculty archives are supposed to be organized by decade. When did you say Cedric taught here?" Professor Rogers inquired.

Malcolm rubbed his nose, thwarting any more sneezes and thought back to when Reconstruction ended and Cedric moved back to Mississippi. "Maybe around 1877. I'm not sure how long he taught though."

"Okay. So, we're talking about the oldest records," Professor Rogers said, leading them all the way to the back of the room. The farther back they went, the fewer materials were on the shelves. Malcolm began to doubt they would find anything from someone who taught more than a century ago.

Deep in the back of the room, a lone box labeled *President Hiram Revels* sat on a shelf. "What about that box there?" Malcolm asked.

Professor Rogers used a step stool to retrieve the box, and set it on a table against the wall at the end of the aisle. With the anticipation of Christmas morning, Malcolm opened the box and pulled out a Bible, some pictures, and newspaper clippings from the day Revels was sworn in as a US Senator. As soon as Malcolm saw Senator Revels's picture, he smiled; it was like seeing an old friend he hadn't seen in over a hundred years. He looked around hoping he'd find a box for Cedric nearby, but he didn't see anything else.

"Sorry, Mal. I don't see anything for Cedric," Jasmine observed, looking around as well.

Malcolm's shoulders drooped in disappointment even as he tried to make himself feel good that at least they'd found materials for Senator Revels. As they began to make their way back through the mostly empty shelves, Malcolm noticed a large tattered envelope on the floor. He picked it up to put it back on the shelf, but didn't know where it belonged because it wasn't labeled. He looked inside to see if the materials were dated and immediately recognized the handwriting on a piece of paper.

A grin slowly spread across Malcolm's face as he went back over to the table and pulled Cedric's diary from his backpack. His hands shook a little as he placed the loose piece of paper next to the open diary and began comparing the handwriting. Professor Rogers joined him at the table, his eyes wide in excitement from seeing the diary up close for the first time.

"This is it!" Malcolm shouted. It wasn't much but it was something. Jasmine walked over and stood behind him.

Malcolm poured the rest of the envelope's contents onto the table, examining each item one by one. Inside he found a newspaper article written by Cedric about John Willis Menard's election on the masthead of the *New Orleans Tribune*, a copy of "Ain't I a Woman" signed by Sojourner Truth, Cedric's Mississippi voter registration card, a receipt of deposit for $250 from Freedman's Bank, and a handwritten draft of the address to President Grant that the congressmen wrote after the Hamburg massacre.

"This is incredible," Malcolm mused as he flipped through the documents. Professor Rogers continued to peer over his shoulders, shifting his stance to get a better look at each prize.

When Malcolm had finished looking at everything, he put the items back in the envelope and turned to Professor Rogers. "Here you go, Professor," he said, picking up the diary and placing it gently in the professor's hands. "Aunt Carol was so excited about the diary, she read it in one sitting and then asked me what I thought we should do with it. It's all yours on one condition."

"Shoot," Professor Rogers said.

"Could you make sure your students learn about it?" Malcolm requested. "I want to make sure Cedric's story lives on and continues to inspire."

"Absolutely! Malcolm, I'm not only going to share it with my students," he said, pausing to place his hand on Malcolm's shoulder, "but with the world."

"Thanks, Professor Rogers," Malcolm said, now cheesing from ear to ear.

"No, thank you, Malcolm, for this great gift to Alcorn State. I'll have the head librarian log it into our archive system. And, rest assured, if the school earns any money off showcasing this diary, the proceeds will go to your family." Professor Rogers patted Malcolm on the back, squeezed his shoulder, and pulled him in for a final hug.

As he was walking out of the university vault holding Jasmine's hand, Malcolm caught his reflection in the side of one of the metal shelves. At first he didn't think anything of it, but then he noticed it looked like there was something on his face above his lip. He walked closer to get a better look and noticed his reflection was sporting a distinctive mustache that curled up on the ends. The two reflections looked at each other for a moment, and then the one on the metal shelf smiled at him, winked, and then turned and drifted away.

Malcolm felt in his heart that would be the last time he saw Cedric, and he already missed him. But now that the farm and Cedric's legacy were secure, Malcolm took satisfaction in knowing that he could finally rest in peace.

After a long summer in Mississippi, it felt good to finally be back home in D.C. Malcolm had missed his mom, his friends, and his hood. As his bus passed through the city streets, Malcolm kept shaking his head, trying to erase the double vision he was having. He couldn't help but see D.C. the way it was in the 1870s superimposed over the way it looked now. He saw the marshes and swamps on top of the roads and manicured lawns, and livestock and carriages intertwined with buses and cars. Yet the Capitol and White House looked the same, and the Washington Monument was still enclosed in scaffolding and under construction. As his bus passed the Capitol, he thought he saw an old Black man sweeping the steps who reminded him of Buddy.

As soon as he stepped off his bus at Union Station, his mom greeted him with *Welcome Home* balloons in hand. "I missed you so much! Aunt Carol says you went down there and saved Mississippi," she said, squeezing him tight.

"Not quite, Mom," he said, laughing while hugging her back.

"Seriously, I'm real proud of you, baby, and I know how proud your dad would be too," she said, holding his chin and looking deeply into his eyes.

"Thanks, Mom," Malcolm responded modestly. Although there was nothing he could do to bring his dad back, he felt a lot closer to him after his stay in Mississippi and being able to save his dad's childhood home was icing on the cake.

Half an hour later, Malcolm was walking through the front door of their apartment. The phone was ringing as they entered. Malcolm answered: "Hello."

"You made it back safely?" Uncle Corey's voice boomed through the speaker. Malcolm smiled.

"Yeah. It wasn't too bad of a trip," Malcolm replied, thinking it was definitely better than the long train rides he took all over the South in the 1870s.

"Cool. So imagine my surprise when I got home from my first day of working at the grocery store and found a voter registration card from the 1800s on my pillow."

Malcolm laughed. "Oh yeah, you found that?"

"Yeah man. What's that about?"

Malcolm had been waiting for this call since he had left Mississippi. He replied encouragingly, "Man, I just remembered you saying no one in our family ever had a say in how this country was run. I wanted to give you proof that even if your dad and grandfather couldn't vote for most of their lives, your great-grandfather did, so don't give up. Our story's not done yet."

Uncle Corey took a second to respond and then mumbled through the phone, "All right, little dude." There was a pause, and Malcolm thought he heard a sniffle coming from the other end of the line.

"Now listen, just 'cause you out of Mississippi don't mean I'm gonna stop checking on you," Uncle Corey continued, his voice having snapped back to its usual bounce. "I'm gonna be calling every Sunday night around this time to see how you doing. Cool?"

"Bet. Congrats on your new job, by the way."

"Thanks man. Uncle Leroy introduced me to a grocer down at the farmers market who was willing to give me a shot. It's not much, but it's a start." Uncle Corey had hope in his voice, something Malcolm knew had been elusive for a long time in his uncle's life.

"A start is good," Malcolm said, smiling, savoring the peacefulness of the moment.

After the call, Malcolm headed to his room. He threw his backpack on his bed and sat down, looking at the empty space on the wall where his dad's posters used to hang. He missed them, especially after seeing them all summer at Aunt Carol's house. He pulled his backpack over to him and pulled out some of the drawings he'd made while in Mississippi. Thankfully, he found some tape in his desk drawer and carefully hung each one on the wall where the posters used to be. He was standing back admiring them when his mom walked in.

"Malcolm, what's this?" she asked, walking up to the drawings to get a better look.

He motioned to them one by and one and said, "These are just some sketches I made of things Cedric wrote about in his diary."

His mother's eyes scanned each piece of artwork in admiration. "They are so lifelike. They have so much detail it makes you feel like you're there. What's this one about?" she asked, pointing to a drawing of a man giving an animated speech in a large ceremonial room before an adoring crowd.

"That's Congressman Robert Elliott arguing in support of the Civil Rights Act of 1875," Malcolm explained.

His mom's jaw fell open, unable to believe what she was hearing or seeing. "But he's Black. I didn't know there were Black congressmen back then." She shook her head, digesting this realization.

Malcolm nodded.

She reached out and touched one of the more intense sketches. "These are really good, Malcolm. I wish there was a way you could share them with people," she said.

His mom's words resonated with him. The journey Cedric took Malcolm on had impacted him deeply, and he couldn't help but wish that other people could experience it too. As devastating as it had been to learn about these events—stripped from the history books and re-created in lies—learning the truth had saved him in a way. It helped him see himself and his place in the world differently. Staring at his drawings on the wall, he had an idea. "Mom, can I borrow your computer?"

That evening after googling *how to start a blog*, Malcolm took pictures of all his sketches and began uploading them into a blog page. He uploaded all of his drawings from Reconstruction and then began to add sketches of present-day Black experiences. Some were sad, like the faces of countless unarmed Black people shot by the police or neighborhood kids killed in gang violence, but others put a smile on his face, like pictures of his family reunion, a game of pickup basketball with Uncle Corey, or President Obama hanging with his family at the White House.

At first he was stumped about what to name his blog, but then it came to him: *Black Was the Ink*. Black like the ink in his drawings that would ensure the lessons of Reconstruction were never lost again. Black like the ink used to write the laws intended to protect his people, but also like the ink used to strip their rights away. And Black like the people who have tried for centuries to hold America true to the words written in her founding documents: that all men are created equal.

EPILOGUE

On a cool autumn day in the fall of 2015, Malcolm decided to attend a rally in front of the D.C. City Council building, where protesters were demanding stronger checks on the police after yet another shooting of an unarmed Black man. Since he had been back in D.C., his mom agreed that he could contribute some time during the school year to a few causes he believed in, as long as it didn't interfere with his schoolwork or basketball. That didn't leave a lot of free time, but now that he had gotten a taste of what it was like to affect change, he was hooked. He always made sure to include drawings of the few events he did attend in his blog.

The sun was beginning to set, and a spokesperson from the mayor's office emerged from behind the double glass doors of the government building and stood at the top of the stone steps to address the crowd. Malcolm was glad he had arrived early, because from where he was standing, he had a front-row view of the spokesperson and could clearly hear what she had to say.

"Thank you for taking such a strong interest in this issue. I just want you to know that the mayor has heard your concerns and is supporting a bill to address this issue. At the same time, we are also doing our best to reduce crime, so it's important for us to be careful in our efforts and not hamper the police department's ability to do its job. Thank you for coming out," she said in an effort to get the crowd to disperse.

Malcolm found her response to the protest to be incredibly unsatisfying. "Excuse me, ma'am," Malcolm said, stepping forward, while searching for the courage to speak. "I just have one question."

"Um, okay, go ahead," the spokesperson said, appearing to be thrown off by such a young person questioning her.

He raised his voice so she could hear every word. "Thank you. It's . . . it's just that, while crime is clearly an issue in D.C., the reason there is so much crime is because there is so much poverty. Most people turn to crime out of desperation. So why not address the real issue by investing in our communities with jobs and training programs instead of sending in the police to hunt us down?" He finished his question and stared expectantly at the spokesperson.

"Um, well, that is a pretty big question, young man. I mean, it is very complicated," the spokesperson attempted to explain, clearly racking her brain for a satisfying answer. "There are budgetary constraints, for instance, and it is difficult to find programs that really work, but please believe poverty reduction is also a high priority for this administration. Thank you. No more questions," she said, before turning to walk away.

Malcolm felt unheard, but he knew better than to stop there. He would follow up later with some letters to city council members. He doubted the budget to reduce or eliminate poverty was anywhere close to the budget for the police department. The more he thought about it, the more he needed to get the day's events out of his mind and down on paper.

Malcolm sat down on some nearby steps, pulled out his notepad and favorite pen, and began drawing a sketch of the protest to add to his blog. He focused on the pained expression on the face of a little brown-skinned girl who couldn't have been any older than seven carrying a sign that said NO JUSTICE, NO PEACE. He hoped with all his heart that she wasn't the daughter of the man the police had shot, but he had seen her pain in too many other faces—including his own—to ignore the truth. As he was adding cheerful bows to the ends of her braids, he felt a tap on his shoulder.

"Hello there, son."

Malcolm looked up and saw a kind-faced Black woman in a purple pantsuit trying to get his attention.

"Hi?" Malcolm responded quizzically, wondering why this stranger was talking to him.

"That was a very good question you asked back there. What newspaper do you work for?" she inquired, assuming Malcolm was much older than he was.

"Um, I don't. I'm in school, but I do have a blog," Malcolm answered.

"Really?" The woman was taken aback by his answer, then she continued in a softer voice, even more intrigued. "Do you have a lot of readers who follow your blog?"

Malcolm, still feeling a bit dejected from the spokesperson's dismissal, replied humbly, "I do all right. Most of my classmates have started checking it out. I'm planning to reach out to other high schools soon."

"Do you mean to tell me you're just in high school?" she asked, bewildered, arching her eyebrows in shock.

"Yeah, I'm a junior this year," Malcolm clarified proudly.

She dug in her purse for something while continuing the conversation with Malcolm. "Very impressive. Well, it seems like you have an interest in helping your community and a desire to find solutions to tough problems. We're in the process of bringing on interns this fall, and I'm wondering if you might be interested in interning for my office?" she said, handing Malcolm her card.

Malcolm looked at it: *United States Congresswoman Regina T. Stevens*.

Malcolm's jaw dropped. "You're a congresswoman?" he asked in disbelief as he quickly rose to his feet.

She smiled tenderly, appreciating the young man's passion, and responded optimistically, "Yes. I was just elected to my first term, and I could certainly benefit from having someone with a youthful perspective, and who has a good head on their shoulders on my team."

Malcolm looked up at the lady and smiled. "Thank you, ma'am. There's nothing I'd rather do more. There's a lot of work to be done," Malcolm said, shaking the congresswoman's hand. He couldn't help but believe that somewhere Cedric was smiling down at him.

MEET THE STATESMEN IN THE BOOK

BLANCHE BRUCE (1841–1898) US Senator from Mississippi (1875–81) and the first Black senator to serve a full term. Born enslaved in Virginia to a Black woman and a White plantation owner. Only former slave to preside over a session of the US Senate. Received eight votes for vice president at the 1880 Republican National Convention. Register of the Treasury (1881–85, 1897–98), making him the first Black person to sign their name to US currency.

RICHARD CAIN (1825–1887) South Carolina state senator (1868–72), member of the US House of Representatives (1873–75; 1877–79). Born free in what is now West Virginia to a Cherokee mother and Black father. Attended Wilberforce University and Divinity School. Ordained minister with the African Methodist Episcopal (AME) Church and pastor of Emanuel AME Church in Charleston, South Carolina. Founder of *South Carolina Leader* newspaper (later renamed the *Missionary Record*). Co-founder of Lincolnville, South Carolina, a large tract of farmland that was subdivided and sold exclusively to freedmen. President of Paul Quinn College in Texas.

ROBERT ELLIOTT (1842–1884) Member of South Carolina House of Representatives (1868–70). Member of US House of Representatives (1870-74). South Carolina Speaker of the House of Representatives (1874–76). South Carolina attorney general (1876–77). Little is known about the early details of his life. He was a trained lawyer who spoke French, Spanish, and English, and frequently quoted the classics. Editor of the *Missionary Record*. Opened the United States' first known Black-owned law firm. Special customs inspector for the Treasury Department (1879–82).

JOHN MERCER LANGSTON (1829–1897) One of
the first Black elected officials in the United States
(elected town clerk in Brownhelm, Ohio, in 1855).
Co-drafter of the Civil Rights Act of 1875. First
Black congressman from Virginia (1890–1891).
Born free in Virginia to a freedwoman and her
former master. Graduate of Oberlin College.
Attorney. Founder of Howard University School of
Law. President of Virginia Normal and Collegiate
Institute (now Virginia State University).

P.B.S. PINCHBACK (1837–1921) Louisiana state sen-
ator (1868–71). Lieutenant governor of Louisiana (1871–72). Louisiana governor (Dec. 1872–Jan.
1873), making him the first Black US governor.
Elected to the US House of Representatives and
US Senate, but never seated. Born free in Macon,
Georgia, to a freed mulatto woman and a White
planter. One of the first Black-commissioned
Union officers. Co-founder of Southern University
in Louisiana.

JOSEPH RAINEY (1832–1887) South Carolina state
senator (1870). First and longest serving Black
member of the US House of Representatives during
Reconstruction (1870–79). Special agent for the US
Treasury Department and owner of a brokerage
and banking business. Born enslaved in South
Carolina, but his father purchased his freedom
during his childhood.

HIRAM REVELS (1827–1901) Mississippi state senator
(1869–1870). US Senator from Mississippi and first Black member of Congress (1870–71). Ordained minister in the AME Church. Chaplain in the Union army and recruiter of Black regiments. President of Alcorn Agricultural and Mechanical College (now called Alcorn State University). Born free in North Carolina to parents who were free people of color.

ROBERT SMALLS (1839–1915) Member of the South
Carolina House of Representatives (1868–70). South Carolina state senator (1870–75). Member of the US House of Representatives (1875–79, 1882–87). Collector of Customs for the Port of Beaufort, South Carolina (1890–93, 1897–1913). Born enslaved in South Carolina in the heart of the Sea Islands to an enslaved Gullah woman and a White man thought to be the plantation owner's son. Trained as a seafarer. Successfully commandeered the Confederate states' ship *Planter* and delivered it to the Union Army, gaining freedom for himself,

his family, and the crew. His refusal to give up his seat to a White passenger on a Philadelphia streetcar in 1864 led the Pennsylvania legislature to pass a bill outlawing segregation on public transportation. Authored language as a delegate to South Carolina's 1868 Constitutional Convention that made South Carolina the first Southern state with a free and compulsory public education system.

TIMELINE OF EVENTS

Before Reconstruction . . . .

1619	Beginning of English-speaking transatlantic slave trade
June 17, 1822	Denmark Vesey's slave revolt in Charleston, SC, thwarted
March 6, 1857	Supreme Court issues *Dred Scott v. Sandford* declaring people of African descent are not US citizens
April 12, 1861	Civil War begins
January 1, 1863	President Lincoln issues Emancipation Proclamation freeing slaves in the Confederate states
May 5, 1863	Freedman's Village created on Robert E. Lee's Arlington estate

Reconstruction Era . . . .

January 12, 1865	General Sherman issues Field Order No. 15, colloquially known as "40 acres and a mule," which President Andrew Johnson later rescinds
March 3, 1865	Congress issues charter for Freedman's Savings and Trust Company (Freedman's Saving Bank) and establishes The Freedmen's Bureau
April 9, 1865	Civil War ends
April 14–15, 1865	President Lincoln is assassinated; Andrew Johnson becomes president
December 6, 1865	13th Amendment ratified abolishing slavery, except for those duly convicted of a crime
July 30, 1866	Mechanics' Institute massacre (New Orleans, LA)

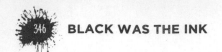

July 9, 1868	14th Amendment ratified granting birthright citizenship and prohibiting states from denying people rights without due process or equal protection of the laws
February 27, 1869	John Willis Menard is the first Black person elected to Congress, but never seated
March 4, 1869	Ulysses S. Grant inaugurated as president
February 3, 1870	15th Amendment ratified prohibiting states from denying or abridging citizens' right to vote on account of race, color, or previous condition of servitude
February 25, 1870	Hiram Revels sworn in as US Senator and first Black member of Congress
May 31, 1870	First Ku Klux Klan Enforcement Act enacted
June 2, 1870	Congress establishes the US Department of Justice, which prioritizes dismantling White domestic terrorist groups
December 12, 1870	Joseph Rainey (SC) becomes first Black member of US House of Representatives
Spring 1871	The following Black people join US House of Representatives: Jefferson Long (GA), Robert De Large (SC), Robert Elliott (SC), Benjamin Turner (AL), Josiah Walls (FL)
February 28, 1871	Second Ku Klux Klan Enforcement Act enacted
April 20, 1871	Third Ku Klux Klan Enforcement Act enacted
March 4, 1873	The following Black people join US House of Representatives: Richard Cain (SC), John Lynch (MS), Alonzo Ransier (SC), James Rapier (AL)
April 13, 1873	Colfax massacre (LA)
January 6, 1874	Congressman Robert Elliott delivers his famous speech supporting the Civil Rights Act on the House floor
June 29, 1874	Freedman's Savings and Trust Company closes
February 5, 1875	Civil Rights Act of 1875 enacted

March 4, 1875	Blanche Bruce (MS) joins Senate; the following Black people join US House of Representatives: Jeremiah Haralson (AL), John Hyman (NC), Charles Nash (LA), Robert Smalls (SC)
March 27, 1876	Supreme Court issues decision in *U.S. v. Cruikshank,* throwing out convictions from Colfax massacre
July 8, 1876	Hamburg massacre (SC)
February 26, 1877	Wormley Agreement reached, resolving disputed 1876 presidential election
March 4, 1877	Rutherford B. Hayes sworn in as president and withdraws remaining federal troops from the South

After Reconstruction . . . .

October 15, 1883	Supreme Court issues decision in the *Civil Rights Cases* invalidating Civil Rights Act of 1875
March 4, 1897	George Henry White (NC) is last Black member of Congress elected from a Southern state for 76 years
March 23, 1900	Freedman's Village is permanently closed
September 9, 1957	Civil Rights Act of 1957 enacted creating Civil Rights Division at US Department of Justice
June 12, 1963	NAACP (MS) field secretary Medgar Evers is assassinated
September 15, 1963	16th Street Baptist Church is bombed
July 2, 1964	Civil Rights Act of 1964 enacted, readopting many of the provisions from the Civil Rights Act of 1875
August 6, 1965	Voting Rights Act of 1965 enacted
January 3, 1967	Edward Brooke (MA) becomes first Black senator since 1881
March 30, 1971	Congressional Black Caucus is founded

January 3, 1973   Barbara Jordan (TX) and Andrew Young (GA) become first Black people elected to Congress from the South since 1897

January 22, 2009   Barack Obama inaugurated as first Black president

June 25, 2013   Supreme Court issues decision in *Shelby County v. Holder* curtailing the Voting Rights Act of 1965

June 17, 2015   Massacre at Emanuel AME Church (Charleston, SC)

January 6, 2021   Challenging the validity of votes from majority-Black jurisdictions, supporters of the defeated incumbent president storm the US Capitol in a deadly coup attempt aimed at overturning the 2020 presidential election

January 20, 2021   Former US Senator Kamala Harris is sworn in as the first woman as well as first Black and South Asian person to serve as Vice President of the United States

AUTHOR'S NOTE

I began writing *Black Was the Ink* in the summer of 2015 because I was frustrated with the pace of racial progress in America. Even as we were making positive strides, I saw signs that the pendulum was about to swing in the opposite direction with the ultimate catalyst being the tragic massacre at Mother Emanuel Church in Charleston, South Carolina on June 17, 2015. At the time, I was on maternity leave with my son, whose middle name happens to be Emmanuel. As I stared into my baby's innocent face, I struggled with how to prepare him for a world filled with so much inexplicable hatred toward people who looked like him.

Following the massacre, I began exploring the church's history and was surprised to learn that Denmark Vesey, the founder of the church, led one of the largest attempted slave revolts on American soil, and that Richard "Daddy" Cain served as pastor of the church before becoming one of the first Black members of Congress in the 1870s. For over 150 years, the church stood as a bedrock for civil rights activism, as evidenced by the church's pastor, Clementa Pinckney, who was also serving as a South Carolina State Senator at the time of his assassination on June 17th.

Learning about Mother Emanuel's legacy crystallized for me the connection between slavery, the collapse of Reconstruction, the civil rights movement, and the danger that White supremacist ideology continues to pose today. Through *Black Was the Ink*, I hoped to teach my children about an earlier period, Reconstruction, where incredible advances toward racial equality took place, only to be unraveled by forces of hate. Perhaps armed with this knowledge, they would be better prepared to face the challenges of their time.

Reconstruction is a rather obscure era in American history, intentionally so, due to the "Lost Cause" myth that was created directly after the war and that continues to be taught in many school curriculums in the South today. However, after some initial research, I was grateful to find a handful of resources that helped elucidate this period, including W.E.B. Du Bois's *Black Reconstruction in America*, Philip Dray's *Capitol*

Men, Charles Lane's *The Day Freedom Died*, as well as several books by Eric Foner, among others. First-hand accounts like Congressman John Roy Lynch's book *The Facts of Reconstruction* and the treasure trove of congressional records at the Library of Congress, and Henry Louis Gates' PBS documentary, *Reconstruction: America After the Civil War*, were also incredibly informative.

During my research, I couldn't escape the parallels I observed between the present and the past: the indiscriminate killing of Black people often without any accountability, the false claims of voter fraud to justify voter suppression, and the failure to address the root causes of poverty in the Black community. Even though it's good to exercise some caution against judging historical people by today's standards, one thing I do hope this story makes clear is that there have always been people, regardless of era, who knew the difference between right and wrong—and some even courageous enough to act on those convictions.

A lot of energy was used to bury the history of Reconstruction and distort its memory, and much injustice was built atop those lies. But remembering the good that the first Black congressmen and their White allies accomplished is one way to fight back against that injustice.

This is why, with few exceptions, most of the people Malcolm meets as Cedric in the book are real historical figures, and in many instances, I incorporated their actual words into the book's dialogue. It is my hope that readers discover in these words the inspiration to take on the mantle of these visionaries and doers, and finish the task of rebuilding a truly indivisible nation with liberty and justice for all.

ACKNOWLEDGMENTS

First and foremost, I am eternally grateful to Lee & Low Books and to Stacy Whitman, the publisher of the imprint Tu Books, for choosing my manuscript as the 2019 New Vision Honor Award for new authors of color and deciding to publish this book. Lee & Low serves such a vital function in providing a vehicle for people of color to have their voices heard and their stories told in an industry where few people look like us. Thank you for seeing the potential in my book and being willing to work with me to find a way to share with a young audience this story about a critical, yet largely unknown piece of American history.

To Elise McMullen-Ciotti, my amazing editor, thanks for "getting" the story and being such a pleasure to work with. Your excellent ideas on how to revamp the structure and flow vastly improved the storytelling. To my copyeditor, Chandra Wohleber, thank you. You are a phenomenal copyeditor. Both your precision and fresh eyes were greatly appreciated. To Emily Robinson, thank you for proofreading the book with a compassionate spirit and open heart. To my book designer Sheila Smallwood, thank you for creating an amazing book design that brought all the elements together to feel historic and modern at the same time. And to my illustrator, Justin Johnson, thank you for literally bringing my words to life with your beautiful, poignant art.

Writing this book has been a labor of love that I could never have accomplished without the unyielding support of my family and friends whose encouragement and belief in me every step of the way fueled my fire to the finish line. To my four beautiful sons, thank you for giving me a reason to write this book in the hopes of arming you with the power of truth so that you are never led astray.

To the love of my life, thank you for entertaining my obsession with Reconstruction for the last six years, for talking through storylines in the middle of the night, for sharing your insights into life as a Capitol Hill staffer, and for giving me space to write in the midst of our bustling and growing family.

To my mom, Maria, thank you for being the only person who read every single draft and for your meticulous attention to detail in making sure that every *i* was dotted and every *t* crossed. To my dad, Mike, thank you for your constant faith in me and for filling me with confidence about my capabilities and gifts from the moment I was born. To my sister, Rissa, thank you for your incredible edits and belief in this book's ability to make a difference. To my wonderful and brilliant cousins, Jenny, Rocki, and Cary, thank you for reading early versions, when it wasn't much more than an idea in my head, and for encouraging me to keep going.

To all the friends and loved ones who read drafts or listened to me drone on about the idea, like my line sisters, especially April, Consuelo, and Brandi; my prophytes, especially Jamila and Erica; my girlfriends, especially Miya, Melyssa, Chantale, Courtney, Devin, Kim, and Anika; my young readers, Amir, Samiya, Shani, and Emma; and my scholastic readers Barbara S., Barbara B., Teffanie W., and Jean, thank you for your encouragement, support, and invaluable feedback. To my HUSL crew, thank you for always being down to get into some good trouble. I couldn't ask for a more supportive and inspiring team.

Special thanks to my loving grandparents, especially Mama Glo, whose stories of childhood summers spent on her family's farm in the country and regular visits to the cemetery to lay flowers on the tombstones of loved ones forged my connection to people who lived a century or more before me and showed me that we never really leave the past behind.

Last, but not least, I thank every American who has tried to help our country live up to the promise of its ideals and truly be a nation that believes all men and women are created equal and are equally entitled to life, liberty, and the pursuit of happiness.

ABOUT THE AUTHOR

Michelle Coles is an accomplished civil rights attorney and a proud alumna of the University of Virginia and Howard University School of Law. As a ninth-generation Louisianan, she is highly attuned to the struggles African Americans have faced in overcoming the legacy of slavery and the periods of government-sanctioned discrimination that followed. She hopes that by revealing oft-hidden Black history, her debut novel will empower young people with tools to shape their destiny. Find her on the web at michellecoles.com.

IMAGE CREDITS

Illustration of Congressman Robert Elliott delivering his speech in support of the Civil Rights Act, page 80. From *The Shackle Broken– By the Genius of Freedom* by E. Sachse & Co., c. 1874. Illustration held in the Library of Congress Prints and Photographs Division in Washington, D.C.

Illustration of Ku Klux Klan members dressed in their disguises, page 177. Illustration from *Harper's Weekly* Vol. XII.—No. 625. Originally published on December 19, 1868.

Illustration of the Colfax massacre, page 242. Illustration from *Harper's Weekly* Vol. XVII.—No. 854. Originally published on May 10, 1873. While the image is pulled from *Harper's Weekly*, the accompanying article on that page is not. *Harper's Weekly* correctly attributed the violence at Colfax to the White terrorists.

Illustration of the Hamburg massacre, page 292. Illustration from *Harper's Weekly* Vol. XX.—No. 1024. Originally published on August 12, 1876.

Portrait of Senator Blanche Bruce, page 349. Portrait photograph taken between 1865 and 1880. Photograph held in the Brady-Handy Collection, Library of Congress Prints and Photographs Division in Washington, D.C.

Portrait of Congressman Richard Cain, page 349. Portrait photograph taken by C.M. Bell Studio between 1873 and 1890. Photograph held the C.M. Bell Studio Collection, Library of Congress Prints and Photographs Division in Washington, D.C.

Portrait of Congressman Robert Elliott, page 349. Image pulled from larger illustration by Currier & Ives, *The first colored senator and representatives–in the 41st and 42nd Congress of the United States*, 1872. Print held in the Popular Graphic Arts Collection, Library of Congress Prints and Photographs Division in Washington, D.C.

Portrait of Congressman John Mercer Langston, page 350. Portrait photograph taken between 1868 and 1875. Photograph held in the Brady-Handy Collection, Library of Congress Prints and Photographs Division in Washington, D.C.

Portrait of Governor P.B.S. Pinchback, page 350. Portrait photograph taken between 1870 and 1880. Photograph held in the Brady-Handy Collection, Library of Congress Prints and Photographs Division in Washington, D.C.

Portrait of Congressman Joseph Rainey, page 350. Portrait photograph taken between 1865 and 1880. Photograph held in the Brady-Handy Collection, Library of Congress Prints and Photographs Division in Washington, D.C.

Portrait of Senator Hiram Revels, page 351. Portrait photograph taken between 1860 and 1875. Photograph held in the Brady-Handy Collection, Library of Congress Prints and Photographs Division in Washington, D.C.

Portrait of Congressman Robert Smalls, page 351. Portrait photograph taken between 1870 and 1880. Photograph held in the Brady-Handy Collection, Library of Congress Prints and Photographs Division in Washington, D.C.

All images reproduced under public domain. These images and others can be found using the Library of Congress website (loc.gov) and HathiTrust Digital Library (hathitrust.org).